BOOKS BY LANI FORBES

THE AGE OF THE SEVENTH SUN SERIES

The Seventh Sun
The Jade Bones
The Obsidian Butterfly

ANTHOLOGIES (CONTRIBUTING AUTHOR)

It's All in the Story: California
Warriors against the Storm

THE
OBSIDIAN
BUTTERFLY

THE
OBSIDIAN
BUTTERFLY

LANI FORBES

BLACK STONE
PUBLISHING

Copyright © 2022 by Lani Forbes
Published in 2022 by Blackstone Publishing
Cover and book design by Kathryn Galloway English

Printed in the United States of America

First edition: 2022
ISBN 978-1-9825-4611-3
Young Adult Fiction / Fantasy / General

Version 1

CIP data for this book is available
from the Library of Congress

Blackstone Publishing
31 Mistletoe Rd.
Ashland, OR 97520

www.BlackstonePublishing.com

To Kevin.
Thank you for teaching me
so much about love and faith.
You are the other half of my duality
and always will be.

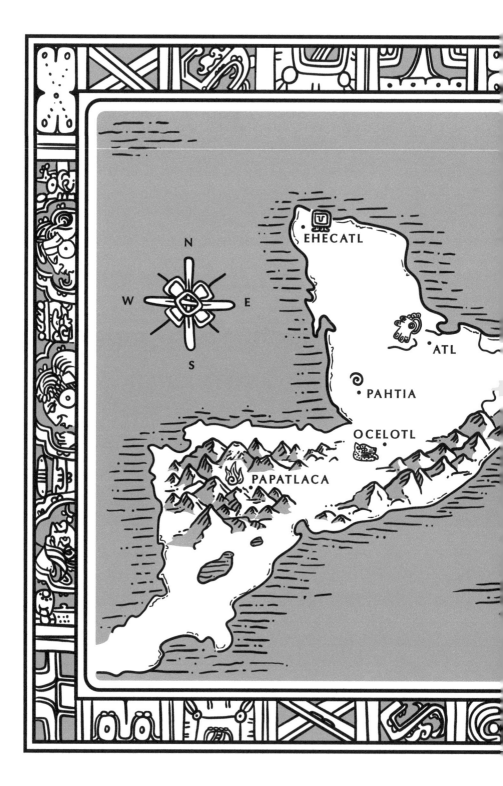

MIQUITZ MOUNTAINS

OMITL

MILLACATL

TOLLAN

CAVES OF
CREATION

ROYAL FAMILIES

OF THE

CHICOME AND MIQUITZ
EMPIRES

CITY-STATE	GODLY ANCESTOR	POWER
Tollan	Huitzilopochtli	to control light and the sun
Atl	Atlacoya	to control water
Ocelotl	Tezcatlipoca	to control animals
Papatlaca	Xiuhtecuhtli	to control fire
Millacatl	Xilonen	to control plants
Pahtia	Ixtlilton	to heal wounds and sickness
Ehecatl	Quetzalcoatl	to control wind/storms
Miquitz	Ah Puch	to possess the soul of another

The Seventh Sun waited just below the horizon, staining the sky in flaming hints of red and gold. Yemania of Pahtia drew in a breath of cool mountain air. Soon, back in the city of Tollan, the empress would use the divine potency of her blood to bring back the sun from its daily trek through the underworld.

For even the darkest of nights could not hold back the dawn.

But unless Ochix did something and did it *quickly*, it was unlikely she'd live to see it rise again tomorrow. Yemania shifted her knees against the earth, her wrists chafing in their binds. Beside her knelt twenty or so other captives, mostly innocent farmers and peasants from the city-state of Millacatl. Their only crime had been living too close to the Miquitz Mountains and the death-worshipping empire that resided there. Now they would pay with their lives.

Not all death worshippers were the demons Yemania had always been taught they were. Ochix, one of their death princes, had stolen her heart and proven himself to be different.

So different that a few weeks ago he'd earned a knife to the gut and a shove off the ledge of a waterfall—at the hands of his own father. The same father who presided as emperor of the Miquitz Empire and their head priest to the gods.

Yemania peeked up through her lashes. Ochix's father, Tzom, paced before the captives, his perfectly smooth head painted an eerie shade of white, black pigment outlining his eye sockets and stretching the corners of his mouth into a sickening smile. Black feathers cascaded down from his headdress and fluttered at his every movement, along with the rattling bones laced around his neck. Yemania suppressed a shudder. With his thin form and crazed eyes, the death priest resembled his ancestor, Cizin, god of death. Or at least what she imagined him to look like. She'd never met the god of death himself . . . and she prayed she wouldn't have to meet him today.

"Welcome, dear brothers and sisters," Tzom chanted. He spread his arms wide as if to embrace the crowd gathered in the large stone amphitheater. Mist clung to the mountain peaks surrounding them like ethereal spirits. Hundreds of cheers rose in response.

"Today, we celebrate our founding and offer our sacrifice to the god of death. For thousands of years, Cizin, my forefather, visited his descendants and their people when the layers between creation destabilized. Should he decide to emerge again, he will devour the first souls he encounters. He thirsts for them as a deer pants for water. And to relieve his thirst, we offer him a plethora of souls to choose from." He turned his skull-like face to the captives, his deadly smile spreading even wider. "And if he chooses to stay within his underworld realm until the next cycle, we will offer him souls in the more *traditional* manner."

Yemania's heart stammered. It didn't matter if the god of death stayed in his domain. The high priest would sacrifice them anyway. Ochix hadn't mentioned *that* part.

She and Ochix had been trying to sneak out of the palace to make it somewhere safe until they figured out the Mother goddess's purpose in bringing them to Miquitz's capital city.

Head for Omitl, she'd told Yemania when she'd helped her escape from the holding cell in Tollan. *You will know what to do when you get there.*

But Yemania had no idea what to do next. All she knew was that it was no longer safe for her among her own people—the Chicome, Empire of the Sun. She was a child of light, now trapped among children of darkness.

She turned her head and scanned the mass of gathered faces behind her, the hungry eyes thirsting for her death. Seated in a great arc around the amphitheater, they all faced the main attraction for the day's events— the cave entrance that led to Xibalba itself. Ochix might be different, but his people seemed as eager for bloodshed as their emperor priest.

Ochix had thought they'd be safe hiding in the city, but they'd never made it that far. The guards had caught up with them yesterday, and he'd had no choice but to continue his ruse as her captor.

"I will not let you be sacrificed," he'd whispered in her ear when the soldiers led her away. "I will find a way to get us out of this. I promise."

Such a different promise from that of her brother, of everyone else she'd known. With the exception of her friend Mayana, people continued to demand she sacrifice her divine blood to the gods. Yemania had studied the intensity in Ochix's dark eyes. The beautiful way his long hair framed the firm set of his squared jaw. The Mother goddess had trusted him, and Yemania trusted him too. "I believe you," she had said as the guards led her to the sacrificial holding chamber. Ochix had watched her go with heartbreak in his eyes. But that had been hours ago, and he was still nowhere to be seen. Would he be brave enough to stand up against his father again? In front of the entire empire?

Pounding drums vibrated within her chest. The booming matched the intensity of her frantic heart. The excitement of the crowd rose along with the music.

A great rumbling sounded from within the depths of the cave. It gaped like the dark mouth of a growling beast, set into the side of the mountain. Yemania's throat went dry. Ochix had said the lord of death hadn't ascended to the land of the living in more than a hundred years. Surely her luck was not that cursed. He couldn't appear for the first time in over a century *now*. Several of the other captives beside her began to whimper.

Yemania narrowed her eyes at the dark hole. Something moved within its depths. *Gods, no.* A large misshapen form was crawling its way out of the underworld. Yemania thought Cizin was a skeletally thin figure, but perhaps the codex illustrations of him were mistaken.

Or maybe he brought a monster of nightmares along with him from Xibalba, the place of fear.

One of the captives beside her collapsed onto his side, fear getting the better of him. Yemania's hands began to shake even harder. *Where was Ochix?*

The Seventh Sun finally broke through the bonds of night—reborn to a new day. The stone amphitheater was bathed in glowing orange light. Just as the drums and rumbling within the mountain reached a crescendo, dust and rubble poured from the mouth of the cave along with . . . along with . . .

The crowd gasped. The drums ceased, and Yemania leapt to her feet. A guard standing beside her immediately shoved her back to her knees. She didn't care.

It was not the god of death that had emerged from the entrance to the underworld. No, it was Mayana. Mayana! She was alive! The princess of water and descendant of the goddess Atlacoya had somehow survived the journey through the underworld. But something was not right.

Her dearest friend's energy seemed exhausted. Her usually rich skin was marred with scars and bruises, angry red blotches, and spots like the signs of sickness. The long, dark hair that hung across her shoulders was limp and lifeless, like her haunted eyes.

Her loincloth skirt was stained and ripped to tatters, exposing far more of her legs than Yemania knew she'd be comfortable with. But she looked far too thin and weak as Ahkin, prince of the sun and rightful emperor of the Chicome, supported her weight with his. He appeared equally starved, beaten, and burdened of soul. His short dark hair glistened with sweat that also coated the muscles of his bare chest. The once-white wrap around his waist was stained gray, brown . . . and red. They were painted in both dried and fresh blood.

They'd done it. *They'd survived.* Though barely, by the looks of them. Yemania's healer heart lurched. She needed to tend to them right away. They stumbled through the entrance of the underworld and collapsed onto the dirt floor of the amphitheater just as the cavern crumbled into a mass of fallen stone and dust behind them. Both gasped for breath as tear tracks glistened on their cheeks. The high priest's smile faltered, and his eyebrows pulled together as he beheld the newcomers who were obviously not the god of death. He quickly regained his composure as realization washed over him. And something about the sick triumph dawning on his face made Yemania's stomach churn.

Mayana sat up and looked around, her eyes widening in horror. She scuttled toward Ahkin, clutching at a bleeding wound on her shoulder. Yemania tried to rise to her feet again, but the soldier shoved her back.

"Stay where you are," the soldier hissed. Rage boiled in Yemania's blood. She glanced up to glare at the soldier beneath the black cloak—and her anger fizzled like magma meeting the ocean. *It was Ochix.* He was posing as one of the guards. Apparently, he did have a plan after all.

He gave her a minute shake of his head. A warning to not give them away. Yemania could have cried with relief. He'd been beside her the entire time. His hand squeezed her shoulder reassuringly while to the rest of the world he looked like a soldier keeping a sacrifice victim in place.

Yemania released a breath, sending tremors of relief down her arms. She turned her attention back to Mayana and Ahkin. It took all her self-control to remain where she was.

Tzom stepped closer. "My dear prince of light," he said. "Welcome to Omitl. I must admit we were not expecting you, but your timing could not be more divine. We are about to partake in one of our most sacred ceremonies." He waved an arm toward Yemania and the other captives waiting on the raised stone platform.

Ahkin's eyes turned shrewd, calculating. He pulled Mayana closer to him.

"After you threw yourself into Xibalba, my plans shifted to your sister, but the goddess has blessed the mission she entrusted to me. What fortune. She has brought you to me after all!"

Yemania's heart twisted. *Of course.* The death priest was obsessed with his patron goddess, the goddess driving him to madness. The Obsidian Butterfly. Ochix had confronted his father about dealing with such a dangerous deity—a choice that had nearly cost him his life.

Sure enough, Ochix shifted uncomfortably beside her.

"What do you want with me?" Ahkin asked, his voice rough. His arms tightened around Mayana.

Tzom motioned to the guards beside him. "Secure our guests. I want to make sure they don't miss this momentous occasion."

Ahkin leapt to his feet. He reached for his knife, but a swift blow to the knees brought him down. Tzom cut his own hand and extended it, bloody palm out toward Mayana. Yemania watched with horror as the mist of possession clouded her friend's eyes. Yemania had seen Ochix use his family's divine abilities before, but it still unsettled her stomach. Mayana did not struggle as guards ripped her and Ahkin apart and pressed a bone blade to her throat.

"Leave her alone," Ahkin roared. He struggled back to his feet, his blade ready in his hand.

Tzom seemed to be enjoying himself. He leered at the prince of light. "Unless you want your companion's blood needlessly spilled, I recommend you drop your weapon."

Yemania's chest heaved as her gaze darted between Tzom and Ahkin. She threw her prayers to the heavens. *Drop it, Ahkin. Please, drop it.*

His fingers loosened, and the knife thudded into the dirt. Yemania sighed in relief.

Tzom inched closer. "Wonderful. You see, I need your blood, son of the sun. My goddess has promised me that it is the only way to save my people. I will help her bring about the darkness that will allow them to descend. They will feast on the flesh of sun worshippers, and in return for my service, spare the Miquitz."

Ochix hissed. Terror washed through Yemania, cold and suffocating. *Oh my gods.* It all made sense. Tzom's obsession with the Obsidian Butterfly, his determination to get to Ahkin's sister, Metzi, after Ahkin fell into the underworld. He needed the blood of the sun god, the blood that ran in the veins of both royal twins. And the Obsidian Butterfly had already been manipulating Metzi. Had this been her ultimate goal? To get Metzi into Tzom's hands somehow?

"What are you talking about?" Ahkin demanded. "Who will descend?"

But Yemania knew the answer before Tzom could say another word. He wanted to bring about a darkness that would allow the dreaded star demons of legend to descend and devour their world.

"The Tzitzimime. The star demons. The followers of the great Obsidian Butterfly." Tzom looked positively gleeful at the prospect. "She will rule the new earth and spare us as her loyal servants. They can only descend during an eclipse, and now that I have the blood of one who controls the sun, I can ensure the eclipse will never end." He paused, his manic eyes focusing on Ahkin. "You will be my guest of honor, son of Huitzilopochtli, as we usher in the age of the *Eighth Sun!*"

A heavy silence hung in the air of the amphitheater. Ochix swore under his breath. Yemania risked a glance up at him. *Did you know?* She asked with her eyes. *Did you know this was your father's plan?*

The fury and surprise on his face gave her the answer she needed, but a shake of his head confirmed it.

Tzom clapped his hands toward the guards. "Take our new prisoners to the holding chamber beneath the temple. The eclipse is set to begin in two weeks, and we have to make sure our new guests do not miss it." He sliced into his hand above the lit brazier and dripped crimson into the sizzling flames. It smoked black and then gray, finally turning an eerie shade of poisonous green. "Cizin is pleased with this new development," he announced.

One of the guards stepped forward hesitantly. "Your majesty, what about the other captives?"

Tzom turned with a swish of his black ceremonial robes. The bones around his neck clattered against each other. His head tilted as he considered them. "Send them back to the holding chamber as well. Their souls will still meet the god of death, but we will make sure we time the gift wisely." He turned toward the expectant crowd and threw his bloodied fist into the air. "My people, we must prepare! The new age shall be ushered in through blood and starlight!"

CHAPTER

2

Metzi's head throbbed as though a stingray spine had stabbed her behind the eye. She'd thrown herself across the furs of her bed, begging the gods to show her mercy and take her pain away. As usual, they remained silent.

The headaches had plagued her for months. They'd started the moment her father told her of his plans to send her to Ehecatl as bride to their storm prince. He could call it a marriage arrangement all he wanted, but Metzi had known the truth. He had planned to barter her like a fish in the marketplace, while her twin brother took the throne. The throne that should have been hers from the beginning.

It was the reason she had taken her fate into her own hands and reached out to the only goddess who would answer her.

The curtains were drawn across her open windows, blocking out the light of the freshly risen sun, though they did little to hold back the humid heat of the day beyond. Light always made the pain worse. How ironic that—as the princess of light—her very element could be her worst enemy. She needed Coatl to hurry with the tea. Though his brews were not as effective as his sister's had been, they were better than nothing.

A bitter taste coated her tongue at the thought of Coatl's sister. Yemania.

Anger and betrayal washed through her, sending a fresh throb across her skull. Metzi hissed into the darkness. She'd expected loyalty from the princess of healing. A shared camaraderie over the wounds of being used by their families. She had lifted her to a place of honor, High Healer of Tollan, and how had Yemania thanked her? By stealing her betrothed, the death prince of Omitl, and plotting to cut her off from the one deity that understood her. The only god or goddess who had taken any concern with her plight. The daughter of healing had used Metzi's generosity to get herself ahead, and then instead of sharing the power with Metzi, had tried to take it all for herself.

Metzi thumped a fist against the pillows beneath her. That's what she got for trusting, for letting her guard down. She could add both Yemania and Ochix to the long list of those who wanted to use and deceive her.

"Tea for my empress," Coatl announced, knocking the beads across her doorway aside and striding into the room as though he were Quetzalcoatl himself, returned from the dead.

Metzi's lip curled and she didn't respond. After the disastrous results of cutting off their relationship to fake an alliance with the Miquitz prince instead, the Butterfly had finally agreed to find a plan that would allow them to be together. But Metzi didn't have patience for his arrogance when it felt as though a dagger was piercing between her eyes.

Coatl came to sit beside her. He placed the clay bowl of tea against the ground with a light clatter. "Is it getting any better?"

"No." Metzi ground her teeth together, then immediately regretted that decision. She reached for the cup and brought the steaming herbal liquid to her lips. It burned her nose and throat, but the aching in her head dulled ever so slightly.

Finally, *finally*, she was able to sit up without her stomach upending itself. She took another sip of tea and sighed, hugging the warmth of the clay bowl close to her chest. "Do we have any news of your sister? Have she and the death demon been captured?"

Coatl fidgeted beside her but did not answer.

She sighed in frustration. "I take that as a no."

He winced. "I'm sorry, my love. I wish I had better news, but it appears they fled into the jungles. We have no idea where they could be headed."

Metzi took another sip of tea. Her fingers tapped impatiently against the bowl.

"Leave me," she said, rising to her feet and turning away.

Coatl dropped to his knees before her, reaching for her fingers. "Metzi, please. Don't send me away again."

Disgusted, she yanked her hand out of his grasp. Her voice came out deadly and calm. "I said *leave me.*"

He blanched. "I didn't—I'm not—"

Something about the sheer panic in his eyes sent a thrill of excitement through her stomach. She hated to admit how much she liked to see him grovel at her feet. Not because she enjoyed seeing him in pain—she wasn't *cruel*—but because she loved seeing how much power she had over him. The power to make him, or anyone, beg. She loved to see someone so desperate for her approval. No one had ever valued her favor before—never cared about what she thought. Now, her favor was the most prized possession in the empire. She was no longer a commodity for men to barter with. Now they saw her, respected her, even feared her.

How quickly tides could change.

And she knew exactly who she had to thank for her sudden shift in circumstances. Someone who might not be very pleased with the news of Ochix and Yemania's escape.

"I'm not telling you to leave me permanently," she snapped. "I just need some time to myself. For . . . prayer." Technically it wasn't a lie. She *would* be communing with the heavenly realms.

"As you wish, my empress." Coatl pressed a warm kiss against her palm, his eyes brimming with emotion, before bowing out of the room. The beads clattered as he parted them, and the slapping of his sandals echoed down the hall. Metzi's heart sank slightly, as though she'd thrown off a stifling blanket only to realize how cold she felt without it. She stuffed the feeling away. Coatl couldn't be here for what came next.

"Stand down at the end of the hall and make sure no one disturbs me," she ordered the Eagle warriors guarding her doorway. They nodded and immediately took their new positions.

Once she was alone, Metzi padded to the shelf that housed her blood chest—a small stone box crafted with magic so that only her blood could open it. How close Yemania and Ochix had come to stealing it. She shuddered to think what might have happened had her only method of contacting the goddess been ripped away.

She removed an obsidian dagger from her beaded belt and sliced it into her thumb. Blood oozed from the small cut, warm and sticky. She smeared a droplet across the top of the box, and it cracked open. The stone sitting inside was worth more than gold. Gray and shimmering, its edges rounded and pockmarked as though water had dripped upon its surface for hundreds of calendar cycles. It was only the size of her fist, and yet it still amazed her to behold.

A star stone. A piece of the heavens that had fallen to earth in a blaze of light and glory. It did not resemble the glittering stars that clung to the night sky. This star was dead, leaving behind a shriveled husk before plummeting to earth. How magnificent it must once have been to be so beautiful even in death.

Metzi slipped her fingers beneath it, and the icy cold of its surface seeped into her skin. It was so much heavier than it appeared, but Metzi loved that too. That something so small could wield so much might.

She placed the fallen star on the golden altar that stood in the back of her room. With the cut on her thumb still bleeding, she held her hand over the stone and squeezed until a single drop of blood splattered the stone's surface. The blood hissed and disappeared, absorbed by the stone as it accepted her offer of payment.

"Bless me with your presence, Itzpapalotl. Great Obsidian Butterfly. I seek your wise counsel."

The torches lining the room began to flicker. Several extinguished altogether. An icy chill swept through the air, raising bumps across her arms. Her breath rose in little bursts of mist. Sound and color seemed to dim as if a shadow had crept close and tainted the world with its infinite darkness.

Finally, above the altar, a face began to materialize. Flowing, night-dark hair framed a skeletal white face. Lines of black paint ran the length of her cheeks while blood dripped from the corner of red-stained lips. She was beautiful and terrifying to behold. Behind her shimmered red-and-black wings, as intricately patterned as a butterfly's, yet they were tipped with claws as sharp as knives—claws as sharp as those gracing her long-fingered hands. Metzi thought she'd eventually grow accustomed to the appearance of the warrior goddess, the queen of the Tzitzimime, but still, her breath froze in her lungs.

"Princess of light." Itzpapalotl greeted her with a voice as cold and void as the space between the stars.

Metzi tugged nervously at one of her gold bracelets. "Forgive me, Obsidian Butterfly, but there has been a change in the plan."

The goddess's star-bright eyes narrowed slightly. "A change?"

Metzi drew herself up to her full height. "I tried to follow your plan to marry one of the death princes of Miquitz. You assured me that it was the only way to find the freedom that I sought. I did not understand, but I trusted your divine providence. The engagement was arranged, but before we could follow through, the prince betrayed me. He escaped Tollan along with my treacherous High Healer. They seem to have been having some kind of dalliance behind my back." She let out a heavy breath.

"I am aware, my dear. Do not forget, the stars see all that happens at night. I had hoped they would fail," the goddess said. "But do not fret. We will get you to Omitl another way."

Metzi frowned. "I don't understand why it is so important for me to ally with the Miquitz. They are our enemies. Surely we can free you and secure my power another way."

The Obsidian Butterfly's lips thinned. "You need to trust me. This is the only way we *both* get what we want."

"Then explain to me. Please. I need to understand."

The goddess was silent for several heartbeats, her gaze seeming to focus on sights that Metzi could not see. "Mortals cannot understand the ways of gods."

Metzi exposed her palms. "Let me try. Do not underestimate me as everyone else has. You know I'm stronger and smarter than that."

The goddess tilted her head, considering. "Do you know how the Tzitzimime became trapped within the stars?"

"The codex only states that they desire to devour humankind should we fail to keep the sun aloft. And the paintings in the codex are rather . . . unpleasant."

The goddess scoffed. "Of course that is all your codex says. Like every deity, we exist in duality, equally capable of what you humans would call good and evil. We are the protectors of the feminine, worshipped by midwives. I protect the spirits of infants who perish before their time. But yes, we also desire to devour humankind. Do you know why?"

Metzi shook her head, swallowing hard. She'd heard the legends of the warrior goddess and protector of women; it was why she reached out to her for help in the first place. She had also read the stories of what the Tzitzimime would do should the sun fail to rise. Her father never let his children forget the importance of raising the sun each morning.

She would be lying to herself if she didn't admit that part of her worried which side of the goddess she was dealing with. Were the promises Metzi was making for her own benefit, or the goddess's? Or could their goals truly be beneficial to both?

The goddess went on. "Ometeotl, the Father and Mother in one, birthed the gods and created the celestial tree, which spans the space between the heavens and the underworld. But she favored some of her children above others. They were spoiled. Fed extra power by the blood sacrifices of humans, all while squabbling amongst themselves like children. Their petty grudges against each other destroyed your world—not once, but many times."

The six apocalypses. Each time the world was destroyed, one of the gods or goddesses had sacrificed themselves to save humanity and create a new age. Those same gods were the ancestors of the royal families of the Chicome. But she had not heard the *cause* of those apocalypses before. Had humanity really been innocent bystanders in the petty arguments of gods? Or had they played a role somehow in their own demise?

"You humans worship their sacrifices as honorable, selfless. You forget the reasons your world was destroyed in the first place. Floods, famines, beasts. The power of the gods unleashed by their descendants in fits of tantrum against each other. The gods were not gracious;

they sought to ease their guilt. Yet everyone still *loved* them . . ." The goddess's voice turned even colder. "But some of us—lesser gods not loved enough to receive sacrifices—were *so* hungry. Starved for the power that comes from human blood. While our spoiled siblings gorged themselves at your expense, we plotted their downfall. We knew we could rule the realms of heaven and earth far better than they ever could. But our Mother grew angry, forever protective of her favorite children. So she imprisoned us, the Tzitzimime, within the stars, doomed to watch humanity prance before us. They were a feast set before the eyes of the starving—yet we were never able to partake. You see, princess, we thirst for blood, and the temptation held before us has driven many of us to madness. The only time we may eat is during times of darkness, in the rare moments one of us can escape our prison before we are forced to return."

"The curfew," Metzi whispered, understanding for the first time why it was considered dangerous to be out at night, why the Chicome enforced such a strict curfew. Her gaze fell to the golden sun etched into the altar. "I thought gods could not die."

"Oh, we do not die. We do not *need* blood to survive. But it energizes us, strengthens us. Gives us a rush of power like nothing else in creation. Not unlike how mankind eats a mushroom or drinks fermented drinks. The power is—" she licked her blood-stained lips "—addicting."

Metzi's stomach twisted with unease. She'd also heard of men lying, cheating, or stealing to obtain the object of their addictions.

"Your blood controls the sun, princess of light. You can summon it or put it to sleep, but your people foolishly believe it is *your* power alone that brings it back from Xibalba each morning. You've never seen what would happen if you *didn't* call it forth."

Metzi blanched. "If I didn't raise the sun, darkness would continue forever. You and your demons would descend and devour us all."

The goddess scoffed. "You humans give yourselves too much credit. The sun would rise regardless because Quetzalcoatl died to set it in motion. But your people are too foolish to see that for yourselves. Besides, the simple instability of night alone is not strong enough for all of us to escape. For that, we require a much greater cosmic instability."

Metzi lifted her gaze from the altar. A tendril of doubt was creeping down her spine. "Like the Nemontemi, the last five days of the calendar year?"

"Or an eclipse." The goddess's smile widened. "We will feast upon the blood we crave, but do not fear, my child. I am also the protector of the feminine, and I have great plans for you. You appealed to me for help, and I took pity upon your plight. You had little control over your own fate. If anyone can understand the feeling of being trapped, of being passed over for a favored sibling . . ."

Metzi's head throbbed. Why did the gods always speak in riddles and stories? Never a straight, clean answer. It made it so difficult to trust. "Then what *are* your plans? You promised me power and an empire of my own."

A glint of something like madness shone within the Butterfly's soulless eyes. "You will still get your empire. But I never promised it would be the *Chicome* Empire."

●●●

Mayana awoke in a dimly lit stone chamber. Two torches burned along the low walls, and the air was humid and heavy, as though too many bodies were breathing all at once. Her blurred vision focused on a face hovering above her. Thick, dark hair framed rounded cheeks and a large nose. Mayana could now clearly see tears pooling in the corner of the young woman's eyes as a grateful smile spread across her dry, cracked lips.

Mayana knew that face. Yemania.

Mayana sat up so quickly her head collided with something hard. Someone hissed in pain. Stars blinked behind her eyes, and she looked back to find Ahkin clutching his nose, his own eyes scrunched in pain. Had she been lying in his lap? She mumbled an apology, but her attention was focused elsewhere.

"Not too fast, Mayana. You need to rest." Yemania placed a firm hand on her shoulder and held her still.

Mayana flung herself into the arms of her friend. "Yemania! Oh gods, I've missed you."

Yemania made a sound somewhere between a laugh and sob as they embraced. "I've missed you, too. I was sure you were dead, but then you tumbled out of the underworld only *half* dead. I finally understand why the Mother goddess wanted me to come here. I was supposed to find you!"

A million images flashed behind Mayana's eyes. The City of the

Dead. The lords of Xibalba. Cizin trading her the bones of Quetzal-coatl for the bones of her mother. The giant owl attacking them. Not escaping in time. Ona jumping to take the blade meant for her own heart. Leaving her precious dog there in that place of nightmares.

Mayana wrapped her arms around herself to stop from shaking. "Where are we? What happened?"

The room was large, as large as any house. And they were not alone. Around them huddled about twenty peasants in varying states of ex-haustion and filth. Some looked as though they had spent a month or more trapped here. Mayana wrinkled her nose. It certainly smelled as though they had been imprisoned for that long.

Ahkin cleared his throat, the torchlight reflecting off his dark unruly hair. "A holding chamber for sacrifice victims. Somewhere un-derground. I think we are beneath the Miquitz temple."

Another rush of memories. Emerging out of the collapsing tunnel, Ahkin supporting her. The amphitheater filled with hundreds of faces. The death priest smiling in triumph.

"We're in Omitl? The capital of the Miquitz?" She turned back to Yemania. "What are you doing here?"

Yemania leaned back on her heels. "The Mother goddess told me to come here, so I did. I was captured and added to their group of captives. We were going to be sacrificed to Cizin, but then you two arrived and the death priest decided to wait until the coming eclipse."

"The eclipse?" Mayana touched the freshly healed skin on her shoulder, where the owl's claws had dug into it. Yemania must have treated her while she was unconscious.

Ahkin's frown deepened. "He plans to sacrifice me and use my blood to hold the eclipse in place. If darkness is allowed to continue for long enough . . ."

Mayana's sluggish thoughts sharpened, and she gasped. She knew the legends. The Tzitzimime. Star demons. Lesser gods trapped in a celestial prison, punished for plotting to overthrow the ruling gods of the heavens. Sentenced to slowly starve as they watched the humans of earth, whose blood served as their source of power and sustenance.

Demons who could only escape in darkness.

Mayana's skin crawled. "He means to unleash the Tzitzimime? Why? Why would he want to destroy the world?"

Ahkin rubbed the bridge of his nose. "He is trying to protect his own people. The ruler of the Tzitzimime supposedly promised she would spare the Miquitz and only devour the Chicome if he helped her."

Yemania made a disgusted sound. "Their ruler is the Obsidian Butterfly, a treacherous goddess that cannot be trusted. Metzi has been communicating with her as well. I don't know what the goddess is planning, but she's guided Metzi's steps from the beginning. It was her idea to poison the emperor."

Ahkin's jaw went rigid, while Mayana's hands flew to her mouth.

"So what do we do?" she whispered between her fingers. Surely Ometeotl, the Mother and Father of all the gods, would intervene. She had to have some kind of plan, just as she had a purpose for Mayana and Ahkin's journey through Xibalba to rescue the bones of Quetzalcoatl. Mayana twisted around, looking for her bag, for the bones she had sacrificed so much to save, but it was gone. Her panic sent her heart thudding against her rib cage. "Where's my bag? Where are the jade bones?"

"They took them," Ahkin said, rising to his feet. He let his gaze wander around the room. "First, we need to escape. We can't do anything trapped beneath the Miquitz temple."

He circled the chamber, assessing every corner and crack. The eyes of the huddled farmers followed him, likely in awe to be so close to their true emperor. But finally, Ahkin shook his head in defeat. "We'll have to come up with some kind of plan for when they roll the stone away from the doorway. Perhaps ambush the guards if we all work together—"

"And go where?" Mayana interrupted. "Ahkin, these people are half starved and weak with exhaustion. There is no way we'd be able to fight our way out."

The hollowed eye sockets of the fellow prisoners voiced their consent. They were in no shape to fight, and yet hope sparked within their eyes.

Mayana laid a hand on Ahkin's arm. "They are not soldiers."

"I know." Ahkin pursed his lips, but then he placed his hand over hers and squeezed. His gaze briefly held that of an older man who leaned against the back wall. Something about the wrinkled face tickled at Ahkin's memory. The old man nodded at him as though in approval and pulled at the black-and-white geometrically patterned shawl around his shoulders. A sudden, inexplicable feeling of calm swept over him.

Ahkin smiled. "But they *are* Chicome. We will find a way."

When he turned back, the old man who had been there was gone. Ahkin turned his head, searching for him. Though he should feel unease at the man's impossible disappearance, the same relaxing calm that had swept over him before kept his muscles loose, his head clear. He couldn't explain it. It was almost as if a gift of peace had been given to him by the gods . . .

Ahkin sucked in a breath. He *had* seen that patterned shawl somewhere before—draped across Ometeotl's shoulders.

—————

"Father," Ochix greeted the head priest of Miquitz, as though nothing unusual had happened. As if the man had not just announced his plans to destroy the world earlier that day. Ochix still couldn't believe what he'd heard in the amphitheater. He knew his father was crazy—but he'd thought the man was just normal crazy. Not strike-a-bargain-with-a-murderous-goddess-to-cause-an-apocalypse crazy.

His father not only ruled the Miquitz as emperor, but spiritually, as their high priest. He had been a brilliant man; his ability to memorize texts and recite them at a moment's notice was unparalleled. As a child, Ochix thought his father knew as much as the gods. As he grew older, his father's eccentricities grew less awe-inspiring. His subjects never questioned him, his divine gifting unquestioned as a descendant of the gods. But Ochix had seen. He'd watched the spark of brilliance ignite into something far more dangerous, a mania that bordered on madness. A madness that was fanned to flame when he started communicating with the Obsidian Butterfly.

His father's chambers were a mix of library, elegant living quarters, and eclectic workshop, currently illuminated by the fading rays of sunlight leaking in through the windows. Stacks of codex sheets and history texts lined the many stone shelves that stretched from floor to ceiling. What wall space was not covered by shelves displayed glyphs and painted images of the gods. Various instruments and weapons fashioned from wood, stone, and even gemstones littered the low tables. Beside them sat a woven bag with something that glittered like jade within its depths. The scent of cloyingly sweet incense hung in the air, burning Ochix's nose. To his right, a waterfall gushed past a wide balcony.

Tzom ignored his eldest son. The table before the death priest was strewn with star charts and ancient religious texts. His fingers were stained with charcoal and paint, and his eyes frantically scanned nonsensical writings and images. Beside him sat a pockmarked gray stone, a star stone descended from the heavens. Ochix's stomach tightened at the sight of it.

He cleared his throat. "Father, I wish to speak with you."

Tzom lifted a hand and waved Ochix away. Ochix knew better than to get too close when he was in one of his frenzies. He'd once seen his father stab a servant who'd interrupted him. Ochix would just have to try another tactic.

"What are the stars saying tonight?" he said conversationally, picking up a discarded piece of charcoal and inspecting it.

Tzom straightened, rubbing his face and smearing the white paint with charcoal dust. "The signs are beginning to confirm the impending destruction. It is as I suspected. The eclipse will begin exactly two weeks from today."

Ochix tightened his hand into a fist, but fought to keep his tone even. "And you mean to sacrifice the sun prince?"

Tzom didn't take his eyes off his charts. "We've had this conversation before, my son, and it did not end well for you last time."

Ochix dropped the charcoal shard, and it fell to the stone tabletop with a clatter. Last time? Last time his father had tried to kidnap the prince of the sun from the battlefield, a move that would have provoked open war with the Chicome. And his father hadn't seemed to care. When Ochix brought his worries before his father, his concern over his father's recent behaviors and the choice to risk open war, his father had possessed him and forced him to shove a knife into his own gut before throwing him over the edge of that expansive balcony. He would have died if Yemania had not found and healed him.

"This is why you sought the sun prince? To sacrifice him and bring destruction on us all?"

Tzom wiggled a finger in the air. "Ah-ah-ah, my son. Not all of us. Just the Chicome. Her plans have ensured that the Chicome are the weakest they have been in centuries. They are ripe for the harvest. The goddess has promised that her demons will destroy the sun worshippers once and for all and that she will reward the Miquitz for their service. We will be spared."

Ochix ground his teeth together. "Except we will all still die when we have no way to raise the sun."

"Well, that is your fault, my son. You were supposed to bring the daughter of light here with you. She would have raised the sun for us, and your children would have ensured the survival of our empire. Now, we will have to lure her here another way. Do not worry, the goddess assures me we will. Just as she found a way to bring the sun prince to us. She knew that if he fell into Xibalba, he would emerge here in Omitl. And she was right. She is *always* right."

Had she known Ahkin would survive? Her explanations made sense to his father, but to him, everything sounded a little too convenient. "And you really trust this goddess? You do not think she is deceiving you?"

"Your mind is small, my boy. You study your art and your poems. You have your clever tongue and know your way around a battlefield, but you lack true *vision*. The foresight to lead your empire to greatness!" His hands gripped the edge of the table as he wheezed a bone-chilling laugh.

Ochix began slowly backing away. "You were once a man of intelligence, of honor. I don't know what you are now."

"I am the man that will save us all," Tzom whispered. He bent forward and began etching the form of a skull across his papers.

A skull with eyes like stars.

●●●●

CHAPTER

4

Though they could not see the outside world from their holding chamber, Ahkin assumed night had long since fallen. He could not take his eyes off the starving bodies of the Millacatl farmers. His subjects—the same farmers of Millacatl that he had failed to save that day on the battlefield. It felt like a lifetime ago. Yet now the Mother goddess was giving him a chance to right his wrongs. A chance to finally save them and take them home to their families after nearly a month away.

"We will escape. I promise you," he assured them. Many nodded gratefully, but Ahkin could tell they struggled to find hope in the darkness. He understood that feeling, having gone through literal hell himself.

Once, the pressure to lead, to save them, might have overwhelmed him. But that was before he had survived the underworld. He'd escaped death. He'd seen gods and goddesses and overcome trials no ordinary man would have.

And he was no longer alone.

A bloom of warmth spread across his chest as he watched Yemania and Mayana walk among the farmers, using their abilities to offer water from the jade skull pendant and heal the peasants' injuries. The Miquitz had given them enough sustenance to keep them alive, but not much beyond. His father's words echoed through his memory. *Your duality will not let you fail. And you will not let her fail either.* No, he would not fail, because Mayana would stand beside him and help him carry the burden. Together.

A strangled sound came from the other side of the large stone blocking the exit. Then several thuds—like bodies hitting the ground. Ahkin's attention shifted to the door. The peasants looked up as well, some clutching cloaks around themselves as if they could shield themselves from whatever was coming. The stone slab began to shift, grinding against the doorframe.

Mayana straightened, her lips pursed, and wiped her bloody finger on the tattered remains of her loincloth skirt. Since their weapons and belongings had been taken from them, she'd had to bite a small cut. She retreated to Ahkin's side. His hand itched for a weapon, even if he was still injured.

He used the sharp sliver of rock Mayana had found to cut into his thumb, releasing enough blood to bend the light around him and hide him from human sight. He'd have the element of surprise on his side. There were a few gasps as he disappeared. He positioned himself in front—whoever came into the room would have to go through him first. Light from the torches in the hall beyond seeped into the room as the stone rolled farther. Someone behind him whimpered.

A male figure stood silhouetted against the torchlight, a small blade in his hand. It might be the only opportunity they had. Ahkin didn't think twice.

He lunged.

There was a cry of surprise. One of his hands closed around the man's throat to cut off a scream while his wounded hand reached for the weapon. The damaged tendons flared painfully as he pried the blade from the man's fingers. It clattered to the floor. But a knee to Ahkin's gut knocked the air from his lungs. His hold loosened momentarily.

"What in the nine hells?" the man gasped, looking around for his invisible attacker.

Ahkin regained his breath and threw his arm around the intruder's throat, forcing him to his knees. Mayana scrambled forward and grabbed the fallen blade. Only then did Ahkin allow himself to re-appear.

"Stay where you are," Ahkin growled.

The captive bucked against him anyway, his hands clawing at Ahkin's arm. He had long dark hair, the strong build of a warrior, and—like other Miquitz men he'd seen—a black wrap around his waist. A necklace of human finger bones dangled against his bare chest.

"Stop!" Yemania screamed. "Don't hurt him."

Shock nearly knocked the breath from Ahkin's lungs a second time. The healing princess ran forward and fell onto her knees before them. "Let him go," she begged. "Please, Ahkin! He's my . . . friend."

"Friend?" Ahkin asked, his voice flat. "How can you be friends with a death demon?"

"Let him go. I promise I'll explain." She focused on the death de-mon's face, which Ahkin assumed must be turning purple. Already his hands were weak in their attempts to pull at Ahkin's arm.

Ahkin's eyes darted to Mayana, who shrugged, eyes wide with dis-belief. At least she still had the knife.

He loosened his arm.

The death demon fell forward, retching and coughing on his hands and knees. Yemania rushed to his side, already checking his throat and assessing him. She helped him sit. The young man rubbed at his throat and glared at Ahkin. His eyes were as cold and dark as death.

"His name is Ochix," Yemania supplied. "He's—uh—"

Ochix coughed. "A prince of Miquitz."

Mayana squeaked and lifted the knife toward him. Ahkin flexed his hands, ready to fight again if necessary.

"Yemania?" Mayana asked carefully. She did not take her eyes off Ochix—or lower the knife. "How do you know a prince of Miquitz?"

"It's a long story." Yemania waved an impatient hand. "The point is, he's here to help us." She looked down at him. "At least, I'm assum-ing so, right?"

Ochix rolled his eyes. "Yes. I possessed the guards outside and knocked them out. I was *going* to lead you all out while the palace is asleep."

"Why would you help us?" Ahkin demanded. "Don't you serve your father?"

Ochix rose to his feet and wiped the dirt off his wrap. "I don't know who that man is, but I can assure you he is no longer my father." He gestured to a puckered scar across his abdomen. "This is how he handles those who question him. Or his patron."

Bile rose in Ahkin's throat. Tzom stabbed his own son? What kind of person tried to kill their own kin? But then the thought of his own treacherous twin came to mind. He clamped the thought down before it could go any further.

"And were it up to me, I'd rather *not* see the world destroyed. I happen to enjoy it far more than I should," Ochix said, an arrogant smirk tugging at his lips as he glanced down at Yemania.

The princess of healing seemed suddenly flustered, tucking her hair behind her ear and refusing to meet anyone's eyes.

Ahkin's head was reeling. Were they more than friends? How any citizen of the Chicome could fall for a death demon was beyond him. "You said you could help us escape?"

"Yes. I don't know when the guards will wake up, so we'll need to hurry."

Mayana was already ushering the peasants to their feet. "If you can walk, please help support any who can't. We have to go now."

An older woman grasped Mayana's wrist and thanked her, tears pooling in the corners of her eyes. Mayana smiled back, but then met Ahkin's gaze with a dawning look of concern.

She made her way to him. "Ahkin, we have to get the bones. We can't leave them here. Not after—" She swallowed hard. "Not after everything we gave up to get them."

He knew her thoughts had gone back to Xibalba, where Cizin, the Lord of Death, had demanded she trade the bones of her mother for the bones of Quetzalcoatl. Where her beloved dog, Ona, had sacrificed himself to ensure they could escape.

"Where would your people take something they confiscated from us?" he asked the death demon.

Ochix took the bone-handled blade back from Mayana and secured it around his waist. "We don't have time to worry about any personal belongings. I'm sorry."

Ahkin's temper flared. He stepped forward and shoved a hand into Ochix's chest. "Those 'belongings' include the jade bones of Quetzalcoatl himself. We are not leaving without them."

The bones were priceless. Not only had they sacrificed so much to retrieve them, the Mother had a specific purpose for them. Ahkin wasn't sure what that purpose would be yet, but he knew it would be important. Quetzalcoatl had been her most favored son, the god who had sacrificed his blood to resurrect humanity in the Caves of Creation at the beginning of the current age.

Ochix muttered a curse and ran a hand through his long hair. "Bones of jade? Were they in a woven bag?"

"Yes!" Mayana cried. "You know where they are?"

Ochix held out his hands in apology. "They are nowhere you'd be able to retrieve them."

"Try me," Ahkin said, his tone flat. The death prince's arrogance chafed at his patience.

"On a table in my father's rooms. I don't think he knows what they are. But if he catches you there your blood might get sacrificed a little earlier than planned." Then his expression darkened. "*I* might be able to get them."

There was no way Ahkin was trusting the bones of Quetzalcoatl to a death prince, not when he knew how valuable they were. "No, absolutely not. I'll get them. You lead the others to safety."

Ochix snorted. "I can't exactly lead your people into Tollan. Your dear sister would rip my heart out of my chest if I tried."

Ahkin started at the mention of his twin. "Metzi? How do you know Metzi?"

Yemania groaned. "Again, it's a long story."

"Regardless," Ochix interrupted, "I can't lead your people, you have to. Let me get the bones."

Ahkin wrapped his hands behind his head and began to pace. They didn't have time to argue about this. His pulse pounded behind his ears. There had to be a way to make this work.

"I'll go with him," Mayana offered. "You need to protect the peasants. I'm not as effective with a blade as you are, but I can fight with my powers well enough. Plus, if the death priest catches you, the world will end. Not as severe if he catches me."

"No," Ahkin said immediately. "Why can't Yemania go with him?"

"I'll need to go with the farmers," Yemania said. "Some of them are still not well and I want to be there if someone needs a healer. Plus, I'm the only other one who knows the way out of the mountains. I traveled the path to get here."

Mayana exposed her palms to Ahkin. "*I* need to get them. I can't explain it. Ometeotl gave me the mission to retrieve them. This is my burden to bear. Please trust me."

Ahkin hated the idea of leaving the girl he loved in the hands of an arrogant death prince he barely knew. But Mayana was right, and he knew better than to argue with her. His blood in the hands of Tzom was infinitely more dangerous, and the peasants needed someone to protect them. Challenge shone in Mayana's eyes. *Tell me not to*, she seemed to say. So this was how it would go. Ahkin and Yemania would leave with the peasants. Mayana and Ochix would try to retrieve the bones.

"If you let anything happen to her, I will personally gut you. Understand, death prince?"

Ochix's eyes glittered with humor. "My father already beat you to that."

Ahkin opened his mouth to show exactly what he thought of humor in a situation like this, but Mayana put her hand on his arm again. He took a deep breath instead. "Fine. We will meet you at the base of the mountains."

He drew Mayana into his arms and pressed his lips firmly against hers. "Come back to me."

Mayana pulled back and gave him a sad smile. "I will do my best. I need to save the bones and you need to save your people. If the Mother wills it, we will see each other again soon."

5

Mayana was more nervous than she let the others believe, but she had to have faith that the Mother would protect her. She still wrestled with trusting, with having the kind of faith that Ahkin did. But the Mother had a purpose for the bones, and Mayana knew her favor would be upon them.

She prayed that was enough.

Ochix explained to Ahkin exactly how to escape the temple so that no one would see them. Apparently he had possessed the guards into compliance and then forced them to eat a bitter root that would render them unconscious for several hours.

"That is utterly terrifying," Mayana admitted, eyeing Ochix with shades of distrust as Ahkin and Yemania organized the other prisoners to leave. "You can possess anyone? And make them do anything?"

"Well, like you, my blood must be exposed. And the more souls I'm facing, the harder it is. It's a battle of wills, and I can only bend so many at once. Luckily my will is pretty strong."

"And you can do this from anywhere?"

"No. From the testing I've done, I need to be close enough to hear the person's voice."

A thought occurred to her. "But it can be fought?"

Ochix shrugged. "I suppose if the other soul's will is strong enough, and again, it's harder with more than one soul at a time. That's why I made the guards eat the root and go to sleep. There were too many for me to hold indefinitely."

Mayana smiled inwardly. Her will would be a difficult one to bend. Hadn't her experience with the rituals proven that? Honestly, Ochix still terrified her. She hoped it wasn't a mistake to let him help. But the thought of trying to break into Tzom's personal chamber alone left her heart pounding and a cold sheen of sweat across her skin.

Ochix turned back to Ahkin. "The guards will not be sleeping for much longer. There is a narrow trail that will lead down the mountain, Yemania can help you find the way. Once you make it out of the temple . . ." He used his hands to further explain their escape route. Ahkin nodded along, his face serious.

Yemania rushed forward and gave Mayana a swift hug. "We will meet you at the base of the mountains. And then we can all go home *together*."

Ahkin made a growling sound in his throat. "And deal with my sister."

Mayana hadn't given much thought to what would happen if they made it back to the capital of the Chicome Empire. She'd been so concerned with escaping the underworld alive, the thought of what would happen after didn't seem as pressing. But now that they were back among the living, she couldn't help but wonder. Would Metzi just hand the throne back to Ahkin? What would Ahkin do with her for killing their parents and tricking him into sacrificing himself? Was it still Ahkin's plan to make Mayana his empress? How would the head priest—or the whole empire for that matter—respond to his decision? Last time she was in Tollan, she had been branded a heretic and dismissed by everyone, including her own family.

More questions that would have to wait.

"Good luck," Ochix said, clapping Ahkin on the shoulder. Ahkin's jaw tensed, but he inclined his head in thanks anyway.

Ochix smirked. "And if anything happens to Yemania, I will return the gutting favor."

Mayana then stifled a gasp of surprise when Ochix drew Yemania to him and kissed her. "I'll see you soon," he told her. He released her and turned to face Mayana. "Ready to rescue some bones, daughter of water?"

She nodded, not trusting herself to speak. A sick sense of foreboding filled her stomach as she watched Ahkin and Yemania lead the small group of farmers out into the stone hallway. Ahkin bent and retrieved one of the sleeping guards' knives and tucked it into the waistband of his once-white wrap. Some of the farmers also picked over the discarded weapons, though most looked unsure how to use them. One older man carried a dagger as though it were a snake about to bite him.

Ahkin turned back briefly, his worried eyes meeting her own. She knew separating felt as awful to him as it did to her. They had survived hell together, and now they were facing incredible dangers without each other. She nodded to him, and he nodded back, a wordless connection passing between them.

Come back to me, he silently pleaded.

I always will, she wanted to say back. Mayana broke their connected gazes, and the weight of his absence settled onto her shoulders. She told herself she would see him again. She had to.

While Ahkin, Yemania, and the group of peasants disappeared around a corner, swallowed by the dark bowels of the temple, Ochix lead her down a separate hall. They carefully stepped over the bodies of four guards, fingers and lips stained yellow from the root, all lying where Ochix had left them. The light of the burning torches flickered across their sleeping faces.

Mayana's head was still reeling from what she'd just witnessed. Yemania—sweet, shy, insecure *Yemania*—was not only friends with a death prince, she'd kissed him! How in the nine hells had that happened?

"So, um. You and Yemania?" she whispered to Ochix's back.

He slowed and turned to face her with a smirk pulling at the corner of his mouth. Mayana got the distinct impression this death prince thought very highly of himself.

"Me and Yemania," he confirmed with an arch of his eyebrow. "Does that displease you, daughter of water?"

"I—I don't—" Mayana swallowed the thick lump that formed in her throat. "No. I don't mind. I just can't—How?"

"If we make it out of Omitl alive, I will happily explain it to you.

The tale is harrowing and dramatic and I want to make sure I do it justice."

Mayana snorted. *Very* highly of himself.

They wound their way through countless dark passageways until the dank stone walls turned brighter and drier, some even hung with woven tapestries or painted in intricate geometric patterns. They were leaving the realm of captives and entering the household of the Miquitz royal family.

Ochix checked each hall, making sure that any servants wandering this late at night would not see them. Soon, windows joined the tapestries and painted designs, offering glimpses of the mountains and winking stars beyond. Mayana swore the stars turned their attention to her, their malevolence cold and unnerving. She could sense their lust for the power housed in her blood. They did not want her to succeed.

They wanted to devour her.

Back home in Atl, her family's palace was a separate structure from their stone temple pyramid. The grand architecture of Tollan, capital of the Chicome Empire, followed the same pattern. But here in Omitl, their royal palace and temple seemed to be one and the same, a gargantuan structure fit for both a high priest and an emperor descended from the gods. Though their path remained confined to the twisting stone hallways, Mayana caught images of the luxurious rooms beyond. Storerooms overflowing with furs and weaving, baskets of fruits and grains grown from the terraced gardens that were rumored to cover the steep mountain slopes of their empire. There were meeting rooms, housing for servants, courtrooms, and libraries—endless libraries of codex sheets and histories and star charts. Mayana observed shrines built to different gods and altars, along with an armory of obsidian blades and weapons. Once, Mayana briefly glimpsed a room with towering jade pillars and a carved throne of the same iridescent green.

Ochix finally darted into a storeroom and motioned for her to follow. She did, slipping inside as silently as a shadow. It was a small room lined with shelves of pottery and baskets of grain. The scent of maize and dust teased her nose, almost making her sneeze.

The death prince drew the curtain closed behind them. "My father's rooms are down this next hallway," he whispered. "I'd hope he was sleeping, but to be honest, I know he's not. He's probably still drawing weird pictures all over his star charts and murmuring about who he wants to kill next. I'm going to go in first and see if I can distract him. Then you'll need to sneak in and steal the bones."

"Where do I go once I get the bag?"

"If you can, meet me back in this storeroom and we will make our way out from here. Then it's just a jolly jaunt back to your capital."

Mayana studied the determined set of his squared jaw, the desperate humor dancing in his eyes, teasing without needing to say a word. He was certainly handsome. But she also sensed a depth to him that he tried to mask with his bravado, like a pool that appeared shallow until you dove in.

"Thank you for doing this. I know it can't be easy to go against your own father."

Ochix shrugged. "It's easy when your father is a psychopath that tries to murder you for questioning him."

Mayana flinched. Her relationship with her own father was tense at best, but she also sensed it bothered Ochix more than he was showing. "Still," she touched his shoulder, "that doesn't mean it doesn't hurt."

Ochix laughed and twitched his shoulder away. But the laugh sounded hollow to her ears and he wouldn't meet her eyes. "Hurts a lot less than a blade to the gut and a tumble off a waterfall, I'll tell you that much."

"Tumble off a waterfall? You didn't mention that part before."

Ochix traced a finger along the scar on his abdomen. "He made me stab myself and pushed me off the balcony of his rooms. I fell and hit the water down below, but I don't remember anything past that. The next thing I knew I had washed up on a riverbank somewhere down in the valley. That's where Yemania found me and healed me."

"And apparently stole your heart in the process?"

"It's hard not to fall for a heart like hers."

Mayana beamed. "I agree."

Ochix cocked his head at her. "Are we going to get these bones, princess, or are you going to keep probing me about my feelings?"

Heat bloomed across the back of her neck. "Sorry, yes. Let's get the bones."

"Wait a few minutes to follow me. I'm going to try to get him to leave the room. Watch through the door and when he does, be quick. The bones should be on one of his work tables. I'll possess the guards outside to make sure they don't notice you." He pulled his bone-handled blade from his waistband.

Panic fluttered in her stomach. "Okay," she said in a small voice.

With a nod, Ochix disappeared behind the curtain.

Mayana waited several minutes, trying to calm her breathing. She was about to walk into the personal chambers of the crazed emperor of the Miquitz. He was a descendant of Cizin, the treacherous god of death who had taken the bones of her mother. The god that had sent the owl to stop them escaping the underworld. The god that had cost them the life of Ona.

Her breath came in angry gasps. Thinking about this now was *not* the best way to stay calm. At least Ochix seemed to be nothing like his ancestor—well, aside from his tendency to possess people's souls without their permission.

Mayana clenched her teeth. She had promised Ahkin and the Mother she would get the bones.

She had to go. Now.

6

Metzi hated council meetings. It wasn't because the endless talks of finances, politics, or warfare bored her—on the contrary, she found those aspects entertaining. A challenge to finally stretch the boundaries of her cleverness.

No. She hated them because it meant being stuck in a room with a bunch of somber old men who didn't have the strength to do what was necessary. They spent hours debating, arguing and posturing, all while lounging on their furs and feasting on the best delicacies the empire had to offer. A waste of everyone's precious time. Metzi had not gotten to where she was because of her inability to act. It was time her advisors showed the same level of decisiveness as their empress.

"The invitations to the royal families of the other city-states have been dispatched," Yaotl, the general of the elite Jaguar warriors said from across the table. For the meeting, he had traded his traditional warrior costume of jaguar pelts for a rich blue nobleman's cloak. "Ehecatl will not stand in opposition for long."

"No, they shall not," Metzi agreed, rising to her feet. "They have rejected every offer of peace and every attempt at intimidation. Those pious wind-worshippers need to bend the knee to their true empress once and for all. They will not do so until they are forced to their knees by the collective weight of the empire. For too long my father tried to appease them, giving in to their demands like a parent bribing a spoiled child. The only way to stop the tantrums of a spoiled child is through strict discipline."

"Well said, your highness," Yaotl agreed, banging a fist on the table in solidarity. Metzi doubted the general would be as supportive of her if he knew the truth about how she had risen to power. Ahkin had been his battle protégé from the time he was a boy. The two had shared a relationship as deep as that of father and son. Still, Yaotl's support of her now provided much-needed confidence.

The other advisors glanced nervously at each other, their movements sending their beaded necklaces rattling into the silence.

"You do not agree?" Metzi said, staring each of them down in turn.

It was Toani, the head priest of the Chicome Empire, who spoke first. He rose, his bloodred cloak pooling at his feet, the feathers of his elaborate headpiece adding to his already considerable height. Deep creases lined his aged face. His voice was slow and deliberate, but as powerful as a lava flow. "You are young and inexperienced in the ways of war, my dear. Gathering the leaders of the other city-states here and presenting a united front may yet persuade the rebels to acquiesce. Ehecatl's submission is a necessity, but when it comes to our divine brothers and sisters, peaceful submission is always preferable to a bloody one."

My dear? He dared to speak to the daughter of the sun as if she were a petulant child? Metzi slammed her hand against the table. "Toani. You know I respect your wisdom, but my intent in summoning the leaders of the other city-states is not merely a show to intimidate. I intend to mobilize and march on Ehecatl and their city on the sea. I need the help of the other city-states to *weaken* their resolve. When we do march, it will be to victory."

Toani tilted his withered chin toward the heavens. She could tell the older man had a distaste for outright displays of strength, preferring to wield his control and influence in ways that were much more manipulative. She hadn't forgotten how he'd lured the daughter of water into that trap before the whole empire to humiliate her. "And how do you intend to weaken their resolve, my empress?" he asked.

At that, Metzi grinned. Let them finally see for themselves the level of her daring. "I have asked the lords of each city-state to bring at least two other members of their bloodline. With the power of the gods, we will bring Ehecatl to her knees. I will have the lord of Atl cut off any supply of water into their city. The lord of Millacatl will shrivel any seedling that attempts to sprout through their earth. Papatlaca will burn the homes of the outer villages to force everyone within the walls of the city. I will have every nagual from Ocelotl harass the citizens with bees, flies, and toads, while Pahtia prevents their wounds from healing. All until the people beg their royal family to submit."

She glared at every slack-jawed face around the table. "So when they are homeless and starving, bitten and stung to the point of desperation, we will march into the city and kill the Storm Lord himself."

There was a collective gasp around the room. The priest narrowed his eyes.

"Your majesty—" one of the advisors began, but Metzi cut across him.

"You cut off the head of the beast and the rest of it loses the will to fight. His sons and daughters will continue the sacrifices that will prevent storms. Our empire will remain safe."

She said the words, but even as she said them, a horrible thought occurred to her. A sense of dread settled in her stomach. The Obsidian Butterfly had promised her an empire, but she had said she did not necessarily mean the *Chicome* Empire. Metzi still wasn't sure what the vague promise meant, but her mouth went suddenly dry. Was it possible that this war with Ehecatl was pointless? She glanced down at the map sketches on the table, to the drawings that represented where Ehecatl's forces had been seen mobilizing. She swallowed hard, her throat aching. Was the Butterfly hinting that there might not even *be* a Chicome Empire in the near future? Would it matter if Ehecatl surrendered, if there was no Chicome Empire to obey?

She would have to consult with the goddess as soon as possible. She needed answers. *Demanded* answers.

"It is an effective battle strategy. Harsh, but effective," Yaotl confirmed.

Metzi exhaled sharply through her nose. The other nobles apparently did not have minds for the military. They were merchants, religious leaders, judges. They did not know what it felt like to strategize, to fight for the upper hand.

Toani cleared his throat, his jaw tight with restraining whatever he was feeling. "Perhaps, your majesty, we can—"

"Am I your empress or not? Do I raise the sun or not?" Again, the Butterfly's words to her made her sick. According to the goddess, her blood did not really raise the sun at all. It could control it, yes, but because of Quetzalcoatl's initial sacrifice, the sun would rise *without* her. Did that mean the sacrifices of the other city-states, the ones done to prevent other forms of disasters, did not matter either? Assuming that was even true, there was no way she was going to tell anyone. Let them continue to think the way they had for generations. She would not hand over her greatest weapon to her enemies.

The head priest pursed his lips but did not argue. He gave her a look of shrewd calculation and assessment that deeply unnerved her. It was almost as if he knew her secret but also knew better than to speak of it in front of the other council members.

"We will meet again once the royal families have arrived," she said, dismissing them.

Benches scraped against the stone floor as the noblemen rose to their feet. Everyone bowed, though some not as deeply as others, before filing from the meeting room. Toani lingered as though he wanted to say more, but she dismissed him with a wave of her hand.

The throbbing behind Metzi's eyes began again. She ran a hand along her temple, pressing lightly with her fingertips.

As satisfied as she was with her newfound power and position, dealing with such small-minded fools still grated on her nerves.

Hopefully the other royal families of the empire would be more agreeable.

———

Metzi retreated to her rooms and sent her guards to stand at the end of the hall.

With a quick sacrifice of blood to her star stone, Metzi paced her rooms, waiting for the Obsidian Butterfly to materialize. The torches flickered, a cold chill swept through the room, and once again the horrifyingly beautiful face of the Butterfly appeared over the small altar. The goddess's hungry eyes focused on the cut on Metzi's finger for the briefest moment. Her lips dripped with fresh blood—Metzi's own blood, she realized with a start. The blood she'd just fed to the stone. Metzi's sacrifice must have been what gave the goddess enough energy to appear for this brief meeting.

"I need to ask you something," Metzi started.

"That is not a reverent greeting for a goddess," the Butterfly's frigid voice answered.

"Sorry." Metzi bowed her head. "Thank you for blessing me with your presence."

The goddess watched her through narrowed eyes, but eventually she seemed appeased. "What is it you wish to know, daughter of light?"

"You mentioned before about giving me an empire that was not the *Chicome* Empire. What did you mean by that? What are your plans for my people?"

"You also asked before why I sought to bring you to Omitl."

A typically confusing answer. Metzi felt impatience burning in her chest, but she could not speak down to a goddess the way she would to one of her advisors. "Are you saying you are planning to give me the Miquitz Empire? Is that why you wanted me to marry their prince, Ochix?"

"The Chicome are unlikely to let go of their obsession for the greater gods. Or their control," was her only answer.

Metzi fought the urge to growl in frustration. "And the Miquitz are?"

"Their loyalty is to Cizin, who also holds little love for our favored brothers and sisters. While we were banished to the stars, Cizin and his followers were banished to rule the underworld. He is fortunate his descendants have not forgotten him."

"And you think the emperor of the Miquitz will just hand over his empire to me?"

The goddess cackled. "I have promised that I will spare his people should he serve me. But the man is a fool, as all men are. I will use him and then dispose of him when he no longer serves his purpose."

Metzi nodded appreciatively, glad to be finally getting some answers. "And what purpose is he serving now?"

"The people of the Chicome fear the death of the sun, and as you know, they believe without your blood the sun will fail to rise. They would never support willingly sacrificing your brother to hold the eclipse in place. Whereas Tzom . . . well." She gave another bloodthirsty laugh. "He has no qualms sacrificing a child of the sun for me."

Metzi blinked. "Ahkin? But he's dead."

"No, my dear. Your brother has survived."

Metzi's stomach clenched in panic. Ahkin couldn't come back! That would ruin everything. *Everything.*

"Do not fear, my child. Tzom failed to capture him on the battlefield, but by convincing him to throw himself into Xibalba, you sent him to Omitl another way. Tzom has already captured him and will sacrifice the sun prince at the eclipse ceremony in two weeks' time, holding the darkness in place long enough for me and my children to escape."

At first, relief washed through her, but then Metzi's hand flew to her mouth, understanding hitting her over the head like a rock. "And then you will descend and devour the Chicome? Leaving the Miquitz Empire with me as their new empress?"

The goddess's eyes sparkled with mania as she cocked her head to the side. "I knew you were a clever girl. See? You are getting all your heart desires after all."

Metzi took a step back, stumbling slightly on the hem of her dress. "You never told me you were going to devour *my people.*"

"They will no longer be your people. They have mistreated you and so many others like you. Their thirst for power and control knows no bounds. You don't even know the extent of their greed. You owe nothing to them. Even now, I watch you fight with your own advisors, trying to make them see reason when their prejudices continue to hold you back from greatness. They will never truly accept you as empress. They are too set in their ways."

Metzi blinked back tears. The Chicome were not perfect; they still had much to learn, that was true. But who better to teach them than Metzi? Who better to force the Chicome to see what greatness was possible? They were still *her* people.

"I sense remorse stirring inside your heart, daughter of light. Are you regretting our deal? Should I take away all that I have given to you?"

Metzi shook her head, panic clenching her heart. "No! I will not lose everything I've fought for."

"Then prove to me you have the strength to do what is necessary," the goddess demanded. "If you do, you will be rewarded. But fail, and I will find another way that involves you perishing alongside the people you seek to protect."

Metzi raged against the sadness clinging to her, the grief begging her to change her course. She had already killed her parents, tricked her brother into almost killing himself. She knew pain, she knew sacrifice. But every step she'd taken was a step toward freedom, a step away from the wretched helplessness she'd felt her entire life. Her memory floated back to the words the traitor Yemania had spoken to her: *There is a difference between strength and cruelty.* No, she'd come this far already. She'd made the hard decisions that were necessary, taken her fate into her own hands for the first time in her life. She had tasted freedom and power, and no one would ever take them from her again.

Metzi cleared her throat, her voice stronger. "Then what am I to do about this war with Ehecatl?"

"Let the Chicome fight amongst themselves all they wish. Let them distract themselves from the true enemy that is coming. The weaker they are, the easier it will be for my demons and I to devour them." She seemed gleeful at the very thought, her gaze again focusing on the cut on Metzi's finger. Metzi recognized the crazed bloodlust inside the goddess's star-bright eyes, the same kind of thirst she herself felt for power. It was a heady thing, intoxicating.

And she knew from experience that once power had been tasted, she would do anything to keep it.

CHAPTER

7

Mayana crept toward the doorway ahead. There was a rushing sound of water beyond that energized the blood in her veins. The jade skull pendant the Mother had given her felt cold against her skin.

Two guards in black cloaks stood sentinel on either side, obsidian-tipped spears glistening in the torchlight as though flames still danced within them. As she neared, she noticed their dark eyes were clouded with a silver mist. They did not turn or acknowledge her as she passed.

"Hurry," one of them whispered in the cadence of Ochix's voice.

"You can talk through them too?" she whispered back. Gods, that was creepy.

The guard did not answer.

Black beads and toucan feathers dangled across the doorway, and Mayana held her breath as she parted them as soundlessly as she could. Several still clattered back into place. She clenched her teeth, frustrated with herself. Hopefully the sound of the waterfall outside had damp-ened the noise.

She stepped into the chamber and felt her jaw drop. Tzom's rooms were lined in jade-green pillars like the throne room, intricate patterns carved around them like geometric snakeskin. An expansive balcony stretched out from a curved opening in the wall, exposing a breathtak-ing view of the moonlit mountains and the waterfall that rushed right past. Her stomach tightened. That must have been where Ochix had fallen.

Wooden shelves sagged under the weight of stacks of maguey papers and engraved stone tablets. The tables littered around the room boasted instruments and tools Mayana had never seen before. Ahkin would kill to inspect some of the star charts draped haphazardly around, as though Tzom had tired of them and thrown them aside at random.

But what unnerved her most was the image drawn over and over across almost every surface she could see: a skull with eyes like stars. It reminded her of the time her younger brother Tenoch had stolen a piece of charcoal and practiced his glyphs around his room. Her father had been furious.

But *this* was infinitely more sinister. Tzom was obsessed with releasing the star demons. The truth of it screamed at her from every star-eyed image.

She scanned the surface of the tables for signs of her woven bag, a simple brown thing that was worthless aside from the priceless bones it held. Male voices sounded from a side room, and her pulse pounded in her ears. They sounded tense, angry. She needed to hurry. *Where was it?* She searched the tables closest and didn't find anything, so she moved to the tables along the walls. It had to be here somewhere. Panic began to squeeze its claws around her chest. She didn't have time to waste.

Finally, *finally*, she spotted it on a table beside the balcony. Next to it sat a random collection of crude knives and farming tools, as well as Ahkin's ancestor's shield. The soldiers had taken it from him when they were captured. Perhaps the other items had been confiscated from the peasants when they were taken.

She darted forward, relief easing the burning panic in her chest. She stifled a sob as her hands closed around the strap. The jade bones winked from within, and she hugged them to her chest. "Thank the gods," she whispered. She reached forward to grab Ahkin's shield too, but a sandal slapped behind her. Mayana's heart leapt into her throat, and she whirled.

It was Ochix.

She lifted a hand to her throat. "Nine hells, Ochix." She released a breath. "Don't scare me like that. I've got them—let's get out of here."

She reached for the shield again, but his hand shot out and grabbed her arm. "You're not going anywhere," he said, a growl in his voice.

"Ochix, you're hurting me, what—"

She turned her head and the breath rushed out of her lungs. Tzom stood in the doorway, the shock in his eyes turning slowly into suspicion.

"What's this?" the death priest asked.

"I caught her trying to steal these," Ochix said, dragging Mayana forward. She swore the sound of her heart breaking was loud enough to hear over the waterfall. How could Ochix betray her like this? Betray Yemania like this?

"You filthy *demon*," Mayana hissed at him, trying to jerk her arm free.

Tzom's eyes narrowed. "How did you escape the dungeons, little princess?"

Mayana clamped her teeth together. If Ochix had been working on his father's orders, she didn't want to give him the satisfaction of knowing his trick had worked.

Tzom's attention shifted to the bag in her arms. "So you escape, and do not run. Instead, you come back for the bag. What is so valuable about the bones inside, my dear? What would be worth taking such a deadly risk?"

Ochix reached to pry the bag away from her, but Mayana elbowed him in the gut. Right over his scar. Ochix grunted, his eyes sharp with warning, but he ripped the bones from her grasp anyway.

"I'll take her back to the dungeons," Ochix said. He started marching her toward the door.

"Wait just a moment." Tzom stepped in front of them, blocking their exit. "While she is here, nothing says we cannot make her useful."

A muscle twitched in Ochix's jaw. "Of course. What do you intend?"

"The Obsidian Butterfly might appreciate a little . . . gift of good faith."

Mayana's chest heaved and she pulled harder against Ochix's grip.

"A gift?" Ochix's brow creased.

"Common servant blood feeds her power well enough, but she might like a treat that's a little more *divine*." Tzom's eyes raked up and down Mayana's body, as if she were a fruit he was examining to purchase in the marketplace. Then he reached into his robes and withdrew a long black ceremonial knife. He ran a finger lovingly along its edge. "She will be so pleased."

Ochix cleared his throat. "Shouldn't we question the princess about the bones first? What the Chicome intend to do with them?"

"The bones will remain in my chambers, and whatever purpose they were intended for will not be served."

Tzom stepped closer, lifting a hand to her neck. "I can smell the water in her blood," he said, his thumb tracing one of the veins. "So cool. So refreshing. I imagine the goddess will *love* the rush of power your blood gives to her."

Mayana had just left the underworld; she didn't want to go back anytime soon. Her thoughts cast around for anything to save herself. If she could cut herself, she could call forth the water from her necklace or even the waterfall . . .

But before she got the chance, Ochix's grip on her loosened. He reached for his own blade and drew it across his palm. His blood glistened like rubies. He shoved the bones back into her arms and threw his bloodied hand toward his father. "Run!" he screamed.

Tears threatened to burn their way down her cheeks. He hadn't betrayed her at all. He was trying to save her.

Silver mist coated Tzom's eyes, and the blade in his hand clattered to the floor. But as quickly as they clouded, the mist cleared.

Tzom roared in frustration. "You dare to possess me? You think yourself strong enough to control *me*?"

Ochix growled, fighting to exert his hold over his father. Tzom's eyes momentarily clouded again as he thrashed against unseen bonds.

But Mayana glanced toward the doorway, where she knew Ochix was also controlling the guards. Hadn't he told her that the more people he tried to control, the more difficult it was? There was no way he could control his father while his attention was divided.

That's when she noticed the knife Tzom had dropped. She didn't think. She dove for it.

Her fingers closed around the bone handle, and in one fluid motion, she drove it up toward Tzom's heart.

But at the last second, the death priest moved. Instead of piercing his chest, the blade sank into his arm. Tzom screamed and ripped the blade out, his eyes clearing. Blood rushed down his arm in a torrent.

Panic reared its ugly head as Mayana realized she'd just released his own power to possess. And if the power of Cizin's descendants worked anything like her own, the more blood that was exposed, the stronger the power became.

Tzom's scream turned into a crazed laugh as he beheld the wound in his arm. He reached toward his son with an open palm. Ochix met her gaze for the briefest moment, her own terror reflected in his black eyes before they clouded over with the mist of possession.

What had she done? Her legs went weak as a wave of dizziness crashed over her. Mayana scrambled back, taking the bag of bones with her.

Ochix prowled toward her like a wolf, his bloody hands reaching for her.

Mayana's heart thrashed inside her chest. "Ochix! Fight it! Fight it, please!" she cried, her vision blurring with tears.

"He cannot fight me," Tzom laughed. "And neither can you." The beads covering the doorway clattered as the guards entered the room, spears raised. Now that Ochix was no longer possessing them, their wills were fully their own.

She was cornered. There was no way out. No way except . . . Mayana turned, facing the waterfall. The same waterfall Ochix himself had fallen down. If he didn't die from his fall, then—

She backed up far enough that her heels kissed the ledge of the balcony. Mist from the waterfall coated her skin and blew at the tattered remnants of her loincloth skirt. A shiver ran down her spine at the sudden chill that swept through her.

Tzom forced Ochix to stop. Her friend now stood—placid and unmoving—mere steps in front of her. Tzom's face split into a grin as gruesome as the skulls painted all over his rooms. "I know what you are thinking, daughter of water. Yes, you would likely survive the fall. But my treacherous son will suffer for both of you. Instead of your blood, I will feed *his* to the Obsidian Butterfly."

A sob ripped its way out of her. She couldn't leave Ochix to die here, not after all he'd done to save them. Yemania would never forgive her. Mayana would never forgive herself.

She watched in horror as Tzom made Ochix turn the blade toward his own neck. Ochix's eyes cleared briefly as he fought his own hand, but the mist quickly stole him back under.

"Hand over the bones, daughter of water. Tell me whose they are and why they are so important to the Chicome, and I might let you live. But leap from that ledge, and my son's body will follow you. And this time, I will make sure he is dead *before* he falls."

Through the haze of panic Mayana swore she could hear Ahkin's voice, his blatant refusal to accept a difficult choice. His determination to find another way. *There is always another way.*

The waterfall was her only escape, and she could not leave Ochix behind. There was one clear answer. But she would only have the element of surprise for so long—

She inched her finger into the bag, finding a sharp edge of one of Quetzalcoatl's bones. Her finger stung as she found it, but she smiled despite herself. She cut deeper, bringing forth as much blood as she could without Tzom noticing.

"Make your choice. I don't have all day to wait," he hissed.

"Then I won't make you wait any longer," she said, flinging her arm wide. Water burst free from the waterfall behind her, barreling in a stream right toward Tzom's face. The death priest flew backward, landing hard on his back. The guards rushed forward. But it was the chance she needed.

Just as Ochix's eyes cleared, his mouth gaping, she grabbed his hand and yanked him toward the ledge.

And together, they leapt into the waterfall.

...

CHAPTER

8

Yemania's eyes never left where the path had spilled the escapees onto the muddy riverbank, illuminated by the light of the full moon. It was still dark, but they'd been waiting at the base of the mountains for what felt like hours, and there was still no sign of Mayana or Ochix.

Yemania chewed her bottom lip until she tasted blood. Her fingers were almost numb from fiddling with the hem of her woven dress. She pulled her knees closer to her chest and hugged them, though her arms longed to embrace someone else. If Mayana and Ochix didn't appear soon, they would have to leave for Millacatl without them.

The peasants had been slow in their descent from the mountain city, the small goat path steep and rocky. Ahkin was patient and kind, helping the older ones navigate the tricky terrain. Still, it took much longer than Yemania anticipated. The Miquitz would soon discover them missing and pursue.

Her stomach twisted itself into knots. There should have been some sign of Mayana and Ochix by now.

They waited along a river cutting through a canyon created by two sloping hillsides. The thick greenery that coated the foothills made it difficult to see the mountainous peaks they had just clambered down. Still, if Mayana and Ochix took the same path, then the gap in the trees should be where they emerged. Next to where Yemania sat upon a flat rock, the river twisted like a brown boa, hugging the ravine walls and rushing past them in a smooth but steady current.

An older man with a weather-beaten face bent over the river's edge, bringing the water to his lips with trembling hands. A group of women dressed in simple tunic dresses stained with mud huddled close together, their eyes darting about the riverbank as though Miquitz raiders might appear at any moment.

Ahkin, however, just paced. And paced. And paced. Yemania half expected him to wear the canyon deeper if he didn't stop.

"Ahkin, you need to sit down. Rest. Please."

"No, I'm fine."

Yemania's gaze dropped to where his sandals had dug angry marks into the skin on top of his feet. "You're not fine. You're anxious to fight, but there is nothing here to fight. All we can do is wait."

"I don't like waiting."

Yemania loosed a sigh. "Neither do I, but you're making me nervous."

"I shouldn't have let her go with him. I knew this wasn't a good idea. How do we even know we can trust him?"

"We can trust him," Yemania almost growled.

"I should go back. What if they've been captured?" One of Ahkin's hands opened and closed as if it itched for a weapon. She didn't want her own fears given a voice. He was going to drive her insane along with him.

"I'm worried too, Ahkin. If they aren't here in another hour, we will have to start moving. We can't still be here at dawn."

Ahkin made a grumbling sound. "I will hold back the dawn if I have to."

Yemania rolled her eyes, not sure she was supposed to hear that last part. "Have a little faith."

The mention of faith seemed to ease his nervous tension. Slightly.

"You're right. I need to have faith in her and faith that the Mother will protect her."

Yemania fiddled with the hem of her skirt again, running her fingernail along the edge. "Why are these bones so important anyway?"

It was Ahkin's turn to sigh. By some miracle, he actually stopped his nervous pacing and settled down on the rock beside her.

"When we first fell into Xibalba, the Mother goddess warned us it would be a dangerous journey," he said. "She gave us gifts to help us survive, but even then she couldn't guarantee we'd make it out alive." He shook his head as though dispelling disturbing memories. "But she also made us promise to retrieve the bones of her son, Quetzalcoatl, from the lord of the dead."

Yemania's hand covered her mouth. They'd taken the bones of Quetzalcoatl from Cizin, the lord of death himself? "How did you get them?" she asked from behind her fingers.

He launched into the story, describing every horrific layer of the underworld and the dangers he and Mayana had narrowly escaped. Had they not been descendants of the gods, they would have certainly perished. He told her about Ona, Mayana's childhood dog that the Mother goddess had resurrected for the journey, how he'd been dying from his injuries and sacrificed himself to make sure they could escape. How Mayana had found the bones of her own mother, and how Cizin had forced her to trade them for the jade bones of the god of wind.

By the time Ahkin finished, Yemania's cheeks were wet with tears. How had Mayana been able to endure such pain? How had her friend not given up hope in the face of so much darkness?

But as she studied the starkly handsome features of Ahkin's face— features that were often darkened with sullenness to hide his true feelings—she knew how.

Mayana hadn't done it by herself. There was strength in companionship, in realizing that you didn't have to face the world alone. There was incredible comfort in knowing that when you fell, another soul would carry you until you could walk again. She'd gotten a taste of that herself with Ochix. But now the thought of him throbbed like a bruise.

"So the Mother mentioned taking the bones to the Caves of Creation . . ." Yemania mused. "Do you think she intends to bring Quetzalcoatl back?"

Ahkin rubbed the back of his neck. "That's what I think. He may be our only hope to defeat the Obsidian Butterfly."

As he flexed his hand again, Yemania's attention caught on the way he couldn't fully extend his fingers, on the oddly swollen, crooked joints. "Ahkin, what did you do to your hand?"

He tried to flex it again, wincing slightly as he did. "It was crushed beneath a rock. The dog, Ona, had the ability to heal with his tongue. He healed the broken bleeding skin, but much of the internal damage was already done."

"May I see it?" She held out her own hand in invitation.

Ahkin looked down at it, a crease forming between his eyebrows.

Yemania sighed impatiently. "I won't hurt it, I promise. Just let me look at it."

Ahkin seemed torn, as if he didn't want to show how badly he was injured, but he finally did as she commanded.

She spread his fingers apart gently, running her own fingers along the bulging tendons. The blood of Ixtlilton, her ancestor and the god of healing, warmed inside her veins. It told her all she needed to know.

The bones were not set properly, and she would need to rebreak his hand to fix it. "I'm amazed you're able to use it at all," she told him.

Ahkin jerked his hand back, flexing it again. "It's painful. But sometimes there are more important things than pain."

"Yes, but if pain can be lessened, there is no need to bear it unnecessarily."

Ahkin met her gaze, hope budding to life within the depths of his eyes. "Can you heal it?"

Yemania sucked in a breath between her teeth. "Yes, technically I can. It may never return to what it was, but I do believe I can lessen your pain considerably."

"Then please." He thrust his hand back into hers. "By all means, heal it."

"I'm afraid that to relieve the pain, you will have to go through much worse first."

Ahkin's eyes went wide. "What do you mean?"

"I will have to rebreak it and set it correctly. The bones and tendons can heal with the use of my blood, but even then, it would be sore for days."

"Rebreak it?" His tone was as flat as the rock beneath them.

"Not now, obviously. But think on it. Perhaps when we get to Millacatl. That way it is healed by the time we reach Tollan."

Ahkin grimaced. "That should be fine. I'd rather wait for you to torture me until after Mayana returns. I'm not sure I wish to handle both forms of punishment at once."

Yemania's cheeks dimpled. "I think that is a wise decision, your highness."

He was quiet for several moments, thoughtful. Then he finally said, "When we return, I would be honored if you were to serve as my High Healer. Obviously there won't be a selection ritual anymore, and you clearly have the heart and skill that—"

A scream suddenly shattered their moment of peace.

Yemania and Ahkin leapt to their feet. Already a small group of peasants was retreating from the riverbank, a woman pointing toward the muddied water.

"There's a beast in the water! Some kind of monster," she cried.

Though the landscape was lit with moonlight, the shadows of the trees still obscured parts of the river. Something was definitely moving within the currents, something bigger than any fish. Had they disturbed a spirit that protected this part of the river?

Ahkin ordered the farmers behind him, his knife already in his injured hand. His jaw clenched in pain as he squeezed the handle.

The water erupted and expelled—not a monster—but two flailing human bodies. A great wave washed them ashore and onto the muddy riverbank. The peasants gasped. Ahkin sprinted to the water's edge, Yemania close on his heels.

It was Mayana and Ochix.

They both coughed and retched, Mayana climbing to her hands and knees while Ochix flipped onto his back. Ahkin was beside Mayana in a heartbeat, helping her to her feet.

"What happened?" he demanded, drawing her into a tight embrace.

Mayana did not answer. She merely coughed and held up the bag of bones in confirmation of their success.

Yemania dropped to her knees beside Ochix, her fluttering hands already assessing him for damage. She didn't sense any beyond cold and shock. Then, she threw her arms around him, thanking the gods above they'd made it back safe.

"How did you end up in the river?" Yemania squeaked.

Ochix pointed to Mayana, a wry smile curving on his lips as he sat up. "Ask your crazy, brilliant friend."

Yemania jumped to her feet and threw her arms around Mayana. "I was so worried about you both." Tears stung behind her eyes. "I'm glad you're okay."

She assessed Mayana for any injuries, but like Ochix, she seemed fine beyond shivering and a rapid, thudding pulse. A deep gash in her finger was bleeding, which explained the wave that had thrown them ashore. Yemania pricked her thumb and used the power of her own blood to seal the cut before any infection could set in.

"Thank you," Mayana said, sounding breathless. "I'm glad to see you all escaped safely too."

Ochix turned his attention to Ahkin. "We need to move. They will already be searching for us."

Ahkin nodded his agreement, twining his fingers through Mayana's. "Then let's get going. You can explain what happened along the way." He lifted Mayana's hand to his lips. "I want to hear every detail."

"Ask her how she attacked my father and then threw us both off the ledge of a waterfall to save our lives," Ochix said, winking at Mayana. He stumbled to his feet and steadied himself against Yemania's shoulder. Then he bent down and pressed a kiss to the side of her head. Yemania felt heat rising up the back of her neck.

"You did *what*?" Ahkin stared at Mayana, disbelief mingling with awe on his face.

"Well, I told you I'd bring the bones back," Mayana shrugged. "So I did."

Ochix leaned down and whispered in Yemania's ear. "I'm glad you're friends with that one. She's going to be one hell of an empress."

Yemania smiled but didn't respond. Of course she agreed with him. She was proud of her friend—always knew that Mayana would make a wonderful empress. But the look of awe on Ochix's face as he looked at Mayana sent a twinge of sadness through her.

Women like Mayana seemed destined to rise to greatness, to make a real difference in the world. But what about her? Would she always be destined to live in the shadows?

Ahkin tried to be patient with the pace of the peasants. He knew many of them were older, some injured, some still weak from hunger. But his nerves rankled at the thought of the Miquitz warriors catching up with them at any moment. The jungle heat grew more intense as day broke and wore on. The canopy of trees began to close overhead, enveloping them like the arms of a loved one welcoming them home into the valley. Ahkin was grateful to put distance between themselves and the Miquitz Mountains. At this pace, if they didn't take many breaks, they should make it to the gates of Millacatl before sundown.

He hovered near the back of the group, his head turning to check behind them so often that the death prince started asking if he had a neck problem.

"Seriously," Ochix said, clearly restraining a laugh. "You should have Yemania take a look at that for you."

Ahkin glared at the death prince. "No, I do not need to have my neck *looked* at. I am trying to make sure we aren't being followed."

Ochix continued to strut like a quetzal bird. "So am I."

Ahkin scoffed. "I haven't seen you do anything but bat your lashes at Yemania and make useless jokes."

Ochix quirked the corner of his mouth and lifted his thumb. A drop of blood glistened at the tip. "While you are giving yourself a neck cramp, I'm scanning for life forces around us." He winked conspiratorially. "And currently, all I am picking up within voice range of us is local fauna."

Ahkin glanced behind them one more time.

"Seriously, sun prince, give your neck a break."

"I am the *emperor*. Thank you very much."

Ochix arched an eyebrow. "I thought your sister was the empress right now."

Ahkin ground his teeth and turned his attention away from the death prince before he punched him in the teeth. "Mayana, could I get some fresh water, please?"

———

The day continued to grow warmer, and soon Ahkin's back was coated with sweat. The trees around them buzzed with the sound of cicadas and the occasional cry of a howler monkey. The older peasants were beginning to lag, and despite his better judgment, he knew they needed to rest.

"Let's stop for a few minutes," he called ahead.

There were audible sighs of relief.

Mayana walked around the group offering water from her jade skull pendant, while Yemania started checking the surrounding plants for anything edible.

"*Minutes*," Ahkin reminded them. "We aren't stopping for long."

Mayana waved a dismissive hand at him, as though he were an irritating gnat. "We will, but we won't make it very far if we end up having to carry half the peasants on our backs because they've collapsed."

He harrumphed, but she just patted his cheek and smiled at him endearingly. Ahkin couldn't help it; the corners of his mouth lifted. Mayana had a way of bringing out a side of him he often kept protected.

"I knew you could smile." Ochix came to stand beside him again.

And just like that, Ahkin felt his smile vanish. He sighed heavily. "Are you always like this?"

"Always," Ochix grinned.

He wanted to make another smart remark back, but Ochix held his hand up to stop him.

"Wait," Ochix whispered, suddenly serious. He closed his eyes in concentration.

Every muscle in Ahkin's body tensed. "Do you sense something?"

Ochix's eyes flew open, and he met Ahkin's gaze with somber confirmation. "Miquitz raiders. Quickly approaching."

Ahkin swore. "Mayana, Yemania, get the peasants moving. Raiders are coming. I'll hold them off."

There were cries of terror as the peasants clambered to their feet and began to run. Mayana met his gaze with a look of fierce determination. *I'll take care of them*, she seemed to say.

His stomach clenched as they all disappeared beyond a curve in the path ahead. He tightened his grip on the blade he'd stolen from a Miquitz guard. He'd spill their blood with one of their own knives.

To his surprise, Ochix remained beside him, his bone-handled blade ready in his own hand.

"You're willing to fight against your own people?" Ahkin asked.

"Well, I'm not going to let them capture you. You're kind of important."

Ahkin usually hated that arrogant smile, but this time his throat constricted when he saw it. He didn't know how to say thank you, so he just bent his head, a sign of gratitude and respect. Ochix returned the gesture.

"How many?" Ahkin asked.

Ochix closed his eyes again. "I'm sensing at least ten other souls."

"*Ten?*" Ahkin never would have been able to hold them off alone. But maybe with Ochix and their godly gifts, they'd stand a chance.

"Better use that invisibility trick," Ochix said, cutting deep into his palm and allowing the blood to pool there. "We're going to need it."

Ochix watched his fellow Miquitz warriors slink out from between the trees all around them. They had them surrounded.

The soldiers wore black cotton bodysuits adorned with brightly colored patterns and feathers. Many wore jewelry constructed of captured enemy bones, from earrings to nose piercings to necklaces like the one Ochix wore himself. His heart ached at the thought of fighting against men he had trained with from the time he was a boy. But they revered his father, followed his orders to any end. They did not see what Ochix had seen, the madness that had stolen his father away from all of them. Even his own younger brothers followed his father without question. They had not been educated to rule, trained to think and question as Ochix had.

They had been taught to obey. Like good soldiers.

He also knew there would be no reasoning with the raiders. He could sense the anger and hatred tainting their souls, almost like a bitter taste that lingered on his tongue. They believed him a traitor. They wished to capture the prince of the sun and as many escaped captives as they could, but they also wished Ochix *dead.*

With an almighty cry, the soldiers lifted their macana swords, wooden clubs inlaid with shards of obsidian fire-glass, and charged.

Two soldiers headed straight for Ahkin, who immediately disappeared. The two soldiers collided with each other, falling to the ground in a tangle of shields and swords. Ochix almost laughed. But then they screamed as an unseen blade found their throats, their blood coating the dirt.

Impressive. The sun prince knew how to hold his own in battle. Which was good, considering Ochix had his own problems to worry about.

A group of three soldiers surrounded him, weapons and wooden shields outstretched. He reached out his hand, and their eyes clouded with silver mist. The three soldiers' arms went slack, their weapons falling to the earth at their feet. With a few swift motions of Ochix's knife, their bleeding bodies joined their weapons.

Ochix turned, trying to judge the location of the sun prince—which he guessed was somewhere near where two soldiers spun and swung at the air in a panic—when another Miquitz soldier appeared right in front of him. The edge of a shield thrust into his gut, and Ochix fell back, his lungs aching. He gasped for breath and leapt back to his feet. Then he charged, his knife sinking into the wooden shield. He kicked out with a sandaled foot and sent the soldier to the ground, the shield sliding off the man's arm.

He ripped the knife free and jammed his own arm into the woven shield strap. He brought the shield down hard on the soldier's head with a sickening crack.

A burst of blinding light shot suddenly across the jungle path. Ochix's stomach tightened with panic: the light momentarily blinded him and hid his enemies from view.

"Hells, Ahkin, watch where you point that thing," he said, swinging his shield out and connecting with another raider's head.

"Sorry," Ahkin grunted somewhere to his right.

Ahkin then appeared, his concentration lapsing as he struggled, locked in hand-to-hand combat with a soldier wearing a skull mask. Another Miquitz soldier raised a sword behind him, ready to strike the sun prince in the back. The weapons were designed more to injure and capture than kill, but Ochix assumed Ahkin wouldn't appreciate a club of glass shards sinking into his back.

He possessed the soldier behind Ahkin, grabbing hold of his will and forcing him to stop. The macana sword froze midswing. Ahkin's knife sunk into the skull-faced soldier's chest. Ahkin then turned to see the frozen soldier standing behind him.

His eyes went wide with shock, then understanding. He drove his knife into the frozen soldier's chest too.

"Thanks," he called, wiping his knife on his already filthy waistcloth.

"Anytime." Ochix felt sorry for these common soldiers; their prowess against normal men was no match for descendants of the gods. And *battle-trained* descendants of the gods, at that.

Another flash of light flooded across his vision. Ochix winced, rubbing his face with his free hand. "Damn it, Ahkin, I thought I said . . ."

A thud sounded behind him. The last remaining soldier fell to the earth, clutching at his own sun-scorched face.

"Oh," Ochix said, bending to drive his knife into the incapacitated soldier's neck. "Thanks for that."

"Like you said, anytime." The sun prince actually grinned.

Ochix looked around, realizing they were now alone—the only two left standing amidst the carnage of fallen raiders.

"Well," Ochix said conversationally, rubbing his face again. "That went quicker than I expected. Of course, I could only see half of it."

Ahkin met his eye for the briefest moment, breathing heavily and coated in blood. Then they both broke into a fit of slightly hysterical laughter. Ahkin felt the pent-up energy and terror of the battle release itself. He clapped Ochix on the back, a moment of shared camaraderie between soldiers, before they rushed ahead to find the others.

Their empires were enemies, but that didn't mean they had to be.

10

Mayana didn't stop running. The bag containing the jade bones bounced against her chest, each thud a reminder of the burden she carried. She had to protect these bones no matter the cost. She could hear the clash of the battle behind her. Grunts and screams, the crashing of fire glass against wooden shields. Any one of those screams could be Ahkin. Or Ochix.

Yemania stifled a sob as she ran too, clutching at what must have been a stitch in her side. Mayana knew her friend's worries were the same as her own.

"They're soldiers," Mayana reminded herself. "They will be fine."

"I know, but it just sounds like there's so many of them," Yemania panted.

One of the captive women tripped, ripping her hands open on the rocky path. Yemania stopped to help her, healing the cuts on her hands and lifting her to her feet as quickly as she could.

"Thank you," the woman whispered before lifting the hem of her skirt to keep pace.

Mayana had no idea how long they ran. It felt like an entire age. Her feet pounded against the earth until each footfall shook through her body in painful throbs. Finally, when the sounds of the battle had long since faded and the older members of the group could not keep going, Mayana led them to a cluster of trees and bushes.

"Rest here," Mayana said. "I think we will be safe for a few moments."

"How close are we to home?" one of the older farmers asked, his lined face grave.

"It can't be far. Once we reach Millacatl, we will be safe," Mayana said, trying to catch her breath. She massaged her aching feet with her hands.

"Look!" a woman shouted, pointing between the wickerwork of branches surrounding them. "We're here!" Her voice broke. "We're *home*!"

Mayana pulled aside some of the branches for a better look. Sure enough, the jungle ahead of them transitioned into rolling hills. Fields of corn maize and other crops stretched out beneath the clouded sky. Mayana sensed water within the clouds. The air itself crackled with the energy of a looming storm. A rumble of thunder sent the birds in a nearby tree to wing.

"Do you sense the storm coming too?" Yemania asked.

Mayana eyed the clouds. "We will likely walk into Millacatl soaked to the bone."

Yemania giggled. "Well, at least we will get a chance to clean off. I'd kill for a steam bath right now."

"Me too."

Yemania reached for her hand and squeezed. "Ahkin told me some of what happened in Xibalba. I just want to tell you how proud I am of you. I'd love to hear more about it when you're ready."

"Thank you," Mayana said, her voice thick. But then she wiggled her eyebrows at the princess of healing. "And I want to hear more about how you ended up with a death demon."

Yemania suddenly became very preoccupied with the hem of her dress, a shy smile tugging at her lips. "We will have much to discuss."

"Indeed." Mayana bumped her shoulder playfully against Yemania's. It felt good to have her friend by her side again. Mayana loved Ahkin, but there was always a place inside a woman's heart that only other women could fill.

The sound of running feet made her ears perk up. She shushed the peasants and inched herself closer to the leaves to see who was approaching their hiding place.

Two pairs of men's sandals appeared on the path, their skin filthy with caked blood and dirt. They spoke in low voices, running at a controlled but steady pace. But she'd recognize those voices anywhere.

Mayana leapt from the bushes in front of them.

"Sweet Mother of all that is holy—" Ochix yelled, clutching at his chest. Ahkin, who had lifted his knife, was already lowering it in recognition.

"Mayana . . ." He ran to her, pulling her into an embrace.

Mayana suddenly drew back. "Gods, Ahkin, you're covered in blood. Again."

Ahkin shrugged. "I thought we've been through this before. When there's a *battle* . . ."

Mayana rolled her eyes and cut him off with a kiss. "The raiders?" she asked.

"Dead. The whole party," Ahkin assured her. "But that doesn't mean there aren't more coming."

Yemania sighed with relief, pulling herself out of Ochix's arms. "We're almost there," she said, taking Ochix's hand and leading him forward. "The farming fields start just beyond this line of trees."

━━━

The storm unleashed its fury just as the gates of Millacatl came into view. The rain was nothing like the rain Mayana had experienced in the underworld. There, it had been icy cold, drenching her heart as much as her body. But the warm tropical rains of the jungle were the same rains Mayana had known her whole life. They filled her heart instead of froze it. They could sweep in over the course of a few moments, then sweep out just as quickly, as though the rain god had passed a fleeting hand over creation. The wet, earthy scent of soil and flowers, the mist rising from the trees once the rain had cleared . . . it was one of Mayana's favorite things in all the world.

She spread her arms wide as the skies unleashed their deluge. It was moments like this she felt most in touch with her godly heritage—closest to the heart of Atlacoya, goddess of drought and floods.

The great stone city of Millacatl, home to the descendants of Xipe Totec, sat atop a low hill, rolling farmlands stretching around it in all directions. It was one of the Chicome Empire's most important city-states, providing most of the food throughout the empire. It was also the richest, as the royal family used their blood to grow the cacao beans the empire used for currency.

"This is Teniza's city, isn't it?" Mayana whispered to Yemania. She remembered the princess of plants from the selection ritual. She had been haughty, full of herself. A fitting princess for a city with such great wealth.

"Yes, I came here with Metzi after Ehecatl declared war."

Ahkin stopped walking. Mayana nearly ran into him. "Wait . . . what? We are at *war*?" he said, incredulous.

Yemania chewed her lip. "I forgot to tell you. But after you fell, Metzi called off her engagement to the storm prince. Ehecatl was furious and declared war, demanding their independence from the empire."

Ahkin ran a hand through his short, dark hair. "Nine hells. She's empress for a matter of weeks and she plunges us into war just so she can marry Coatl."

Yemania wrung her hands at the mention of her own treacherous sibling. "She broke up with Coatl, for a while actually. And made me High Healer of Tollan instead."

Ahkin grumbled. "Well, at least *that* was a smart decision."

"So she could marry me instead," Ochix cut in, picking at his nails with the blade of his knife.

"Marry *you*?" Mayana blanched.

"Don't look that surprised. Believe it or not, I had quite the pick of brides back in Omitl."

Yemania gave him a flat look, which made Ochix's smile turn sheepish.

"Not that I wanted to marry any of them, of course," he added quickly.

"Why on earth would she agree to marry you?" Ahkin asked.

"Again, I had quite—" Ochix started.

Yemania punched him in the arm and Ochix fell silent. He rubbed his arm and beamed at Yemania as if she were the sun itself. Mayana didn't think she'd ever understand how that relationship came to be.

Yemania sighed and explained, "She was trying to secure an alliance with the Miquitz. She claimed it was to help in the fight against Ehecatl, but she was really following the commands of the Obsidian Butterfly."

A horrible thought occurred to Mayana. She suppressed a shudder, looking to Ahkin. "What if Tzom only wanted Metzi for her blood? The same way he wanted Ahkin. For the blood of the sun to bring about unending darkness."

"The Butterfly must have tricked her to try and get her to Omitl," Ahkin agreed.

"I'm offended. I'm not just a piece of meat to barter with," Ochix said, arching an eyebrow.

Mayana snorted a laugh. "Welcome to how half the princesses of the empire feel."

Ahkin frowned at that. "I don't like how marriage is used so politically."

"Neither do I," Ochix agreed. "I'm the one that almost had to marry Metzi."

Ahkin's eyes narrowed toward the gate of Millacatl. "Once we are inside, I will meet with the lords of Millacatl and discuss how we are going to take the empire back from my sister. When I am emperor again, there are a lot of things that are going to change."

11

The last time Yemania had come to Millacatl, she'd been with Metzi and Coatl. She'd wandered into the forest, sick with grief over losing Mayana and all that had transpired after. She'd been a shadow of those more important around her. There to serve, but always in silence.

She looked at Ochix now, alive and healthy because of her. She'd done that. She'd saved this handsome prince's life . . . and he had helped save her heart.

The peasants grew anxious the closer they got to the gate. Yemania couldn't blame them; their families probably thought them dead. Tears of anticipation already tracked down several of their faces. The guards on either side of the gates lowered their spears, likely having difficulty seeing through the torrential downpour.

Ahkin ran ahead. "I am Emperor Ahkin of Tollan," he called, his hands raised in supplication. "Lower your weapons."

The guards did not move, and their weapons remained pointed at Ahkin's heart. A thrill of fear spiderwalked down Yemania's spine. What would they do if Millacatl turned them away? Where else could they go?

"Ahkin is dead," one of the guards said. "He threw himself into the underworld."

"And he—*I* survived. I escaped the underworld and have come back. I bring with me the captives stolen by the Miquitz."

One lowered his spear. "You—they—they are alive?"

"Yes," Ahkin insisted. "And so am I. Please take me to Lord Millacatl."

Recognition blossomed in the eyes of the guards as they took in the faces of the peasants. Finally, they all lowered their spears and knelt before Ahkin.

"My emperor. Forgive us for not recognizing you," the guard on the right said. "We will take you to the palace right away." His eyes swept over them all, noticing the filthy state of their clothing. "And to a steam bath for cleansing."

Ahkin sighed in relief. "Please."

Yemania's heart leapt as they entered the stone gates, but when she turned to look at Ochix, she noticed his jaw was clenched and his eyes darted around as though waiting for an ambush. He was now a man without an empire. An outsider walking among his former enemies.

"You're with us," she reminded him. "No one will hurt you."

Ochix swallowed hard. "I hope you're right."

———

The palace of Millacatl still took Yemania's breath away. Perched upon the low rolling hills, the stone city exuded an ancient sort of elegance. It was as if the earth itself had grown a palace, tree trunks weaving their way through curving walls inlaid with different colored stones and tiles. Every building within the city itself burst with color and life, planter boxes overflowing with growth or baskets hanging with blooms from every post, throwing their floral scent into the air to mingle with the scent of freshly cooked maize.

Nobles and servants darted about, the entire palace buzzing like a hive of nervous bees. No one seemed to know what to do with the newcomers besides cover their ripped and filthy clothing with clean cloaks before presenting them to their lord.

Especially Ochix. A small group of guards had appeared behind him, trailing him like dogs guarding against an intruder. Ochix kept glancing back, his jaw tight enough to crack his teeth. Yemania slipped her hand into his and squeezed.

"They are just being cautious," she whispered to him.

He nodded, but he didn't loosen his grip on her hand. Yemania's heart lurched with pity. She knew how it felt to walk into the palace of the enemy, unsure of the future.

They were led into the main hall, where the stones of the walls were so interwoven with trees it felt as though they were still walking through the jungle. At the head of the hall, in his throne woven from branches, sat Lord Millacatl. The older man towered over them, a ceiba tree amongst shrubs. His gaze landed upon Ahkin, and he rose to his feet.

"Prince Ahkin. I—I do not understand. We all believed you dead. You fell, and the girl jumped in after—" His dark eyes fell on Mayana and widened in surprise. "How have you both survived?"

Ahkin drew himself up to his full height. "We trekked through the underworld and escaped more horrors than you can imagine." He went on to explain what had transpired in Xibalba, how Metzi had fooled them all into believing the sun was dying so that she could steal the throne, and about their escape from the Miquitz. Yemania did not miss how he left out the bones of Quetzalcoatl and what the Mother had told them about the rituals.

By the time Ahkin finished, Lord Millacatl had slumped back into his throne. He gripped the armrests with white knuckles. "Tomorrow we were planning to leave for the capital upon the summons of the empr—I mean, your sister. It seems we have much to discuss. Much to plan before that happens."

Ahkin nodded his thanks.

"And what of the death demon in your company?" Lord Millacatl jutted his chin in Ochix's direction. "I will not have his murderous kind in my home."

Yemania tightened her grip on Ochix's hand. He swallowed hard beside her.

"Ochix is a prince of the Miquitz," Ahkin started. There was a sharp intake of breath as the guards aimed their spears. Yemania glanced at Ochix's serene face. Though Ochix tried to hide his fear, beads of nervous sweat gathered along his hairline. Ahkin continued, "As a prince of the Miquitz, he will be afforded the respect that royalty of any city-state is afforded. He is more than a death demon." Ahkin's mouth quirked into half a smile, as though he couldn't believe what he was about to say. "He is also my friend. We would not have escaped Omitl without him."

Yemania held her breath. Lord Millacatl drummed his fingers upon his armrest, seeming unsure how to proceed.

Ahkin cleared his throat. "The last time I was here, Lord Millacatl, you saw me as a child. A young man too inexperienced in the ways of the world to truly lead the Chicome Empire."

Lord Millacatl did not contradict him. Ochix squeezed Yemania's hand even tighter.

"But the boy that fell into Xibalba is not the man that emerged. I have been through the fires of hell, and I will lead my people with or without your help, though I would much rather have it than not."

Yemania's heart lifted at the authority that rang within Ahkin's voice. He hadn't just spoken those words, he'd *meant* them. She didn't know all the details of what transpired in the underworld, but she agreed with Ahkin. He was not the same person that fell that day.

Lord Millacatl considered him. "Very well. The *prince* of Miquitz shall not be harmed as long as he resides under my roof. He will be treated as any visiting dignitary would be treated."

"Thank you." Ahkin bowed his head in gratitude.

Beside her, Ochix finally relaxed his grip on her hand as he too thanked Lord Millacatl for sparing his life.

"Let's get you all cleaned up and properly fed." Lord Millacatl signaled to his servants before rubbing his hands together. "Then tonight, let the real politics begin."

———

"What do you think will happen from here?" Mayana asked, sorting through the selection of clothing laid out upon the bed mats of their guest room.

Yemania fingered the simple white tunic dress. It wasn't her family's color, but it was clean, and right now that was all that mattered. "I'm not sure."

Their skin was fresh and raw from the steam bath, and Yemania felt as though a new person had emerged from the layers of mud she'd washed off.

"You will accompany us to the capital," came a cool voice from the doorway. Yemania and Mayana both straightened as Princess Teniza of Millacatl entered the room. She looked exactly as Yemania remembered, willowy in height and frame, her long dark hair cascading down her back like an ebony waterfall dotted with jungle blossoms. Her face was beautiful in a way that made Yemania's gut clench for a moment, but she quickly dismissed the feeling. She knew it wasn't right to compare herself.

Mayana's lips pursed, but she didn't respond as Teniza swept inside. The princess of plants' usual haughty demeanor seemed somewhat faded, as though a shroud of sadness and defeat had settled on her shoulders.

"You are princesses," she said with a wave of her hand. "You will be dressed much finer than this when we return to the palace. Come, my rooms have a far better selection."

Mayana arched an eyebrow. "What do you mean?"

"You think I would allow you to walk into the throne room of Tollan and not look the part of an empress? Then you do not know me at all." She did not smile, but motioned for them to follow her out into the hall.

Yemania felt just as confused as Mayana looked. Teniza had always seemed so . . . arrogant, so superior. And though she still seemed cold, she was here offering to help them?

Mayana leaned in and whispered. "Do we go with her?"

Yemania shrugged. "I don't see why not. And she's right, when you march back into Tollan, you will need to look the part of an empress."

"You'll need to, too."

Yemania's heart lurched. "No one will care about me. You are the one that matters."

"That's not true." Mayana grimaced, and together, they followed Teniza into the labyrinthine hallways of the palace.

12

Mayana stifled a gasp when they entered Teniza's rooms. She guessed she shouldn't be surprised; Millacatl was the wealthiest city-state in the empire, after all, but the sheer size and scope of its luxury still stole the breath from her lungs.

What little stone she could see between the tree trunks lining the walls glittered with inlaid crystal geodes, like drops of rain falling in a gentle afternoon shower. From the benches to the tables to the shelves, the furniture itself was all carved from rich, dark mahogany, intricately designed with patterns of vines and flowers. Teniza's bed mat, elevated on a wooden dais, overflowed with soft, thick furs. Brightly colored cushions dotted the wooden furniture like bright flower blossoms.

"Help yourselves if you are hungry," Teniza said, flicking a lazy hand to a bowl overflowing with succulent fruits. She busied herself with opening baskets and throwing elegant garment after elegant garment across every surface of her room.

Mayana reached for a mango, but her head was reeling. Why was Teniza being so helpful? Hadn't she sided with Zorrah during the selection ritual? Hadn't she treated Mayana like she was a beetle worthy only of being crushed beneath her sandal?

"I'm sorry," Mayana finally said. "I appreciate your generosity, but I don't understand. Why are you helping us?"

Teniza's gaze dropped to the green dress in her hands. Her voice softened with grief. "Ahkin is back. You are back. I assume that means the sacrificial ceremony for your wedding is still going to take place. And . . . I . . . I need to ask that you do one favor for me before I die."

Mayana stumbled back a step. No, there was no way on Ometeotl's great green earth she would allow the other princesses to be sacrificed to bless her marriage. Especially not after the Mother goddess told her such a sacrifice was not even necessary. "No, the ritual will not take place. Ahkin and I would never allow it."

Teniza's eyes met hers, hope blazing to life within them. "What do you mean? The head priest—"

"The head priest can jump into Xibalba himself if he doesn't like it. Ahkin and I are both in agreement. The ritual will not take place." Mayana crossed her arms over her chest.

At first Teniza seemed frozen in shock, but then her hand shot to her mouth and a sob shook through her body. She lowered herself onto a bench, clutching at her heart as though it had burst inside her chest. "I'm s-s-sorry, I just thought—"

Mayana's own heart twinged with pity. How awful to think that you'd escaped the selection sacrifice, only to have Mayana and Ahkin show up and make your greatest fear come true. Again.

"I'm so sorry if I made you think your life was in question again," Mayana said softly. "I assure you that it isn't." She reached out a hand and laid it on the plant princess's shoulder.

Teniza's sobs quieted after several moments. She wiped a hand across her nose. "You would risk the wrath of the gods and the cursing of your reign just to save us? I know Zorrah said you hated the rituals, but—"

Mayana flinched at the mention of Zorrah, the brutal animal princess of Ocelotl who had tried to kill her on more than one occasion. "It isn't just because I despise the rituals." She paused, knowing how crazy she was about to sound. "The Mother herself appeared to us in Xibalba, explained that she wanted us to honor her with life, not death. She said she'd seen enough of death and suffering and didn't want us offering blood that her children had already spilled for us. She said it minimizes their sacrifice."

Teniza's tear-swollen eyes narrowed. "The council would never agree to that. What you speak is blasphemy. They will never let you marry Ahkin if you say things like that."

Mayana's stomach tightened. She worried about the exact same thing. She and Ahkin might hold different views than the rest of the empire, but that didn't mean the rest of the empire would agree, emperor or not. The ways of the Chicome had become so ingrained in their society, the rituals and sacrifices were a part of daily life. They made the people feel safe, as if they were in control of their fates. But as Mayana had learned in Xibalba, you had to trust. You couldn't try to take all of the control onto yourself because you couldn't see the bigger picture. That was the definition of faith.

"It's the truth," Mayana said. She lifted the jade skull pendant around her neck, the gift given to her by the Mother goddess. "This is the amulet of Atlacoya, my ancestor. Given to me by Ometeotl herself. I will follow what she wishes of me, no matter who stands in my way."

Teniza's gaze fell to the necklace, her eyes widening in shock. "*The amulet? The one that—*"

"Captured the flood waters that destroyed the First Sun?" Mayana finished for her. "Yes, I can call them forth with the power in my blood."

Even Yemania gasped. Mayana realized she had forgotten to explain that part of the story as well.

"You were going to ask me a favor, before. When you still thought you would have to be sacrificed?"

Teniza gave a watery laugh. "It does not matter now, but I was going to ask if there was a way for you to postpone your wedding. Until . . . until after my own."

"You're getting married?" Yemania squealed.

Teniza shushed them both, glancing toward the doorway. A spark of mischief twinkled in her eye.

"It is a secret. I plan to marry him under the guise of nightfall, a ceremony before the gods alone."

"Why must it be a secret?" Yemania asked.

Mayana remembered a long-ago conversation, when Metzi had

probed the princesses with personal questions during the selection ritual. Teniza had mentioned a lover back home, a lover who was willing to kill himself to join her in the underworld. She had been trying so hard to win Ahkin's heart—not to save her own, but to save the boy she loved.

Teniza's cheek dimpled. "He is not someone my father would approve of. But once we are bonded before the gods, there is nothing he can do to stop me."

Mayana raised her eyebrows, impressed. She admired Teniza's stubborn refusal to give in. She could very much relate. "He's a commoner, isn't he?"

"Not to me," she said quietly, glancing toward the door. "He's one of my guards."

"A warrior then." Yemania nodded.

"I'm happy for you, Teniza," Mayana said. "And I'm happy your marriage will not have to be short-lived."

"Me too," Teniza agreed, the weight seeming to lift off her shoulders. Then she slapped her hands on her thighs, immediately serious again. "I believe you about what the Mother said. I can see the conviction and truth of it in your eyes as well as around your neck. I will proudly bend my knee to you as empress, Mayana. But not everyone will be convinced so easily, especially with your views on the sacrifices." She rose to her feet, eyeing her baskets of clothing with newfound purpose. "So when you march into that throne room, we will make sure you look as majestic as the sun itself."

Tears stung behind Mayana's eyes as she watched Yemania and Teniza laugh and compare different necklaces and bracelets. Maybe she had been wrong about the princess of plants all along. She had been willing to help dress Mayana while she still thought she would be a sacrifice. Yes, she had wanted to ask a favor, but she still cared about Mayana looking her very best. She also believed Mayana about the Mother's wishes. Every ally she could have on her side was crucial, and Teniza would be an excellent ally.

Likely even an excellent friend.

Ahkin was amazed at how quickly the royal family of Millacatl was able to throw together a celebration feast. Their great hall was filled with the scents of spices and roasted meats, fresh fruits, and cooked maize. Dancers twirled about in elaborate costumes made from feathers, beads, and animal pelts. The thudding of the dance drums vibrated in his chest.

Ahkin himself lounged upon cushions spread out across the dais, shoving every bit of food he could find into his mouth. It was his first real meal since falling into the underworld.

"Don't eat yourself sick," Mayana teased from beside him. He had noted how well she'd hid her displeasure at the rituals to bless the meal. It had been a brief reminder of the strength and determination he so admired about her. She also looked magnificent, as regal as the empress she would soon become. A tunic dress of greens and gold clung to her womanly figure, accentuating the curves of her hips in a way that made the back of his neck grow hot. Her hair was plaited into a crown atop her head, accented with a beaded jade headband. The jade skull amulet dangled from the cord around her throat.

"Aren't you as starved as I am?" he asked, trying to keep his attention on the food.

"Yes, but I know better than to choke myself on it." Mayana popped a berry into her mouth.

It felt surreal to Ahkin to be sitting at a feast, watching the people around him dance with levity and life, when mere days ago he'd been trapped in a nightmare of death and torment. Colors felt brighter, fruits even sweeter. He felt blessed, grateful for another chance at life.

"So I assume you have chosen your bride," the lord of Millacatl said conversationally. Beside him, Mayana looked up, equally interested in his answer.

"We can worry about weddings later. First, I need to secure my throne back from Metzi."

He could have mentioned the imminent threat to the empire from the Obsidian Butterfly, but Lord Millacatl was one who admired strength above all else. He did not need to learn about another danger that had developed under Ahkin's leadership without his knowledge—at least, not just yet. Better to ensure the lord's support before disclosing the additional threat waiting upon their doorstep.

Lord Millacatl snorted. "I am afraid you will have to pry your power out of her grasp. She is ruthless and cunning, and to be honest, I rather think she makes an excellent empress."

He couldn't be serious. "She murdered our parents and tricked the empire into thinking the sun was dying."

"She also tricked you into killing yourself," Lord Millacatl pointed out, taking a sip of fermented pulque.

"And did she succeed?" Ahkin arched a brow.

Lord Millacatl laughed. "No, I guess she did not. You descendants of Huitzilopochtli truly are children of war."

Ahkin didn't want to play games. He needed a straight answer. He also knew that if the city-states decided to back Metzi's claim to the throne, the result would be catastrophic. He needed to know that Millacatl was on his side. And he needed the backing of their army, if it came to that. "Will Millacatl stand beside me in my rightful claim? Or will you support the usurper?"

The older man tapped his chin, clearly thinking. A wickedly sharp gleam shone in his eyes. "There's a chance I would stand beside you if I knew my daughter would *sit* beside you on the throne."

Mayana dropped her bowl of pulque, the liquid spreading across the floor. Its pungent scent burned Ahkin's nose. She muttered an apology and a servant hurried in to help her clean up the mess.

Ahkin clenched his teeth. "I told you I want to wait on any discussions of my marriage until after we've dealt with the politics."

"Weddings and politics are one and the same, my *prince*. If you want my support to reclaim your throne, then you have my price."

Ahkin did not miss his emphasis on the word *prince*. Lord Millacatl thought he had Ahkin good and trapped, and unfortunately—he did. There was no chance Ahkin could dethrone Metzi without Millacatl's backing. And Lord Millacatl would help only if Ahkin agreed to marry Teniza.

Ahkin glanced over to where Teniza sat beside Mayana and

Yemania, her eyes wide with horror at her father's suggestion. She noticeably wasn't interested in marrying him either. So what game was Lord Millacatl playing?

"Let me think on it," Ahkin managed to get out.

"What is there to think on, prince of light? You need my support should the empress resist your claim, and my support you shall have. Without it, the other city-states will never follow you. Millacatl controls the food for most of the empire, and I know the others will be afraid to go against whoever I decide to support. Would you really turn down such an offer to follow your heart and marry a heathen that spits upon our sacred ways?"

Mayana stiffened beside him as sparks of fury lit inside Ahkin's chest. He longed to punch the man in the face—but seriously doubted such an action would accomplish much in the ways of diplomacy.

Lord Millacatl continued, a caiman smelling blood in the water. "You cannot honestly think the council, let alone the empire, would support your marriage to the disgraced daughter of Atl? What kind of empress would she be? News of her refusal to sacrifice a dog spread throughout the empire faster than a plague."

Several prominent nobles nearby chuckled.

"Excuse me." Ahkin leapt to his feet, knocking over a platter of flatbreads as he did so.

Lord Millacatl called after him. "Take your time, prince of light. Though I warn you, tomorrow Millacatl marches to Tollan one way or another. We will be marching to support Empress Metzi, or to dethrone her. The choice is yours."

Ahkin slammed his fist through the beaded hanging separating the feast hall from one of the pleasure gardens outside. The majestic greenery and flowers overflowing from every surface should have calmed him, but instead, the sight of it made him want to rip the leaves off every single one.

He loved Mayana. They'd literally been through the *hells* together. There was no way he was marrying anyone else.

"Mother, please. I need an answer. There has to be another way.

Any other way," he threw to the heavens. "You said yourself Mayana is my duality. Surely you would allow us to be together when the rest of the world would tear us apart?"

He turned his face toward the stars. But there was no answer. The truth was, the world had done nothing but try to tear them apart from the moment they emerged back into the overworld.

He lowered himself onto a stone bench and threw his head into his hands. This was one decision he did not want to make.

A soft hand touched his cheek. Ahkin leaned into the touch, knowing who it was before he even looked up.

"I can't do it, Mayana. We have to find another way to take the empire back."

Mayana settled down beside him. "You're already at war with Ehecatl, and the Miquitz want your blood to end the world. You know we can't do anything without the support of Millacatl."

Ahkin lifted his head. "What are you saying? That I should agree to marry her?"

Mayana flinched as if his words had caused her physical pain. "I don't want you to, of course. But we also know that any wedding would have to wait until well after these wars are finished. Perhaps," she leaned in and kissed him softly, "we will find a way once this is all over. I know Teniza doesn't want to marry you either."

Ahkin drew her into his arms, holding onto her as though he'd never let her go. "She hates me that much?"

Mayana shook with silent laughter. "No, it's because she's in love with one of her guards. They plan to wed in secret as soon as possible."

"So you think I should agree, under the condition that the wedding waits until after the war with Ehecatl is settled?"

Mayana pulled back, looking deep into his eyes. "It's not my favorite solution, but I think it is the only one we have. The truth is, no one wants me as their empress. If we march into Tollan together, the people will be furious—"

He started to cut her off, but she held her fingers to his lips to stop him.

"I know *you* do. But there has been so much instability. Maybe once everyone is settled, once we are not at war or trying to save the world from ending, the people will be less afraid. Maybe then we can convince everyone of the truth." Her smile seemed genuine, but there was also a tenseness to it. He wondered how much she believed in what she was saying.

Ahkin leaned his forehead against hers, heart cracking in half at the thought of agreeing to this. "So we will have to pretend that I am engaged to Teniza?"

Mayana's lip quivered, but she nodded before dropping her gaze to her lap.

He reached up, cradling her face in his hands. They'd always managed to find their way back together before. A tear tracked its way down her cheek and he wiped it away with his thumb. Her eyes finally lifted to meet his, and when they did, Ahkin couldn't stop himself.

He pulled her face toward his and their lips found each other. She tasted of salt and water and life itself. He couldn't imagine letting her go, pretending to not love her as much as he so clearly did. She met his need for her with equal intensity, her own hands wrapping around the back of his neck to hold him closer. She made a small whimpering sound, and their kisses became desperate, devouring, consuming one another as a starving man might consume a last meal . . .

A throat cleared.

"Um, if you're going to follow through on the offer to marry his daughter, I recommend *not* kissing another woman in the garden of his house," Ochix said behind them.

Ahkin broke the kiss, pulling back and leaving part of his heart behind as he did so. His breath came in gasps. "So you think I should agree to it too?"

Ochix shifted his shoulders uncomfortably. "Well, I was supposed to marry Metzi and got myself kicked out of Tollan for getting caught with Yemania, so I'm not *exactly* the best person to give advice on such matters."

"It doesn't mean you have to go through with it. You can agree now and change your decision later," Mayana reminded him in a low voice, checking around for anyone that might be watching their conversation without their knowledge. "But we can't do anything without Millacatl's backing now. He's right, the other cities will follow his lead in which ruler to support."

Ahkin heaved a sigh. "All right," he finally agreed.

He knew in his gut it was the only way. The only option they had moving forward. But he wouldn't have to go through with it. He could act the part for long enough, just long enough to bring peace and stability, and then he and Teniza could each be free to marry the ones they truly loved.

He had a newfound appreciation for Metzi's desperation to get out of her arranged marriage. But a voice in the back of his mind reminded him exactly what had happened when Metzi had broken off her engagement to the storm prince and triggered a war . . .

He prayed Lord Millacatl didn't have the same thirst for vengeance as Ehecatl.

13

Mayana supposed she shouldn't be surprised. Just because the Mother goddess told her she was right about the rituals didn't mean the rest of the empire would believe her. To them, she fell into the underworld a heretic and emerged a heretic all the same.

Ahkin seemed pacified with the idea that they would someday be married, but as she watched Teniza and Ahkin lift their joined hands before the gathered assembly in Millacatl, she had a sinking feeling that she'd never sit by his side on the throne. No matter the depth of their love for each other, the empire would never allow it.

They wanted someone like Teniza.

The rest of the night continued in celebration, culminating in an intimate dance between Ahkin and Teniza. They danced in tight circles around each other, hands clasped as the beat of the drums intensified. Mayana fought back tears. That was supposed to be *her*.

She couldn't watch a moment longer, her stomach heaving at the sight, so she blamed the pulque and headed back to her room early.

Yemania came in shortly after. She closed the curtain across the guest room doorway and found Mayana huddled into the furs of her bed mat. She wasn't crying as much as just staring into nothing, praying that this whole evening had been a nightmare from which she could wake. How could she and Ahkin have been allowed to go through so much together only to get torn apart?

"Teniza is heartbroken too," Yemania whispered, settling down beside her.

Mayana sniffed and hugged the pillow in her arms tighter against her chest. "I know."

Yemania chewed her lip, visibly concerned. "It won't actually happen. You know that, right? Ahkin won't actually marry her. It's just a ruse to get Teniza's father to agree to support him."

Mayana loosed a shuddering sigh. "That's the plan."

Yemania patted her back in a maternal sort of way. "Then why are you still so upset?"

Mayana pushed herself up into a sitting position. The ache inside her chest throbbed painfully. "Just because it's *our* plan, doesn't mean it will happen. No one wants me to be the empress, Yemania. All my life, I have been branded selfish. A heretic. Unwilling to follow the will of the gods above my own. My family shamed me for it, and now the entire empire shames me for it." She pressed a hand against her heart, the pain within it building to a pressure she struggled to contain. "I don't know how to ever escape it. I'll never be what they want me to be. I hate this feeling that there's something fundamentally broken inside me and—" The pain cut off the rest of her words and escaped, pouring out of her as she cried, unable to hold it back any longer.

Ahkin loved her. Ahkin saw the truth of who she was and still cherished her. He alone had been there to hear the Mother's words, the words that were a balm to her wounded soul. *She had been right.*

But what did being right matter, if no one would listen? If everyone else accused you of selfishly following your own will above the gods', when in reality you were the one fighting to honor their true will? Well, the true will of the *Mother* goddess, at least.

Why? Why couldn't Ometeotl just force everyone else to see the truth? How could she just *let* them continue in their ways? Ways that were costing people and animals their very lives? Ways that kept Mayana beaten down into a place of ridicule.

Yemania shushed her gently. "No, Mayana, you know that isn't true. You know who you are. *I* know who you are. Ahkin knows who you are. Forget what everyone else thinks and focus on the people that matter."

Mayana growled, throwing the pillow onto the bed mat. "I'm afraid that even after this war is finished, I won't be allowed to marry him. That we will all end up sacrificed anyway when he marries Teniza. We never really escaped the selection ritual, Yemania. We were just fools to think that the decision was ever Ahkin's alone."

"No," Yemania said, shaking her head. "Mayana, I love you, but you're wrong. The selection ritual is over. Ahkin has chosen you. He will choose you no matter what happens. It's only in your own heart that you're not worthy of it."

Mayana collapsed back onto the furs. She remained quiet for a long time, running through Yemania's words over and over again. But it wasn't just in her own heart—it was in the hearts of the entire empire. She'd heard what Lord Millacatl said at dinner. Everyone had heard. She didn't want to talk about herself anymore. "How is Teniza handling the news?"

Yemania grabbed her hand and pulled Mayana to her feet. "Come ask her yourself. You're not as alone as you think you are."

———

They found Teniza in her rooms, and—Mayana noticed with a start—she was not alone.

A young man dressed in simple guard's attire—green loincloth with a matching embroidered cloak fastened around his shoulders—hurried out of the room the moment Mayana knocked on the doorframe.

She'd bet all the gold in Tollan he was Teniza's secret lover.

Teniza was already on her feet, bustling about the room as though nothing unusual had just happened.

"Teniza?" Yemania asked tentatively. "Is it all right if we come in?"

"Of course." She waved them in and perched her hands on her hips as though assessing the best way to pack her belongings in her travel baskets. "There's so much to do before we leave tomorrow. I want to make sure I have everything."

"Can't you have your servants help you pack?" Mayana asked, taking in the sheer number of garments. They were strewn across the bed mat and laid over stone benches, hanging from branches on the wall and overflowing from the already full baskets.

"They wouldn't do it right," Teniza said distractedly.

Mayana unhooked the jade bracelet she'd borrowed and held it out. "Thank you for letting me borrow this, by the way. It's beautiful."

But Teniza closed Mayana's hand around it instead. "No. You keep it." Her eyes were kind, but then she shifted back into a kind of frenzy, as though she wanted to use busyness to bury whatever feelings were coming up inside her.

She turned back to her baskets and began sorting every garment she owned according to color. "My father tells me that he agreed to postpone the wedding until after the war with Ehecatl is settled. That should give us plenty of time to—" She flinched, as if an emotion had tried to make itself known and she shoved it back down. "—to figure a way out of this."

"Was the guard who just left—?" Yemania started to ask.

Teniza thrust a pile of jewelry into Yemania's arms instead. "Would you mind sorting those according to size? Thank you so much, my dear."

Mayana and Yemania exchanged significant looks. Teniza was a bowstring wound a little too tight. The tighter it pulled, the more tense it became.

"I—um, sure." Yemania sat on the floor and started sorting.

Finally, after almost half an hour of sorting and organizing and reorganizing, Teniza dropped the garments she was holding and pressed her fists into her eyes. "I didn't think I'd have to say goodbye to him." Her voice cracked and she slid to the floor. "Again."

Mayana settled herself on the floor too. She'd been waiting for this to happen. The stretched bowstring had finally snapped. "I know. It's not fair to you at all."

Teniza's breaths were shallow and quick as she tried to contain herself. She wrapped her arms around her chest. "I don't want to marry someone else. I'm so tired of trying to s-s-seem perfect all the time, of following all the rules. I want the strength to follow my own heart for once." She glanced up at Mayana through tear-stained lashes. "Strength enough to jump into the underworld if I had to."

Mayana blinked, unsure how to respond.

"I know everyone thinks you're a heretic who will bring about the end of the world with your heathenish ways." She waved a hand dramatically. "But all I could think when you leapt off the edge was how brave you were. How I wish I had that same level of conviction you did."

"Um, thanks? I think." Mayana laughed uneasily.

"I want to stand up for myself. What if we can't find a way around this? What if the council forces me to marry Ahkin and sacrifices the rest of you with or without his consent?" Teniza's voice climbed, her shoulders heaving with her panicked breaths.

"We won't let that happen," Yemania said, abandoning the jewelry to join them. She drew Teniza into a hug. "We have to have faith and stay strong together."

Mayana's stomach twisted with anxiety. They could hope and dream and plan all they wanted, but despite what Yemania said, the council and the rest of the empire *could* make it happen.

Fear could drive people to do terrible things, and if the people were afraid of causing an apocalypse, they could pressure Ahkin to decide between his bride or his empire.

Between the survival of all their hopes and dreams—or the death of them.

"It is a pleasure to welcome you back to Tollan, Lord Atl." Metzi inclined her head in greeting.

The golden sun throne was hard and uncomfortable to sit on for this long, and with each arriving delegation, she felt her impatience growing. She really should have ordered a servant to fetch more cushions. Still, as the banquet hall filled with the rumbling voices of the gathering nobility, she knew she must appear collected, controlled. She must be the living incarnation of a goddess in regality and dominance.

But gods above, she'd almost trade Coatl for a cushion right now.

The older man swept out his deep blue cloak and bowed. "Of course, my empress. Atl is—as always—a servant of Tollan."

Metzi considered him. Around him stood three younger men, undeniably his sons. They were all warriors, judging from their builds. Good. That would be useful in the weeks ahead.

The lord himself was relatively young, gray just beginning to tint his temples. His face was aged, but not too deeply lined. If she looked hard enough, she could see traces of Mayana in the curves of his cheeks and the rounded shape of his eyes. What an embarrassment the daughter of water must have been to him. Metzi herself had spoken with the girl on several occasions, had thought her beautiful and clever enough as a match for Ahkin, but not even she had seen what lay dormant inside the girl's heart. The rebelliousness that would lead her to anger the gods and humiliate her family in front of the entire empire. The foolishness to fling herself into Xibalba after Ahkin.

Hopefully Lord Atl did not harbor such similar beliefs. "I am pleased to hear your pledge of service," Metzi told him. "After the actions of your daughter, actions that hinted at sympathies with the beliefs of Ehecatl, I feared that Atl . . ." She let her voice trail off suggestively.

Panic flashed across Lord Atl's face. He bowed quickly. "My empress, I assure you the actions of my late daughter do not speak for the royal family of Atl. We were as outraged as any at her refusal to honor the gods with a proper sacrifice."

"Though she seemed to have no qualms with sacrificing *herself*," Metzi smirked. Several of the council members standing beside her chuckled their agreement.

Laughter echoed around the hall. Lord Atl's jaw tightened, but his voice remained calm. "No one was more surprised to hear of her actions that day than I, I assure you."

"Had she shown such heretical tendencies before the selection ritual?" Metzi asked, inspecting one of her fingernails. "I'm just curious."

The sons of Atl glanced nervously at one another.

Ah. So she'd struck a nerve. Excellent. Knowing the weaknesses of your allies was as crucial as knowing the weaknesses of your enemies. And one never knew when allies could turn into enemies.

"Mayana is—" The lord of Atl cleared his throat and blinked several times. "—*was* a sensitive child. She did not like offering blood, be it her own or the blood of sacrificial animals. She had a very kind heart."

"A kind heart that put its own emotional discomfort over the safety of the entire empire?" Metzi arched an eyebrow.

The lord of Atl flinched. She was being too harsh with him, pressing on a wound that could make him lash out in pain, but she also sensed something there that could be of use to her.

Shame.

Shame could be a powerful ally in terms of keeping Atl obedient to the empire. He would want to prove his worth and loyalty. And she would make him do just that.

"I do not say such things to shame you, my lord," Metzi said. Which, of course, was far from the truth.

Lord Atl looked up, the hope of forgiveness shining inside his eyes.

"I merely bring up the unfortunate circumstances with your daughter to make an important point." Now she spoke louder, rising to her feet and addressing the entire assembly. "When we put our own interests above the interests of the empire as a whole, we risk everything. We risk angering the gods that have the power to protect or destroy us at their pleasure. Ehecatl has put its own desires above the needs of the collective. And in doing so, they risk angering the Mother herself. The Mother, who allowed her beloved children to die for us, to sacrifice themselves upon the altar of creation to birth each new sun. We shall not now, or ever, allow any city-state to dishonor the sacrifices that were made, to insist that the debt paid for us does not need to be repaid. Ehecatl wishes to exert its own selfish independence, when they should be submitting not only to their empress, but to the gods themselves. And if they will not bow, then we will ensure the gods feast upon *their* blood and not our own."

Roars of approval flooded the hall. Men and women rose to their feet and stomped or slammed spears against the stone floor, rattling the bowls of drinks laid out for the coming feast. Their adoration soaked into her skin like sunlight after a long night, like fresh breaths of air after drowning beneath the waves. Metzi wallowed in it, savoring every cry and chant that followed her declaration.

The Obsidian Butterfly had revealed that the sacrifices were not necessary, that the gods desired them out of their own thirst for the rush of power they provided. The sun would rise with or without Metzi's blood. But the people did not know that. Nor would they. Fear was the strongest arrow in her quiver. She knew their fears, and she played them as deftly as a flute in the hands of a master musician.

They did not see her as powerless now. No, now she was a warrior. A goddess of light determined to save them from the wrath of the gods.

A true empress.

Even if she would not be *their* empress for long.

———

The head priest, Toani, led the sacrifice of a black iguana to bless the welcome feast. Beside her on the dais sat the patriarchs of the other royal families of the Chicome Empire.

Well, most of them. Ehecactl's lord of storms, descendant of Quetzalcoatl, was not in attendance. And Metzi's eye continually darted to the empty cushion where the lord of Millacatl was supposed to be seated.

She grabbed a nearby servant and whispered harshly in her ear. "Have we heard anything yet?"

The young woman shook her head. "I'm sorry, your highness. There have been no messengers nor any sign of the lord of Millacatl."

Metzi ground her teeth together. How was she supposed to fund this war campaign without the support of Millacatl?

"Calm, my love." Coatl leaned in and rubbed a hand along her thigh. "They'll come."

Metzi slapped his hand away. "Not in front of the council," she hissed.

Her stomach roiled with tension. She tried to eat, but the deer meat tasted dry and sinewy, sticking in her mouth and refusing to go down her throat. If Millacatl wasn't coming . . .

She'd just have to hope the other lords did not suspect anything was amiss.

Directly to her right sat the lord of Papatlaca. The man was a mountain as large as the volcano his family hailed from, and he tore into the leg of deer meat with the ferocity of a wolf. Honestly, he terrified Metzi, but as his family controlled fire and made every fire-glass weapon in the empire, he was a necessity. Beside him sat his older son and daughter. The latter she recognized from the selection ritual. Yoli. Another princess whose life was spared by Metzi's ascent to the throne. Yoli's hair was cut to her shoulders with sharp fringe above her eyes. A thick black bead protruded through her lower lip. Though they were at a royal banquet and her brother beside her ate as ravenously as their father, the girl looked utterly bored, poking at her food with a shard of obsidian as long as her forearm.

On the other side of the family of Papatlaca sat the royal naguals of Ocelotl, the fiercest warriors in the empire. Descendants of Tezcatlipoca, the naguals not only commanded the battlefield, they commanded the ferocious beasts that fought beside them. Eagles, jaguars, snakes, and wolves—all could be used as weapons. Their men and women alike trained from an early age to compete for positions in the elite Eagle and Jaguar forces in the capital. Indeed, the river beside their battle temple often ran red with the blood of fallen warriors. The naguals believed the strong survived, and those that were not . . . well . . . Metzi respected their love of strength and willingness to do what was necessary to obtain it.

The lord of Ocelotl sat beside his wife, a feral-looking woman who reminded Metzi of a vulture, and the one who remained of their two daughters. Metzi had heard rumors of the princess Zorrah, who had defeated and killed her older sister in ritual combat. Her hair was pulled back into a severe style that accented her artfully pointed teeth. Dressed in the cloak of a jaguar, she seemed to have recently attained a coveted position amongst the elite Jaguar warriors. Supposedly she'd gotten into a fight with the daughter of water last time she was here. She must have seen the truth about her as well.

Lord Atl sat on Metzi's other side, his three sons beside him. They all ate in silence, trying and failing to hide their grief over the lost princess. Perhaps being back in the place she had perished was difficult for them, but they never should have allowed the girl's heresy to go as far as it had. Her death was on their own heads.

Coatl was most uncomfortable with his own father, who sat on the other side of the lord of water. When the lord of Pahtia—descendant of Ixtlilton, god of healing—had been presented to her, Coatl actually snarled. She knew he hated the man, from every deep wrinkle on his wide face to the red feathers around his ankle. His temper was legendary throughout the empire, as was his reputation for taking that anger out on his children. Metzi found it ironic that the lord of healing could cause so much harm. Coatl still bore marks on his back from his father's "discipline." Metzi imagined that if she didn't get the chance to kill Yemania for her betrayal, her own father would happily see the job finished.

Servants wound through the mass of guests seated below them—the judges, distinguished warriors, and other nobility of common blood forever separated from the divine royalty that sat a step above them. The room soon filled with the haze of pipes and incense while everyone finished the last remains of the meal.

"So what is the purpose of the royal summons, my empress, if I may be so bold?" came the deep, thunderous voice of the lord of Papatlaca. "As you know, it is not an easy journey for my family to make."

Metzi suppressed the spark of irritation that flared inside her chest and gave the lord of fire a saccharine smile. "We have devised a strategy that will considerably shorten the conflict with Ehecatl, but we are in need of a *divine* intervention of sorts."

A servant tapped on Metzi's shoulder, but she swatted the girl away.

The lord of fire stabbed a sliver of meat with a long knife and brought it to his gash of a mouth. "Divine intervention?"

Metzi's eye twitched. "Yes. We will discuss more tomorrow at the official war council, but our plan requires the use of the divine gifting of each royal family. That is why we asked you to bring several of your descendants with you as well."

"Joy, more use for our blood," Yoli drawled. Her father gave her a dark look of warning and Yoli fell resentfully silent.

The lord of Papatlaca opened his mouth to respond, but before he could, the servant tapped on Metzi's shoulder again with increased urgency. "Your highness, I'm so sorry but—" she whispered.

"What?" Metzi snapped. "What could possibly be so vital to make you interrupt me in the middle of an important conversation?"

"It's Millacatl, my empress."

A stone settled in the pit of Metzi's stomach at the look of shock clearly painted across the young servant's face.

"What about them?" Metzi asked, the words coming out less

powerful than she intended. Had they been attacked on the way here? Had they betrayed her and joined the enemy?

"They have arrived at the gates with a regiment of warriors . . . and . . . and . . ."

Metzi grabbed the servant's wrist and yanked her closer. "And *what?*"

The girl's lip trembled, but she forced the words out in a rush. "Your brother is with them. Emperor Ahkin has returned."

The golden pyramid glinted in the light of the setting sun. It was a monument to Ahkin's ancestor, Huitzilopochtli. The great god of the sun. The god of war.

The city of Tollan perched upon a volcanic plateau that rose high above the jungle canopy. Every building shone with gold. In the reflected light of its many torches, it was a city that never knew darkness.

A surge of relief overtook him upon seeing the plateau, releasing a tension he'd been carrying in his chest since falling into the underworld. Ahkin drew a deep breath. He was finally home.

Millacatl had brought a small company of warriors with them. They weren't enough to take the city, but all Ahkin wanted was to give his own warriors pause long enough for him to get into the throne room. To get in front of Metzi.

He didn't know what he'd do once he saw her, but he knew he would never let her get away with what she'd done.

Luckily, the confusion at his appearance, along with the obvious support of Millacatl, stayed the hand of the Eagle warriors guarding the city. They allowed him to pass, many of them even bowing as he did.

The city streets teemed with people, residents pouring out from their homes onto the main avenue to see for themselves that Ahkin was alive. That their emperor had returned.

———

Metzi ran to the window overlooking the main plaza. The crowd that had gathered along the main avenue and filled the plaza itself swelled and rolled like the sea, many people throwing flowers at the feet of the approaching delegation. The members of Millacatl's royal family along with thirty or so warriors parted the throngs of people like a great ship cutting across the water. And at the boat's helm marched her twin.

Ahkin.

"I thought he was dead," Coatl said, coming to join her at the window. The guests of the feast had abandoned their meals and pressed against every other window along the side of the banquet hall. There were shouts of joy and celebration, cries of disbelief and wonder.

But what disturbed Metzi most were the gleeful looks of triumph upon the faces of the council members. As if they had been biding their time, waiting for their true emperor to return.

Metzi wanted to scream and claw out every single one of their eyes. They would disown her so quickly?

Ahkin was supposed to be in Omitl! Hadn't the Butterfly said as much? That Tzom had captured him and was planning to sacrifice him during the eclipse? This couldn't be happening.

She couldn't have her power taken away from her like this. What if Ahkin forced her into marrying the storm prince to end the war with Ehecatl? Everything she'd been working toward, everything the Obsidian Butterfly had promised. Gone. In the blink of an eye. Just . . . gone.

"Metzi?" Coatl asked. He reached for her hand, concern written across the planes of his handsome face. She wouldn't lose Coatl like this. She'd almost given him up to follow the Obsidian Butterfly's plan and marry Ochix, and her heart had suffered for it. She'd finally convinced the goddess to let her keep him, and she wasn't going to allow Ahkin to separate them ever again.

What could she do? A million ideas, a million strategies raced through her mind. She couldn't fight him; there was no way she would win. The council obviously supported his claim. They would be of no use to her. With Millacatl behind him, the rest of the city-states would follow, fearing repercussions from the city-state that provided most of their sustenance.

No, she had to be clever about how to play this next move. There was only one way forward.

"Trust me," she whispered to Coatl.

"Always," he said, squeezing her hand.

Metzi turned from the window and spread her arms wide to the banquet hall. "My brother has returned to us! What a fortunate and blessed day this is! We must welcome him back to his palace and throne in a manner befitting the emperor of the Chicome!"

More cheers rose from the guests, blending with the voices of the crowd below.

Metzi ordered servants to prepare more food, for even more dancers to be summoned from the temple. If she was to welcome Ahkin back, she would do so with such enthusiasm that none would suspect the true intentions of her heart. The smile frozen on her face made her cheeks ache, but she held it in place. Her smile would be her battle mask.

"Show him to the throne room immediately," she said to the Eagle warriors stationed around her. "I wish to welcome my brother home and see him properly seated on his throne."

The guests returned to their seats, eager anticipation of Ahkin's arrival sending a frenzy of energy into the air.

The only one who did not return to her original seat was Metzi. Instead of sitting on the golden throne, she stood patiently beside it, her gaze fixed upon the entrance to the throne room.

Waiting.

The roars of the crowd outside dulled slightly, and the clamor of voices within the halls grew louder. Servants were clapping and crying just outside the room.

Metzi's hands began to shake, her pulse pounding so loudly in her ears she was surprised she could hear anything else. She folded her hands in front of her, trying to hold them steady. No matter how her cheeks screamed in protest, she never let the smile slip from her face.

The moment he appeared, she would have to play her part perfectly. She would be the humbled sister, overwhelmed with joy at her beloved brother's return. She would graciously thank him for saving her from the *burden* of the empire.

The thudding in her ears intensified, and the moment Ahkin actually appeared in the doorway, all sound seemed to cease entirely. She was numb. Numb with anger, numb with disbelief. It felt as if she'd walked into her greatest nightmare.

Ahkin looked incredibly handsome, dressed in a fresh white waist-wrap trimmed with gold. His fingers grasped a long obsidian blade. On his other arm was a simple wooden shield with the symbol of Millacatl engraved upon it.

He was the warrior sun god incarnate, radiating a soft glow of light using the power in his blood. Metzi wanted to snort in disgust. Really? He was making himself literally *glow*?

Instead of snorting or rolling her eyes, Metzi ran to meet him, the guests that had risen to their feet in jubilation parting for her. She threw herself into his arms, tears streaming down her cheeks.

"Ahkin! Ahkin! You're alive! It's a miracle!" she sobbed. Though her tears were real, she pretended they were tears of joy.

Ahkin grunted and stumbled back, a look of shock and disbelief contorting his face. Whatever response he'd been expecting from her, worshipful joy was apparently a surprise.

Had he expected her to fight him? To try to keep her place on the throne through brute force? Good. Let him be surprised. And let everyone around them see how *graciously* she handed her reign back to him. She would play the part of the dutiful and obedient princess as long as she needed. She'd schemed her way onto the throne through cunning and cleverness, and she would do it again. Ahkin did not know that she had tricked him into killing himself. He did not know she and Coatl had murdered their father. There was no way he could. And not he, or anyone else, would ever need to know.

"My dear brother." She fell to her knees before him, kissing his feet as a sign of reverence. "My *emperor*."

Ahkin bent down and grabbed her arm, jerking her back to her feet.

Metzi lifted her tear-blurred gaze to meet his, expecting to see his gratitude and pride at her humbling show of submission.

Instead, the rage that burned within his eyes took her breath away. Metzi actually flinched. "Ahkin? What—?"

"Guards," he yelled to the Eagle warriors flanking him—the Eagle warriors *she'd* just sent to welcome him. Then, he spoke loud and clear enough for the entire room to hear. "Seize her. She is responsible for the death of our father, and for faking an apocalypse to deceive the empire."

Ahkin thought he'd feel fulfilled, watching Metzi and Coatl dragged from the throne room kicking and screaming about their innocence.

Instead, he felt a hollow sadness.

Coatl had been his friend, but Metzi was his twin. His sister. His blood. The ghost of a memory faded across his vision as he looked to the throne. He could see her there, no more than seven years old, round cheeks split into a playful grin as she climbed atop it, imitating their father as she pointed and commanded imaginary servants. The phantom trill of her young laughter filled his ears, drowning out the sound of her screams fading down the hall.

But Metzi was no longer a child.

And neither was he.

He was not the foolish young man who had been too afraid of his own power to truly embrace it. He was the emperor of the Chicome. And for the first time in his life, he *felt* he was.

Ahkin strode forward with purpose. The sun throne waited for him, a subtle aura of power emanating from the sharp points that radiated out from the seat like rays of the sun itself. His father's throne, his birthright.

Already the head priest Toani stood waiting for him, holding the elaborate white-feathered headdress of his father. Tears burned behind his eyes at the sight of it, but Ahkin did not let them escape. He kept his face smooth, calm . . . regal.

He stepped onto the dais, and a hush swept over the crowd as Ahkin sat down.

"It is good to see you again, your highness," Toani said quietly, his wizened face alight with joy. He lowered the headpiece onto Ahkin's brow.

It fit perfectly.

All around him, every member of the royal families, every Eagle and Jaguar warrior posted around the room, every nobleman and servant before him, sank to their knees and bowed.

He finally knew he had the strength to wear his father's headpiece and deserve it. He could be the emperor his people needed.

But as he looked around, at every bowed figure, he noticed the cushion beside the throne was empty. The cushion where his mother, the former empress, had sat beside his father. An overwhelming feeling of loneliness crashed over him.

His parents were gone. Metzi was gone. His best friend, Coatl, was gone. Mayana was supposed to be seated there beside him, the empire bowing to her just as they were bowing to him.

His duality. The complement to his soul.

This didn't feel right, sitting upon the throne without her. He needed her. She was the moon to his sun, the dusk to his dawn.

When his subjects rose from their bows, he looked for her, needing the assurance that if she wasn't beside him, that she was at least still *there*. His heart thudded in sudden panic, needing to see her, to see the love in her eyes—

And then he spotted her.

Ahkin almost gasped in relief.

She stood at the very back of the room, half concealed in shadow. Her long dark hair flowed almost to her waist, the green dress she was wearing showing her every curve. But what caught his attention more than any of her beautiful physical attributes was her smile—a smile that said everything he needed to hear without her uttering a single word.

I'm proud of you. I love you.

He swore to himself that she would be seated beside him one day, not upon a cushion, but upon a throne of her own. A true empress. Not a singularity to rule the empire, but a duality. Just as Ometeotl existed in duality.

Across a sea of faces and expectations, he held her gaze, unwavering, as if they were the only two individuals in the room.

As if they were the only two individuals in all the world.

———

"The council wishes to convene immediately," the high priest bent down and whispered in Ahkin's ear. "There is much to discuss."

The dancing and drinking in honor of Ahkin's return promised to last late into the night. After all the celebrating, he was beginning to crave a moment of privacy. Even outside the main palace, the streets were alive with celebrations. But Ahkin knew the leaders of the royal families as well as his generals and advisors wanted to enlighten him on recent events. Presumably, the most pressing of which was the looming war with Ehecatl.

"Have everyone gather in the council chamber in thirty minutes," Ahkin commanded.

"Of course. I am at your service, your highness." Toani bowed his head and swept from the room.

The lords of the royal families were gracious, congratulating Ahkin on his return and swearing their immediate allegiance. Ahkin's stomach tightened at the sight of the strong-jawed face of Lord Atl, Mayana's father. He approached the throne and swept low into a bow, his older sons hovering nearby like flies.

Ahkin fought to keep his gaze from flickering to Mayana. "Lord Atl, I am pleased to receive your pledge of loyalty."

"I am pleased to give it, my emperor. The city-state of Atl remains faithfully in your service. In all ways."

Ahkin nodded in acknowledgment, then lowered his voice. "I'm not sure if you were aware, but your daughter, Mayana, survived the journey through the underworld as well."

A swirl of emotions flitted across the lord's face, first wide-eyed shock, then a tight-lipped smile of restraint, as if the news brought him more pain than joy. "I had not yet been informed. Thank you."

The lord of Millacatl was next. Ahkin had to force himself not to grimace at the lord of plants, who had been lingering nearby like the scent of incense long since burned. "Your highness," the lord said, "I look forward to the joining of our families and the final conclusion of the selection ritual."

The lords of Ocelotl, Pahtia, and Papatlaca stiffened, their attention shifting to focus on the conversation.

Ahkin shifted uncomfortably on his throne. He hadn't wanted to address the looming matter of the selection ritual so soon. "We will discuss our next steps moving forward at the council meeting. As members of the empire's royal families, you are all invited to attend. I hope to see you in thirty minutes."

With that, he rose to his feet and headed for the nearest doorway. The crown upon his head suddenly felt as if it were made of stone instead of feathers, the golden sun pendant around his neck as heavy as a weight. He longed to tear them off and throw them into a corner.

Out in the hallway beyond, he returned the welcoming smiles of the servants that rushed past, grateful for their enthusiasm at his return. But what he really wanted was a moment to himself. A moment to catch his breath before the political constraints of the empire tried to strangle it out of him. He leaned against the wall, sweat dripping into his eyes.

"Well, you look like you've taken a punch to the gut," Ochix said, appearing seemingly from the shadows.

Ahkin jumped. "Do you have to walk out of the darkness like that?"

Ochix shrugged. "I have to maintain an aura of mystique somehow, it's the only way you sun worshippers will show me any respect."

Ahkin snorted. "Let them see you on the battlefield. That will earn you their respect very quickly."

Ochix ignored him and leaned against the wall too. "You nervous about the meeting?"

Ahkin grimaced. "I feel confident in my own ability to lead, more than I ever have before. But what I'm not looking forward to is the politics, the maneuvering between multiple voices and opinions all pulling me in different directions. I want to marry Mayana and forget the stupid selection ritual entirely, but I'm afraid they're just going to tell me not to. They aren't going to like me suggesting the rituals aren't necessary."

Ochix nodded thoughtfully. "Who says you have to do what they say?"

"I'm *supposed* to. They're my advisors. The greatest minds in the empire. Government officials and military leaders, religious leaders and royals of their own city-states."

"I was trained to lead too, sun prince. And despite my father's many flaws, he did teach me one thing that I agree with. Advisors are there to offer advice. Listen to them, hear their thoughts and opinions, take them in and consider them. But if you are going to be a true emperor, remember that it's just that: advice. In the end, you have to weigh their opinions and then make decisions for yourself."

Ahkin gave him a flat look. "And your father made his own decisions right into the claws of the Obsidian Butterfly."

"Well, I didn't say *he* was a good leader. When your mind has been tainted by an evil goddess, it's hard to make the right decisions no matter the advice you're given."

"And you think I am?"

"Am what?"

"A good leader?"

Ochix was silent for several moments. He tapped his chin thoughtfully. "I do, sun prince. I think you have a good heart and a mind for battle. I think you have the courage to do what is right. But you also need to be careful. It is difficult for good men to be good leaders."

Ahkin narrowed his eyes. "Why do you say that?"

"Because it's easy for good men to fight their enemies, but it is much more difficult for them to question those they are supposed to trust."

Ahkin blinked at him. There was a deep truth to those words that unsettled his stomach even more than it already was. "Where did you hear that?"

Ochix arched an eyebrow. "I like poetry."

Ahkin chuckled. "I've never had much time for the arts. Any free time I had away from battle training I spent studying the religious texts and star charts."

"Pity," Ochix said, pushing himself off the wall. "That's probably why you're so boring."

"*Boring?* I'm not boring."

Ochix yawned. "You're getting better," he said with a wink.

Ahkin rolled his eyes, but then a thought occurred to him. "Come with me. To the council meeting."

It was Ochix's turn to snort. "Right. I'm sure the elite leaders of the Chicome Empire would love to listen to the thoughts of a prince of Miquitz. They almost keeled over when Metzi announced she was going to marry me."

"You said I need to be comfortable making decisions for myself, and this is one of my decisions. Besides, you can help inform them about the situation with your father and the Tzitzimime star demons."

"If you say so."

Ahkin straightened his spine. "I do say so."

Ochix grinned. "There you go. All right then, *your highness.* Lead the way."

17

Mayana had hoped to avoid the eye of the high priest, Toani, but sure enough, the old vulture's gaze found her as quickly as buzzards circling a carcass. The hatred and fury radiating from him made her stomach turn. He'd humiliated her in front of the entire empire and set a trap to expose her "heathen" ways to Ahkin. She was everything he loathed, and she could tell he longed to crush her beneath his foot like some kind of poisonous beetle. Mayana looked away, itching to run from the room and put as much distance between herself and Toani as possible.

After the feast, Mayana bolted back toward the room that had been hers during the selection ritual. She wasn't really sure where else to go. It wasn't like she could set up residence in the empress's quarters, and she wasn't sure who to ask about where she'd be staying. Ahkin was so busy she couldn't get near him. Toani probably wouldn't let her anyway.

The palace of Tollan was overwhelming in its size and splendor, rooms upon rooms overflowing with the finest luxuries the empire had to offer. Guest rooms and residence rooms for the royal family, court-rooms, meeting rooms, steam baths, storerooms, and servants' quarters. She knew that if she ventured out of the palace itself, she'd find aviaries and zoos managed by the naguals of Ocelotl, the renowned terraced plea-sure gardens of Tollan bursting with every kind of jungle bloom and fruit, and the intricate pool and waterfall system weaving through the gardens.

Just the thought of the garden pools twisted Mayana's belly into a knot. The memories flooded back of the night she and Ahkin had spent together, enjoying the cool water against their flushed skin. The hours they'd spent talking and appreciating each other's company in the garden's temazcalli steam bath.

After passing several servants rushing around on palace business, she finally reached the long stone hallway located deep in the heart of the palace, where hangings of various colors and symbols represented the six city-states. A black curtain with a woven pattern of fire for Papatlaca, green with a sprouting shoot for Millacatl, red with a healing swirl for Pahtia, golden yellow with a jaguar for Ocelotl, purple with the symbol for wind for Ehecatl, and finally blue with the symbol of water for Atl.

These rooms had belonged to the princesses during her previous stay, but from the rumbling sound of voices within, they also served for whatever royal family members were visiting. Which meant her room was no longer just hers; it likely held her father and brothers.

She froze in front of the blue curtain of Atl, watching it billow slightly. The image of her father's face the last time she'd seen him burned behind her eyelids. The heartbreak, the disappointment hanging heavily upon his shoulders. And—the memory that hurt the most—the resigned defeat, the apparent acceptance that she'd ruined everything with her foolishness. The acceptance that she was going to die as a sacrifice. He had walked away from her that night without looking back.

Mayana lifted her hand to knock on the doorframe, but she hesitated. Her vision blurred with tears. Did she even want to see her family? Did they even care that she'd survived the underworld?

The curtain was suddenly yanked back, and Mayana yelped in surprise.

Her older brother, Chimalli, stood before her, his muscled frame taking up most of the doorway. He looked no different: the same short tousled hair, same humor dancing within his dark eyes. He jumped back, not expecting someone to be standing there—but then his eyes went wide with recognition. "Mayana?"

Mayana's lip quivered, her hand half lifting to reach for him, but then she drew back. Would he just shove her away in disgust?

But then, without a moment's hesitation, her oldest brother threw his arms around her and crushed her to his chest.

Mayana couldn't breathe, but she didn't care. Tears leaked out of the corners of her eyes as she embraced him back, savoring the solid, reassuring strength of him. She'd seen the false image of his brutalized body hanging from a post in Xibalba. To see him whole, and healthy—

"Chimalli, I—" she choked out.

But he shushed her, holding her tighter. "I thought you were gone forever," he whispered. "I'm never letting you go again."

"Mayana?" Her twin brothers Achto and Aquin, slightly younger than Chimalli's twenty-three years, were still impossible to tell apart. Their gangly frames appeared behind Chimalli's back briefly before they fought to get her into their arms next.

Hope blossomed inside her chest. Her brothers still loved her—forgave her for her choices during the selection ritual. Perhaps her father did as well. Perhaps she had a home still.

"Did you really survive Xibalba?" Achto asked, pulling back to look at her. "What was it like? Did you see demons and monsters—?"

Chimalli elbowed him in the gut.

"What?" Achto groaned, rubbing the tender muscles of his abdomen. "You know she's got some wicked stories."

Mayana arched a brow. "I'll tell you about the rock monsters and demon jaguars later."

Achto and Aquin exchanged glances that were equally awestruck and horrified, but before they could pepper her with more questions, a throat cleared loudly. Her brothers leapt away from her as though they had been caught playing with a forbidden toy.

Her father, Oztoc, lord of Atl, stood behind her in the hall. His arms were folded tightly across the expansive muscles of his chest, the torchlight glinting off the turquoise jewels inlaid on his deep-blue cloak. He looked like moonlight reflecting off the surface of a lake—a turbulent lake, caught in a sudden squall.

Crow's feet wrinkled the corners of his eyes, which swirled with lurking shadows of danger.

Mayana's spine stiffened. Suddenly she was ten years old, frozen under the scrutiny of her father's unending disapproval. She was the girl who'd sneaked into his brood of sons, like a bird laying its egg in the nest of another. She was never enough for him, could never make him proud. The memory of his joy at watching her selected as Ah-kin's bride stung like salt in a wound, especially when she remembered his horrified rage when she'd refused to sacrifice the dog. When she'd proved his reservations right after all.

Never able to silence her heart to do what was necessary. That's what he always said. Her father's voice was the same one that plagued the back of her mind, constantly questioning her and holding her back.

"What is she doing here?" her father asked, his tone as dark as his expression. "Did I not expressly forbid you from reaching out to her?"

Achto and Aquin dropped their chins to their chests, both kicking nervously at the stone tile beneath their feet. Chimalli balled his hands into fists, but he knew better than to question their father's authority.

Mayana, however, jutted her chin into the air. "And why would you forbid my brothers from seeing me? Aren't you happy I survived the underworld?"

Her father's eyes were black pools of sorrow. "It would have been better for us all if you hadn't."

Mayana recoiled as if he'd slapped her. "You're saying it would have been better if I had *died*?"

"Yes," was all he grunted before storming past them into the room. "Excuse me. I need to prepare for the council meeting."

Her brothers hovered nervously by the door, torn between their desire to obey and their desire to support their only sister.

"Go," she finally told them. Her voice quivered with restrained emotion. "I'll see you again soon."

The twins gave her sheepish smiles before retreating into their rooms. Chimalli, however, embraced her quickly one more time.

"I meant what I said. I will not lose you again." His gaze burned with intensity as it bore into her own. It spoke of promises and a stubbornness she recognized all too well. She wasn't the only member of their family cursed with such a double-edged gift. He was just much more skilled at wielding it than she ever was.

And then the curtain fell back into place, separating her from her family. But she knew a veil far thicker had separated them for years now, and she had no idea how to pull it back and join them again.

CHAPTER

18

Yemania *refused* to go anywhere near where her father was staying. That man had given her countless scars, both seen and unseen, and she would not give him the satisfaction of glimpsing her.

Ahkin had promised to reinstate her as High Healer of Tollan. Since Coatl and Metzi were supposedly imprisoned within the temple awaiting their fate to be decided by the council, she figured the healer's quarters were available to her. And as much as she wanted to rub the appointment in her father's face, she knew it would not do her any good. Her accomplishment was her own, and she didn't need anyone else's validation to be proud of it. Plus, it gave her an excuse not to go anywhere near the palace apartment reserved for Pahtia's royal family members.

Still, when she entered the rooms that had once belonged to her brother, Yemania felt an aching sense of loss. Coatl's betrayal still left a bitter taste on her tongue—that he'd been willing to sacrifice her life to restore his favor with Metzi. Now it was his turn to await judgment in the bowels of a temple. She should have felt vindicated, but instead, there was an aching, throbbing emptiness deep inside her chest.

Yemania shoved the feelings down and set to refamiliarizing herself with the room. Work tables, stone shelves sagging under the weight of hundreds of jars and clay pots, a smattering of comfortable cushions for patients. She breathed in the thick sweet scent of herbs and earth and felt more at home than she had anywhere else in her life. This was where she belonged, finding new cures and treatments for ailments. Ahkin may even let her resurrect her dream of using her gift to benefit the entire empire and not just the royal families.

A knock sounded behind her.

"Come in," Yemania said, too busy with her jars of herbs to see who was visiting.

"Can I hide in here?" Mayana's voice answered. She sounded tired, fragile, like pottery teetering on a ledge.

"Yes, but be warned, I might put you to work." Sometimes distraction could be the best medicine.

"Is there anything here to mend a broken heart?" Mayana shuffled to the table and began lifting jars to her nose, testing their scents.

Perhaps it was her healing spirit, but Yemania couldn't help studying her friend. The way Mayana's shoulders hung low, as if a weight was pressing them down. Shadows flickered in her eyes like ravens of ill omen taking flight. Her friend was troubled. Deeply so.

"Ahkin will not marry Teniza. You don't need—" Yemania started.

But Mayana flicked a dismissive hand. "It's not that. Though that's definitely a problem too."

Yemania waited for her to elaborate.

Mayana silently inspected the herbs and tonics, but then she finally gave up and wrapped her arms around herself. "I knew my father would be angry about what happened when I refused to sacrifice the dog. I just thought—" she drew in a shaking breath, "—I just thought he'd be happy I wasn't *dead*."

Yemania flinched. She knew that pain all too well. "Well, *I'm* glad you aren't dead."

"You'd probably be the only one." Mayana hugged the bag of Quetzalcoatl's bones against her chest like a talisman against further injury.

Yemania's cheeks dimpled. "I bet Ahkin would disagree with that statement. And so would the Mother goddess." She nodded pointedly toward the jade bones in Mayana's arms. "She needed you to save those for a reason."

"Yeah, I meant to ask you earlier," came a dry, sarcastic voice from the doorway. "What's with the creepy bag of bones, daughter of water? You never really struck me as the hoarding type."

Yemania clenched her teeth at the sight of Yoli of Papatlaca. She wore a simple black tunic dress edged in red, and the severe cut of the dark hair across her eyes cast her face in shadow. A thick obsidian bead protruded through her lower lip and—just as she had the last time they'd met—she twirled a long, thin fire-glass blade between her fingers. Her painted lips split into a wicked grin.

"Yoli," Yemania said stiffly. "Nice to see you again."

"I doubt that." She winked, making Mayana snort with laughter.

Yemania sighed and set to sorting the sheets of healing documents stacked on the shelf. She wasn't going to argue. She didn't have anything *against* the princess of fire. She just didn't feel particularly comfortable around her. Yoli seemed to revel in pain. Yemania preferred to see it healed. She could still remember the ease with which Yoli had stabbed herself in the arm and let her blood drip onto the floor, as though she enjoyed shocking people.

But gods bless Mayana, she'd seemed to have a fascination with the ironically *dark* princess of fire. And sure enough, she jumped up with a squeal and ran to embrace her.

Yoli's eyes went wide with surprise, as if she wasn't used to such a welcoming reception. But she still embraced her back, even if she withdrew rather quickly.

"So how in the nine hells did you survive, well, *the nine hells?*" she asked conversationally.

"Eight," Mayana corrected. "I didn't go through to the final resting place of souls."

"But you managed to steal a bag of worthless bones while you were there?"

Mayana cradled her bag protectively. "They are the bones of the god Quetzalcoatl, ripped from the throne of Cizin himself."

Yoli blinked. Then, she burst into a fit of laughter.

"I'm sorry, I'm sorry. You just should have seen how serious your face looked!" She wiped at tears forming in the corners of her eyes. "The bones of Quetzalcoatl himself. The underworld must have done a number on your head."

"The Mother goddess charged me with retrieving them, and I did."

"Now you're saying you met the Mother goddess? Ometeotl herself?"

Yemania knew how it sounded. She wasn't even sure she would have believed Mayana . . . if the Mother goddess had not also appeared to her.

"She's not lying," Yemania said, continuing to sort through the paper sheets on the shelves. There were recipes for various remedies, records of ailments treated. Typical of what she'd expect to find in the High Healer's workroom.

But then Yemania's fingers paused on a folded sheet that had been shoved into the corner. The moment she touched it, a shiver ran across the back of her neck. Mayana and Yoli's banter faded to the background.

She unfolded it with shaking hands—and then dropped it. It was a sheet ripped from a set of historical texts. A sheet she recognized because she had personally taken it from the temple library.

It fluttered to the floor, and the face of the Obsidian Butterfly stared up at her.

Yemania gasped.

"What is it?" Mayana asked, her eyebrows scrunching together.

"Nothing," Yemania said quickly. "I just dropped something." She didn't feel like discussing it in front of Yoli, so she swept the paper up and folded it. There were lines of glyphs on the back she hadn't had time to read before, and something told her it was important. She slipped it delicately beneath her waistband.

"So, daughter of water." Yoli flopped down on a cushion. "When's the wedding? I'm surprised I didn't see you up there with Ahkin."

Mayana nervously chewed her bottom lip, not meeting Yoli's eyes.

"Things not go so well in Xibalba?"

Mayana shook her head. "No, it's not that. It's just . . . politically a little complicated."

"Ah, you mean committing heresy and leaping into the underworld didn't endear you to the high priest?"

The corner of Mayana's mouth quirked up. "Not exactly."

"Good. Who cares what that old turkey thinks anyway."

Yemania sputtered. "Did you just call the high priest of the Chicome a turkey?"

"An *old* turkey," Yoli clarified. "The man's practically as old as the gods."

"I call him a vulture in my head," Mayana giggled.

Yoli snapped her fingers in Mayana's direction. "Maybe your head isn't damaged after all."

Yemania rolled her eyes. "Her head is not damaged. First, I can sense injuries, and second, the Mother goddess appeared to me as well."

Yoli narrowed her heavily kohled eyes. She assessed them both for the length of a heartbeat before she finally shrugged. "Okay, I believe you."

It was Yemania's turn to snort. "Just like that?"

"I don't see what reason you'd both have to lie. Besides, anyone lucky enough to survive Xibalba must have some kind of divine blessing."

Yemania pursed her lips.

Yoli groaned. "Okay, fine, that, and I'd much rather hang out with you than be stuck with my stupid family or talk to the Tree or the Wild Cat. So if believing you two talked to the gods lets me do that, then so be it."

"Aw," Mayana teased. "You like us."

Yoli crossed her arms over her chest. "Don't push it, princess. You are just the least annoying of anyone else here."

A crease appeared between Mayana's eyebrows. "Why are you all here? Didn't you go home after the selection ritual ended?"

Yoli deftly twirled her blade between her fingers. "Metzi summoned the lords of the city-states and told them to bring at least two members of their families. Apparently she wanted to use our abilities to harass Ehecatl."

"And you don't want to be with your family?" Yemania asked.

The air around Yoli seemed to grow cold, as if the fire in her eyes had gone out. There was a sharp edge to her voice when she answered. "Not really." She did not elaborate.

Yemania's heart lurched at the pain she sensed in the daughter of fire. "Well, you're welcome to stay with us as long as you need."

"I don't *need* to. You're just the least annoying, remember?"

"Right," Yemania said, fighting not to laugh. She couldn't help but notice Yoli was showing just the hint of a smile.

There was a sudden crashing sound, and the curtain covering the doorway flew up.

Yemania, Yoli, and Mayana jumped up, eyeing the doorway with apprehension. Yemania's already frayed nerves flared as every muscle in her body tensed. What could possibly be going on?

A small group of Eagle warriors marched into the room. Their polished wooden helmets were carved to look like the deadly beaks of predatory birds. Their spears were tipped in flints equally as sharp.

"Princesses of Pahtia, Atl, and Papatlaca," the nearest one said, his voice harsh. "You have been ordered to come with us."

Yoli stepped in front of them, sparks dancing on her fingertips and a fresh cut glistening on her palm. "And where are we going?"

For once, Yemania was happy to fade into the background.

"You will be escorted to a temple holding chamber until the selection ritual sacrifice is ready to be completed."

Yemania's heart slammed itself against her ribcage so hard she almost blacked out. *No.* She couldn't have heard correctly. There had to be some kind of mistake. She'd heard Ahkin say the ritual would not take place.

"*The selection ritual?*" she squeaked. "But what about—"

"His majesty, Emperor Ahkin, has made his choice. His wedding to Princess Teniza will take place at the end of the week, and your blood is required to bless the reign of the divine couple."

The Eagle warriors moved to grab Yoli, but flames licked their way up her arms. The closest warrior leapt back with a yelp.

"Yeah, I don't think we're going anywhere," she said calmly.

Several spears lowered at her all at once. Yoli's lip curled as if in anticipation.

Before any sparks could ignite into violence, Mayana jumped between them, her arms out. "Stop! We're coming. I'm sure this is just some kind of misunderstanding." Mayana turned to Yoli, her eyes wide with warning. *Trust me*, she mouthed. Yoli's jaw went rigid, but she calmed her flames.

Yemania wanted to speak, but her throat seemed to stop working. Her legs began to shake as hands closed around her arms and dragged her from the workshop. In front of her, Mayana and Yoli shuffled along with their heads held high. Why couldn't she be as brave as they?

She glanced back at the healer's workshop as it disappeared from view, her dream once again slipping between her grasping fingers. Ahkin had promised her, and now he would have her suddenly sacrificed? It wasn't like him.

He loved Mayana. She'd seen the truth of that clearly with her own eyes.

Like the sting of a wasp piercing her thoughts, she realized this wasn't Ahkin's command at all. It couldn't be. There was no way Ahkin would allow this, let alone order it to happen.

This was someone else's doing.

But with Metzi and Coatl imprisoned, then whose?

Ochix immediately regretted his decision to attend the council meeting.

The curtains to the entrance parted, exposing a large room flanked in painted red pillars of stone. The flickering torchlight against the paint gave the impression the walls were bleeding. Ochix suppressed a shudder. Always an ominous sign. The Chicome and their endless demand for blood.

And that was before the eyes of about ten or so older men turned to him with looks ranging from confusion to pure hatred.

"Well, this is pleasant," Ochix said. He took a seat on an empty cushion and waved cheerily at the closest Tlana priest, who was glaring daggers at him.

The priest harrumphed and turned toward Ahkin, ruffling the feathers of his ceremonial headpiece. "What is the death demon doing here? I thought he ran back to Miquitz with his tail between his legs when he was caught dallying with the healer girl."

"A tail is *not* what you would find between my legs," Ochix mumbled.

Ahkin cleared his throat to mask his laugh and took a seat at the head of the table. "Ochix is here with my personal invitation. He saved my life when we escaped from Miquitz, at great personal risk to himself." He spoke with a finality that dared to be questioned.

None of them did. Though several clearly wanted to. So at least they weren't as stupid as they all looked.

Ochix got comfortable and grabbed one of the sweet honey drinks set out on the table. "*Great personal risk*," he repeated, lifting his bowl in salute toward the general of the Eagle warriors. The thick-necked general clenched and unclenched his fists.

Ahkin cleared his throat again, commanding the attention of the council. "I want to thank you all for coming. I know the last few weeks have been difficult. Believe me, they have been difficult for me as well." The corner of his mouth quirked up.

Ochix snorted a laugh, impressed that Ahkin made a joke. But he was the only one. "Oh come on," he whispered to the advisor sitting beside him. "Difficult? Get it? Cause he just went through—eh, never mind." Apparently no one here had a sense of humor. Ochix raised his eyebrows and took another sip of his drink.

The head priest bowed his head in Ahkin's direction, rattling the beads and jewels around his neck. "We are so honored to have you back, your highness. May the last weeks be forgotten like a bad dream as we move forward."

"Thank you, Toani. I want to first discuss what will be done with Metzi and Coatl. Chicome law requires a fair trial to convict them of their crimes. I will leave the interrogation—and their punishment—to the discretion of our high judge." Ahkin lifted a hand and indicated a heavily wrinkled man whose flowing green cloak resembled a toad.

"Of course, your highness. I will begin preparations immediately," the judge croaked.

"Yaotl, where do we stand in the war with Ehecatl? What negotiations have taken place?" Ahkin addressed the general of the Jaguar warriors. At least, Ochix assumed that was his position, based on the spotted pelt he wore draped across his massive shoulders.

"We have attempted negotiations, but failed to secure Ehecatl's loyalty. They remain steadfast in their desire to withdraw from the Chicome Empire. We cannot allow their rebellion to be successful."

And it did make sense. If one city-state thought they could leave, then what would stop the rest from following suit? Their empire as they knew it would crumble into chaos.

"I agree," Ahkin said. "What attempts have we made?"

"After friendly reminders of the benefits of being part of the empire, we resorted to threats and intimidation," Yaotl said. "Your sister had the weapon masters of Papatlaca send them an arsenal of new weapons. Along with the gift, she sent a message that said we are so confident in our imminent victory that we are willing to supply them with weapons to fight against us."

Ahkin's eyes went wide with surprise. "That was Metzi's idea?"

"She might have been cruel, but she has a keen mind for strategy, your highness. I must admit that I was impressed with her plan."

Ahkin frowned. "But it was unsuccessful?"

"It accomplished a halt in open hostilities, at the least. I think it scared them enough that they retreated into the city, barricading themselves against invasion."

Ochix let out a low whistle. He had heard the rumors of the towering stone walls built around the city of storms. Supposedly they were to protect the city from the raging sea at its back—but they were also effective at keeping out storms of the political nature. "Good luck reaching them in there."

The council members ignored him.

"Your sister had a plan to flush them out like rats," Yaotl continued. He gestured to the lords of the loyal city-states gathered around the table. "She summoned the lords of Pahtia, Ocelotl, Papatlaca, Millacatl, and Atl and at least two of their blood relatives to use their abilities against the city. The plan was to burn their crops and prevent more from growing, spread disease, harass them with insects, and cut off their water supply. When they surrendered, Metzi planned to have the lord of Ehecatl executed as a warning against future rebellion."

This time, it was Ochix's eyes that went wide. He had seriously underestimated the cruelty that Metzi was capable of. Then again, the princess did consult with a wrathful goddess to kill her parents and trick her brother into thinking the world was ending, so arguably he shouldn't be so surprised. Ochix blew out a heavy breath. "Nine hells. Why is it so important to you people that they submit? Wouldn't it be easier just to let them worship the way they want to?"

The silence that fell over the table was deafening. Ochix actually felt bumps rise up the skin of his arms. "Apparently that wasn't the right question to ask," he said nervously.

Toani, the head priest, rose delicately to his feet. He smoothed out the folds of his bloodred robes and fixed Ochix with a glare as black and soulless as the space between the stars. "We are a united empire, forged through the flames of death and destruction. We have survived as long as we have in this seventh age because we have worked tirelessly to appease the gods. If Ehecatl fails to uphold their responsibilities, if *we* fail to uphold our responsibilities—" He hissed. "—then the world as we know it shall end again, and the Miquitz shall perish alongside us. So instead of mocking and questioning our ways, prince of death, perhaps you should be thanking us."

Ochix shifted on his cushion. These sun worshippers had to be drinking a little too much pulque. The Miquitz believed that the emperor of Tollan raised the sun each morning. That much was obvious. Still, beyond that . . . there was no real evidence that their precisely timed rituals supposedly appeased the gods. The Chicome claimed the holy codex sheets given to them by the gods demanded it, but no one from Miquitz had ever seen them, and the Chicome weren't inclined to share.

He lifted his exposed palms to plead with the men gathered around him. "You don't actually think you save the world with all your little rituals, do you? You really think you have that much power? Ehecatl doesn't believe that. Not even Ahkin does anymore."

There was a collective intake of breath. The council members' gazes shot toward Ahkin like a volley of arrows.

"What does he mean, your highness?" Toani demanded. "Surely you still understand the importance and significance of our divine responsibility? Surely you are not so young and naive as to think that the safety we have enjoyed these last hundred years has been unearned?"

Ahkin gave Ochix a warning look and gripped the side of the table until his knuckles went white. "No one speaks for me," he said through gritted teeth.

The room broke into a frenzy of whispers and angry buzzing. Ochix's chest squeezed. He shouldn't have blurted out the prince's secret like that. He hadn't meant to. It had just slipped out in his frustration. The reaction around him suggested it was far more grievous a mistake than he could have imagined.

Toani suddenly slammed a hand against the table, and the buzzing stopped. The priest's voice was as calm and deadly as a snake about to strike. "You still have not answered the questions. Tell us it is not true. Tell us you still intend to uphold the traditions that your ancestors have upheld for generations, starting with the selection ritual and your marriage."

Ahkin's jaw tensed, and he dropped his gaze to the table in front of him. Ochix swore he could hear the sun prince's mind scrambling to find an adequate answer. He wished he had one to throw to him, like passing a ball to a teammate in a ceremonial ballgame.

The priest sighed. "Your highness, may we speak?" He spoke with the air of an exasperated father about to discipline his son. "In private?"

Ahkin finally lifted his head. "Yes, I think that would be wise."

Toani nodded to the general of the Eagle warriors, almost as if a silent signal passed between them. Ochix's stomach swirled with unease, but before he could say or do anything, the sun prince and the high priest disappeared behind a curtain. He hadn't even gotten the chance to tell them about his father and the star demons as Ahkin had planned.

And then Ochix felt the sharp edge of a blade pressed against his throat.

CHAPTER

20

The curtain whispered shut behind them. Ahkin led the way down the hall to a smaller meeting room with plain white walls. The stone table at its center could only seat about six men instead of the twenty or so in the main council chamber.

Toani, however, did not sit down. He stood as rigid and tall as a ceiba tree. "I will say it again. Assure me that what the death prince said is not true." He folded his hands in front of his chest and waited.

Ahkin gritted his teeth. "I can't do that."

"And why not?"

Ahkin took a deep breath. "Because what he says *is* true. The rituals are not necessary to protect us from an apocalypse, or even to secure the gods' favor. I agree with the urgent need to ensure Ehecatl remains part of the empire, but I don't understand why they can't worship as they wish. Ometeotl wants to be worshipped with life, not death. Through singing, dancing, offerings of fine foods."

Ahkin expected some kind of reaction, but not even a muscle on Toani's withered face twitched. It was as if the priest had turned temporarily to stone. The distant bustling of servants echoed around the empty room.

Ahkin coughed. He resisted the urge to start tapping the table with his fingers.

"And where did you hear such a thing?" Toani finally asked.

Ahkin felt flustered, like a child who had broken a pot and was trying to explain why he wasn't guilty. "I—uh—the Mother goddess told me."

Silence.

"The Mother *and* Father, technically," Ahkin clarified, his confidence slipping with each passing moment. "You know, the divine coupling. Ometeotl. The embodiment . . . of . . . duality?"

Finally, after several more painful moments of silence, Toani narrowed his eyes ever so slightly. "You are telling me that you spoke to the divine creator and that she told you personally the rituals are not necessary?"

Ahkin swallowed hard, his throat dry. "Yes?"

"And I assume you wish to marry the daughter of water and forgo the selection ritual entirely?"

The back of Ahkin's neck grew hot. "Well, that would be my eventual plan, yes." The sickening swirling in Ahkin's stomach solidified into a heavy stone. "But that's not what we are discussing right now. I'm just saying we need to negotiate peace with Ehecatl, and the best way to do that is to just let them worship as they wish. It is why they resent Tollan as they do. I don't see why that is so unrealistic a request to grant them."

Toani held up a hand. "Let me stop you right there, your highness. I think I have heard all that I need to hear."

"What do you mean?"

"I mean I have heard your explanation. Let us return to the council chamber to discuss our next steps."

That was it? After everything he'd just said? Ahkin felt deeply unsettled, but he didn't know what to say to argue. "All right, fine."

Toani shuffled along behind him, not a word passing between them. When they emerged into the council chamber, Ahkin immediately noticed Ochix was missing. None of the council members seemed willing to meet his eyes.

"Where did Ochix go?" Ahkin asked.

Quauhtli, the leader of the Eagle warriors, grunted. "He said it would be better if he left. Probably ashamed of his irreverent actions. And rightly so, in my opinion."

The unsettled feeling in his stomach grew even stronger, but Ahkin knew he had to appear calm. His council needed him to be strong, dependable. Regal. So he nodded and took his seat at the head of the table. Toani resumed his position immediately to Ahkin's right.

"I apologize for the delay, gentlemen," Toani said, offering a tight smile to the room. "There were some matters I had to attend to, and I think we finally have the answers we need."

Ahkin returned Toani's tight smile with one of his own.

"His highness has confided in me some of the events that transpired while he ventured through the underworld, including—as he puts it—discussing our religious practices with the Mother goddess herself."

Several council members exchanged significant looks. Ahkin suddenly felt as though he were a rabbit walking into a snare.

Toani turned to face him. "Did you suggest to me that we let Ehecatl worship as they wish, including their desire to no longer perform the rituals essential for our survival?"

The high judge and Quauhtli leaned forward, eager for Ahkin's answer.

Ahkin rubbed the flaming back of his neck, and the sound of his heartbeat thudded in his ears.

"Isn't that what you told me, Ahkin?" Toani tilted his head like a curious dog.

He hadn't said *your highness*.

Ahkin took a deep breath to calm his nerves. He wished Ochix was still here so that he could have an ally. He couldn't deny Toani's allegations, and the council needed to hear what he thought whether they approved or not. "Yes, that's true."

"And what did the Mother goddess tell you while you were in Xibalba? That the rituals—including the same selection ritual that joined your parents—is no longer necessary? Ometeotl appeared to you herself and told you she preferred us to worship her with acts of life instead of death? Acts like singing, and dancing, and offering fine foods?"

Ahkin pursed his lips. When Toani said it like that, it made him sound . . .

Toani smirked. "As the council can see, our young prince has emerged from Xibalba quite changed from the boy that fell. His head is filled with dangerous ideas of changing the way the Chicome have lived for centuries, from the ages before our current sun. He has been bewitched by the whims of the heathenous daughter of water, who I fear may in fact be an agent sent from Ehecatl to destroy us from within."

"That is preposterous," roared the lord of Atl from the other end of the table. "Mayana's views are blasphemy, it's true, but my daughter has never had any contact with Ehecatl, nor would she conspire against her empire. She is nothing more than a foolish child who rejected my teachings."

"Perhaps," purred the leonine lord of Ocelotl, his golden eyes focusing on the lord of Atl, "if the lord of water had not indulged his daughter's tantrums, spoiling her into thinking she is above the ways of—"

"Do not speak of my future wife in such a way," Ahkin demanded, his tone turning deadly.

The lord of Millacatl leapt to his feet, his willowy height towering over the men around him. "Your future wife? Are you insinuating you never had any intention to fulfill your promise to marry *my* daughter? Was Millacatl a political game piece to be moved across the board as needed? You lured us here to betray us just as your sister betrayed her engagement to Ehecatl?"

"No! That's not what I—" Ahkin started, throwing his hands in the air.

But the council exploded into a cacophony of shouting and threats.

"I will not stand by and allow such disrespect—"

"If you had tamed your daughter instead of letting her run wild—"

"We came all the way from the volcano for *this*—"

"In the name of the holy gods above, STOP!" Toani's deep, ominous voice cut through the chaos.

To Ahkin's surprise, the various lords and council members obeyed, though the simmering tension between them was now about as thick as the smoke from a sacrificial brazier. Chests heaved, glares were thrown, but they stayed their voices.

"This," Toani stood and began to pace slowly, methodically, across the length of the room, "this is exactly why our way of life is to be preserved. The alternative is war, bloodshed, and worst of all, attracting the ire of the gods. The rituals unite us under a common purpose, a common divine mission to appease not only the gods but our own desire for rebellion. Ehecatl needs to be brought back where it belongs, whether it understands why or not. We are the leaders of this great empire. It is our job to fight for and protect the unity of our people against any who threaten to tear it apart, either from the outside—" his gaze fell pointedly on Ahkin "—or from within."

Ahkin's jaw dropped. Was Toani accusing him of treason against his own subjects? Was this how Mayana had felt her whole life? Fighting against a giant when you were nothing more than a mouse? But Mayana was no mouse.

And neither was he.

Ahkin pulled his blade from his waistband and drew blood across the length of his palm with a quick flick. Before anyone could notice, Ahkin called all the light of the room to him. He ordered it to surround him, illuminating his body until he glowed as brilliantly as the sun itself. The council members shielded their eyes.

"I am the son of Huitzilopochtli. The son of the sun itself. It is my blood that raises the sun each morning and I will not allow the council that has sworn to serve *my* family—"

A firm hand settled on his shoulder and shoved him back to the cushion. Toani's voice whispered harshly in his ear, "You are a child that is unfit to lead. If you do not do as I say right this moment, I will ensure that your little friend from Miquitz joins his ancestor in the underworld."

Ahkin's light extinguished in an instant. Ochix's words floated back to him. *It's easy for good men to fight their enemies, but it is much more difficult for them to question those they are supposed to trust.* He felt lost, as though the man he had discovered himself to be in Xibalba never truly escaped. He was a child again, a child trying to wear his father's crown.

Toani addressed the council once more. "It is clear that the prince is unfit to lead in his current state. I fear his experiences in the underworld have affected his mind. As his council, we must act not only in the best interest of the empire, but in the best interest of the prince himself. Until he can recover, we will keep him contained and manage the empire in his stead. For his own safety, of course."

Of course. Ahkin felt numb, as though his limbs had stopped working. He knew he needed to fight, to stand up and push back against Toani. He still needed to warn them about the Tzitzimime and Tzom's plan to release them. The head priest was supposed to guide Ahkin, serve him as a spiritual advisor. Ahkin had trusted him, valued his wisdom and knowledge. But in calling him a child in front of the council, in threatening Ochix's life, Toani had struck a blow that knocked the wind from Ahkin's lungs. It had knocked the fight from his very spirit. Hands closed around his arms and lifted him to his feet.

Eagle warriors marched Ahkin toward the doorway, Toani following close behind. The councilors again erupted into a frenzy of shouting.

"I hate that it had to come to this, Ahkin. I really do," Toani said so quietly that only Ahkin could hear. "You will be comfortably contained while you recover. With some rest and perspective, your mind will return. In the meantime, I will handle the arrangements for your coronation and wedding to Princess Teniza of Millacatl. I will also prepare the other princesses for the selection sacrifice."

A rushing sound filled Ahkin's ears as Toani's words washed over him. *The selection sacrifice?* Mayana. Yemania. Yoli. Even Zorrah. Their deaths would be pointless. Ahkin's spirit returned in a blazing glory. He ripped his arms out of the grip of the Eagle warriors and dove for Toani. "NO! You can't do this!"

His hands had just closed around the front of the priest's bloodred robes, the gemstones of Toani's necklaces cutting into Ahkin's palms, when more warriors rushed in to restrain him. They yanked him back before he could do any further damage.

"I am the emperor! You can't do this! I AM THE EMPEROR!" Ahkin screamed as they started to drag him away. Blinding flashes of light ricocheted around the room. Several guards clutched at their eyes in pain.

But a warm hand grasped his own, and the stinging cuts began to heal. Ahkin looked up to see the deeply lined face of the lord of Pahtia, Coatl and Yemania's brutal father. He was healing Ahkin's wounds to prevent him from using his powers.

"Stop! You can't do this! I am—" Ahkin yelled before a hand clasped over his mouth.

"You are not truly the emperor until you are married and crowned, little princeling," the lord of Pahtia said, his voice dancing with cruel laughter.

"Perhaps it would be best to secure him so that he does not hurt himself." Toani straightened, adjusting the feathered headpiece that had been knocked askew in the scuffle. "Such a shame. He was a sharp and intelligent boy. I had such high hopes for him."

CHAPTER

21

Mayana paced the length of the temple holding chamber. It wasn't much larger than a single-room house. The ceiling hung so low, the top of her head nearly scraped it. There were no windows, only a single doorway currently blocked by an enormous rolled stone. It smelled of wet rock, mildew, and something distinctly like human excrement.

"This is ridiculous. Ahkin agreed to marry Teniza, but there is no way he'd allow the selection ritual to continue," Mayana growled. She kicked the stone door, which accomplished nothing but making her toes hurt. Her empty arms ached for the comforting weight of her bag, of the jade bones. But the guards had taken them away when they were captured.

Yoli sat in the center of the floor wiggling her fingers, watching the sparks she ignited dance across their tips. "I told you, you should have just let me torch them."

Yemania, who was crouched in a ball in the corner, lifted her head from her knees. She twittered like an angry sparrow. "Life has worth, Yoli. We don't just *torch* people because we feel like it. Those soldiers have families too. Wives and children that would miss them."

"Then they shouldn't follow stupid orders," Yoli countered.

Yemania groaned. "And you should stop cutting yourself just to play with your powers! It's killing me to watch you sit there and injure yourself over and over!"

Mayana sighed in frustration. Whatever temporary truce Yemania and Yoli had found seemed to evaporate when the guards seized them. But Mayana had more pressing concerns. Where was Ahkin? Was he searching for her? Did he even know they'd been captured?

"How are you making flames like that?" Mayana asked Yoli, suddenly distracted. "Doesn't your blood just allow you to manipulate fire? I can only manipulate water, not summon it."

"I thought you could summon water from that necklace of yours," Yoli said, watching a feather of flame that flickered on the end of her thumb.

Mayana looked down at the amulet of Atlacoya. "Yes, but I can't summon water from nothing."

"I can't summon fire from nothing."

"But you are right now."

Yoli shrugged. "Fire is energy, daughter of water. Energy is all around us. In the air itself. All I do is call forth the energy from around me and it condenses into flame. I bet you could do the same with the water in the air if you tried."

Mayana blinked. She'd never imagined such a thing was even possible. Perhaps she should try.

The rock across the doorway suddenly shifted, crunching and grinding against the stone floor as several guards rolled it aside.

Yoli and Yemania rose to their feet. The flames in Yoli's palm grew in size. Mayana stepped forward to demand to speak to someone, but before she could say anything, *someone* was shoved into the room with them. Whoever it was collided with Mayana, and they both fell to the floor in a tangle of arms and fur.

Yemania rushed forward to help while Yoli unleashed a burst of flames from her hand toward the open door. The stone rolled back in place and Yoli's flames sputtered uselessly against the rock. At least they left an impressive scorch mark behind.

Mayana tried to scramble back away from the new arrival, but there was a gasp of recognition, and then Mayana felt fingers close around her throat.

"I didn't kill you before, but I sure as hells won't fail this time," Zorrah, princess of animals, growled.

Stars blinked in Mayana's vision as she gasped for air.

Yemania cried out. "No! Please! Stop!"

Zorrah's nails dug like claws into the skin of Mayana's neck, drawing warm, sticky blood. In her panic, the feel of her own blood at least gave Mayana an idea. She focused, and a jet of water burst from her jade skull pendant, striking Zorrah squarely in the chest.

The princess of animals flew back and hit the opposite wall, where she collapsed into a heap of soaked jaguar fur. She scrambled back to her feet, spitting her long, dark hair out of her mouth. With a hiss, she bared her teeth, which—like her nails—had been filed into sharp points. Instead of the revealing pelt dress she had worn at the banquet earlier, she now wore the tight-fitting hide bodysuit of a Jaguar warrior, complete with the pelt of the beast draped across her shoulders as a cloak.

"You're a Jaguar warrior now?" Mayana said in surprise.

"And you're alive. For now." Zorrah's chest heaved. She lunged toward Mayana again, but this time a wall of flame erupted between them.

"Go after Mayana again and I will torch you," Yoli said, sounding utterly bored. "Is that all right this time?" she asked Yemania, arching an eyebrow.

Yemania let out a sound somewhere between a laugh and a sob. She lifted her hand to her chest as though bracing her thudding heart. "Yes, in this case, I think it's warranted."

"Excellent." The corner of Yoli's mouth curled into a wicked smile.

"To injure of course, not kill." Yemania added quickly. "Then I can heal her."

Yoli let out a sigh of exasperation. "Damn healer . . ."

"Or," Zorrah hissed, "how about you tell me why the *hells* we are in a sacrificial holding chamber?" She backed herself as far against the wall as she could, the flames dancing alongside fear in her feral eyes.

"Haven't you heard?" Yoli asked, picking at her nails. "Ahkin chose his bride. They are going to sacrifice us."

Zorrah's wild eyes swiveled toward Mayana. "So he didn't pick you after all."

"He didn't pick you either," Mayana said, her voice as cold as ice.

They stared each other down. Mayana swore the fire between them grew even hotter.

Yemania stepped forward. "Can we put out the flames and just talk about this? Please?"

Yoli cocked her head to the side. "Depends. Can the animal princess tame herself?"

Zorrah gave Yoli a look of pure disgust. "What's to talk about? We are going to have our hearts ripped out and burned on the sacrificial altar."

"No we aren't," Mayana said.

Zorrah snorted. "Right, are we going to escape and flee into the jungles? Live among the *monkeys*?"

Mayana clenched her teeth. Zorrah had sent a monkey to steal her cacao beans during one of the selection competitions and then another one to destroy Mayana's rooms.

Instead of responding—Mayana really didn't trust herself not to say something that would ignite another fight between them—she summoned more water from her necklace. She coaxed the glistening silver stream to extinguish the flames with a sputtering hiss. Steam filled the chamber so thick it became difficult to see. It reminded her of a steam bath that grew a little too hot.

"We need Itza," Yemania coughed, waving a hand in front of her face. The steam swirled around her hand like smoke.

"You'll see her soon enough," croaked an old woman's voice.

Mayana froze. She knew that voice. She *knew* that voice . . .

Yemania squeaked and covered her mouth with her hands.

An old woman, humpbacked and bowlegged, stood before them. Her face resembled a dry, cracked riverbed in the height of summer. White and black hair swirled into a bun that sat atop her head like a coconut in a tree. The dress she wore alternated black and white geometric patterns. A radiant glow clung to her wrinkled skin as though a bright star shone just behind her.

Zorrah howled in surprise, while Yoli . . . well, Yoli looked utterly unfazed by the old woman's sudden appearance in their midst despite no entrance or exit through the solid stone. She just blinked curiously.

"My darling granddaughters." The old woman clapped her hands together. "I must admit, I am disappointed in your behavior toward one another."

Zorrah lifted a shaking hand and pointed at her, her face as pallid as if she'd seen a ghost. "Who—how—this isn't possible! How did she get in here?"

Yemania fell to the floor and prostrated herself. Mayana probably should have done the same, considering this was *the Mother goddess*, Ometeotl herself. Or himself. Though the creator clearly preferred to take her female form with them. But Mayana couldn't bring herself to feel anything more than frustration. And something else . . . Was it . . . anger?

Yes, it was anger she felt bubbling to the surface as she beheld the Mother goddess standing before her. Ometeotl hadn't prepared her or Ahkin at all for what they experienced in Xibalba. She'd let them wander through the hells, barely surviving, tortured body and soul to the point that Mayana knew she'd never be the same.

The goddess had let her beloved dog Ona die to save them. She even let Mayana think she could bring her mother back from the dead, just to force her to trade her mother's bones for the jade bones of Quetzalcoatl. How could she ever have asked that of her? Did the Mother have *any idea* what a choice like that would do to Mayana's heart?

"Yes, I do have an idea, my dear," Ometeotl said, turning to face her. Her aura glowed slightly brighter.

Mayana shrank back, her anger evaporating and replacing itself with fear.

"I had to choose between saving my godly children or saving my human ones. For a mother to choose between her children, which to live and which to die . . . Mmmm—" Ometeotl closed her eyes and shook her head, as though finishing her statement was too painful.

She took a deep, shuddering breath. "Do not think for a moment, daughter of water, that you are unique in your suffering. Sometimes suffering is the path we must take to reach our destination. I hope you know me well enough to trust that I do have a destination in mind. Your suffering does matter to me, more than you could ever imagine, but sometimes I am trying to protect you from an even greater one."

The words pierced straight through Mayana's heart and she fell to her knees, exposing her palms to the creator. She dropped her head. Tears rolled hot and thick down her cheeks. "I'm sorry. I'm so sorry," she cried.

Yoli chose that particular moment to swear loudly and violently.

Everyone's heads turned toward her.

"Sorry," Yoli said, lifting her hands in apology. "I just realized . . . that's *Ometeotl*."

The Mother rolled her eyes. "My darling daughter of fire," she chuckled. "It is wonderful to finally speak to you in person."

"Uh—yeah. Thanks. You too—um—Mother Ometeotl. Welcome to our humble—" she waved a flippant hand around the rank stone chamber "—prison."

The last time Yemania had seen the Mother goddess, she had been in one of these exact same holding chambers. Metzi had just discovered her affair with Ochix and sentenced Yemania to death, but the Mother goddess had helped her escape and reminded her that no one else got to decide her worth.

"I agree. We really must stop meeting in places like this," the goddess said, reading her thoughts. Ometeotl bent down to tilt Yemania's face up from the floor. "Up, my child. You do not belong in places as low as you think. You have one of the most important roles to play."

Yemania's heart swelled at the Mother's words. *She* had a role to play?

The Mother goddess winked. "Presumably the most important of all. But I'll let you discover that for yourself. You're a smart girl."

Yemania sat up from her prostrated pose. Beside her, Mayana was trying to discreetly wipe the tears from her eyes. The Mother goddess turned to her next.

"I do not blame you for your doubts, Mayana, nor for your anger. Sometimes the lessons we must learn are painful ones. Be angry at me. Your anger will not hurt me. I would rather you work through it than let it fester in your heart. I promise that at the end of everything, you will finally understand."

Mayana sniffed and then nodded. The Mother goddess rested a hand on the side of her face. Mayana placed her own over it and pressed it harder into her cheek, as if she were begging the goddess not to let her go.

Ometeotl gave her a reassuring smile before withdrawing her hand. She snapped her fingers and the clouds of steam still permeating the room dissipated in an instant. "Now," she said, clapping her withered hands together. "There is much to discuss. Can I trust you to stay your hand, daughter of beasts?" She arched an eyebrow in Zorrah's direction.

Zorrah still looked as though she was going to jump out of her skin. Her feet twitched as if she wanted to run but had nowhere to run to. She stared at Ometeotl with a mix of horror and fascination. "I—yes—I will stay my hand."

"Thank you." Ometeotl winked at her. "Because I will need your skills, if you are willing."

Zorrah dipped her head in obedience. "Of course. I am your servant."

The Mother then turned to Yoli. "And yours as well."

Yoli just nodded with her eyes wide, her usual witty remarks apparently stuck in her throat.

"First things first." Ometeotl snapped her fingers again, and Mayana's woven bag containing the jade bones appeared within her hand. "You really need to stop getting these taken away from you. We went through quite the ordeal to rescue them."

Mayana gasped and took them, placing the strap across her shoulder. "Thank you." Yemania could see the relief washing over her.

"The mission ahead is full of danger, and the only way you will succeed is if you work together. *All* of you." The Mother's eyes swept across every princess in the room.

Yemania's stomach clenched. Danger? Work together with Yoli and Zorrah?

"And Itza of Ehecatl, though you will need to pick her up along the way," the Mother said. "I have plans for Teniza as she remains here, but you will be united with her eventually as well."

"What exactly are we doing?" Zorrah cut in.

Ometeotl pointed at the bag at Mayana's hip. "These bones are our last hope to save humanity. You must venture to the Caves of Creation and use Itza's blood to resurrect her ancestor, Quetzalcoatl, before the Obsidian Butterfly and the Tzitzimime unleash their fury upon the world."

Yoli blinked. "The Tzitzimime? The star demons?"

"But Ahkin is safe in Tollan," Mayana cut in. "Tzom can't use his blood to hold the eclipse if he doesn't have it."

Ometeotl's eyes swam with ancient wisdom none of them could understand, with futures none could see. "Ahkin is not the only child of the sun, daughter of water."

Yemania gasped in understanding. Ahkin was not the only descendant of Huitzilopochtli.

So was Metzi.

———

Rage burned through Metzi so hot she thought it might devour her. She was helpless, back in the exact position she swore she'd never be again. Waiting for a room full of old men to decide her fate. Ahkin had stolen everything from her. Again.

She screamed her frustration, beating her fists against the cold, heartless stone blocking the doorway. How long would they leave her in the bowels of the temple? What would they decide to do with her now?

"They still need your blood," Coatl assured her. "They don't need mine, but whatever happens, they won't risk the sun not rising."

Metzi ripped her sandal off her foot and threw it at Coatl's head. He ducked and it slapped against the wall behind him.

"What was that for?" he snapped.

"You idiot! They don't need my blood at all. The sun will rise with or without it."

A crease formed between his brows. "What? No. Metzi, I think you're just confused."

"I'm not confused," she shrieked. "They think our blood is needed, but what will they do when they discover it isn't?"

She knew she was letting her emotions get the better of her, but she felt desperate, and Coatl just didn't understand. The pity in his gaze incensed her even further. "The Butterfly told me everything. The ritual isn't needed, and if you don't believe me, then you are more of a fool than I thought."

A twinge of guilt pricked in her gut at the wounded expression that crossed Coatl's face. Especially when he said, "I was just trying to give you some hope to hold on to." He turned away from her, his hands now clenched into fists.

"I put my hope in my goddess." Metzi squatted down on the floor and hugged her knees. She fought against the hopelessness threatening to wash over her. "She will deliver us. She has to."

"Just like she delivered us into a holding cell in the temple?" Coatl's sarcasm cut deep beneath her skin.

"Don't question her," Metzi said, her voice low and dangerous.

Coatl threw his arms wide in frustration. "I have not questioned you, or her, or anything we've done from the beginning because it allowed us to be together. But I can't help it. I'm starting to wonder if the Butterfly really has our best interests at heart, or if we're just being used."

Metzi ignored him. He didn't have the connection she did to the Obsidian Butterfly. He'd never felt that same hopelessness, that sense of feeling trapped with no control over your own life.

So instead, she threw frantic prayers to the stars. Repeating her desperation over and over until it became a steady chant, a chant that calmed the panic rising in her chest. *Set me free. Set me free. Set me free. Set me free. Set me free . . .*

A boom suddenly shook the temple walls. Dust rained from the cracks above their heads and tiny pebbles danced across the stone floor. Metzi tumbled against the wall.

Coatl was beside her in an instant. "What in the nine hells . . ." he started to say.

But then, outside their cell, came the sound of men screaming.

Metzi's heart threw itself against her ribcage. The sound of screaming grew closer, tainted with a strange rattling sound she'd never heard before in her life, like beads scattering across the floor.

Like . . . like . . . shells.

Something heavy thudded against the door. Bright-red blood the color of cinnabar oozed from beneath the stone. Metzi screamed, then covered her mouth with her hand.

What was going on out there?

"Stay behind me," Coatl instructed, which was brave considering he'd spent all his days learning to heal, not to fight. The calluses on his hands were from grinding pestles, not grasping weapons. Still, Metzi positioned herself behind his back just as the stone across the doorway began to shift.

Metzi slammed her eyes shut, the side of her face pressed against the hot skin of Coatl's bare back. She could hear the frantic thrashing of his heart against her ear. It matched the frenzy of her own.

She could hear the grinding of the door sliding open. Whatever guards had been posted outside were silent. The rattling grew even louder.

Coatl sucked in a breath. The muscles of his back contracted.

Then Coatl screamed.

Metzi couldn't help it; she opened her eyes and peered around his back.

The mutilated bodies of the guards lay strewn about the hallway beyond. And there, framed in the doorway, was a creature pulled straight from her nightmares. Skeletal and pale, like the skin of a lizard left to bleach in the sun, the figure stood so tall, it had to stoop over to fit beneath the low ceiling. It was humanoid in shape, but its arms, which ended in needle-sharp claws, were far too long and spindly. Black, pupilless eyes blinked from the joints of its arms and legs.

But its face was the most horrific.

A skull with no skin at all—just white bone exposed to the world and red eyes gleaming within the black depths of its sockets. Blood dribbled down from its teeth and coated its feathered necklace and chest, where its ribcage protruded grotesquely. Atop its head, a feathered headpiece of long owl feathers bent beneath the stone ceiling. And around its waist, a tasseled skirt patterned with snakes the color of blood rattled with shells tied around the edges.

A tzitzimitl, one of the Tzitzimime star demons. Metzi had seen painted images in the religious texts, but nothing could have prepared her for the horror of witnessing one of the monsters in person.

No, not a monster—a servant of her goddess.

"How . . . how have you escaped your realm?" Metzi whimpered.

The star demon's voice wheezed and crackled in response. "My queen has sent for you, princess of light. We had to wait for nightfall so that one of us could escape, but I have just enough strength to deliver you before I am forced to return."

"Deliver me? Deliver me where?"

The skeletal head cocked to the side. "To *freedom*."

"And what if she will not go with you?" Coatl demanded, his voice shaking.

"I am afraid she has no choice," the demon rasped.

"That doesn't sound like freedom to me," Coatl said, his voice getting stronger.

But the tzitzimitl did not answer. Instead, it whipped out its arm like the tongue of a chameleon, and its needlelike claws sank deep into Coatl's stomach. So deep, the points stuck out through his back and spattered Metzi's white dress with his blood.

Metzi screamed again as the demon withdrew its claws with a quick jerk. Coatl's body slumped to the floor.

"Coatl!" She dropped to her knees beside him. The ground was already warm and slick with his lifeblood. He looked up at her, the arrogant spark of life in his eyes flickering like the last ember of a doused fire.

Metzi cradled his head in her arms, her body trying to force itself to believe what it was seeing. Coatl, her Coatl, the one she'd risked everything to be with. He was gone. *Gone.* Tears streamed down her cheeks as a sob ripped its way out of her.

Claws as cold as a corpse wrapped around her arm and yanked her to her feet. Metzi pulled back, her grief and rage mingling and bursting to the surface.

"You didn't have to kill him! I would have gone with you!" she cried.

"Do not mourn for the man-child, princess. You have much greater things to worry about." The skeletal smile widened, making Metzi's stomach lurch.

And with a strength far greater than she expected from a frame so thin, the demon swept her from the room. The last image she saw was of Coatl's blank and lifeless face. His words echoed inside her head . . .

I'm starting to wonder if the Butterfly really has our best interests at heart.

CHAPTER

23

Yemania and the other princesses looked around, bracing themselves after the violent shaking of the temple.

"Was that an earthquake?" Yoli's face seemed to pale with fear.

The Mother goddess paced to the stone doorway. She placed a withered hand against it.

"No, I am afraid it did not come from the earth. It came from the stars."

Fear traced its way down Yemania's spine like a spider. "The stars?"

"It's already here," Ometeotl whispered, her gaze focusing on things they could not see.

From the hallway outside came the sound of many sandaled feet running past. Then men screamed before they were quickly silenced.

"Wh-what's going on?" Yemania whimpered, inching closer to Mayana. She reached out a hand and Mayana squeezed it reassuringly.

Zorrah marched forward, positioning herself between the door and the other princesses. She crouched into a defensive stance. Yemania felt a surprising surge of gratitude. She had never imagined Zorrah would be willing to protect *her*.

"Shhhh," hissed Ometeotl. "We must wait until it's gone."

"What is *it*?" Zorrah said through gritted teeth.

There was a pregnant moment of silence. Then Ometeotl whispered, "A tzitzimitl."

Yemania gasped. Even Yoli looked as though she'd taken a blow to the gut.

"They've escaped?" Mayana squeezed Yemania's hand even tighter.

"It can sometimes happen at night, when the force that holds them weakens without the strength of the sun. Though usually only one or two of the demons can escape their celestial prison at a time," Ometeotl said.

There it was: the faint rattling of shells, the sounds that had haunted Yemania's nightmares from the time she was a child. Then, the crunching of a stone doorway grinding open echoed from the cell beside their own. A female scream, a rumble of voices, then more screaming.

The hairs on Yemania's arms rose and her pulse thudded in her ears. She recognized that scream.

"That's Metzi!" Yemania whimpered. "Shouldn't we do something?"

"Do *you* want to fight a star demon, daughter of healing? Cause I sure as hells don't." Zorrah bared her pointed teeth.

But Ometeotl shushed them again. "There is nothing we can do now. The Butterfly has made her move, and we must make ours. It will be the only hope for the Seventh Sun."

At last, silence fell.

"When I tell you to, you need to run. Do you understand?" the Mother finally said, speaking to all of them at once. "Run. Flee for the jungles. Make your way to Ehecatl and find Itza. She and her people are familiar with the ritual. You must take Itza and Yemania to the Caves of Creation. Resurrecting Quetzalcoatl will be the only way." Ometeotl began running her hands across the surface of the stone, as though searching for something.

Then, with what must have been divine strength, she single-handedly rolled the stone away from their doorway.

Terror clawed at Yemania's gut. As much as she wanted to escape this cell, she was terrified of what they'd find waiting for them outside.

Then, the Mother motioned frantically. "It is time."

Yemania stuck as close to Mayana as moss on a tree as Zorrah led the way at a run.

"Try not to look down," Zorrah warned.

So naturally, it was the first thing Yemania did. And she immediately regretted it.

The savaged bodies of Eagle warriors littered the hallway like acorns scattered haphazardly beneath a tree. Their skin was tinged with blue, and Yemania realized their bodies had been drained of lifeblood. She cast about with her divine senses, seeking any fluttering sign of life amidst the carnage.

She did not find any. Her heart nearly burst from the realization. They had died so quickly.

"Come on, there is nothing we can do for them now," Mayana said, gently tugging her forward.

Yemania fought back tears. "But they could have families, wives, *children*."

"Their souls are already in paradise," Ometeotl assured her. "They died as warriors and have been rewarded for their bravery."

Yemania pressed her hand over her mouth and tore her gaze away.

The princesses began stepping carefully around the bodies of the guards. Yemania tried very hard not to focus on their faces.

Mayana's hand suddenly shot out and grabbed her arm.

"Ouch! Mayana! What—"

"Yemania, please trust me. Do not look into the cell beside us."

Her stomach tightened, knowing that she should follow her friend's advice. She was already undone by the sight of the guards so needlessly slaughtered by the star demon. She couldn't imagine what would be serious enough to warrant such a direct warning.

But what if someone was gravely injured? What if it was someone who needed her healing abilities?

She had to check. She owed whoever-it-was's family to see if she could help in some way.

Peeking through her lashes, Yemania glanced inside the cell as they passed. And then the breath rushed from her lungs.

It was Coatl.

Yemania lunged for the doorway, but Zorrah was there faster than a blink. Her arms wrapped around Yemania's stomach and wrenched her back. "You cannot help him," she growled.

"He's my brother! I have to do something!"

"He's gone too, daughter of healing. Surely you can feel his spirit is no longer there."

Ometeotl stepped between them and Coatl's body. "You must go now. The chaos that reigns in the wake of the star demon's attack will soon fade. This will be your only chance to escape."

Yemania wailed and sagged in Zorrah's grip. She turned to the Mother goddess, desperation coursing through her. "Tell me if he's at least made it to a paradise?"

Ometeotl smiled reassuringly. "He died protecting Metzi. Though he failed, such an action does not go unrewarded."

Mayana gasped. "The demon took her?"

Ometeotl's thin lips pursed. She nodded. "The Miquitz may not have Ahkin's blood, but they will soon have hers."

Yemania straightened and Zorrah finally loosened her hold, though she looked concerned about whether or not to trust that Yemania wouldn't bolt for her brother's body. Yoli, who had stood silently through most of the ordeal, eyed Yemania with a look of horror, as if watching Yemania cry over the body of her brother had summoned ghosts of her own.

But Yemania always had the strength to do what was needed. She may not have liked it; she may have wallowed in the fear and hopelessness of her fate.

But she never ran from it.

Never.

And as she looked around at the worried eyes of the other princesses, at the reassuring warmth radiating from the Mother goddess, she knew they would all have to find the strength to do what was necessary.

"Yes," Ometeotl said, agreeing with the thoughts Yemania had not spoken out loud. "I know you will all have the strength to do what is necessary, because you will have each other. Hold on to that, because it may be the only way you'll all survive what is to come."

———

Ahkin paced anxiously around his chambers. His *father's* chambers, actually. Carved images of the gods glared down at him from the high stone ceiling. Towering red pillars stood sentinel around the main room, framing his father's elegant collection of furs and gifts of weapons or treasures he'd amassed throughout the years. He hadn't had the heart to have them removed. Though much had joined his father's body in his tomb, it would feel like blasphemy to send away what remained. As if the memory of his father would truly be gone forever, once his belongings were. He tried not to think about what had happened the last time he was here. Since then, he never had the courage to move into the emperor's quarters, claiming that he wanted to wait until his official wedding and coronation.

But he knew the real reason.

Though the basalt stone floor had been scrubbed clean weeks ago, he swore he could still see the faint traces of his mother's blood. He knew it was just in his mind, but the images were burned into the back of his eyes.

His mother standing in this very room, as proud and regal as a goddess of fire, before plunging the dagger into her chest. Her blood soaking down the front of her dress as she sank to the floor, Tlana priests surrounding her like buzzards circling a kill.

Ahkin blinked back the burning in his eyes. It hadn't been necessary. The ritual she'd been upholding wasn't even what the gods required of her. If only they'd known sooner, if only the priesthood believed him . . .

Then there was his father. Murdered by his own daughter, a daughter sick of obedience and bent on taking power for herself no matter the cost. His best friend, Coatl, had betrayed him to help her.

This room swam with ghosts determined to haunt him. If he hadn't tipped over the ledge into madness already, as Toani claimed, remaining trapped here long enough would certainly push him.

"Ahkin, my dear? Are you in here?" came the overly enthusiastic voice of Atanzah. He hadn't seen the old matchmaker since before he fell into the underworld. He wasn't sure his nerves could handle her at the moment.

Though she wasn't blood, Atanzah had been his mother's dearest friend. So in a way, she was still that obnoxiously flamboyant aunt that always embarrassed you at family feasts.

"Where else would I be?" Ahkin sighed and ceased his restless pacing.

Atanzah swept into the room as plump and ruffled and feathered as a brightly colored canopy bird. The tinkling of bells from her shawl accompanied her into the room along with the strong smell of whatever flowery perfume she had bathed in. The scent of it enveloped him along with her arms.

"Oh my dear boy. I thought we'd lost you forever. *Forever.* To think I wouldn't get to plan the wedding I'd always dreamed of for you. It nearly broke this old woman's heart."

Ahkin rolled his eyes and pulled himself out of her embrace. "You aren't that old, Atanzah."

"Oh stop," she trilled, smacking his arm playfully. Then she clapped her hands together, suddenly every shade of serious. "Now. We have much planning to do. Your wedding will need to take place before the eclipse next week. The empire is on edge enough as it is. War with Ehecatl, instability in the heavens, the betrayal of their princess of light." Atanzah clucked her tongue disapprovingly. "No, no, no. It will not do. We will give the empire something to *celebrate.* And what better way to celebrate than with a royal wedding!"

Ahkin felt his temper rising. "I don't—"

"Ah-ah-ah," Atanzah said, pressing her stubby fingers against his lips to silence him. "Don't you worry about a thing, my dear. I know your nerves are frayed already as it is. I will handle all the arrangements, of course, so all you have to do is show up and be your handsome—if somewhat surly—self!"

Something inside of Ahkin snapped. "I'm not marrying Teniza! I demand—"

"There you are, darling. I wondered where they were keeping you." The sickeningly sweet voice of Teniza of Millacatl joined them before he could continue. Behind her, Ahkin could see a contingent of guards stationed just beyond the doorway.

"The bride to be!" Atanzah gushed. Her eyes went distant and dreamy. "I'm having a vision of vines and white blossoms, accentuating a golden altar where the ceremony will take place right as the sun rises. Gods, it will be *stunning*!"

Teniza's smile became rather fixed. "That sounds lovely. Would it be all right if I steal my future husband for a few moments? Alone?"

Atanzah winked. "Of course, my dear, just remember that some things must wait until *after* the wedding ceremony." She wiggled her eyebrows suggestively.

The back of Ahkin's neck blazed like the sun itself.

Teniza gave a false laugh that sounded too high even to Ahkin's ears, but Atanzah seemed satisfied and finally sashayed from the room, the bells of her shawl tinkling as she went.

Ahkin's head immediately dropped into his hands. "Sorry, I'm not really in the mood to discuss wedding plans."

Teniza waved an impatient hand. Her bright and airy tone disappeared in an instant. "We have more important things to worry about. Did you hear what happened at the temple?"

Ahkin lifted his head and narrowed his eyes at her. "The temple? Something happened at the temple?"

"I heard my father talking about it. The priest is trying to cover things up, but apparently, a star demon attacked last night and killed many guards. The cells were found open and the princesses are missing. *All* the princesses are missing."

A cold feeling like water filled up his chest. *Missing.* Mayana, Yemania, Yoli, Zorrah? They were all gone?

"Were they taken? Where are they?" He hadn't realized he was shouting until Teniza flinched. "I'm sorry," he said quickly and softened his tone. "Where are they?"

Teniza took a tentative step closer, her eyes darting to the doorway.

"From what I heard," she whispered, "a priest was hiding and saw the star demon take Metzi. No one knows where the others went . . . well, no one except me."

Ahkin reached out and grabbed her wrist. "Where? Are they okay? How do you know?"

She held out a scrap of maguey paper etched with tiny hieroglyphs. "A bird brought this into my room. I know it's from Zorrah, but I don't know what it means."

Ahkin took the small strip of paper between his fingers. He scanned the symbols, immediately recognizing the symbols for Ometeotl, Quetzalcoatl, and finally, the symbol for a cave.

"She's helped them escape," he said quietly, pressing a hand to his thudding heart. He half collapsed onto one of his father's wooden benches.

"Who?" Teniza breathed, sitting delicately beside him. "Ometeotl?"

Ahkin ran a hand through his hair. "Yes. They are going to the Caves of Creation."

Teniza sucked in a breath. "The Caves of Creation?"

"Mayana and the others must be going to try and resurrect Quetzalcoatl." He felt a sudden rush of sadness, of being left out of the important journey he had planned on taking with her himself. Every future he'd envisioned seemed to be disintegrating like sand between his fingers.

Teniza's voice cracked with concern. "But the caves are forbidden. My father always said that if someone ventured too far in, they would never come out."

Ahkin shrugged. "They said that about the underworld too, and yet, here I am. I just feel useless, stuck here while they risk their lives."

Teniza perched her hands on her hips. "Useless? Are you kidding me? Don't you understand what it means if Metzi's been taken by a star demon? The Miquitz may not have your blood anymore, Ahkin, but they don't need your blood if they have Metzi's!"

Nine hells. How had Ahkin not realized that before? He'd been so worried about Mayana and the other girls, it didn't immediately register that Metzi had been taken. If Tzom and the Obsidian Butterfly had Metzi, then they had their sacrifice to hold the eclipse in place. Without him.

They had the means to unleash the star demons upon the earth.

"Oh my gods," Ahkin breathed.

Tears swam in Teniza's doe-brown eyes, clinging to her lashes. "If they don't resurrect Quetzalcoatl in time, does that mean we'll have to fight them? We can't be fighting amongst ourselves or we'll all be destroyed."

"You're right," Ahkin said, rising to his feet. A plan was already forming in his mind. He didn't have to sit here uselessly while Mayana and the others resurrected the god of wind. "We need to stop this war with Ehecatl and march to Miquitz instead. We need to save her."

"How are we going to do that? The priest announced to everyone that your mind has been damaged from your journey through Xibalba. No one will listen to you."

Ahkin let his face split into a grin. "I have an idea. But I'm going to need your help."

"What can I do?" Teniza sniffed and dabbed at her eyes.

"Can you stall the wedding as long as you can?"

To his surprise, Teniza laughed as high and clear as one of Atanzah's many bells. "Oh, Ahkin. That will be easier than catching flies with honey."

24

Ahkin summoned Toani to his father's chambers. The head priest took his time, grating on Ahkin's nerves with every hour he chose to wait. Was he trying to prove Ahkin's powerlessness?

Finally, with the air of an emperor himself, Toani swept into the room.

"I apologize for my lateness. We had some . . . issues to attend to at the temple."

Issues indeed. Did he think Ahkin did not know about the star demon's attack? Ahkin sat upon a low stone bench and motioned for Toani to join him. "I wanted to apologize for my behavior last night in the council chamber. I don't think I've had a decent night's sleep since my return to the overworld. I believe you did the right thing in forcing me to rest. Especially in my father's rooms, where I am reminded of the great legacy I bear upon my shoulders. I woke up this morning with a renewed spirit and a sharpened mind."

Toani pursed his lips and considered him. "I see." He did not sound at all convinced.

Ahkin fidgeted with the golden chestpiece hanging from his shoulders. "I mean to say, that I am ready to fulfill my responsibilities as the council sees fit and end the war with Ehecatl as quickly as possible."

The head priest folded his hands delicately across his lap. "Ahkin, do you know why we have the rituals?"

Ahkin blinked. "Of course. They were given to us by the gods to protect us from another—"

"Let us be frank with one another, shall we?" Toani interrupted. "I do not for a moment believe that you have suddenly come to your senses after a good night's sleep. Perhaps the rest of the council could be fooled by such a pronouncement, but I am not the rest of the council."

The air flew from Ahkin's lungs as though he'd taken a blow to the stomach. "Then why did you agree to meet with me?"

"Because if we are to come to an agreement that works for both of us, dear prince, it is time for you to act like a man and bear the responsibilities of a man."

Ahkin swallowed. "What do you mean?"

Toani rose to his feet and slowly paced toward one of his father's stone bookshelves. He absently selected a stack of papers and star charts and began flipping through them. "This is a conversation I was hoping to have with you *after* your coronation."

He placed most of the papers back on the shelf, but kept several in his hands. He sighed heavily and threw down a painted image depicting Quetzalcoatl offering his blood upon an altar in the Caves of Creation—an altar piled with human bones he had rescued from the underworld. "It has been many generations, but after storms destroyed our last sun, you are aware the god Quetzalcoatl resurrected humanity and then gave his life to create the Seventh Sun?"

Ahkin nodded, but he did not trust himself to speak. He had the horrible feeling that whatever he was about to hear would steal far more than just his voice.

"We were not a united empire then, before the age of the Seventh Sun. We had angered the gods with our constant fighting, our disagreements about the best way to worship our creators. City-state fought against city-state, each thinking their way was better. The gods took sides, protecting their own descendants, and it was all of humanity that paid the ultimate price when the Sixth Sun was destroyed. Our ancestors were resurrected into our new age, and the lord of Tollan, city of the sun—your ancestor, I might add—recognized that if we did not want to anger the gods, to force them to take sides against us and each other again, we had to remain united ourselves. And there was only one way to do such a thing."

"A treaty?"

Toani clicked his tongue impatiently, as though Ahkin were a young priesthood student who had given the wrong answer during a lesson. He threw another picture onto the table before them, an image depicting warriors bearing the symbol of the sun locked in battle against those wearing the blue of Atl. "Fear," he corrected. "Fear alone is strong enough to demand obedience. The sun emperor conquered each of the city-states in turn, all except the city of death. Omitl used its position in the mountains to protect itself, uniting the villages around it into what we now know as the Miquitz Empire."

Ahkin wasn't sure where this was going, but he continued to listen with his arms crossed over his chest.

"The emperor met with his priests and decided that to keep the empire truly united, they had to be united around a *common purpose*. The purpose of preventing another apocalypse. As long as the people remained occupied with their responsibilities, united in their fear, they did not have time to fight against each other or rebel. You see, each city had a *role* to play. Tollan's leadership was assured by the claim that it was your family's responsibility to raise the sun each day." He threw down another painting, this time showing an emperor raising the sun while everyone bowed beneath him. One bleeding hand was outstretched, while in the other he clutched what appeared to be sheets of the codex.

Ahkin felt suddenly dizzy. He gripped the side of the bench for support. "My ancestor created the rituals," he breathed. "Are you saying . . . my blood isn't needed to raise the sun?"

"You can manipulate it, force it to rise or to set, but no, it is not essential. It will continue on its course without you. The first emperor created the rituals, and he was not alone in his endeavor. The priesthood was an essential component, creating the additional codex sheets to support his claim. It is a burden and responsibility that has been passed from head priest to head priest for generations. Emperor to emperor upon each coronation."

Ahkin lifted his gaze to Toani's. "My . . . my father knew?"

Toani threw his hands in the air. "Of course he knew, child! He also understood the importance of keeping the empire united. It was the entire reason Metzi's marriage to Ehecatl was so essential, to ease the tensions and keep them within the family of the empire."

"But Metzi never wanted to marry the storm prince. It's the whole reason she faked the apocalypse."

"I am aware of that now. She did not know any of this, of course. But I admit her stunt had even me convinced the sun was dying. She has no idea the damage she has done with her selfishness."

Ahkin jumped to his feet. "So you know about Metzi colluding with the Obsidian Butterfly? About what she's planning?"

Toani rolled his eyes. "The Obsidian Butterfly? Your friend from Miquitz was rambling something about her as well. That is nothing more than a fantasy of a child desperate for her own power and willing to make up whatever she has to to try and keep it."

"No, it's not. The Obsidian Butterfly is trying to unleash the star demons upon us all. They *took* her! Surely you can't deny the star demon's attack upon the temple."

Toani studied him. Ahkin was sure he was wondering how Ahkin had received news of the attack. But finally, Toani waved a dismissive hand. "The gods took Metzi as punishment for her deceit. Nothing more."

Ahkin ground his teeth together. He wanted to tell him everything he had learned in Miquitz of Tzom's plans, of the threat the star demons posed to them all, but Toani was already questioning his sanity, his judgment. Surely Toani wasn't so entrenched in his own power and importance that he refused to see the truth right before him? But the firm set of the priest's jaw answered his question. Yes, yes he was. There would be no convincing him. Which meant only one option moving forward. "So what do you want with me? If my blood is not even needed?"

Toani lifted a wrinkled hand and rubbed the side of his head. For a moment, his strength and authority seemed diminished, as though all that stood before Ahkin was a tired old man. "I need your cooperation, Ahkin. We may know the truth, but the rest of the empire does not. They need to believe in the rituals. We need to keep the empire united as one while avoiding outright warfare if we can. That is the real threat to our existence. Far more than star demons, or rebellious wind worshippers, or selfish sun princesses."

Ahkin dropped his head into his hands. This was not what he had been expecting. *His* family had created the rituals. The very rituals that had taken his mother's life. Had that been his ancestor's doing too? To ensure he had a companion when he finally began his trek through the underworld? The rituals that had cost so many lives, for how many generations? How many princesses had been sacrificed for nothing?

No, not for nothing, at least according to Toani. They had been sacrifices: not to the gods, but to the rituals themselves, to the greater good of maintaining control and peace within the empire.

Ahkin wasn't sure what to believe anymore.

"You want to do what is best for your empire. So the question you need to ask yourself is—are you willing to do what is best for your people? No matter the cost?" Toani gave him a sharp look.

Ahkin held his ancient gaze for a long time. Thoughts raced through his head like rabbits through the underbrush. Just when he thought he caught a glimpse of a solution, it disappeared just as quickly.

He took a steadying breath. "What do you need me to do?"

———

Ochix was really beginning to despise these sun worshippers. He cared for Mayana, Ahkin, and Yemania, but they were unmistakably the oddballs in the empire. The rest of these ritual-obsessed, narrow-minded fools were going to get them all killed.

And eaten.

By star demons.

Granted, his father wasn't helping matters. Why was he surrounded by so many idiots?

He looked around his guest room. It was luxurious, and every detail screamed comfort—from the bed mat overflowing with rabbit and deer pelts to the jars of fresh water and baskets overflowing with fruit. Everything except for the large host of armed Eagle warriors guarding his exit.

The worst part was, the guards didn't even have a sense of humor. They just stood there like toads on a lily pad, refusing to move or speak. Ochix lounged on his bed mat, convinced he was going to die of boredom. His muscles ached to be moving, to be training. If his muscles could not work, then at least his mind craved to. He should request they bring him some poetry sheets to pass the time.

He finally started tossing berries at the guards, just to see if he could get some kind of reaction.

A fat, delicate purple-fleshed berry bounced off an Eagle warrior's carved wooden helmet and rolled pathetically onto the floor. The Eagle warrior didn't even crack a smile.

Ochix sighed.

He supposed he could try to fight his way out, but one look at the obsidian-tipped spears the guards held chased the thought from his mind. He could try to possess them, but that was likely the reason they had so many guards posted. Fifteen seemed a little excessive for a single prisoner. He couldn't control that many at once.

He had to hope that Yemania would notice him missing *eventually* and come searching for him. She could go to Ahkin, and the sun prince would immediately demand his release.

Still . . . with each passing hour, and each rolling berry collecting on the floor, Ochix felt a sense of unease rise in his stomach.

Why hadn't Yemania come looking for him? Or Ahkin? Surely Ahkin noticed that he had left the council meeting. Unless the scheming council members came up with some excuse for him?

Ochix ground his teeth together and threw another berry. This time, it stuck to the guard's helmet with a small *splat*. The corner of the guard's mouth twitched ever so slightly and he reached up a hand to flick the berry remains off with an impatient swipe of his finger.

He dared a taunt. "You know, you could give me one of those spears and we could make things a little more entertaining for all of us."

"But then you'd just make a mess of things, and after we've fixed this room up so nicely for you, too," Ahkin's teasing jest answered.

The Eagle warriors parted and the sun prince entered the room, dressed in a fine golden chestpiece and with a clean white wrap around his waist. A circle of tiny yellow feathers crowned his head. Though he appeared whole and well, he walked with a stiffness that set Ochix's nerves on edge. Behind him marched the leather-faced high priest, tailing him like a mother hen following her chick.

Ochix leapt to his feet. "Gods, Ahkin! There you are! What the hells? Your lovely council members forced me out of the meeting at knifepoint, and I've been stuck in here for a day—"

But Ahkin held up a hand to silence him. "I already informed the council of the agreement we made."

Ochix frowned. "Agreement? What—?"

Ahkin's eyes went wide, imploring Ochix to play along.

Ochix choked his words back and forced his features to appear understanding. "Ah—yes. Our agreement. The agreement that was made. Together. That agreement." He arched an eyebrow at the prince. *If you want me to play along, you gotta give me more than that.*

"The council was wary, but I explained your intentions to overthrow your father after he disowned you. How, in exchange for Chicome support, you will join our empire and serve as lord of Omitl instead of emperor of the Miquitz."

Confusion swirled like a fog inside his head, making him dizzy. Overthrow his father? Submit to Chicome rule? What the hells was Ahkin playing at? But with the priest watching them both as closely as a spider eyeing a fly, Ochix knew better than to blink. "Overthrow my father. Yes. Of course. Join the empire. Mmmhmm. That agreement."

"Excellent. We can discuss the details of our arrangement after

Ehecatl is subdued and the wedding takes place. In the meantime, I hope you will remain here at the palace as my distinguished guest."

At least there was one piece of news that made sense. "Oh, the council approved you marrying Mayana?"

Ahkin's jaw went rigid. "The heathen daughter of water will be sacrificed at my wedding to Teniza along with the other fugitive princesses. Once they have been hunted down and apprehended, of course."

Ochix's calm demeanor nearly slipped. "I—I cannot wait to hear the details of how such a development came to be. The princesses are fugitives now, are they?" His thoughts raced to Yemania, suddenly understanding why she'd never come to search for him. Something had happened. She and Mayana must have fled the capital.

"Much has transpired since yesterday."

Clearly much had transpired. This time Ahkin averted his eyes. Whatever was going on, Ahkin was hiding it from the priest.

"So it seems," Ochix agreed. He felt as though snakes were wrestling inside his belly, but he had a part to play.

"Anyway, now that the council's concerns about you have been eased in light of your desire to join the empire, I came to see if you would like to join me on the training fields this afternoon. I could use a sparring partner." Ahkin's right eye twitched ever so slightly.

Ochix swept into an exaggerated bow. "I would be honored, my . . . *my prince.*"

The high priest tucked his withered hands into the scarlet sleeves of his ceremonial robes and tilted his chin in the air. He gave Ochix the impression of a ruffled squirrel collecting nuts in his nest—as though Omitl was another treasure to be added to his trove.

Ochix resisted the urge to punch the old man in the face. He didn't think it would be a wise decision, considering how careful a game Ahkin was playing.

The question was, what game *was* he playing?

Mayana had never been alone in the jungles at night. Though she wasn't technically alone, it was certainly the first time without any of her family's guards.

She didn't know why she expected it to be quieter, more peaceful. But the jungles were as alive in the moonlight as they were beneath the sun. The air hung heavy and humid, teasing with the scent of jungle blossoms and earth. What little moonlight filtered down through the canopy above dappled the leaf-strewn ground at their feet.

And she knew it was not only animals that lurked between the trees, under the cloak of darkness. The Chicome had a strict curfew that prevented them from venturing out after the sun descended into the underworld.

And for good reason.

The layers between creation were less stable without the sun, though not as unstable as during the last days of the calendar or during an eclipse. But the slightest shift in stability was enough for a powerful de-mon or spirit to slip through and venture into the land of the living. She imagined that was how the star demon who had taken Metzi escaped.

A monkey cried out somewhere nearby, making them all jump.

"I don't like being in the jungles at night." Yemania inched closer to Mayana's side.

"I don't either." Mayana frowned. "Where exactly are we?" she called ahead to where Zorrah led them through the underbrush. Yoli followed close behind, her forearm lit like a torch and giving them just enough light to see. Still, Mayana tripped on the roots and vines littering the jungle floor, and the brush was so thick in places that it tore at their arms and legs as they pushed through. More than once she had to dislodge the bag containing the jade bones from where it had gotten stuck between branches.

Zorrah bent down and dug her sharpened nails into the dirt. She lifted it to her nose and sniffed. "We are going the right way," was all she answered.

"Yes, but how do you know?" Mayana countered.

Zorrah did not look at her but kept trudging forward. "How does a monkey know which tree is its home? How does the jaguar know where to hunt?"

Mayana exchanged a glance with Yemania, who shrugged.

"Call it a sense for tracking, daughter of water. I cannot explain it. I just know which way is right."

Yemania leaned in and whispered in Mayana's ear. "I wonder if that's part of the gifts of the family of Ocelotl."

Zorrah grunted, which Mayana took as confirmation. However, she wasn't sure how Zorrah had heard them. Perhaps her senses were sharper than an average human's, just as Mayana could sense the presence of water. She couldn't hear a stream or river, but the coolness across her skin told her water was close.

"I'm sure she gets her pleasant manners from her family, too." Yoli snorted.

Zorrah hissed and finally turned around to face all three of them. "If you don't all stop talking, you are going to attract every beast in the jungle toward us. Now *shut up!*"

"Definitely gets them from her family," Yoli mumbled.

Zorrah growled in frustration and stomped ahead of them again. "Just keep the light going, daughter of fire, I don't want to get caught off—"

But she suddenly plunged out of sight. There was a terrified scream as she disappeared. Then, the sound of a loud splash.

"Zorrah!" Mayana and the others ran ahead. A massive hole gaped open in the jungle floor, like a mouth waiting to swallow unsuspecting meals. A cenote, like the many sinkholes that surrounded her home in Atl. The rock ledges surrounding it were covered with leaf debris and greenery right up until the sudden drop-off into darkness below. Mayana threw out her arm just in time to keep Yemania from toppling over the ledge too.

"Holy hells," Yoli said, lifting her flaming arm to light the shadows inside the sinkhole. The flames reflected off the turbulent surface of the water far below, rippling out from where Zorrah had fallen. "Zorrah, are you okay?" Her husky voice echoed into the pit.

Zorrah suddenly broke the surface, thrashing like a deer caught in the jaws of a river caiman. Her arms clawed at the water, but her jaguar cloak seemed to be dragging her back down. Mayana immediately registered the panic painted across her features, recognizing the inexperienced way she moved in the water. Her chest squeezed with fear.

Zorrah couldn't swim.

"Hold these." Mayana thrust the bag of Quetzalcoatl's bones into Yemania's arms.

Yemania took them willingly and then fixed Mayana with a knowing look. "You're going in after her, aren't you?"

Mayana gave her a quick smile. "Would I be me if I didn't?"

Yemania sighed. "I suppose not. You do have a horrible habit of following people off ledges."

"Keep your fire going," Mayana told Yoli. Then she jumped feet first into the cenote below.

She had made such jumps dozens of times back home with her brothers. They loved finding new places to swim, and forgotten cenotes were their favorite finds. She knew how to position her arms and her legs to keep herself from getting winded by the impact. If she pretended, she could be back home in Atl like nothing had changed. The air was cool and still, nothing like her plunge into the underworld. It was also infinitely shorter. Instead of falling for what felt like hours, Mayana barely had time to register the feel of the air against her skin before cool, clear water closed over her head. She kicked out with all her strength back toward the surface.

"Mayana, hurry!" Yemania cried from above.

Treading water, she scanned her surroundings, the flickering light from Yoli's flames dancing across the water but making it very difficult to see. The walls of the pit hung with ominous shadows. She could still hear Zorrah thrashing, but with the cave echoing the sound all around them, Mayana could not tell where she was.

"Where is she?" Mayana yelled, turning herself around and around.

"I can't see!" Yemania cried. "I think she's gone under!"

Mayana shrieked in frustration. She may not like Zorrah, but there was no way she was going to let her drown. Somewhere nearby a bat shrieked back, agitated by the noise they were all making. Mayana had a sudden idea. She could find Zorrah the same way she had found Ahkin in the Sea of the Dead, by sending out small pulses of water the way bats used sound to see.

Her finger found the sharp edge of the bracelet she was wearing, and the moment her blood was exposed, she sent out a pulse of water in every direction.

The current quickly ran up against Zorrah's sinking body.

Mayana sucked in a breath and dove, kicking harder to reach the princess of animals before she took much water into her lungs. She reached out, feeling nothing but water until her hand finally closed around Zorrah's flailing wrist. She yanked Zorrah upward, willing the water around them to push them faster toward the surface.

The moment the cool air above hit their faces, Zorrah began clawing at Mayana's face and arms, desperate to stay afloat.

"Stop," Mayana hissed as Zorrah's sharp nails sliced across her cheek. "You're going to make us both drown. Calm down."

Mayana had never seen such panic in someone's eyes. It was literally as if Zorrah were a helpless cat someone had thrown into a river.

"I can't swim! I can't swim!"

"I know," Mayana assured her. "Trust me, please. I won't let you drown. I'm forcing the water to hold you up. Relax."

Zorrah stopped clawing at Mayana's arms and froze, her chest heaving and her eyes still wild. But she was not sinking. Mayana kept a steady current around her, keeping her head above the water.

"How are we going to get out?" Zorrah whimpered. Mayana had never heard fear tainting Zorrah's voice before.

"Actually, if you promise not to scratch me again, I think I can get us out of here too." Mayana reached up and touched her cheek, which was warm and sticky with the blood Zorrah had drawn. Hopefully it was enough.

Mayana concentrated, willing the water around them to rise. It swirled into a giant crystal mass, suspending them. Just as she had saved Ahkin and herself from the great crocodile Cipactli by floating above the sea, she lifted herself and Zorrah slowly toward the opening of the sinkhole.

Higher and higher they rose, until Mayana could clearly see the looks of awe on Yemania and Yoli's faces. Then they crashed to the jungle floor in a cascade of water and mud.

Zorrah flopped onto her back, staring up at the canopy with her chest still heaving, heavy breaths escaping through her clenched teeth.

Mayana sat up, and Yemania was already there, healing the cuts on her cheek and finger.

"Zorrah? Are you all right?" Mayana asked, looking over at her.

Zorrah didn't answer at first. She just kept breathing harshly and staring up at nothing. But finally, she turned her head. "Why?" she asked, her voice cracking.

"Why what?"

"Why did you jump in after me?"

Yoli forced her way into the conversation before Mayana could answer. "That's kind of her thing. You know, jumping off ledges to save people without really thinking about the consequences."

"I just couldn't let you drown," Mayana answered simply, wringing out her soaking hair. "I may not like you, but that doesn't mean you deserve to *die*."

Zorrah's wild eyes swam with emotions Mayana couldn't recognize. Anger, confusion, fear, helplessness. She knew Zorrah was used to feeling competent, in control of herself and her surroundings. The experience had clearly shaken her to her core, but she did not know how to handle it. Mayana had seen such reactions before. Anger usually masked much more vulnerable emotions. Emotions Zorrah would likely do anything to avoid.

They fell into an awkward silence. Yemania, seemingly desirous of something to do, began plucking berries from a nearby bush. She passed them out to each of them, but still no one seemed to know what to say.

After a while, Zorrah stumbled back to her feet, shaking out her long ponytail and adjusting her soaked jaguar cloak across her shoulders. She turned her back to them and started marching forward. "Are we ready to keep moving? It's a two-day journey to the coast from Tollan."

"Yes," Mayana said, shoving the rest of the berries into her mouth. Their tartness burst satisfyingly across the surface of her tongue.

And so they resumed their trek toward Ehecatl, the only sounds to be heard were the chattering of the night beasts and the rush of feet through the foliage. Mayana wasn't sure if she imagined it or not, but she swore a whispered *thank you* drifted back from somewhere ahead of her.

26

The warrior district was a collection of elegant gold-trimmed stone structures that graced the eastern edge of Tollan's volcanic plateau. At its center, a training field sprawled in front of a smaller temple reserved for warriors to worship and offer gifts or sacrifices for blessings. The houses of the different ranks of warriors framed the field, organized according to level of prestige.

The House of Jaguars had been Ahkin's home from the time he was a boy of seven. Only the most elite students, or families who could afford the greatest warrior mentors for their children, were invited to join. Naturally his family had secured the mentorship of Yaotl, the leader of the Jaguar warriors himself and the head general of the Chicome forces.

Yaotl had become like a father in many ways, training Ahkin not only in basic combat, but in ways to use his divine abilities on the battlefield. If Ahkin closed his eyes, he could still see Yaotl lining their recruit class up on the field and putting them through their exercises, his loud voice echoing over them like the call of a harpy eagle over the canopy.

Ahkin still liked to come back and train when he was feeling restless. Yaotl was always happy to oblige in a sparring match.

And best of all, as Yaotl was a member of the council, Toani trusted Ahkin to be alone with him.

"Remind me again why you invited the death demon to train with us?" Yaotl grunted, shoving Ahkin back with a foot pressed against his wooden shield. Though the practice field was busy with classes of students running through their exercises, he and Yaotl had the corner relatively to themselves.

Ahkin grunted and regained his footing, matching Yaotl's macana sword blow with one of his own. "Because," Ahkin said through gritted teeth, "I need to explain my plan to him. We are going to need his help."

Yaotl pulled back and wiped sweat from his heavy-lidded eyes. His mountainous shoulders shifted. "I'm still not sure I like this plan."

Ahkin bent forward and braced his hands on his knees, breathing heavily. "Yaotl, you trust me, right?"

Yaotl pretended to ponder his answer, making Ahkin smirk.

The hint of a smile graced Yaotl's ever-serious countenance. "You know I trust you with my life, young prince. You are my emperor, yes, but I also consider you my friend." His massive hand clapped Ahkin on the shoulder with such force that Ahkin nearly fell over. "Even if you are smaller and weaker. And of course much less handsome."

"Thank you," Ahkin laughed, rubbing his shoulder. Then he turned serious. "I'm sure you saw what happened to the guards in the temple. You know Metzi was taken. I promise I have a reason. I'm not as crazy as the council wants me to seem."

"I know those guards were not killed by human hands. But are you going to tell me exactly what we are dealing with here?"

Ahkin glanced around before leaning in and telling him. Everything. From what happened in Xibalba to Tzom's proclamation in the amphitheater to Toani's treachery.

Yaotl made a low sound of disapproval. "The council is nothing but a bunch of old turkeys with no courage. They sit in the palace and give orders that the rest of us have to carry out. They do not know you as I do. If you say we are in danger, then I believe we are in danger."

Ahkin's throat thickened with emotion. He cleared it and turned his gaze away. That's when he saw Ochix striding toward them, his air of confidence evident even across the field.

Yaotl let out a disgruntled huff at the sight of the death prince.

Ochix marched right for them, ignoring the stares of the younger warriors training with their mentors. He still wore the black wrap of Miquitz, and coupled with his long dark hair and necklace of human finger bones, he looked like a lord of Xibalba taking a stroll through the sun.

"Prince of light," Ochix greeted him with a nod of his head. "Pleasure seeing you *without* your priestly shadow."

Ahkin sucked in a breath through his teeth. "Sorry about earlier."

"I figured you had a good reason for promising my empire to my mortal enemies." Ochix shrugged a flippant shoulder. "I mean, not that I don't want to start a fight with my father, but still."

"Good, because I do." Ahkin motioned with his sword to a laid-out selection of other weapons. "Care to vent some of that frustration?"

Ahkin could tell Ochix was itching to get out some of his energy, and sure enough, his eyes lit with excitement. He wiggled his fingers over several different options before selecting an obsidian-tipped spear.

"Oh, you're a pretty one," he said with reverence, examining it as one might inspect a fine piece of pottery. Then, to both Ahkin and Yaotl's surprise, Ochix began to whirl the spear with such speed and precision, it was as if he were dancing. With each thrust and arced swing, Ahkin felt his eyes go wider.

"Why didn't you fight like that on the road?"

Ochix brought the spear down into the dirt and looked up, an arrogant grin plastered upon his face. "Well, all I had was a dagger. And besides, you kept shining that damn light in my eyes so I couldn't get too fancy."

Yaotl barked a short laugh, but then frowned as though it had escaped without his permission.

Ahkin and Ochix both turned to face him. There was a moment of awkward silence.

"Anyway, about this plan of yours." Ochix shook his head and leaned against the spear. "I'd like to actually hear what it is."

Yaotl leaned in, clearly eager to hear the details.

Ahkin let his gaze sweep their surroundings, ensuring no one else was listening. Then he turned his attention back to his friend and his mentor. "How do you both feel about going to war tomorrow?"

———

Ahkin was drenched with sweat from sparring by the time he returned to his father's chambers, but he felt lighter, as if at least one of the worries weighing on his shoulders had been plucked away.

He looked forward to a few moments of solitude before someone from the council would inevitably appear. Toani would watch him like an owl with a mouse until he was sure Ahkin would comply with his wishes. Ahkin suppressed the desire to snort. Here he was, emperor of the mightiest empire in the world, and he was being treated like a naughty child. Power was a funny thing, ironically more fragile than anything Ahkin had ever owned.

The palace halls bustled with activity. Servants rushed back and forth like ants in a colony, some carrying baskets of food or decorations, others running errands for the judges and lords that used the council chambers or seeing to the daily maintenance of the royal residences. It seemed even more hectic than usual, as Atanzah had begun her wedding preparations.

He couldn't wait to reach the quiet peacefulness of the emperor's chambers. At least, until he actually walked through the beaded curtain.

The moment the beads clattered back into place behind him, he was rushed by a flock of twittering servants dressed in white.

"What the—" Ahkin took a step back and swatted them away as they started measuring and prodding him like a deer before roasting.

"Oh good, darling, you're finally here." Teniza's bright and cheery voice carried across the room. She was standing next to his bed mat and laying out various outfits in a collage of white and gold fabrics. Dressed elegantly in the traditional green of Millacatl, she towered over the flustered-looking Atanzah, who harrumphed from the corner of the room. The older woman crossed her arms with the faint tinkling sound of bells.

Ahkin momentarily considered making himself disappear, but instead settled for slipping around the servants with a quick, fluid movement. They squawked in complaint and continued to swarm after him like gnats.

While they continued their measurements, Ahkin looked between Teniza and Atanzah, the tension in the room thicker than cold honey. He swallowed hard. "Everything all right?"

"Oh yes," Teniza trilled. She laid out three more wraps upon the bed mat and eyed them. Her finger tapped thoughtfully against her chin. "Atanzah and I are planning *every detail* of the wedding ceremony. I want to make sure it's the most spectacular event the empire has ever seen."

Ahkin bit back a laugh.

Atanzah sighed dramatically. "If only Lady Teniza would stop changing her mind and making such outrageous demands. At this rate the wedding won't be ready to take place for another month." The matchmaker pouted. "I'm all for extravagance, but I want to see you married before I die of old age!"

Ahkin swore he saw a glint of triumph sparkle in Teniza's eye. She hadn't been joking when she said she'd handle postponing the wedding.

"Don't be so silly," Teniza giggled. "It won't take a month. We just want to make a statement, don't we darling? Set the proper tone for our reign?"

Atanzah eyed him, imploring him to intervene.

Ahkin cleared his throat. "Um, yes. I agree. I want the empire to know how powerful and important we are. And of course, I want my future bride to be happy."

Teniza pretended to beam, while Atanzah mumbled something under her breath that sounded strangely like "stealing the show."

Ahkin fixed a smile on his face and motioned to the outfits laid across his bed mat. "Is one of those for me?"

"They're *all* for you," Teniza said with complete seriousness. "A different look for each part of the ceremony. Of course, I will want fresh garments prepared with even more gold embroidery. Can we get working on that?" she called over her shoulder toward Atanzah. "All six outfits? We both want the prince to look his best, don't we?"

Atanzah groaned and threw her hands in the air. "Let me hunt down the royal seamstresses. *Again*." She marched away and threw aside the beaded curtain with much more force than was really necessary.

Ahkin chuckled. "I knew trusting you to postpone the wedding was a good idea, but you're going to be the death of that poor woman."

Teniza grinned slyly. "Oh, she hasn't even seen the plans for *my* dresses yet."

Yemania's feet ached to the point that she took her sandals off and began walking barefoot. Angry red marks throbbed where the straps had cut into her skin. Now, roots and rocks cut into the bottoms of her feet, but at least it was different. They had been traveling for almost two days, but she knew they couldn't stop. They had to be nearing the coast by now.

The sun had long since traveled across the sky, and hot sweat stuck to the back of her neck.

"How much farther?" she panted, stumbling over yet another root.

"We should be nearly there," Zorrah snapped. "Keep going, daughter of healing. You are stronger than that."

Yemania huffed and clutched at an ache in her side. She was not as fit as her siblings had been, a fact her health-obsessed mother loved to berate her for anytime she got the chance. Zorrah might think her strong, but Yemania was beginning to let the seeds of doubt creep into her mind like insidious vines. They hadn't stopped for sleep at all that first night, wanting to get as far away from the capital as possible. The second night, Zorrah had let them rest for only a few hours before shaking them awake.

Mayana glanced back, chewing nervously at her lip. She summoned some water from her necklace and floated it back. Yemania caught the water gratefully in her hands and brought it to her lips. It did little to ease the ache in her side, but at least her tongue was no longer parched.

Yoli slipped on a wet patch of mud and hit the ground on her backside. "I think she means to kill us," Yoli grumbled as Mayana helped her back to her feet.

"I mean to get us there before they hunt us down and drag us back. This is pathetic. None of you would survive for a moment in the training camps of the Jaguar warriors." Zorrah hiked her jaguar cloak a little higher as though for emphasis. Yemania noticed that she slowed a little as she talked.

"I'd have no desire to," Yoli said.

But Yemania was desperate for any kind of respite. Hopefully if she got Zorrah talking, they could enjoy a break from the grueling pace she was forcing them to keep. "Why did you become a Jaguar warrior?"

Sure enough, Zorrah slowed slightly. "I don't know. I just wanted to be part of the strongest warriors the empire had to offer."

"There aren't many women who qualify," Mayana said. "I'm surprised they let you."

Zorrah bared her teeth. "The Jaguar warriors care about skill more than anything. Though I will not lie; it helped coming from a royal family to secure me an adequate battle mentor. And of course the final test is to capture and kill a jaguar for your cloak. That was easy for me."

Mayana grimaced. "They let you use your divine abilities for the final test? That doesn't seem fair."

Zorrah whirled and withdrew a long sharp knife. She pointed at Mayana, who took several steps back with her hands raised. "Are you insinuating I *cheated*?"

Yemania's heart leapt into her throat. "No, of course that's not what she's saying. We are just curious how—"

Zorrah rounded on her next. "I did it the same way every warrior does. I killed it with only a knife and my strength."

Yemania eyed the point of the dagger and felt her lower lip tremble. "I'm sorry, I n-n-never meant to of-f-ffend you."

Yoli stepped between them. "What do you feel the need to prove, princess of beasts? Are you that insecure of your own strength you feel the need to prove it to everyone?"

Something dangerous flashed in Zorrah's eyes, not unlike the look Yemania sometimes saw in the eyes of a scared, wounded animal. Yemania's heart lurched with pity. Was that the wound she was hiding? Worrying she wasn't strong enough? It made sense, coming from a city where strength meant everything. Even your literal survival. Yemania had heard the rumors that Zorrah had been forced to kill her sister in their ritual combats. She couldn't imagine the pressure that would lead one to do such a thing. "I'm grateful for your strength. I don't think we would have made it this far without you."

The dagger in her hand quivered, and Zorrah's eyes shimmered with tears. But before a single one could fall, she turned away again and marched forward.

"I sense a wound there that needs to be healed, but it isn't one of flesh or bone," Yemania whispered to Yoli and Mayana. They both silently nodded their agreement.

Mayana's face scrunched suddenly in concentration. "Do you hear that?" she asked.

"Hear what? Zorrah's pride shattering to pieces? I'm pretty sure that's what *I* hear," Yoli said, a wicked smile pulling at her lips.

"No . . ." Mayana reached into the brush next to them. "I hear . . . water."

The moment Mayana's arms pushed the greenery aside, Yemania gasped. Yoli stared with her mouth gaping wide.

The edge of the trees opened onto a thin strip of white sand, but beyond the sand . . . an expanse of water greater than Yemania had ever seen. It stretched like a sparkling blanket of turquoise, glistening and lapping at the shore like the foaming tongue of a great beast. Out of the trees ahead of them, backing up to the beach itself, rose a city of stone. But unlike the cities of Millacatl or Tollan, its pyramids and towering walls were not made of gray stone or gold. They were made from a lighter stone, identical to the cliffs that rose in the distance, almost the color of bone. "Is that . . . ?" she started to ask.

"The ocean," Mayana finished for her. "I think we made it to Ehecatl."

———

Metzi awoke in the dark. It was not the cool stone of the temple holding cell beneath her, but the soft fur of a bed mat. Though the haze of sleep still clung to her mind, she wondered if it had all been a horrendous dream. She was back in her father's bedchambers. *Her* bedchambers. She was still empress. Ahkin had never returned, the star demon had never fetched her from the bowels of the temple.

Her fingers reached out across the furs, expecting to find Coatl's warm body lying beside her. They brushed against air and nothing more. Coatl must have risen early for his meal, just as he always did.

Metzi rolled luxuriously onto her back, stretching and rubbing the remnants of sleep from her eyes. When they cleared, she sat up so quickly it made her head spin.

This was not any room in the palace of Tollan at all.

A waterfall rushed outside of the stone-framed window. The walls were painted white with jade and green accents, and green pillars framed the room. The pottery decorating the stone shelves were painted with skulls.

Oh gods. *Where was she?*

The damned star demon had killed Coatl and brought her here . . . wherever *here* was. Thoughts of Coatl rushed over her and stole the breath from her lungs. She pressed a hand against her chest, wishing she could soothe the sharp stabbing that his memory caused. He really was dead. It hadn't been a dream. He had tried to protect her. Even in the end. He'd taken the claws of a star demon right through the gut to try and save her.

The aching pain inside her crested and brought with it waves of tremors and tears. He was gone. *Gone.*

She looked down at her once-white cotton dress, where spatters of his blood still coated her. Panic rose inside her chest like water, and she rubbed at the stains, frantically trying to wipe away the memory of what had happened to him. She was about to tear the dress off completely, when the obsidian beads covering her doorway clattered.

She froze.

A man stood there. As old as her father had been, he was tall but thin, draped in robes of black across a painted bare chest. A necklace of black toucan feathers and bones dangled from his neck while a small crown of equally black feathers ringed his perfectly smooth head. His face was painted to resemble a skull, ghostly white with black ink filling his eye sockets and stretching out from the corners of his mouth into a skull-like grin.

He spread his arms wide as though in welcome. "My dear princess of light. It is such a pleasure you could join us at last."

Metzi's arms began to shake and she hugged them against her chest. It was so cold here, much colder than she was used to in Tollan. "W-w-where am I? Who are you?" She tried to force herself to sound regal, like an empress, but her fear betrayed her, making her voice tremble as much as her body.

"Oh my dear, I thought that would be obvious," he chuckled lightly.

Bumps rose over Metzi's arms, making the hairs stand on end.

"You are in Omitl, the capital of the Miquitz Empire."

"Omitl?" Metzi squeaked. Had the Obsidian Butterfly ordered her brought here to finally rule as their empress? Had she heard her prayers after all? Hope blossomed like a flower inside her chest . . . but then the memory of Coatl plucked away the petals. She knew the Butterfly disapproved of her relationship with Coatl, but had it really been necessary to *kill* him? Just to ensure her plan was carried out? Her gut swirled with nausea.

"Why am I here?"

"*She* brought you to me," he answered simply. "As she promised she would."

"Do you mean Itzpapalotl? The Obsidian Butterfly?"

The death priest folded his hands in front of his chest. His crazed eyes went distant and dreamy. "My patron, yes. She always rewards those who are loyal to her."

Something about the death priest unnerved her, as though he might lash out with a blade at any moment just because he felt like it.

Metzi rose uneasily to her feet. "I am her servant as well."

The death priest swept into a quick bow. "Of course, my dear, of course. You may call me Tzom. I am emperor and high priest of the Miquitz. As a fellow servant of the great Obsidian Butterfly, you are most welcome here."

"Has the goddess informed you of her plans regarding my brother?"

Tzom's smile twitched ever so slightly. "Yes, I am aware. They have been difficult to carry out with his escape, but the goddess and I have a new plan to ensure we have everything we need for the ceremony. Ahkin will come for you, I'm sure. And when he does, well . . ."

The eclipse was still a week away, but Ahkin's blood would be an essential component. She had to trust that the goddess was working to ensure their plans would succeed. Despite the constant blunderings of humans always complicating matters, the Butterfly seemed one step ahead. Always prepared. "Our goddess and her will shall prevail."

"Indeed." Tzom's smile stretched wider. "Your devotion to her is both evident and admirable. I do regret your marriage to my eldest son did not come to fruition, but he is no longer my heir. You are welcome to discuss the possibility of marrying one of my other sons. I believe it is still your intention to become our empress? When the sun prince is gone, you alone will be able to raise the sun, and the Miquitz would treat you far better than the Chicome ever have."

The wound left by Coatl's death throbbed. Metzi winced. "Thank you. Perhaps we can discuss marriage arrangements after the eclipse ceremony?" As if she would ever agree to marry one of his sons. She would not let herself be manipulated into marriage for politics ever again.

"Of course. If that is what you prefer."

"It is."

Metzi and Tzom assessed each other, smiling with their teeth but not with their eyes. The cordiality between them felt hollow somehow, as though there were secrets both sides were withholding. She was reminded of a snake slowly tightening its coils around unsuspecting prey. But Tzom had no idea the viper he was really dealing with. The

Obsidian Butterfly had told her she would become empress of the Miquitz, that the kingdom would be handed to her and her *alone*.

I will use him and then dispose of him when he no longer serves his purpose, the goddess had said of Tzom.

The Butterfly needed the high priest to sacrifice Ahkin because the Chicome never would, but beyond that, he was unnecessary. Metzi almost felt pity for him. Poor man, he had no idea he was being used, and by those far more clever. She and the Butterfly would tighten their coils around him until he fell, just like every other man who tried to stand in her way.

Tzom turned to leave with another quick bow. "In the meantime, you will be my *honored* guest. It is our desire to make you as comfortable as possible in your new home."

Metzi strolled toward the window, taking in the beauty of the waterfall beyond it. "Thank you. I think I am really going to love it here."

She was well on her way to the control and freedom she had always dreamed of. Coatl would always be her only regret, especially when she didn't understand why the goddess saw it as necessary to kill him.

She took a deep breath, reminding herself that the goddess knew far more than she did. She had to trust. To have faith. After all, only six more days and this palace would be hers.

The council decided that the time to march upon Ehecatl had come. With Toani's support, Ahkin argued that for the sake of keeping the empire unified it was essential to crush Ehecatl's rebellion swiftly and effectively. The supplies were gathered. The armies from the various city-states were already assembled and adequately trained to work in unison.

The time to act was now.

"Are you sure your mind is ready to handle a military campaign?" one of the judges asked, his shadowed eyes narrowing with suspicion. All heads turned toward Ahkin at the front of the council chamber.

Ahkin cleared his throat. "Yes, my mind is sound and ready to lead my empire into battle. I have already discussed the strategy with Yaotl, who agrees with our plan of action."

"I do." Yaotl gave the nod to confirm Ahkin's proclamation.

"And what of the death prince?" The judge leaned around his neighbor to glare at Ochix.

Ochix gave a little wave from where he leaned casually against the wall.

"Ochix has agreed to fight with us against Ehecatl. His ability to control the spirits of others will be an asset on the battlefield."

Several heads around the table nodded in agreement. Toani looked particularly pleased. Ahkin knew the priest was anxious to quell

Ehecatl's rebellion as soon as possible. "And when you return, we will witness your wedding to the daughter of Millacatl," Toani said.

Ahkin avoided looking at Mayana's father when he answered. "Yes. And at the coronation ceremony that follows, we will perform the necessary sacrifice."

"Have the other princesses been found, then?" the lord of Papatlaca rumbled.

"No." The answer came from Quauhtli, head of the Eagle warriors. He pushed back his wooden eagle helmet, frowning in frustration. He was an older man, his head completely shorn aside from a small bit of hair tied at the nape of his neck. "We are searching the jungles for them as we speak. No city-state would hide them."

Ahkin knew it didn't matter, because the princesses wouldn't be seeking refuge within a city-state. They would be making their way to the Caves of Creation. They had only until the eclipse started to resurrect Quetzalcoatl.

He threw a prayer to the Mother goddess that should his plan to save them fail, the princesses still would find a way to make it in time.

"The prince and I have devised our strategy moving forward." Yaotl rose to his feet and addressed the council. "If the lords are still in agreement, we will cooperate in beginning the assault on Ehecatl. When we arrive, Lord Atl and his sons will cut off all water supplies going into the city, while Lord Millacatl and his sons wither their crops. Lord Papatlaca, you will be ready to burn the homes of the outer villages, forcing everyone to retreat into the city itself. Once they are trapped, Lord Ocelotl will lead a campaign to harass the citizens with beasts, and Lord Pahtia will address any injuries our side sustains. Our hope is to have the city begging for forgiveness before the month's end. If we can lure the Storm Lord from his city, we can negotiate and urge him into surrender. We hope to avoid any unnecessary loss of Chicome life."

While the lords of the various city-states voiced their agreement, Ahkin dropped his gaze to the table. He knew it was Toani's greatest wish to avoid open warfare with Ehecatl—to avoid the gods' ire for fighting amongst themselves. Ahkin wanted to avoid open conflict for another reason. Each warrior's life would be essential, should his plan fail and a war with the stars commence.

The head judge turned down his toad-like mouth. "What about the signs? The eclipse will begin in a week. Is that not an unlucky time to begin a military campaign?"

Ahkin deferred to Toani. The priest shook out the sleeves of his robes, sending the jewels about his neck dancing. "The far more unlucky occurrence will be to allow the gods to think we do not honor their wishes. They are angered by Ehecatl's rebellion, furious at their disregard of the true methods of worship. I am confident they will bless our endeavors to honor their will."

"I have read similar signs in the heavens," Ahkin agreed, though in truth he had seen no such thing. He was sure the stars themselves were trying to hide their secrets. "We must march before the eclipse."

Toani nodded his approval, and Ahkin fought the urge to smack the smug smile off the man's face. He would unknowingly lead them all to their deaths.

The head judge looked around to his fellows, who each nodded their agreement. "The judges defer to the judgment of the religious leadership," he croaked.

"And as always, the religious leadership submits to the will of the divine emperor," Toani purred.

Ahkin's hands clenched into fists, but he kept his voice steady. *Sure they did.* "It is settled then. Let us begin our preparations and depart immediately. It is my intention to have Ehecatl's surrender and be home before the eclipse even happens."

The council convened, and Ahkin pulled Yaotl aside. "Have your men ready when I give you my signal."

Yaotl frowned as he looked over to where Ochix was still leaning lazily against the wall. "And you are sure this is the best way?"

Ahkin smiled and waved at the passing lords and judges wishing him luck on the campaign. He leaned in and whispered, "I'm afraid this is the only way."

———

The limestone walls around the city-state of Ehecatl were taller than any Mayana had ever seen. As they made their way closer, the tops of the towering temples within the city limits disappeared behind them. With their pale color and ominous presence, the walls almost resembled a bank of clouds rolling in from the sea. The girls stuck to where the trees kissed the edge of the sand, trying to stay out of view of the guards patrolling far above them.

"How are we supposed to get in?" Yemania asked, her gaze roving over the sheer size of the walls. Now that they were closer, Mayana could see bits of shells embedded into the stones themselves.

Zorrah scrounged through the pockets of her cloak. "Maybe we don't have to get in. We just need Itza to come out." She withdrew a scrap of maguey paper, the kind usually used for bloodletting sacrifices. "I stole a few of these when we sneaked out of the temple." She dug into another pocket and pulled out a chunk of charcoal.

"Oh! Like the message you sent to Teniza with the bird!" Yemania clapped her hands together in excitement.

"And what do we do if she doesn't come out?" Yoli bit at the dark ring of obsidian piercing through her lip.

"Well," Zorrah said. She carefully drew hieroglyphs onto one of the strips of paper. "Then we go in and *get* her."

"That should be fun." Yoli took out her long shard of obsidian and started picking at her nails.

Yemania wrinkled her nose. "You have an odd definition of fun."

The animal princess summoned a small shorebird. She rolled the paper into a tiny scroll, and the bird clamped it in its beak. Then, with a flick of Zorrah's hand, the bird took flight, soaring into the endless expanse of blue sky that waited just beyond the trees.

"Do you think it will be able to find her?" Mayana asked, squinting after the bird's retreating form.

Zorrah clenched and unclenched her hands. "I hope so."

There was nothing left for them to do but wait.

Mayana wanted to use the time they waited to jump into the sea, but glancing up at the guards still pacing the top of the city walls, she knew it was not a wise idea. They would have a clear view of the exposed beach. It was essential to stay hidden in the protective folds of greenery engulfing them. She hunkered down in the shade of a palm, resting her back against the coarse ridges of its bark, the bag of jade bones resting heavily against her hip. She would have to settle for listening to its gentle waves lapping upon the shore instead.

Yemania wandered off to collect more food for them to eat, while Zorrah patrolled their perimeter, neither able to just sit still. Yoli eventually meandered over and sat beside Mayana, stretching out across the sand and folding her scarred arms beneath her head.

"Not at all how you pictured things going when you got back to the overworld, is it?" Yoli said.

Mayana sighed and rubbed her face. "Not exactly."

"I don't think the council was ever going to let him marry you."

Mayana bent forward and hugged her knees to her chest. "I don't think so either."

"But you're still going to, right?"

Mayana made a sound of disgust. "How could I marry him now? After everything? The empire would never accept me as their empress."

Yoli arched a brow at her. "The empire would never accept you? Or you would never accept *yourself* as empress?"

"Is there a difference?" Mayana huffed a laugh, though there was no humor in it.

Yoli sat up and stared at her, concern painted across her face. "Of course there's a difference. You can't care what other people think, or let them decide what's best for you. You do what's right. That's what I've always admired about you. You can't give into them now."

Mayana hugged her knees even tighter, tears starting to burn behind her eyes. "But it's so hard. When everything in your life feels like a fight, like you are constantly pushing uphill while everyone around you is pushing you back down."

"Not everyone is pushing you back down. You have to find the ones willing to reach out a hand to help you up. They're the ones you want by your side during a fight." Yoli playfully kicked at Mayana's foot.

"You just love anything that involves a fight," Mayana kicked her foot back.

Yoli shrugged. "Of course I do. Makes this life a little more interesting. Life's too short to just go along with what everyone else wants."

"Speaking of fighting . . ." Zorrah materialized beside them, making both Yoli and Mayana jump.

"Gods, animal princess, a little warning next time." Yoli clutched at her chest.

Zorrah just bared her teeth. "You should be on your guard at all times. Not *lounging* in the sand."

"Maybe a little lounging would do you some good." Yoli looked her up and down with a sneer.

If Zorrah had real fur, it would be standing on end. Mayana leapt up and lifted her arms between them. "Yoli, remember what you just told me about people offering hands to help you up? Zorrah *is* one of those people, so can we please stop picking fights with her?"

"She can pick fights with me all day long," Zorrah spat. She threw her shoulders back with the arrogant air of an empress herself. "It's not like she'd ever win one."

Yoli let out a feral growl of her own, and flames erupted up her arms.

Without really thinking, Mayana nicked her finger on the edge of her bracelet and summoned water from her necklace. It rose out of the small mouth of the jade skull pendant, a crystal snake that condensed into a sphere as she curled her hand into a fist. Then, she willed the water over Yoli's head and released her hand.

The water crashed over Yoli, plastering her hair against her head and smothering the flames with a loud hiss. Steam rose from her drenched body.

She turned her anger toward Mayana. "Did you just . . . *extinguish* me?"

Mayana shrugged innocently. "Call it another helping hand?"

Yoli was silent for several tense heartbeats, then she narrowed her eyes. "Well played, daughter of water. Well played."

Zorrah looked as though she was about to say something else, but be it fate or the will of the gods themselves, a swift wind carried a piece of paper right into her face before she got the chance. It smacked into her nose, and Zorrah clawed it off looking murderous. She crumpled it in her hand, likely wanting to punish the scrap for *daring* to attack her in such a way, but Mayana gasped and snatched it out of her hand.

"It's from Itza!" Mayana smoothed out the paper and squinted at the charcoal written there. "Part of it's smudged, but I think . . ." She tried to interpret the images. It looked like a setting sun, the symbol for north, and the symbol for a gate. "She wants us to meet her at the northern gate at sunset!"

Yoli rubbed her chin, looking worried. "It could be a trap. How do we know that's really from Itza?"

Zorrah, of course, was ready to move. "We'll just be careful. If we have to fight, we fight."

"Excellent," Yoli purred, clenching her obsidian shard in her fist.

Yemania, arriving just then with a bundle of bulbous yellow fruits, whimpered but followed them into the trees.

Mayana silently prayed it was Itza waiting for them when they got there . . . and not something worse.

Ochix would be lying if he said the swiftness with which the Chicome could gather and train an army wasn't impressive. He'd seen smaller war parties they sent out to defend against Miquitz raiders, but he had never seen such an assemblage before. At first, he thought the only warriors present were those staying in the military district of the capital. But no. Apparently, entire camps of warriors had been summoned from every city-state in the empire, and they now camped around the base of Tollan's volcanic plateau.

They'd been waiting for Metzi's—well, now *Ahkin's*—call to war.

"Uh—how many warriors are we taking to Ehecatl?" he asked Ahkin as they stood along the plateau's edge, looking down over the sprawling war camps.

"Yaotl estimates we've gathered around ten thousand or so. It's not the largest army the Chicome have ever mustered, but . . ."

Ochix rubbed the back of his neck. "Remind me again how you sun worshippers have never conquered the Miquitz?"

Ahkin barked a laugh. "Let's just say you are lucky that you death demons have lots of hidey-holes in the mountains."

"Better than living in a city made of crap."

"Crap? Tollan is made of gold." Ahkin waved a hand around the shining golden building behind them.

"Exactly. Where do you think gold comes from. It's the crap of the sun god."

Ahkin snorted. "No, it's a precious holy metal left in the earth to remind humanity of the gods' presence."

Ochix shook his head with a smirk. "That's not what we were taught in Omitl."

"By your insane father? Sounds like a perfectly reliable source of information."

"True, true," Ochix agreed.

They laughed, and then both lapsed into thoughtful silence. The Chicome certainly were different than his father always taught. Ochix wondered how many others things they'd been taught about each other were false. "So tell me again why you aren't just marching into Ehecatl and destroying them? I thought you Chicome loved warfare."

The corner of Ahkin's mouth lifted into a somewhat cocky grin. "We do, just not against our own people. We are a holy empire, ruled by the descendants of the gods themselves. Other empires—too far away to be of any consequence to us—are ruled by ordinary men. But Toani believes that when the holy descendants fight amongst ourselves, we anger the gods. It's why he wants me to try and subdue Ehecatl without force first. But if it comes to it, it is better for our empire to be united than not."

"Miquitz are holy descendants as well, aren't we?" Ochix arched a brow.

"Yes, but Cizin himself lives separate from the other gods."

"He's not everyone's favorite, you mean."

"Well . . ."

Ochix playfully punched Ahkin on the shoulder. "Hey, we are all technically family, right? Even the gods. There's always plenty of bickering and rivalry to go around."

Ahkin shook his head, amused. "I guess you have a point. The gods don't seem to mind that he's separate, and having met him myself, I can kind of see why."

Ochix grimaced. "So back to Ehecatl—we are going to try and intimidate them into submission first, and then if they don't, you'll kill them?"

Ahkin flinched. "I am hoping to find a way to appeal to the Storm Lord and get him to agree to a truce. But if he does not . . . then I will do whatever ends this as quickly as possible. I need to get the armies to the base of your mountains before the eclipse begins. I think I can convince the council to fight on your behalf if it means potentially ending hostilities with Omitl."

Ochix picked up a small stone and absently threw it off the cliff's edge. "Good. Because you know if I succeed in saving Metzi, my father is going to come after her. He'd unleash the might of the entire Miquitz Empire to get ahold of one of you. You know, can't let a perfectly good eclipse go to waste."

Ahkin looked down at his feet. "If it works the way I'm hoping, then Ehecatl will surrender quickly and join with us. We will all meet you at the base of the mountains. If you succeed, we will defend against your father's retaliation. If you fail, we must be prepared to face the Tzitzimime."

Ochix nodded. "So no pressure, right? Save your backstabbing sister from my stomach-stabbing father, and no one has to worry about star demons at all."

Ahkin reached out a hand and gripped Ochix's shoulder. "It doesn't rest solely on you. I am not foolish enough to put all of my hopes onto one strategy. If you are not able to save her in time, the star demons will descend. Then our only hope will be to hold them off long enough for Mayana and the others to resurrect Quetzalcoatl."

They stood in silence for several moments. Ochix's worried thoughts had wandered to where Yemania was at the moment, and he wondered if Ahkin's were also with Mayana. He wasn't used to allowing silence this long without some kind of smart comment to break his own nervousness.

"So again, no pressure. From the guy living in a palace of sun crap."

Ahkin rolled his eyes.

Ochix knew that Ahkin had faith in him to trust him with such an important mission. But if he was honest with himself, he was nervous. If he could save Metzi, the star demons wouldn't descend, but he'd unleash the wrath of his father. But if he couldn't . . . well, he just had to trust Ahkin's backup plans were ready to be tested. He had never met someone as strategic as Ahkin, someone who loved mapping out every little detail. But he also knew from experience that sometimes life didn't go as planned.

And everyone seemed to have plans. Metzi. His father. Ahkin. The priest. The Obsidian Butterfly. Even the Mother goddess herself. They all had some outcome they were maneuvering toward, the people around them pieces in this deadly game of worlds ending. But what worried Ochix most was whose plans would succeed and whose would fail, and what lives would be lost in the process.

———

Yemania didn't have a good feeling *at all* about meeting Itza at the northern gate. One exchange of nervous glances with Mayana told her the daughter of water felt the same.

But it didn't stop Zorrah from charging through the underbrush, her hunched shoulders under her jaguar cloak making her appear more than ever like a jungle cat on the prowl. Yoli followed close behind, her hand twirling her pointed obsidian shard with—in Yemania's opinion—wholly unnecessary excitement. The two of them were competent with weapons, but Yemania had only ever healed. She wasn't sure she could intentionally cause someone harm.

The light around the jungle dimmed, casting shades of gold and orange across the greenery. The sun was already nearing the end of its daily trek through the overworld.

"Will we get there in time?" Yemania called ahead. Her dress caught on a thornbush and she struggled to extricate herself.

Zorrah, who continued to slink through the trees as if nothing was an obstacle, slowed and glared back at her. "If we stop getting distracted, perhaps."

Mayana helped Yemania rip her dress free from the long thorns. Yemania sighed in frustration, but broke several of the thorns off and stashed them in her pocket. She gave one to Mayana to do the same.

"These will work better than your bracelet," she whispered. "And you can fight well enough with your power."

Mayana thanked her with a tight-lipped smile.

Finally, when the light around them began to fade even more, Zorrah held up a hand for them to stop.

"There," she whispered, motioning them forward as a general might summon his soldiers to the front. They gathered along the brush in the last line of trees. Zorrah pointed a sharpened nail toward a stone archway in the Great Wall. It was covered with strips of wood and was much smaller than the front gates they had sneaked past on the way here. They couldn't see any guards from where they stood, but that didn't mean they weren't still there.

"What are you going to do? Just walk up to it?" Yemania asked.

Zorrah's lip curled unpleasantly. "*I'm* not going to, no. But you are."

"*Me?*" Yemania nearly shrieked. "Why me?" She wanted to play an essential role in the trials to come, but she hadn't meant as *bait*.

"Because if I march up to the gate dressed as a warrior and looking as fearsome and intimidating as I obviously do—" Zorrah started.

Yoli rolled her eyes.

Zorrah bared her teeth briefly, but continued, "I will be considered a threat. But you, you are the weakest among us. You will inspire curiosity, if not outright pity."

"That's not very kind," Mayana huffed.

"This is war, daughter of water. There is no place for kindness."

"Kindness reminds us what we fight *for*," Mayana threw back at her. "And if I remember correctly, it was my kindness that stopped you from drowning."

"It's fine," Yemania broke in. She didn't need Mayana protecting her either. "She has a point, even if I don't like it. I am the least threatening of you. It makes sense to send me out first."

"Yemania, you don't have—" Mayana started.

But Yemania held up her hand. "No, I want to do what I can to help. Let me. Please."

Mayana nodded, tears rimming her eyes. She embraced Yemania briefly. "If that's what you want, then of course I will support you."

Zorrah grinned unexpectedly. "Perhaps I was wrong. You are stronger than you appear, daughter of healing. I thought I would have to throw you out there. May the gods protect you on your mission."

Pride warmed her chest. Of course, she would hardly consider walking into the open a "mission," but there was certainly a substantial amount of risk involved. "Thank you," she said, rising to her feet.

She threw her head back and clasped her hands in front of her to keep them from shaking. Her pulse thudded loudly in her ears and she worried she might black out from how shallow her breathing had become. *Forward*, she told her feet. They moved, albeit with trembling footfalls.

Itza could be waiting for them, just beyond the wooden planks blocking the archway. Based on the vine growth covering the wall and archway itself, this gate was not used often. Yemania's confidence grew with each step forward she took, until she left the line of trees entirely and crossed the open sand that separated the wall from the grasping fingers of the jungle.

Of course Itza would choose this gate, one that would be easy to sneak through. No one would even notice her leaving, just as no one would notice Yemania arriving. It was a clever idea, really. Yemania didn't know why she had been so worried in the first place. There was still no sign of guards, of any threat at all.

She was about to motion the other girls forward when the wooden planks covering the doorway began to shift.

Yemania froze, her heart leaping into her throat. She told herself it was just Itza moving the planks. Of course she would have to move them to escape. Even if the planks seemed much too large for someone as small as Itza. But she did have her ability with wind, so perhaps she was using her gift . . .

No matter how many encouragements or excuses she tried to make, Yemania could not stop herself from shaking. She looked back at Zorrah's intimidating face, knowing there was no way the animal princess would let her retreat. In fact, her eyes narrowed as though to warn Yemania to *stay out there*. Mayana leaned forward, but Zorrah shot out an arm to hold her back. "Give her a chance." Zorrah's voice carried across the sand.

Yemania swallowed and turned her attention back to the archway, which had finally been cleared of the wooden beams.

But instead of Itza, a stream of guards dressed in elegant purple cloaks emerged. There were ten, fifteen, then twenty of them, each carrying shell-tipped spears dangling with white feathers. They lowered their spears and pointed them directly at her.

Yemania gasped and felt her knees give out.

Itza *had* led them into a trap.

Mayana watched in horror as Ehecatl's guards flooded from the small gate and surrounded Yemania. She moved to join her friend, to help her somehow, but Zorrah clamped a hand over her mouth and pulled her farther back into the trees.

She bit her hand, and Zorrah withdrew it with a yelp. "Stop it! If they hear us, they will capture us too," the animal princess said.

Mayana arched against Zorrah's restraining arms. "I'm not letting them take her like this."

"Wait," Yoli said softly, lifting onto her toes to get a better view. "It *is* Itza . . . and nine hells, it looks like her entire family is with her!"

"What?" Zorrah's grip loosened in surprise. Mayana scrambled out of her arms and back to the bushes for a better look.

Sure enough, the guards had emerged from the gate and surrounded Yemania, but they were not alone. Next came a short but heavily muscled man whose dark hair was flecked with gray. He wore a flowing robe, and a necklace of shells encircled his neck. His shell-encrusted headpiece rose tall and proud with bright purple and white feathers. But what he lacked in stature, he made up for in presence. His eyes danced with sparks of lightning, and he moved as if he feared nothing in the world. As a descendant of the god whose bones rested in Mayana's bag, it's entirely possible he didn't.

Behind him paced his wife and son. The lady of Ehecatl was tall and regal like Teniza, moving with a grace that reminded Mayana of the rippling waves of the sea. Her son took after her in height but channeled his father in fearlessness and authority. His brooding eyes crackled like his father's, and his own purple cape danced out behind him like a gull riding an ocean breeze. He had to be the prince of storms. The one that Metzi was supposed to marry. Mayana wondered if Metzi had ever actually *seen* the prince. If she had, she might not have fought so hard against the match. Even Mayana was struck by how handsome he was.

Last came Itza, who looked just as Mayana remembered her. Small and lithe like her father, as if a simple breeze might carry her away, but powerful in both presence and—from what Mayana had seen during the selection ritual—in her ability to wield her godly gifts. She had always remained distant from the other girls in Tollan, lost in prayers or quoting scriptures. But when Zorrah had attacked Mayana in her rooms that long-ago night, it was Itza who had separated them with the gale-force winds of a hurricane.

Itza rushed forward, lifting Yemania off her knees and embracing her in a warm welcome. The guards lifted their spears and stood at attention. Mayana felt her jaw drop. Itza and Yemania spoke in hurried whispers and a smile stretched wide across her friend's face. Finally, Yemania turned and motioned for them to come out of hiding.

"It could still be a trap," Zorrah said, eyes darting back and forth as though expecting to be surrounded herself.

"I think we are fine," Mayana said. "And if we aren't, I promise you can summon every beast within earshot and start a war right here on the sand. I will even fight by your side and drown as many of them as I can."

"Really?" Zorrah's eyebrows shot up.

"I don't think it will be necessary, but of course, I'd fight by your side."

"I would too," Yoli agreed, the corner of her mouth ticking up. "Even if I do think you need to loosen up a bit."

Zorrah just looked between them, obviously lost for words, so

Mayana grabbed her hand and dragged her out to join Yemania. Yoli trailed close behind.

Itza ran to embrace Mayana next, pulling back with tears of joy in her eyes. "You are most welcome, daughter of Atl. You will find yourself among kindred souls here in Ehecatl."

"Kindred souls?" But Itza had already moved to embrace Yoli next. Yoli looked pleasantly surprised, but allowed herself to be hugged and awkwardly patted the storm princess on the back. Itza then opened her arms to Zorrah, who stepped back as though Itza were a poisonous snake about to strike. Itza laughed and settled for waving at her in welcome instead. Zorrah returned the gesture by baring her teeth in a slightly less menacing way.

Itza took a deep breath and gestured to her family. "The lord and lady of Ehecatl, and my brother, Patlani, prince of Ehecatl. We are so blessed that you have come to us."

Mayana hugged the bones of Quetzalcoatl a little tighter. "Do you know why we have come?"

"I do not know the details, but the Mother spoke to me in a dream and told me that I was to go on an important journey with the other noble daughters of the empire. I have been waiting for you to arrive ever since."

"A dream," Yoli repeated flatly. "And you just believed it?"

"The gods always speak to those who are willing to listen," the storm prince answered, his deep voice calm and reassuring.

Yoli met his eyes and blinked, dumbstruck. "Uh, yeah, sure."

Itza's father stepped forward. "You have been brought to us from the Mother, and we welcome you to our city. Though it is a time of great tension between us and the empire, please know that our quarrel is not with you and your cities."

"Tension" was a gentle way of describing that their city was at war with Tollan, thereby the rest of the empire itself. But Mayana was not going to argue. She was just grateful they were not being treated as enemies.

"Come." The lady of storms swept an elegant arm toward the gate.

"Let us show you the hospitality Ehecatl has to offer. You look as though you could all use some rest and good food."

Yoli slapped her hands together. "Gods yes. Show us the way."

Itza looped an arm through Mayana's and Yemania's, walking between them as if they were old friends. "Where's Teniza?"

"She's back in Tollan, engaged to Ahkin last we heard," Yemania said.

Itza frowned and looked at Mayana. "But I thought he loved you."

Mayana dropped her gaze to her feet. "He does. But love matters little when you are the emperor and have the responsibilities that go along with the title."

"That won't matter in the end. He will still choose you."

"Speaking of your dream, did the Mother show you where we are going?" Mayana asked in a low voice, wanting to change the subject away from Ahkin.

"She did not, but I know it is important."

Mayana slowed and brought the bag on her shoulder into her hands. She opened the flap and showed Itza the glittering jade bones inside its depths. "It is. These are the bones of your ancestor, Quetzalcoatl. I retrieved them from the underworld, from the throne of Cizin himself. We have been tasked with bringing them to the Caves of Creation to resurrect him."

Itza stopped walking and—as her arms were still looped through theirs—Mayana and Yemania jerked to a stop with her.

"Wha—?" Yemania started to ask.

But Itza pulled her arms free of both of them, fixing Mayana with a look of awe. Then, she dropped to her hands and knees and prostrated herself upon the sand before them.

The guards and the rest of the royal family of Ehecatl froze, observing their daughter's odd behavior.

"What is she doing?" Yemania whispered, looking to Mayana for direction.

Mayana met the gaze of the lord of storms and watched as his attention fell to the glittering jade bones she held in her arms. His eyes went wide, and without warning he too prostrated himself upon the sand. His wife and son followed suit, and then each of the twenty or so guards.

Mayana whirled around, half in shock and half fearful about what to do. Yoli trotted up beside her. "You showed her the bones, didn't you?"

"Yes," Mayana said in a small voice.

"And you told her whose bones they were?"

Mayana nodded.

"Ah, okay. That explains it." Yoli began picking her nails again, completely unfazed by the fact that everyone around them was lying facedown in the sand with their arms outstretched.

"Can you explain it to me?" Mayana said through gritted teeth.

Itza lifted her head from the sand, tears streaming down her cheeks. "Because he has come home. The great feathered serpent, Quetzalcoatl, has come home at last."

The Chicome army finally began its march to the sea. Ahkin took his seat upon the golden throne suspended between two poles. It would be carried on the shoulders of four warriors for the two days it would take to reach the coast. Ahead of him, Tlana priests led the way with effigies to the gods, and at his back, the might of the Chicome Empire marched with thundering footfalls. The wolves and jungle cats of the naguals of Ocelotl padded between the warriors, anxious to taste the flesh of their enemies. Not only were there close to ten thousand warriors, there were also half as many young recruits and apprentices, tasked with carrying the army's supplies upon their backs.

The citizens of Tollan lined the edges of the volcanic plateau, throwing flowers and feathers at them as they made their way down the sloping path toward the jungle below. Ahkin glanced back to where the lords of the other city-states rode upon their wooden thrones, each leading the contingent of warriors from their home cities. The lord of Millacatl watched him with an eye as keen as his daughter's.

"At least you don't have to walk the whole way," Ochix grumbled from somewhere below him. The council hadn't wanted to elevate him to the same status as the other lords, instead insisting he prove his loyalty during the coming battle. At least they'd agreed to provide him with his own spear.

Yaotl was assigned to watch over him, the council figuring that the most elite warriors in the empire would be able to contain him should he decide to go rogue. That worked perfectly in Ahkin's favor, as he planned for Ochix to secretly depart for Omitl with a small band of Jaguar warriors the moment an opportunity presented itself. Yaotl still didn't like the idea of sending some of his men with a death prince into the heart of the Miquitz Empire, but he had agreed. Rescuing Metzi from the clutches of the death priest before the eclipse began could save everyone.

They covered a considerable distance the first day of marching, and when they stopped that evening to make a temporary camp, the nobles gathered around Ahkin's fire to solidify the tactical plan for the following day.

Ahkin used the end of a spear to draw diagrams in the dirt, outlining the location of Ehecatl's forces. Spies had sent their findings through message runners stationed along the road, an effective means of communicating across long distances. The latest message assured Ahkin that the vast majority of Ehecatl's forces had gathered at the front gates to the city, the wall at their back to prevent being surrounded.

"We will send a small force of common warriors to engage their largest force here." He indicated the location with the tip of his spear. "While they are distracted, we will disperse the divine lords to the agreed-upon locations, here, here, and here." He pointed to different corners of the city. "When the smoke signal is sent into the sky, the common warriors will feign retreat. At that point, we will attempt to make our first contact with the lord of storms."

The group of nobles and military leaders around him nodded their approval. Yaotl in particular puffed his chest out in pride as he watched Ahkin.

"We will use the divine abilities of our royal families to get their attention and draw them out of the city. If they do not respond or agree to our terms of surrender, we will increase our assault with our divine abilities and begin launching strategic attacks at the major force gathered here at the main gates. Meanwhile, Ocelotl and the naguals attack the forces gathered in the south. Lord Atl and his men will be stationed to the north. With any luck, we will lure the Storm Lord onto the field of battle himself."

At this point, someone cleared his throat. Ahkin looked up from his drawings. "Is there a question?"

The head of the Eagle warriors stepped forward. "My prince, what is your plan for the Storm Lord if he agrees to surrender?"

A tension settled over the group as they waited for Ahkin's answer. The fire crackled and popped into the silence.

"I don't understand your question. What do you mean, what is my plan for him?"

Quauhtli cleared his throat again. "Your sister intended to execute him as a warning."

Ahkin sucked in a breath. Had his sister really planned on murdering the lord of Ehecatl? He quickly smothered his shock and tried to maintain his composure. He had no desire to see the lord of storms executed, especially not when he was hoping to avoid the battle entirely. He planned to meet with the lord in secret, explain the situation, and ask for his help and support in fighting the Tzitzimime.

His gaze met with Yaotl's briefly before he answered. "I will consider our options and communicate our intentions in the event he does not immediately surrender." Yaotl gave him the most minute nod of approval.

The rest of the leaders did not seem appeased, but Ahkin dismissed them to their camps for the night anyway. As everyone else dispersed, Ahkin motioned for Ochix and Yaotl to follow him. When they were out of earshot of any encampments, Ahkin took a deep breath. "Are your men ready? I will tell the others I have sent them on a special assignment."

"Yes, my prince. I have selected six of my most trusted Jaguar warriors. They understand that they will be accompanying Ochix into the heart of the Miquitz Empire to rescue Metzi, and they are prepared to follow his lead."

Ahkin nodded, his throat feeling suddenly tight. So much depended on this moment. "Ochix, are you ready to go home?"

Ochix clapped him on the back. "Not particularly looking forward to it, but I'm ready to save your sister."

Ahkin let a smile pull at his lips. "Well then, death demon, go save the world."

Ochix flourished his hand and bowed. "We're saving it together, sun worshipper."

———

If Mayana thought the beaches were the most beautiful thing she'd ever seen, it was because she had not yet laid eyes on the city of Ehecatl. Palms swayed in a gentle breeze that coated Mayana's tongue with the taste of salt. Though the air was still humid, there was a coolness to the breeze, which held gliding seabirds aloft in its currents. The buildings were made of the same light-colored stone as the city's great walls, encrusted with shells and swirling with inlaid jadeite designs. The roofs were made of sandy-colored fronds, woven together to protect the inhabitants from summer storms sweeping in from the sea. The tallest structure by far was the temple pyramid in the center, a massive carving of Quetzalcoatl gracing its face.

Together with Itza, they ascended the stone steps leading up to the family's palace. Servants were already bustling about, preparing for the day's festivities.

The Storm Lord pulled aside one of his advisors, an older man also dressed in a flowing purple cloak, and whispered something in his ear. Surprise flickered across the man's features, and then, with a quick nod of understanding, he disappeared back into the winding halls. Mayana hugged the bag of bones a little tighter to her chest.

Itza grabbed Mayana's hand, pulling her and the other princesses down another hallway lined with pearlescent abalone patterns. "Come, we need to get you ready."

"Ready?" Mayana asked. "Ready for what?"

"The celebration feast, of course. Our people have studied the prophecy of Quetalcoatl's return for generations, and you better believe we are going to celebrate!"

Yoli wiggled her eyebrows. "Well, not gonna lie. A feast is a much better welcome than the one we were expecting."

Itza led them to a large guest room, the walls encrusted with the same abalone shells as the hallway, and signaled the servants to bring them fresh clothes and refreshments. The days of trekking through the jungle had left their muscles tired and their clothes dirty and torn. Tiny scratches seemed to cover every surface of Mayana's skin, and her skirts were muddied rags. She selected a simple white sleeveless dress hung with pearls from the neckline. Zorrah refused to change at all. She merely washed her face from one of the stone basins in the corner and deemed herself appropriate. Yemania changed into a tunic dress the light purple color of a jacaranda blossom and immediately set to work healing each of their minor wounds.

"You can't heal yourself?" Yoli asked, nodding toward a particularly nasty cut that ran along Yemania's cheek.

Yemania healed the last of Yoli's cuts along her shoulder with her tongue wedged between her teeth. "There, that should feel better." She pressed a strip of clean cloth against the blood dewing on her thumb tip. "And to answer your question, no. I can't heal myself."

"That doesn't seem fair," Yoli said.

Yemania lifted the strip to see if the pressure had stopped the bleeding. "Our power requires sacrifice, to keep balance with the cosmos. For every gift received, there must first be an offering. Healing myself is not true sacrifice. At least, that's how my aunt explained it to me."

"Huh," was all Yoli responded.

"Do we really have time for a *feast*?" Zorrah complained, pacing impatiently across the room. "The eclipse starts in four days."

Mayana had been wondering the same thing, but she also didn't want to insult their hosts. She knew how important an event like this was to them. It was the moment their entire city-state had been waiting for since the time of the Seventh Sun began. "I'm not sure they would let us just leave without explaining everything. And it might be better to set off in the morning anyway after we've rested. We are all so exhausted and we have another long journey ahead of us."

"I don't like it. We shouldn't be wasting time like this," Zorrah growled. "These pious fools will do nothing but fall on their faces and let the world destroy them, as long as they are worshipping as they die."

"Not everyone does things the way they do in Ocelotl." Yoli flopped back on one of the bed mats, her black dress still torn and stained from the trek through the jungle. "Do we even know how to resurrect him? I mean, I know we take the bones to the Caves of Creation and whatnot, but what in the nine hells are we supposed to do with them when we get there? Dump them on the ground and hope for the best?"

Mayana and the others exchanged nervous glances. She felt that familiar pang of doubt, the scratch of frustration grating against her nerves. The Mother hadn't told them *how* to resurrect him. Just to take the bones to the Caves of Creation. But where in the caves? What would they be looking for? What would they do with the bones when they got there? Gods, why couldn't anything be easy and straightforward when it came to Ometeotl?

"Do you think Itza might know?" Yemania asked, lowering herself gently onto the bed mat beside Yoli. "Quetzalcoatl is their ancestor. She said her people have studied this prophecy for generations."

"That's very possible," Mayana said. "We can ask her family tonight. Another reason to go to the feast."

"That, and I'm so starving I could devour an anteater by myself," Yoli grumbled. Her stomach growled for emphasis.

Zorrah glared at Yemania. "Forget the feast. I can just go kidnap Itza and force her to come with us instead."

Yemania squeaked in alarm. "No! I don't think that's a good idea either. Why can't we go and get the information we need and explain everything? I'm sure Itza would agree to leave with us immediately if they understand the urgency of the situation."

"Fine. We can go to the stupid feast. But then we leave immediately," Zorrah said.

Mayana didn't say it out loud, but she couldn't deny that she was curious to see how feasts were handled here in Ehecatl. Itza had mentioned that she would be among "kindred souls" here, and if Mayana was honest with herself, part of her longed to see what it felt like to belong.

Even if for just a single night.

A cacophony of sound echoed around the pale stone pillars of the feasting hall. If the back wall had not opened to the most spectacular view of the ocean below, allowing some of the noise to escape, Mayana feared she would have lost her sense of hearing entirely. It seemed as though Ehecatl had tried to pack the entire city into one room. Unlike in Tollan, where everyone sat upon assigned cushions in neatly organized rows with the royal family elevated above the rest on a golden dais, the people of Ehecatl were on their feet, swirling about in dance and mingling amongst each other like bees swarming a hive. It reminded Mayana of the difference between a funeral and a wedding; reverent, solemn respect versus raw, unbridled joy.

And her starving soul soaked it all in.

At the center stood the Storm Lord himself, the calm eye of this great whirlwind of festivities, looking on with pride, his wife and children by his side. The moment the princesses appeared in the doorway, every face turned toward them and began cheering. Mayana felt as if they were war heroes returning home from some far-off battle. Tears pricked behind her eyes. This city knew who she was and what she believed, and instead of casting her aside as a worthless heathen, they welcomed her.

A flurry of hands reached forward and grabbed them, enveloping them in the sea of celebration. The ebb and flow of the tide of bodies eddied them toward the center, where Itza welcomed Mayana with open arms. A young woman with a round face stood beside her, looking shy but beautiful in a royal purple dress that matched Itza's. Her dark eyes found the bag in Mayana's arms, and they immediately filled with joyous tears. She leaned over and whispered something in Itza's ear. Itza squeezed her hand in response and nodded. The girl placed a hand to her heart, the emotion seeming to overcome her.

"This is Nitia," Itza said proudly.

Each of the princesses greeted Nitia with enthusiasm—well, with the exception of Zorrah, who didn't really seem capable of showing an emotion like enthusiasm anyway. Mayana's cheeks dimpled as she watched Itza beam at introducing her companion. She remembered how uninterested in marriage to Ahkin Itza had been during the selection ritual, and now it made so much more sense.

"Gods," Yoli yelled over the cacophony of voices. "I thought you wind worshippers were all prayers and no party."

"That's the impression we give to the rest of the empire." Itza smiled back and exchanged an amused glance at Nitia, as if they shared a secret. "But we do not offer sacrifices of blood. Instead, we burn offerings of another kind, and offer our hearts and our adoration." She waved a hand toward an altar piled with succulent foods and obscured by the smoke of incense. A female priest dressed in flowing purple robes lifted a basket into the air with prayer, blessing it before placing it back on the altar.

Mayana had never seen a female priest before. Hundreds of questions hovered on the tip of her tongue. Ehecatl still performed their own rituals, just differently from how it was demanded in Tollan. Her gaze met that of Patlani, who gave her a smile that warmed her to her toes. The prince walked toward them to join the conversation.

"I have heard much about you, daughter of water," he said with an amused quirk to his mouth.

"I imagine the entire empire has heard much about me," she said, trying to sound casual but letting the bite of her pain seep into her words.

"Perhaps, but unlike most, what I have heard has impressed me." He held her gaze for several intense heartbeats. With a shake of her head, she broke their momentary connection and turned back to Itza. She desperately wanted to stay and relish the acceptance her heart had always sought, and yet they also had a mission to accomplish. "How long will the celebration last?"

"Well into the night, I am sure," Nitia said.

Mayana sucked on a tooth, wondering how to best proceed. "I'm afraid we don't really have that kind of time. We need to get the bones to the Caves of Creation before the eclipse."

A shadow fell across Patlani's countenance. "Before the eclipse? Why so soon?"

Mayana looked around, echoes of joy and laughter floating across the waves of revelers. "Is there somewhere we can talk? With your father as well?"

"Of course." Itza urged Nitia to go welcome some new arrivals to the feast, and then she went to find her father. After a quick whispered conversation, the lord of storms lifted his gaze to Mayana's, concern creasing the wrinkles between his dark eyebrows. He motioned with his head toward a side doorway.

Mayana nodded and signaled for the other princesses to join them. Zorrah looked thoroughly relieved to be leaving the party, the chaos and motion around her had been overwhelming. Yoli pulled her gaze away from the female priestess with a curious expression.

Mayana followed Itza and Patlani through the pressing crowd. They finally emerged into a small courtyard. Water splashed merrily from a fountain the shape of a fish into a small pond that teemed with shining silver bodies identical to the stone version above. Baskets of jungle greenery overflowed from wooden trellises, while a winding path of abalone shell cut its way across the sand. Somewhere beyond the walls, the sound of waves crashed through the cooling night air.

With a swish of his purple cloak, the Storm Lord turned to face them. "Itza tells me there is something important you wish to discuss." Beside him, Patlani crossed his arms in silent expectation. Mayana tried not to notice how the muscles of his arms bulged impressively.

She swallowed hard. "How aware are you of recent events that have transpired in Tollan?"

The lord of storms scoffed. "We do not care what happens in your city of gold, just as they have never cared about us. With Metzi's betrayal of our agreement, we have finally found a reason to justify our move toward independence." He glanced toward his stoic son.

"Ahkin has retaken the throne from Metzi," Mayana said.

"We are aware of as much. Just as we are aware of his continued efforts to suppress our rebellion. My spies tell me his forces have departed Tollan and march toward the sea as we speak."

"What?" Mayana took a step back. "Ahkin doesn't want to go to war with you."

The Storm Lord gave her a flat look. "Then why does he march against us?"

Mayana looked back at Yemania, Yoli, and Zorrah, as if they held answers she did not. Yoli shrugged while Yemania frantically shook her head. Zorrah's eyebrows rose almost to her hairline, her surprise as evident as the others'.

"I don't know." Mayana nervously chewed her lip. "If he marches against you, he must have his reasons."

Even as she spoke the words, she worried about the truth within them. She didn't know why they had been arrested and thrown into a temple holding cell, aside from being told by the guards that the selection ritual was continuing and Ahkin chose Teniza. She didn't want to think it was Ahkin who'd given the order. Her heart told her it was an impossibility. He loved her.

Yet her head marched its own forces against her heart. Just because he loved her didn't mean he could stand up against the might of his entire council, the pressure from the head priest. Teniza's father surely had a hand in everything, as he always did. Had Ahkin succumbed to the reality of what it would take to become emperor? Did that mean they'd pressured him into denying his heart altogether and doing what they believed to be best for the empire? Including marching to war against Ehecatl when they should be worrying about what was about to happen in Miquitz?

Tzom had Metzi. The Mother goddess had made that clear. And if Ahkin wasn't going to do what he could to save them, then it was up to them. The princesses. She tightened her hold on the bag. Everything depended on their mission to resurrect Quetzalcoatl, and she would not let them fail.

"I don't know what Ahkin is doing, but I know what the Mother goddess has commanded me—all of us—to do. The Miquitz have taken the princess Metzi. They intend to sacrifice her blood at the eclipse in four days to hold the darkness in place indefinitely."

Patlani uncrossed his arms, his jaw going slack. The lord of storms creased his brows in confusion. "How can that be? If the darkness is held in place for too long, then . . ."

"The Tzitzimime will descend and devour us all," Yoli said, looking rather bored. "Yes, we all know the legends."

The Storm Lord looked between them. "I don't understand. Why would Tzom endanger his people in such a way?"

"We believe he might have made some kind of deal with *her*," Yemania said, pulling a scrap of a codex sheet from the pocket of her dress. She threw the image onto the ground, where the pale-striped face and bloodred lips of the Obsidian Butterfly stared up at them. "We believe he has conspired with the goddess Itzpapalotl to spare his own people in exchange for devouring all of the Chicome."

Mayana had no idea where Yemania had gotten the painted image of the Obsidian Butterfly. Still, she was grateful for the ripple of shock it sent through everyone as they beheld it. The malevolence in her gaze was enough to raise the hairs on the back of anyone's neck.

"And as much as I want to stay," Mayana's eyes flitted to Patlani for just a moment, "it's why we don't have time to celebrate the return of Quetzalcoatl's bones. The Mother goddess has commanded us to resurrect him, because your ancestor is the only one who can defeat the Obsidian Butterfly if she and her demons descend. We need to unite against them and not fight amongst ourselves."

The Storm Lord rubbed his chin. "This is a lot to take in. How can I be sure that what you say is true? That this isn't some great trick to distract us from the real enemy?"

"I have seen it, Father," Itza said, brushing her hair back from her face. The familiar crackle of power ignited around her like an aura. "I have seen in my dreams that I must go to the Caves of Creation."

Patlani cleared his throat. "I have seen visions in my dreams as well. A great battle at the foot of a mountain range. But in my dream we fight alongside Prince Ahkin, not against him."

The Storm Lord roared in frustration. "You expect me to fight *with* the Chicome? Give up on our freedom? And you just tell me this now?"

"It was a dream, Father, I did not know what to make of it. But this face—" Patlani said, his lip curling with disgust as he glared down at the goddess's image—"it was in my dream as well. It cannot be an accident."

"So you are all suggesting I send my daughter with you on this journey and surrender our only opportunity for freedom from the empire? Submit to yet another emperor determined to keep us under his control?"

"Yes," Zorrah said simply.

The Storm Lord narrowed his eyes at them. Though he was a head shorter, he still intimidated Mayana.

"I cannot say what you should do about a battle; I am no warrior. I only know that I must carry out the mission given to me," Mayana pleaded. "And we need Itza. The Mother goddess said so."

"So you're willing to sacrifice the blood of *my* daughter and your healer to resurrect Quetzalcoatl?"

Yemania's hands shot to her mouth. Mayana sucked in a breath. What did he mean, sacrifice Itza and Yemania? Ometeotl hadn't mentioned *sacrificing* them.

"What—?" Mayana started to ask.

But Itza cut across her, her temper turned on her father. "You have always taught us to listen to the gods, to follow where they lead. The Mother has given me my path. I am going with her, Father. I am willing to do what I must to save us. Will you?" Itza tilted her chin defiantly in the air.

Her father ran his hands through his gray-streaked hair. He paced in a small circle, mumbling prayers for guidance under his breath.

The silence that hung heavy between them suddenly grew in intensity, as though a sound that had been unnoticed until this moment unexpectedly ceased. A strange sensation ran across Mayana's skin, warm and prickling.

"Wait," Yoli said, pointing toward the fish fountain. "What happened to the water?"

The happy splashing of the fountain had stopped. Mayana peered over the pond's ledge to find the silver fish, their open mouths gasping for air against nothing but dry sand. The greenery in the hanging baskets began to shrivel, the once-lush vines drying into husks before their eyes. A strange buzzing sound came from inside the palace, followed by screams, as a cloud of bees erupted from the banquet hall. The flaming torches along the halls extinguished, while in the distance, from the direction of the outer villages, feathers of smoke rose into the air.

Then, the unmistakable sound of a conch-shell horn. The Chicome signal to charge.

The lord of Ehecatl whirled back to Mayana, anger churning like the clouds of a coming storm across his face. "It is too late for peace between Ehecatl and Tollan, daughter of water. The war has already begun."

Yemania's stomach clenched with panic as everyone ran back toward the feast hall. The lord of Ehecatl whipped a dagger out from his waistband and, in a flash of obsidian, drew the blade across the palm of his hand. Patlani mimicked him without hesitation. They all rushed back through the doorway they had left through. Yemania beheld what had once been a joyous celebration, and her throat closed shut.

Chaos reigned.

Yemania saw the Seventh Sun disappear beyond the glittering horizon through the opening at the back of the hall. In the deepening darkness that filled the room, the once joyous sea of revelers had turned frenzied. Swarms of bees swirled through the masses, attacking and harassing whoever stood in their path. The lord of storms let out a roar, and he flung his hand toward the bees. A great wind rose through the room, lifting the hair on Yemania's head and pulling at her dress. She pressed the skirts down with her hands as bees were swept out into the open air. The Storm Lord held them in place as they continued to fight their way back inside, the buzzing bodies colliding repeatedly with the wall of wind as though they searched for points of weakness.

"Get everyone out of here!" he yelled to his son.

Patlani raised his arms and used his own power over wind to buffet everyone toward the exits. Itza ran to his side, with determination etched upon every plane of her fierce face. She raised her bleeding palm to combine her power with that of her brother's.

Yemania's sandals slid against the polished stone floor as she fought to maintain her footing against both the wind and the bodies scrambling to escape. Mayana slid to the floor beside her, one hand attempting to hold back her wild, flailing hair, the other gripped tightly around the strap of her bag.

"We need to leave!" Zorrah yelled over the rushing sound of the wind.

"Not without Itza!" Mayana yelled back.

Zorrah nodded in understanding. Her feral eyes scanned the chaos, finally focusing on the cloud of bees. She withdrew her blade and slid it into the flesh of her hand. She threw it toward the bees, possessing the swarm herself and sending them plunging to the sea below. The waves swallowed the tiny beasts, and they did not rise again.

The Storm Lord and his children lowered their hands as the last of the straggling citizens of Ehecatl fled for the safety of the halls. "Thank you," he said, sounding breathless.

Patlani and Itza were also panting hard, as if summoning the wind had pulled the air from their lungs. Nitia ran forward and steadied Itza as she stumbled sideways.

A group of Ehecatl warriors carrying flint-tipped spears burst into the room. One of them strode forward and addressed the lord of storms. "The Chicome have begun their assault on the city. It appears the lords of the other city-states are using their godly abilities to try and render us helpless."

"My divine brothers have united against us. I guess it is to be expected. Their fear holds them captive to Tollan as much as their ignorance." He signaled for the warriors to follow him. "We must do what we can to protect the city. Summon the other generals and meet me in the war room immediately."

"Yes, my lord." The warrior nodded his head and sprinted from the room, his fellows at his heels.

Itza gave Nitia a grateful smile. Her father strode purposefully from the room without so much as a glance at the remaining princesses.

Patlani, however, reached down and helped both Yoli and Mayana back to their feet. "You must go now," he said. "Before it is impossible to escape."

Yoli's eyes focused on the smoke rising from the outer villages in the distance, barely visible against the stars. The fires were likely the work of her father and brother. "Are we sure it's even still possible?"

Itza and her brother exchanged a look. She nodded briefly. "We can take the tunnels."

Patlani cast a nervous glance over the other princesses. "Can they make it to the beach from there?"

Yemania's chest tightened. "Tunnels?" she asked. She had never been fond of tight spaces.

"We will make it," Itza said. She turned to the other princesses. "There are tunnels below the palace that lead out to the cliffs. Very few know about them. They are a secret in case the royal family ever needs to escape."

Patlani's jaw went rigid. Yemania guessed he didn't like the idea of teaching the princesses of the other city-states where to find them. But he had to know that they could be trusted. That they were different from their families.

"We are not your enemy, prince of storms," Mayana told him. "We must unite together if we want to defeat the true enemy."

He seemed to consider for a moment, his eyes darting to the bag of bones still held in Mayana's arms, then back up to her face. "I know what the Mother has shown me. It is time I put my faith to the test."

Itza brushed a swift kiss across Nitia's cheek. She had not left her side since the attack had begun. "Stay hidden, Nitia. I promise I will return to you."

Nitia nodded, tears streaming silently down her cheeks. "Be safe," she whispered.

Izta straightened her spine and turned her back, her own eyes shining. "Let's go."

A scream cut through the sound of the chaos outside, followed by a rumbling *boom*. Dust shook from the walls, coating their hair and skin.

Yoli pricked her finger and ignited the extinguished torches with a flick of her hand. "Lead the way."

Yemania took a deep breath to calm her nerves, and followed Itza and Patlani out into the halls. They descended a series of stairs, going deeper and deeper into the underbelly of the palace. The polished stone walls turned rough, rounding and sloping toward the north where they had seen the cliffs rising behind the city. These corridors had not been carved by man, but by the gods themselves. Or at least, Yemania thought, by the power of the sea eating away at the stone over the last age.

They continued to run, stopping only briefly when Yemania tripped on an outcropping of rock. The air was moist and tangy with salt, and soon the gentle crashing of the waves grew louder. The darkness of the caves lightened, revealing an opening ahead.

Patlani stopped. "The Caves of Creation are quite a ways from here. But follow the river into the hills, and it will lead you to it."

"I know where we are going," Itza assured the princesses. "We make the trek to worship there every summer."

Patlani rubbed the back of his neck. "I must go back and support our father. I don't know how I am going to convince him to join with the Chicome and march for Miquitz, but I know in my heart that we must."

"Find Ahkin," Mayana said, imploring him. "You can trust him."

Patlani frowned, doubt swimming with something darker in his eyes. "You mean the sun prince himself?"

"Yes," Mayana said, reaching out her hand and placing it on his arm. "You do not know him as I do. Please, you will be able to trust him."

Yemania noticed how Mayana's voice seemed to tremble as she spoke, as though she was not sure she believed what she was saying either. How could she possibly doubt him after everything they'd been through? Yemania had seen Ahkin's heart for herself. She'd watched him every moment since they'd escaped Omitl and knew without a shadow of a doubt that he loved Mayana. She feared her friend's heart wounds were beginning to fester.

"You can trust him," Yemania agreed. "I don't think he wants to fight this battle either. He knows a greater one is at stake."

Patlani still seemed unsure, but instead of arguing, he turned his attention to his sister. "I will do what I must. And so must you. The ritual will not be an easy one, but if the world truly is at stake, then you will not have a choice."

"I know," Itza said, embracing her brother and then shoving him back toward the palace. "Look after Nitia for me, please, if I do not return."

Patlani gave her a reassuring grin, and disappeared back into the winding tunnels.

"What do we do now?" Yemania asked.

Zorrah was already standing at the edge of the opening, her hands gripping the cave wall as though it were the only steady thing in the world. Mayana went to stand beside her. Instead of looking out through the opening, she looked down. Yemania chanced a peek through the opening and gasped. The caves did not open up onto the beach, as Yemania expected.

They opened onto a cliff face with the ocean churning far below.

"Nine hells, that's a long drop," Yoli said. "Who's jumping first?"

Zorrah took several steps back, her head shaking frantically. "I—I can't. Maybe I should go back to help with the battle."

But Mayana grabbed her hand. "Zorrah. We need you. You are the reason we made it this far. Without you, Yoli and Yemania and I would probably still be wandering lost in the jungles."

Zorrah jerked her hand free. "I can't . . . swim."

Mayana laughed. "I know. But I will help you, I promise. I didn't let you drown before, and I won't let you drown now."

"I can support us with the wind so that the fall is not as extreme," Itza assured them.

Yemania breathed a sigh of relief. She was not looking forward to crashing into the sea from such a great height.

Zorrah's chest rose and fell with frantic breaths. She glanced over the ledge once more. "You promise you won't let me drown?"

Mayana held her gaze. "I promise. I will even jump with you if you need me to."

Zorrah gritted her teeth, obviously warring with something inside herself.

"It's okay to accept help sometimes, Zorrah," Yemania reminded her. "It does not make you weak. Sometimes it takes more courage to admit we can't do something alone."

Mayana reached for her hand again. "I will jump with you."

"And I will cushion your fall," Itza said again.

Zorrah did not speak for several heartbeats, but then she swallowed hard and gave the most minute nod.

A surge of warmth spread through Yemania's chest as she watched Mayana and Zorrah jump together into the open air. Perhaps if they could learn to work together for the greater good, there could be hope for Ehecatl and the empire to work together too. She prayed Patlani would reach out, and that he and Ahkin would find a way to bridge the differences between them.

Yemania just knew one thing to be true. The only way they were going to survive the coming apocalypse was together.

"You're not letting me near the front lines?" Ahkin repeated, unsure how to process what he was hearing.

"I'm sorry, my prince. The orders come directly from the council." Quauhtli, the head of the Eagle warriors, shrugged his shoulders. "With Metzi gone and you as the last remaining descendant of the sun, you are to remain safely protected here."

"Safely protected" indeed. Ahkin ground his teeth together. The damn council was keeping him tightly under their control. There was no way he would be able to speak with the Storm Lord in private if he could not go anywhere near the city.

"And what of the planned negotiations with the lord of Ehecatl? If he decides to emerge from the city after the assault . . ."

"We have been given instructions."

"And they are?"

"I am not authorized to share them with you. I'm sorry."

Ahkin slammed his shield into a nearby tree. Toani was making every decision from the safety of the temple, undermining Ahkin every time he got the chance. Did he suspect Ahkin's plan to appeal to the Storm Lord? To negotiate peace and take the armies to the base of the Miquitz Mountains instead?

"Do you forget who is the emperor here? Whose commands

really matter?" Ahkin arched an eyebrow at Quauhtli.

He gave Ahkin a flat look. "I serve the emperor, my prince. When you are officially married and crowned, I will be at your command entirely."

It was a pretty answer that made sense to everyone who was not part of the council. But Ahkin sensed the man's disrespect, the lack of trust in Ahkin's ability to make sound decisions. Toani had done an effective job of turning the leaders of the empire against him.

Fuming, he dismissed Quauhtli back to his men. A new plan was already beginning to form in his mind. If they would not let him meet with the Storm Lord as part of formal negotiations, he would have to find another way to meet with him. He was tired of having to operate in secrets and shadows, but his counselors were giving him no choice.

Ahkin threw himself on the ground beside his fire and discarded his wood and gold shield. His macana sword soon joined it upon the dirt. Balancing his elbows on his knees, he stared into the crackling flames, his mind buzzing with possible solutions to this new obstacle. He could hear the distant sounds of the battle taking place at the city's gates, but instead of fighting beside his men, he was stuck here in the clearing, waiting at camp with the other strategic leaders. He felt so helpless. He was pushing against an immovable wall, trying to force it to bend to his will. But there had to be a weak spot somewhere, an alternative he had not yet realized. If only he could think *harder* . . .

"If you aren't careful, you're going to make that head of yours explode," Yaotl said, settling down beside him. While the small contingent of warriors was poking at Ehecatl's defenses, waiting for the signal to feign retreat, Yaotl and the elite warriors were preparing for the next phase of the plan. If the Storm Lord refused to negotiate terms after the siege, the true battle would begin.

Ahkin threw his head into his hands. "Every time I think I manage to take a step ahead, they stick out their feet to trip me."

"Mmm," Yaotl grunted, his gaze following the retreating back of the Eagle general. "I assume they told you then."

"That I'm not allowed anywhere near the battle? Yes, I've heard."

Yaotl pursed his lips. "I don't like it. This is not at all how an emperor is supposed to be treated."

"I know," Ahkin groaned. "But what can I do? Skip up to the city while it's under attack and ask for an audience with their lord?"

"Pray," Yaotl answered. "Pray the gods provide a path forward. Sometimes it is all we can do when we cannot see the way ahead."

Ahkin dropped his head into his hands. He should pray and have faith, but part of him struggled to release his control to the gods. He had his plans; he knew what he thought needed to happen. Perhaps Mayana was having more of an influence on him than he realized. A pressure tightened inside his chest until he thought he might suffocate. He pressed a fist against his breastbone to try and ease the tension.

The Mother had seen them through Xibalba. She had brought him and Mayana together. He knew she intended to save the world, not to allow it to succumb to darkness.

Ometeotl, he prayed. *Great Mother and Father of creation, please show me my next steps. Every plan I make falls to pieces in my hands. What is your plan? How do I stop this war with Ehecatl?*

He lifted his face toward the heavens, where the bloodred comet had appeared after his father's death, Ometeotl's warning to creation that the end was near. The comet had faded, but she was watching, just as she always was. He could feel her presence in the warm breeze that whispered across his skin like a caress.

All he could do now was trust.

———

Since Ahkin had been old enough to fight, he had never missed an important battle. He didn't know what to do with himself besides pace around the makeshift camp and wait for news. The other council members had retreated to their reed-mat tents, at ease with their roles as manipulators of fate without actually participating themselves. The lords of the different city-states were still on assignment at their various locations, using their abilities to hopefully bring Ehecatl to her knees.

When morning began to scratch at the sky like an impatient beast, Ahkin maintained appearances by performing his duty to raise the sun. Its glowing face bathed the new day with fresh light. A conch horn sounded in the distance, and the smoke signal to retreat rose from the distant tree line.

The first phase of his plan was complete. Now, they would send an invitation to the Storm Lord to surrender. If he refused, the actual siege would begin. The warriors they'd sent to provoke Ehecatl's forces slowly began to return. Ahkin continued to pace around his fire. A warrior ran past, likely in a hurry to determine the fate of a friend.

He had to think of a way to be included in the peace negotiations, or else he might never get the chance to speak with the Storm Lord at all. He glanced toward the heavens. Were the star demons watching him as he failed? Were they reveling in the possibility that their freedom was near and that the empire would be too busy fighting amongst themselves to stop them?

Three more warriors ran by, chattering excitedly as they passed. Ahkin lifted his head. A buzz of voices carried over from the edge of the camp, and a large group of warriors was gathering around what appeared to be one of the lesser generals. Ahkin's curiosity was piqued. What could possibly have them all so riled? Around him, the council members and other strategic leaders were emerging from their tents.

Something had happened.

Ahkin joined the growing mass of bodies and pushed aside the young men around the edges of the group. Once the others saw their prince, they stepped aside willingly. As his way forward cleared, Ahkin got a suddenly clear view of what had the men so excited.

The general was one that Ahkin did not know by name, only in passing as a tradesman-turned-warrior who had risen up the ranks with his many captures in battle. He wore the traditional red-and-black hat of a warrior of his rank, and his red shield dangled with black toucan feathers. At his sandaled feet, however, knelt another figure wearing a purple cloak. Noticeably a young captive from the skirmish. A deep wound upon his leg rendered him unable to stand, staining the dirt beneath him with a steady stream of blood. The general held him by his hair, forcing his face up for all to see. His throat bobbed nervously, and his tanned skin glistened with nervous sweat.

As Ahkin looked closer, taking in the young man's crown of white feathers, the necklace of shells that hung across bloodied gashes on his chest, a realization washed over him. This was not just any warrior they had captured.

They had captured the storm prince himself.

CHAPTER

35

"What should I do with him?" the arrogant young general called to the crowd now gathering. A strange sensation coursed through Ahkin's veins. He knew he should be proud of the warrior; taking captives was how those of common birth distinguished themselves within the army ranks. It was probably how he had risen to a place of leadership among his fellows. But instead, all Ahkin felt was a desire to chastise him into a thousand tiny pieces.

The Storm Lord would be unlikely to negotiate peace if the Chicome killed his son. Must his plan be thwarted in every way imaginable? It was probably Ahkin's imagination, but he swore the last stars of morning seemed to cackle with delight as they faded into the daylight.

There were shouts and jeers, and then finally, stones lobbed at the storm prince's bleeding body. His eyes crackled with defiance and a blast of wind burst out from him, knocking those standing closest flat onto their backs. But his strength was obviously waning with the amount of blood he'd lost, and he didn't seem able to muster any more energy beyond that. Ahkin felt a twinge of pity.

One of Yemania's many cousins from Pahtia, a battlefield healer, rushed forward and began healing the storm prince's wounds to prevent any more outbursts of his power. Ahkin's memory flashed back to the lord of Pahtia healing Ahkin's own hand in the council chambers to subdue him. How overpowered he'd felt when he was only trying to fight for . . .

"Stop!" Ahkin called.

The warriors froze, some with stones still in their hands, and turned to face him. The young general tilted his head in curiosity as Ahkin moved in closer.

"My prince," the general said, dropping his chin to his chest in respect. The red-and-black hat on his head tipped precariously. "I have captured the prince of Ehecatl and present him to you as a gift."

Ahkin took an involuntary step back, his stomach souring in disgust. The storm prince glared up at him, hatred pouring from his eyes as venomous as poison from a snake.

"Ehecatl will never submit to the rule of a puffed-up prince who thinks he's a god," the prince said, spitting at Ahkin's feet.

The general, who still held him by the hair, jerked him back and struck him across the face. "That is not how you speak to your emperor, heathen." The crowd around them heaved in an uproar, surging forward like an angry beast determined to devour the storm prince whole.

Ahkin had prayed for Ometeotl to open a path for him: a way to negotiate peace with Ehecatl, or at least some kind of truce, before the world would end. Was this her answer?

Once again a warm breeze caressed Ahkin's cheek—and the idea burst into his mind like the sun breaking through a bank of clouds.

"Take him away," Ahkin commanded. "Make sure he is secured and isolated at the edge of the camp. I will meet with the other leaders to decide his fate. If he is to be sacrificed, you must not take that gift away from the gods."

There were general rumblings of understanding and agreement.

"Yes, my prince." The general gave a quick bow of his head and jerked the storm prince along, half dragging him.

"Mayana was wrong about you," the storm prince growled as he disappeared between the shuffling bodies of the crowd.

Ahkin took his words like a blow to the stomach. Mayana?

Yaotl tapped on his shoulder. "My prince, the other generals wish to see you at your fire."

Ahkin gave his head a little shake. "Yes, of course. I will be right there."

His head buzzed with possibilities as he and Yaotl made their way back toward Ahkin's tent. Youthful apprentices were flitting about like bees, busy keeping the camp stocked and comfortable for the more experienced members of the army. Someone had freshened the wood in his fire, casting a haze of smoke across his section of the clearing.

The other leaders were already gathered, mumbling to each other in hushed tones. Ahkin's jaw clenched. They were probably already deciding without him.

"Ah, my prince." One of the generals greeted him with a low bow that sent his many necklaces rattling. "We were just discussing this recent development. The Mother has smiled most fortuitously upon us, wouldn't you agree?"

Ahkin forced a tight-lipped smile. "Indeed."

The older man cleared his throat and turned back, half excluding Ahkin from the conversation.

Irritation pricked at Ahkin like a wasp, but he knew better than to disturb the hive right now. He positioned himself so that he was more included. "What are we discussing?"

The general eyed him up and down. "We have decided to hold him for the time being and see if we can use his life as leverage to force the Storm Lord's compliance. He would be more likely to surrender if doing so would ensure his only son's survival."

"And who will be handling those negotiations?"

The general heaved a sigh of impatience. "The council has given us their instructions, my dear prince. You have enough responsibility on your shoulders with the sun; we do not wish to burden you with more." The older men around him chuckled and waved dismissive hands.

The air rushed out of Ahkin's lungs. A faint ringing in his ears grew louder, blocking out all sound. Their cruel laughter faded to background noise as Ahkin's greatest insecurities flooded back. Yaotl's firm hand on his shoulder steered him away and back toward his tent.

"Do not listen to them, my prince," Yaotl said.

Ahkin threw off his hand. "How can I not? They are supposed to be my most trusted advisors and generals. How am I supposed to trust them when they don't even see me as a man, let alone an emperor?"

Yaotl grunted and placed his hand back on Ahkin's shoulder, harder this time. "Does a true emperor submit to his critics? Or does he lead his empire and do what is right regardless of the opinions of others?"

"A leader cannot lead without others willing to follow," Ahkin countered. "And advisors are supposed to advise their leaders, not make the decisions for them."

But then Ahkin remembered something Ochix had said back in Tollan. *Advisors are there to offer advice. Listen to them, hear their thoughts and opinions, take them in and consider them. But if you are going to be a true emperor, remember that it's just that: advice. In the end, you have to weigh their opinions and then make decisions for yourself.*

The words were an encouraging whisper in his ear, a reminder that perhaps it was still possible to lead his people. He had to decide to do what was right, even if his advisors didn't understand.

And if he was careful, they'd never even have to know it was him.

———

The salt water filling Mayana's mouth brought back horrific memories of the sea of the dead. The darkness of the sky above only added to the feeling. Her heart threw itself against her ribcage, panic filling her lungs until she reminded herself that they were not in the underworld. No monster crocodile was waiting beneath her to devour them. Now the danger came from the stars winking awake above them.

She kicked herself back to the surface and immediately scanned the water for Zorrah. Their hands had separated upon impact with the sea below, but she found her quickly, flailing against the whitecaps slapping her in the face.

"I've got you," Mayana said, reassuringly. "I'm willing the current to support you, so you can relax."

Though Zorrah's pupils were still dilated with fear, her arms and legs calmed. The jaguar cloak billowed out around her.

Two more loud splashes, followed by a third. Mayana forced the water to draw them all together.

"The beach is that way," Itza said, pointing north along the cliff's face. "Follow me."

The princess of storms was an excellent swimmer, Mayana noticed. She didn't need any support in the water, so Mayana focused her attention on the others. Unfortunately, their lack of experience in the water was evident. Yemania paddled like a wolf pup, while Yoli flailed as badly as Zorrah. It was slow going, Mayana needing to draw even more blood to keep them afloat, but eventually the cliffs ahead gave way to an expanse of white sand illuminated in the moonlight with dense jungle beyond. The waves rolled gently against the beach, beckoning them forward, and then finally expelled them all, gasping for breath like the fish from the dried-up pond. Zorrah flopped onto her back, staring up at the stars as though she couldn't believe she had survived. Yoli sat up and whistled with excitement while Yemania began wringing out the folds of her soaked dress.

"That wasn't so bad, was it," Mayana laughed, turning to Itza.

But Itza was not smiling. Her face was turned toward the jungle, her eyes narrowing in suspicion at something behind Mayana's back.

Because they were not alone on the beach.

Mayana whirled around. From the shadows between the trees, warriors slowly emerged, their looks of confusion matching the ones dawning on Yemania's and Yoli's faces. Zorrah was already up, her dagger in her hand and a growl in the back of her throat.

But Mayana's stomach dropped faster than it had when she'd jumped into the sea. The warriors were dressed in costumes of blue and jade—the warrior costumes of Atl. Then, from the trees, came the hulking form of her father, his cloak fanning out behind him. At his shoulders, her brothers stared with eyes as wide as the moon.

She and her father held each other's gaze, heartbreak warring with rage so clearly on his face. For a wild moment, she thought he might run to her and embrace her. But instead, he lifted a hand and gave a signal to his men. "Seize them," he ordered. "And tell the generals we've located the missing princesses."

CHAPTER

36

The message to the lord of Ehecatl went out immediately. Ahkin was sure he knew what the letter contained, something along the lines of, "We have your son, surrender now or he dies." Effective for their goals and objectives . . . but not so much for Ahkin's. The leadership was giving the Storm Lord until sunrise, leaving four days until the eclipse began. If they received no answer, the Chicome would unleash all of their forces and decide for him.

He knew Ehecatl would not go down without a fight. Using his son's life as a bargaining chip would accomplish nothing but to incite the Storm Lord's ire further, solidifying their resolve to be free of the oppression of the empire. Ahkin hated to admit it, but he understood their frustration. He, too, felt the suffocating weight of their control threatening to crush him. No, they would not surrender. Ehecatl was a prominent city-state with an established military force. Their lord could summon the force of a hurricane if necessary. There would be mass casualties on both sides.

And then they would be too weak to fight anything else. He had to get every warrior he could muster to the base of the Miquitz Mountains before the eclipse began. Even if Ochix succeeded in saving Metzi, Tzom's retaliation would follow. And if he didn't succeed, something much worse than the death demons would come for them all.

No, they had to be ready in time. The price of being unprepared would be too costly to pay. The blood of his people would feed the Obsidian Butterfly and her demons while his army was on the other side of the empire. Millacatl would be the first in their path if the Tzitzimime flooded down from the mountains. He had to end this war with Ehecatl as soon as possible—and in a way that kept everyone alive.

Ahkin bided his time throughout the day, resuming his anxious pacing and trying to get some training in with Yaotl and the Jaguar warriors. He knew he had to wait until nightfall, when prying eyes would be less sharp.

After the evening meal had been served and the other generals had retreated to their tents, Ahkin feigned exhaustion and retired to his own as well.

"Is there anything you need, my prince?" A young warrior apprentice whose voice had barely deepened stood at the entrance of the reed-mat structure.

"No, I am just going to rest for the evening. Tomorrow will be an ordeal for us all. You had better prepare yourself for the battle; many of the young men will likely not return."

The apprentice squeaked with apprehension and scurried off. Ahkin felt a hint of guilt for scaring the boy away, but there were greater things at stake now.

With a quick swipe of his dagger, blood pooled in the palm of his hand. There wasn't much light left in the gathering darkness, but what little remained, Ahkin bent around himself until he disappeared from sight.

He kept himself hidden from his advisors as he sneaked toward the edge of camp. The storm prince was tied to a post with his hands behind his back. His head bobbed against his chest as he fought the exhaustion threatening to pull him under. They had healed his flesh wounds, but his body was still weak from blood loss. That would take time to replenish. Several Eagle warriors stood watch from a few yards away. Still, they talked among themselves in quiet voices, bored with their assignment of watching a prisoner who obviously wasn't going anywhere.

Though he was invisible to the human eye, Ahkin could still be heard, so he removed his sandals and continued the rest of the way on his bare feet. The clearing was littered with sharp stones waiting to assault him, but he managed to pick his way across the campsite without gasping each time his foot found one.

This next part would be tricky.

The guards were far enough away that a whisper would not carry, but anything louder would definitely catch their attention. Ahkin sneaked as close as he dared to the storm prince's back, keeping the wooden post between them.

He reached out a hand and gently tapped the storm prince's shoulder to wake him.

The prince's head snapped up, suddenly alert.

"Don't say anything, but I'm here to help you," Ahkin whispered quickly.

"Who's there?" The storm prince stretched against his bindings to try and see behind him.

"Stop moving. You will get their attention."

The storm prince stilled, though his chest continued to rise and fall with heavy breaths. "Did my father send you?"

"No," Ahkin whispered harshly. "It is your father I wish to speak to."

The muscles of the prince's back suddenly tensed. "Who are you?" he asked again.

Ahkin pulled the dagger out of his waistband and began sawing at the thick ropes around the storm prince's hands. "A puffed-up prince who thinks he's a god, of course."

"*Ahkin?*" The prince spoke a little too loudly.

The guards standing nearby hushed and looked over toward them. Ahkin's blade froze on the bindings as he waited with his breath held tight. They watched the storm prince for several tense moments before returning to their conversation.

"Be quiet, or I'm going to leave you tied to this pole," Ahkin whispered harshly.

"I don't understand. How come they didn't see you?"

"Human eyes see with light, and I can bend the light around myself until I can't be seen."

"Hmmm," was all the prince answered.

"What is your name anyway? I feel stupid just calling you 'storm prince' over and over in my head."

"Patlani," he whispered back. "Patlani of Ehecatl."

"Well, Patlani, I know we were supposed to be brothers a lifetime ago, so consider this my gift of apology for my sister's broken promise to you."

The bindings finally snapped through and fell to the dirt. Patlani flexed his hands and rolled his wrists at the sensation of freedom.

"Thank you, but why—" Patlani started to ask, pulling his arms around to his front.

But Ahkin grabbed the prince's fingers and held them back in place behind the post. "Don't move just yet. Pretend you are still bound. Give me time to return to my tent so that no one knows it was me that let you escape."

"Why *are* you letting me escape? I don't understand."

Ahkin felt a smile pull at his lips. "I want to meet with your father. I don't want to fight this war. We have a much greater one we need to worry about."

"Mayana told me," Patlani whispered. "She and the other princesses were here and explained everything."

Hope bubbled up like a spring inside Ahkin's chest. "Mayana was here? In Ehecatl?" *Why would she travel all the way here when she was supposed to be going to the Caves of Creation?* he almost asked, but then fear crept in and took the place of hope. They had just attacked a city with the girl he loved inside its walls.

"She's fine," Patlani answered before he got the chance to ask. "My sister Itza joined her and the others, and they are heading for the Caves of Creation."

"But why come here at all? It will take them days to get to the caves from here."

"What choice did they have? They need the blood of my ancestor to resurrect him. They had to get Itza."

Ahkin ground his teeth together. This timeline was cutting

everything so close. The girls might not even make it before the eclipse began. His own time was running short to get the armies positioned where they needed to be.

"Then it is even more essential I speak to your father. My advisors and the other military leaders cannot be trusted. They do not see the threat that looms above us like a macana sword waiting to drop on our necks. All they care about is maintaining their own power and control, and because I haven't been officially crowned yet, my authority is still limited. Please assure your father that if he agrees to meet with me, I will personally work out a deal in both of our favors. But I have to be able to talk to him."

"Then come back to Ehecatl with me. Let's leave right now."

"I can't leave. My council does not trust me enough as it is. But I have to end this war with you so I can convince everyone to march to the mountains instead."

"Mountains . . . mountains covered in mist . . ." Patlani said, sounding suddenly distant and far away.

He had learned long ago not to question when a wind-worshipper suddenly quoted scripture or faded off into prayer.

"So, will you speak to your father or not?" Ahkin said, losing his patience.

"Yes," Patlani answered. "I have to. We are destined to fight together. I will convince him to meet with you and tell him how you saved my life. Mayana was right. You are not the puffed-up sun prince I thought you to be."

"And you aren't the heathenous rebel I thought you to be, so can we call it even?"

Patlani shook with silent laughter. "Yes, sun prince, we can call it even."

Ahkin sneaked back into his tent and collapsed onto the furs of the bed mat. His heart nearly burst with pride. He'd done it. He had found a way to get a message to the Storm Lord. Now he just had to wait for . . .

A flurry of shouting. The short blast of a shell horn. Ahkin stumbled to the doorway of his tent, pretending to be just waking up from sleep.

"Search the jungle!" a man's voice yelled from nearby.

Several military leaders were already out of their tents and gathering beside Ahkin's dwindling fire. Ahkin gave a particularly dramatic stretch and yawned, ensuring they saw him emerge from his tent.

"What's going on?" Ahkin demanded.

"Your highness, I'm so sorry. But it appears the prisoner has escaped somehow." Yaotl bowed his head in apology.

"What?" Ahkin roared. "How could we let him escape?"

Quauhtli pursed his lips. "I don't understand how he managed to escape his bindings. I tied them myself."

"He had help," a lesser general complained. "The bindings were cut. Someone has betrayed us."

"My guards did not see anyone near him at all. He managed to blow them over and escape into the trees before they could stop him."

Yaotl's gaze shot to Ahkin. "And no one saw who helped him?"

Ahkin's stomach clenched, but he tried to appear surprised at this news. Yaotl's eyes narrowed.

The Eagle general spat into the dirt. "No, and now we have no leverage to convince Ehecatl to surrender. I hope you're all ready to go to war in the morning." He stormed off, barking orders at his subordinates as he passed. The other generals followed suit, coordinating their next steps to prepare for attack.

"Ahkin," Yaotl said, rubbing his eyes. "How did the storm prince escape?"

"I don't know. Someone must have—"

Yaotl cut him a look.

Ahkin sighed. "Fine. I let him go."

Yaotl gritted his teeth and turned away in frustration. "Why, Ahkin? That was our chance to avoid open warfare. I thought you wanted this over with quickly?"

Ahkin straightened his spine. "I do. And do you honestly think for a moment that Ehecatl would have surrendered? That the Storm Lord wouldn't have used his son's death as martyrdom and rallied his men to fight against the oppressors who killed him? Tell me *that* would have ended things quickly."

Yaotl dropped his gaze and kicked at the dirt, but did not contradict him.

"You know I am right. If we want to resolve this peacefully, then I need to reopen negotiations and show the Storm Lord that I can be trusted."

"So you freed his son," Yaotl said with a nod. He lifted his head and looked at Ahkin with a strange look Ahkin didn't recognize.

"You think I'm a fool?" Ahkin's throat tightened, waiting for the reprimand from his mentor.

"No," Yaotl said. "I think you are going to be a better emperor than anyone realizes. They are the fools for not seeing it."

Mayana rose to her feet in the sand, cold water from the sea curling around her ankles. Her father's warriors closed in around the half-drowned princesses, spears lowered and pointed directly at them.

"What do we do?" Itza whispered out of the corner of her mouth.

"We fight!" Zorrah yelled, charging at the nearest warrior beside her.

"Zorrah, no!" Yoli called, but it was too late. They watched in horror as her father's best guards engaged her.

Mayana immediately understood how Zorrah had managed to earn her distinction as a Jaguar warrior. The sea ran red with blood as her dagger found the necks of two, three, four warriors before she was overpowered. One hand grabbed at her wrist and forced the dagger from her fingers. A foot collided with her stomach. Zorrah fell to her knees, her breath coming in gasps. A blade pressed against her throat, but still she arched against her captors. Zorrah's feral scream of frustration tore at Mayana's insides, until she couldn't stand to watch another moment.

"Stop!" Mayana screamed at her father. "Please! Make them stop."

Her father held up a hand, and the warriors stilled but held Zorrah in place. Out of the corner of her eye, she saw sparks crackling at the ends of Yoli's fingers. Mayana lifted her hand to stay Yoli.

"I will order her blood spilt without a moment's hesitation. Ocelotl has other heirs," the lord of Atl said, his voice as cold as the darkest night. "If you want her death upon your conscience, then, by all means, attack."

Yoli gave Mayana's father a look that spewed pure hatred, but the sparks dancing along her fingers sputtered.

Mayana's hand tightened around the soaked bag at her hip. The heavy weight of Quetzalcoatl's bones weighed upon her heart. "Father, you don't understand what you're doing. We have to—"

The lord of Atl slapped Mayana hard across the face. Stars danced in front of her eyes, and sound momentarily ceased. The world tipped sideways, and her hands dug into the sand to catch her fall. Her cheek throbbed with numbness that slowly turned to an ache that brought tears to her eyes.

She looked up at her father as he stood above her, his mouth open with horror at what he'd just done. The memory of the last time he'd struck her burned in her mind, a lifetime ago when he'd humiliated her in front of the entire city. When she had refused to sacrifice a lizard. She wondered if he remembered too: how he'd lifted his hand to strike again, but her mother had run between them and taken the blow instead. She let the memory wash over her, let it strengthen what little resolve to fight she had left.

"You brought this on yourself, Mayana." Her father's voice cracked with emotion, his anger laced with his tears of frustration. "You have humiliated our family again and again. Refusing to bend that stubborn will of yours and costing us more than you can ever know. It is time you learn your place. And if you can't, it is my job as your father to put you there."

"Why?" Mayana sobbed. "Why can't you just accept me for the way I am? *Listen* to me for once instead of constantly silencing me! I have a voice. I have thoughts and feelings of my own!"

"No one wants to hear them. No one cares what you think." Her father's voice went low and dangerous. "You are fighting a battle that cannot be won." Then, with a swish of his cloak, he turned away from her.

Mayana choked out a sob, watching as though everything was moving as slowly as sap dripping down the side of a tree. The guards seized Yoli, Yemania, and Itza, dragging them after Zorrah back toward the jungle. Hands closed around her and dragged her to her feet. Someone ripped the strap of her bag roughly over her head, relieving her of the burden of the bones.

Of course they wouldn't let her fulfill the mission given to her by the Mother goddess. Their own plans were far too important. How foolish had she been to think she could defy her family? Defy the empire? Defy the ways her people had lived for generations? She might be correct, and the gods themselves might agree with her, but it was men controlling her fate now. This way of life had been in place for far too long, was far too ingrained in the way everyone thought and acted. Who did she think she was to try and change it?

She watched Itza struggle against the warriors tying her hands behind her back. Even Ehecatl could not stand against Tollan, against Toani, and the ways of the Chicome. How many times had they tried to fight for their freedom? To worship and live as they saw fit? If an entire city-state could be silenced, forced into submission, who was she to think she was any different?

She may have been right in what she believed, but so was her father.

She was fighting a war that could never be won.

By the time Ahkin raised the sun the following morning, Ehecatl still had not sent any kind of response. The armies of Tollan were prepared to launch an all-out assault against the city of storms.

Ahkin had hoped to hear something from the Storm Lord before this moment came, but perhaps Patlani never made it back to his father. Or worse, perhaps they were laughing at his foolish trust. Ahkin wanted to punch a tree. How could he have been so stupid? To think that releasing Patlani would buy enough favor with the Storm Lord to grant him an audience? Maybe he shouldn't have helped him escape after all.

Yaotl's head popped through the flap of his reed tent. "It's time, my prince."

Ahkin sighed and slipped a wooden shield onto his forearm. It was light, the worn handle comfortable against his skin. Simple, but adequate for the job it had to do. For a moment he flashed back to the glorious shield of his ancestor that the Mother had gifted him in Xibalba—the engraved golden sun that could call forth the light of the sun itself. But Tzom had taken it when he had been captured, and he had not seen the shield since. It was likely sitting somewhere in Tzom's palace, a trophy for having captured the son of the sun.

"I'm surprised they are even letting me come," Ahkin said, his tone flat. A hot feeling of shame bubbled in his stomach.

"It's more for show than anything else. You are expected to remain behind the lines with the other generals. Able to watch but not participate."

"A figurehead for them to show off and use, but not an emperor with any real power."

Yaotl lowered his chin and gave Ahkin a stern look. "For now, my prince. Your time will come."

Ahkin chewed his lip for a moment, the burning in his stomach finally bubbling up to his tongue. "I'm sorry," he burst out.

Yaotl frowned. "For what, my prince?"

The burning feeling spread out to the tips of his fingers, consuming him until he wanted to do nothing more than crawl into a dark hole and hide forever. "I'm sorry. I was wrong to let Patlani escape."

To his surprise, Yaotl winked. "Do not give up hope. The battle has not yet begun."

Ahkin ran a hand through his hair. There was nothing to do now but wait. Wait to see if his gamble would pay off or not.

The spies they'd sent to assess Ehecatl's response reported that the Storm Lord had moved all of his forces to the front of the city, preparing for the invasion. Therefore, the Chicome condensed their warriors into a massive force that would attack Ehecatl's main gates like a battering ram. Ahkin tried not to think about how many lives were about to be lost for the sake of protecting a system created by his own ancestor. Toani was willing to let this many lives be lost to maintain his control . . .

Though Ahkin itched to be at the front with the men he'd trained with for more than a decade, he resentfully took his place alongside the other commanding generals as they marched along the main path toward Ehecatl. The trees around them finally thinned to expose a large expanse of sand that stretched between the edge of the jungle and the gates to the city itself. The sky hung heavy with clouds, tendrils of fog reaching down to the earth like grasping fingers of the gods. But between them and the gates stood a sea of Ehecatl's warriors, spears and macana swords drawn and waiting behind wooden shields inlaid with shells. Ahkin tried to estimate their numbers from sight—somewhere in the realm of two or three thousand. He shook his head. Unless they had more waiting inside the city gates, they were nowhere near enough to stand up against the might of the Chicome.

It would be an unnecessary slaughter.

The Chicome warriors began to fan out along the edge of the jungle until they almost extended the length of the city walls. The younger, less experienced warriors waited in the trees themselves, ready to test their skills once the majority of the threat had been contained.

One of the common generals lifted the conch horn to his lips and gave three short, loud blasts.

Yaotl lifted his hand to give the signal for the front line to charge. But before he could, another horn blast answered from Ehecatl, cutting through the light morning fog that clung to the tops of the trees.

Yaotl's hand hesitated.

The wooden gates of the city began to open. Ehecatl's warriors parted down the center, and two figures with billowing purple cloaks marched out between them. Ahkin immediately recognized the tall, muscular form of Patlani. Beside him, a shorter but equally strong older man with dark hair mixed with gray. As they neared the open expanse of sand, a gust of wind rushed out—not strong enough to knock the Chicome off their feet, but enough that many were forced to brace themselves behind their shields.

Ahkin's arm came up to block his eyes from the blowing sand. When he lowered it, the Storm Lord and his son stood alone between the two armies, perfectly exposed.

"I wish to speak to Prince Ahkin," the Storm Lord boomed into the silence like a peal of thunder. "And *only* Prince Ahkin."

Ahkin's heart thudded harder than a war drum inside his chest. Patlani had done it. He'd convinced his father to speak with him. Ahkin's generals turned to face him, their faces a mosaic of confusion and fear, some contorted in outright distrust.

"We cannot allow our emperor to go out there alone; what if he is captured?" one general asked.

"They would be foolish to capture the sun prince with an army at his back," Yaotl answered. "Let him go and speak to them."

"What if they kill him?"

"Then they doom us all to die when the sun can no longer rise. I don't think that is a realistic threat." Yaotl scoffed.

Ahkin fiddled with the handle of his shield and did not meet their eyes. No one besides himself and Toani knew that Ahkin didn't *really* raise the sun each morning. He could manipulate it, but it would still rise without him.

"I'm going," Ahkin said. "If there is a chance I can convince him to surrender without spilling blood on either side, I must take it."

His leadership's sullen silence answered him. He took that as confirmation of their permission.

Ahkin drew a deep breath of salty air into his lungs and began his solo trek to the rendezvous point. The Storm Lord watched him with a mixture of curiosity and concern, as if he wasn't sure yet what to make of the sun prince. When he finally reached them, Ahkin whispered, "Gods, Patlani, you kept me waiting long enough."

The corner of Patlani's mouth curved up. "My father can be a bit stubborn."

Ahkin's thoughts shifted to Mayana, and he almost smiled. Luckily she'd given him plenty of experience with stubbornness. The Storm Lord crossed his arms and looked Ahkin up and down. "Why did you release my son?" he asked with a voice as deep as his son's.

Ahkin swallowed. "I knew that if we tried to use him to barter for your surrender that we would all end up bloodied on the battlefield. And that is not what I want."

"So you released him because you knew we would not surrender?" Ahkin blinked. "Yes."

"How did you know?"

A breeze off the ocean slipped across Ahkin's skin, making bumps rise along his arms. He rubbed them absently. "I just know what it feels like to try and fight for what you believe in and to be constantly silenced. I didn't think threatening to kill your son would calm the rebellion as much as adding wood onto an already burning flame."

The Storm Lord considered him for the length of several heartbeats.

Ahkin's palms began to sweat. "You are nothing like your father," he said at last.

Ahkin's chest tightened uncomfortably. He didn't need another reminder. "I know. I'm not."

The Storm Lord tilted his chin higher. "That was a compliment."

Ahkin nearly swallowed his tongue. "W-what?"

The Storm Lord laughed. "Your father and I disagreed on many things. But I am willing to listen to what you have to say, prince of light."

"Oh, uh. Yes." Ahkin cleared his throat. "We do not—" He stopped. No, that wasn't right. "—*I* do not want to lose Ehecatl as a part of the Chicome Empire. We are family, united all of us by our divine heritage. If I allow you to defect from the empire, you know it will make us appear weak. Then what is to stop the other city-states from following suit? I cannot allow my empire, my divine *family*, to fall apart either."

The Storm Lord cocked his head. "I understand, Ahkin. I really do. Ehecatl does not wish for our independence simply for the sake of being independent. There are many benefits to being part of the empire. But we cannot submit to the level of control that you and your priesthood exert over us. We wish to be free to worship as we see fit."

Ahkin's father had always made it sound like Ehecatl wanted power, that it was a battle of who would lead and who would follow. But he saw clearly that this was a battle of wills, a battle for the right to embrace their identity. As he looked at the Storm Lord and Patlani, he saw Mayana. The young woman he loved. The one willing to sacrifice everything to stay true to her heart and what she believed. Just like with her, there would be no convincing them to give that up either.

Ahkin leaned in and kept his voice low. "What if Tollan was willing to give you the religious freedom you seek?"

Patlani exchanged a wide-eyed glance with his father. "You would consider such a thing?"

"I can promise you that if you come back to Tollan with me and agree to open negotiations, I will do everything I can to find a solution that works for us both. I want you to find the freedom you seek while still keeping you part of our empire."

"Come to Tollan?" The Storm Lord's face wrinkled in disgust. "I have traveled to Tollan many times for negotiations. The last journey I made was when your father offered his daughter in marriage to my son. Your blood did not follow through on those promises."

"My *sister* did not follow through on those promises. I am sure you are aware of what happened, as you saw our moment of weakness as the perfect opportunity to reach for your freedom."

The Storm Lord nodded. "This is true. I will not deny it."

"I do not wish to fight with you. I do not wish any Chicome blood to be spilled on this sand. And you are Chicome, like it or not. You are a part of the seventh people. I need all of you, every warrior we have, for an even greater battle ahead."

He did not seem surprised. "Yes, your princesses mentioned as much."

"Then you know what is at stake. Please, come back to Tollan, and we can reopen negotiations. We only have four more days until the eclipse begins, and we must reach a deal before then. Or none of us may live to see another age."

The silence that hung between them was so heavy, Ahkin nearly collapsed under its weight. He wanted an answer, to grab the Storm Lord by the shoulders and shake him until he saw sense.

"What do you think?" The Storm Lord asked his son at last.

Patlani shrugged his shoulders. "Father, you know my thoughts on the matter."

The Storm Lord heaved a heavy sigh. "All right. We will return to Tollan with you to negotiate."

Joy exploded in Ahkin's chest. "Thank you. I know this is a great risk for you—"

But the Storm Lord's eyes crackled with warning. "I pray we can find an agreement. We will see if you are truly different from your father or not, and if not, we will find ourselves back on the battlefield."

Bile rose up Ahkin's throat, but he swallowed it back down. He nodded in understanding. *This* battle had been avoided, but there were many more looming on the horizon.

It was a miracle. Ehecatl had agreed to march back to Tollan with the rest of the empire and begin peace negotiations. Ahkin had accomplished what everyone else thought was impossible.

But now the harder challenge. He must find a way to negotiate this agreement and convince his council to send all the gathered armies to the base of the Miquitz Mountains. In four days. Two of which would be spent marching back to Tollan.

The march back was uneventful, though many common-ranked warriors seemed disappointed at the lost opportunity to advance their position by taking captives. The Storm Lord remained quiet and contemplative, occasionally glancing over at Ahkin with an assessing look—as if waiting for signs of betrayal.

Ahkin couldn't really blame him. His own father had tried for decades to appease Ehecatl and failed. He would just have to do better. Whatever it took.

They reached Tollan's volcanic plateau just as day was beginning to fade. The armies camped out around its base while the leaders and generals ascended to the golden palace. News of their attempted peace negotiations had already reached the capital city. The citizens of Tollan, dressed in fine white garments accented with gold, lined the streets in greeting. Children wove between their parents' legs for a better look, while men and women cheered and threw flowers. They certainly believed in Ahkin's ability to negotiate peace.

He could not let them down.

The palace itself was alive with activity. When they entered the receiving hall, the servants carrying him upon their shoulders lowered his golden chair to the floor. Ahkin swept to his feet, intent on beginning negotiations as soon as possible, but Teniza immediately intercepted him.

She stepped in front of him, a fake smile plastered upon her face while her eyes screamed in panic. "Welcome back, my prince. I am sure they informed you about the recent developments for our wedding? The wedding that is taking place *tomorrow morning*." A shrillness seeped into her voice at the end.

"No, it can't. I ordered Atanzah that nothing could take place until the princesses had been captured."

Teniza's eyes went wide, begging him to understand. "*Exactly.*"

A fist seemed to close around his heart. Teniza looked over at her father, who had just disembarked from his own carried throne, and watched the two with keen interest.

Teniza threw her arms around Ahkin's neck. To all the world, they were an engaged couple embracing upon her fiance's return from battle.

"*They've been captured. They have the princesses.*" Teniza whispered harshly in his ear before drawing back. "I'm so glad you have returned safely."

Ahkin's thoughts were swirling around his head like a flock of birds taking flight. "I—um—yes, I am glad to be back. Thank you, Princess Teniza." He lowered his chin in a brief nod. He tried to tell her without words that he understood her meaning. *Thank you for the warning.*

"Ah, my prince," Toani's calm, deep voice called behind him. "Welcome home. You arrived precisely when we were expecting you."

Ahkin forced his face to appear triumphant as he turned to face the head priest. "Thank you, Toani. I trust my messengers relayed the situation to you?"

"Indeed." Toani grabbed him by the arm and began steering him down the hall. "I must say, I am impressed, Ahkin. You managed to get Ehecatl to agree to negotiations when I thought there was no way they would ever do so. How did you manage it?" He tipped his head sideways, his gaze shrewd and calculating.

"I convinced them that I am willing to listen to what they desire and discuss it. The Storm Lord said he agreed because I seem different from my father."

"Hmmm." Toani pursed his withered lips. "I hope he does not think he can manipulate you. You are not your father. That much is clear."

Ahkin's face burned. Toani had not meant it as a compliment the way the lord of Ehecatl had.

"But do not worry, my prince. Your counselors are here to guide you, and we will not let you fail."

Ahkin ripped his arm out of Toani's clawlike grip. "I am so fortunate to have counselors so concerned for my success." He strode purposefully back toward his rooms, leaving Toani glaring after him in the hall.

———

"Well, that went well," Yoli said. She lay on her back in the middle of the temple holding cell, igniting the tip of her finger and studying the flame that flickered there. "All we accomplished was retrieving Itza for them so that she could be sacrificed too."

Yemania flipped back the hair that had fallen into her face. It still smelled faintly of salt from their ocean swim two days before. Mayana's father's warriors had bound them and marched them straight back to the capital, undoing all of their hard work to escape and retrieve Itza.

"You should have just let me fight," Zorrah grumbled, still nursing her wounds in the corner. The injuries to both her body and pride had left her temper shorter than usual.

"Yes, because that was going *so* well for you," Yoli said.

"You don't have to be sarcastic about everything, Yoli," Mayana snapped suddenly. "You don't have to make a joke or laugh about it to

make yourself feel better about how awful life is. Sometimes it's just awful, and that's all there is to it."

The flame on the tip of Yoli's finger went out. Yemania worried for a moment that she would have to jump between them, that Yoli would try to burn Mayana to cinders for her harshness. But to her surprise, Yoli's arms did not light up. Instead, it was as if darkness began to claim her, slinking its way across her body until her eyes were dark pools of emptiness.

Mayana had landed a blow that was far more effective than she'd probably meant. But Yoli's darkness seemed far more dangerous than her flames ever were.

Yemania's heart lurched with pity. "Yoli, she doesn't mean that."

"No, she does. And she's right." Tears fell from the corners of Yoli's eyes, dripping into her dark hair.

Yemania shot a look toward Mayana as if to say, *Can you help me fix this, please?*

But Mayana remained curled in on herself, the darkness around Yoli seeming to cling to Mayana as well.

It was a darkness Yemania knew too well. Hopelessness. Its depths were truly endless, if you let yourself fall in.

"Itza?" She turned to the princess of storms, who remained prostrated across the damp stone floor. She mumbled prayers and seemed unmindful that the rest of them were even there. "Um, never mind," Yemania said. She'd just have to deal with this alone.

"Yoli—" she started to say.

"Do you know why I love death so much?" Yoli said suddenly, staring blankly at the ceiling.

Yemania chewed her lip. "Um, no, not really."

"Because you can't escape it. It's always there, hovering, just waiting for each and every one of us. Once you've been marked by it, there is no escape. It's a beautiful thing, really. That everything we have here on this earth is temporary. While everyone else would rather pretend it doesn't exist, frantically try to protect themselves from it with whatever rituals they can, there's a kind of peace in just accepting it. Embracing it. It makes you that much more appreciative for what you do have, instead of always being so afraid to lose it."

Yemania had never really thought about it like that before. When she thought she was going to be sacrificed the first time, she'd been so afraid. Was she as afraid this time? She didn't know the answer to that. Maybe part of her hoped there was still a way they could escape.

"You've lost someone, haven't you?" Yemania asked her.

Yoli blinked. "My younger brother."

Yemania flinched. She, too, knew what it felt like to lose a brother.

"He was just a child, but he was so sick," Yoli whispered. "We tried so hard to save him, but even the healers could do nothing in the end."

Mayana lifted her head from her knees. "I'm so sorry," she said. "I had no idea."

Yoli shrugged, though Yemania could still see the sheen reflecting off her eyes. "That's the will of the gods sometimes, though, isn't it? You can beg for them to take your life instead, plead that he's far too young, but sometimes there is nothing you can do about it. Not even healers can heal everything."

"I can tell you loved your brother very much," Yemania said, suddenly understanding why Yoli had held such animosity toward her when they first met. She struggled to forgive the healers who couldn't save him.

"I did. I—I used to love to make him laugh. Even that last time, I—" Yoli's voice cracked, and she turned her face away from them.

Yemania scrambled forward and lifted Yoli off the floor. Mayana was beside her in a heartbeat. They both embraced Yoli as she tried to fight back her grief. Itza even lifted herself from her prayers to rub Yoli's back reassuringly.

"I'm sorry. I never should have said that," Mayana said, tears streaming down her cheeks. "Maybe we could all use a little humor right now."

Another hand dropped onto Yoli's shoulder. Yemania looked up and almost gasped in surprise.

Zorrah had left her corner and joined them. Though she still kept her distance, her stretched-out hand spoke volumes. She had lost a sister. They had all lost someone. But maybe that was part of the beauty of sharing your pain instead of keeping it buried under humor, or shows of strength. By exposing it, you could discover that other people were in pain too. And sometimes, Yemania realized, learning you aren't alone heals almost as well as the blood of a healer.

"I first want to thank Ehecatl for being here." Ahkin addressed the gathered council members and lords. "I know the hour is late and that it is with great risk that they even agreed to these negotiations."

The lord of Ehecatl glared around the stone table as if he did not trust a single pair of eyes he met.

Ahkin cleared his throat and continued. "The first matter I would like to address is Ehecatl's demands."

The lord of storms rose from his cushion and splayed his hands across the stone. "Ehecatl has thought long and hard about what we are willing to concede in order to reach an agreement of peace. As long as we feel that Tollan is also willing to make concessions."

Toani tittered like an angry sparrow. "Concessions? What kind of concessions, Storm Lord? You are aware that you are coming from the position of weakness—"

But Ahkin lifted a hand to silence him. "What concession is Ehecatl willing to make?"

"We are willing to remain part of the empire. We are even willing to perform our quarterly sacrifices to ensure the empire is protected from storms."

There was a rumble of appreciation. It seemed that it was a new proposal Ehecatl had never put forth before.

Ahkin smiled, feeling encouraged. "That is—and I am sure our head priest will agree—the most important agreement of all." Not that he personally cared about whether or not they did their quarterly blood sacrifices. He knew it all to be a ruse. But Toani would never budge on an agreement that did not involve the quarterly rituals, not when his power hinged so closely upon them.

"But we will not engage in animal sacrifice or human sacrifice of any kind. Starting with allowing our daughter's life to become a so-called blessing for the emperor's reign."

Toani leapt to his feet. "You demand that the selection ritual not take place?"

Ahkin couldn't help but notice that the ears of the various lords perked up. Perhaps Ehecatl was not the only city reluctant to lose a royal daughter. He also rose to his feet. "Toani, I am sure you would agree that the quarterly rituals are the most important. Forgoing the selection ritual risks only my reign, not the fate of the entire empire."

"The entire empire depends on you, my prince. *Remember?*" Toani growled through gritted teeth.

"Agreed. Which is why if we can rescue Metzi from the Miquitz, we will have another option to raise the sun until I sire children."

One of the judges leaned forward. "Princess Metzi has been found?"

Ahkin straightened his shoulders. "My spies tell me she is being held captive in the Miquitz Mountains. I have sent Ochix along with a small group of trusted soldiers to extract her. While he is there, he will get as many of the Miquitz army as he can to defect from his father and follow him instead. This will likely ignite the ire of the Death Priest, so we will need to be prepared to defend should he decide to attack."

"And did you get authorization for such an assignment?" Quauhtli scoffed.

"As I am sure Toani informed the council, Ochix desires to over-throw his father's rule and take the throne of Miquitz. In exchange for Chicome support in his campaign, he has agreed to join the empire. The lost brother in our divine family finally come home."

Toani smiled like a greedy child hoarding treats. But the head judge's toad-like eyes narrowed. "And how have we solidified this alliance?"

Ahkin had a sudden idea, and hoped very much that Ochix didn't mind what he was about to do. "A marriage alliance."

An explosion of buzzing broke out amongst the council members.

"Do you intend to reinstate his engagement to Metzi?" the judge asked.

"No," Ahkin said, fighting back his own smile. "And this would go along with what Ehecatl is suggesting as well. Instead of sacrificing the princesses, I would propose that one of them be used for the higher calling of ensuring peace in the empire. Ochix has already expressed interest in Yemania of Pahtia. If the lord of Pahtia agrees, we can solidify the alliance with their marriage."

The lord of Pahtia shrugged his muscled shoulders. "If she can be of use to someone, then, by all means, take her."

Fury rose in Ahkin's throat to hear Yemania's father talk about her in such a way. But then again, the man had raised Coatl. And the stories he had heard from his former friend were not pleasant ones.

Ahkin plowed ahead. "If we agree, then we forgo the selection ritual and march for Miquitz immediately to secure my sister and Ochix's throne."

The buzzing of voices seemed optimistic, meaning they had not yet turned against him. Hope began to glow inside his chest like a fresh ember, warm and comforting. Toani seemed to be considering it. The old man knew the selection ritual wasn't really necessary. Ahkin could practically see him weighing the costs and benefits of agreeing to Ehecatl's proposal. Did he give up on one unnecessary ritual to gain control over Ehecatl and Omitl all at once? *Come on*, Ahkin silently pleaded with him. *One concession to get more power than you even hoped for. Just one . . .*

"It is possible," Toani finally said, stroking his chin thoughtfully. "I will consult the codex about the consequences associated with failing to uphold the selection ritual."

Ahkin clenched his fist in victory beneath the table. Toani would make up whatever he needed in order to support his agenda. And no one would dare question him.

But when his gaze met that of the lord of Ehecatl, he did not see pride or excitement. He saw distrust shadowed with . . . disappointment? The warmth inside his chest dissipated.

"Is there something else, Lord of Storms?" Ahkin asked.

"You are willing to arrange a marriage to secure your alliance with Miquitz," the Storm Lord said thoughtfully. "I wonder if you are willing to make such an agreement with Ehecatl?"

Ahkin's stomach squirmed, as if a part of him knew he would not like what he was about to hear.

"That depends," he said carefully.

"My son has taken a liking to one of the other noble daughters, and if the selection ritual is indeed conceded to reach our peace agreement, I would like to arrange their marriage to secure our alliance. Perhaps it could even undo some of the insults we suffered at Metzi's broken engagement to my son." He observed Ahkin carefully.

Ahkin's palms began to sweat. He rubbed them absently on the wrap around his waist.

"Of course such an arrangement could be made. Which of the daughters did you have in mind?" Toani's lip was already curling as if he, too, could sense the coming danger.

"Mayana of Atl," the Storm Lord answered. "My son wishes to marry the daughter of water."

Ahkin's breath left him as though he'd been kicked in the gut. Surely the man must know, as everyone else in the empire did by now, that Ahkin loved Mayana. A *concession*, the Storm Lord had asked for. A sacrifice for a sacrifice. But how could he ask for Mayana's hand? The one thing in all the world Ahkin would not concede.

Toani's curling lip broke into a triumphant smile. "What an *excellent* suggestion. Wouldn't you agree, my prince? Such an easy price to pay for peace? To achieve what your father never could?"

The Storm Lord watched him, eyes seeming to bore into his very soul. Questions flowed wordlessly between them. *Are you willing to do whatever it takes to secure this peace? Are you willing to give up the woman you love to save your empire?*

Toani grinned, taunting. "You've gotten everything you've hoped for, my prince. You will marry the daughter of Millacatl, you will earn Ehecatl's allegiance, and we will move our united armies first thing tomorrow morning to secure your sister and defeat our enemies in the mountains once and for all. History will remember you for your accomplishments—and you aren't even officially crowned yet."

Ahkin floundered for reasons to object. "But what does the lord of Atl think of sending his daughter to Ehecatl? Surely he—"

"Send her," the lord of Atl barked. "It sounds like the perfect solution to all of this."

"I need a moment," Ahkin said, heat rising up his neck, dizziness threatening to knock him off his feet. "Let's break and reconvene in two hours. I have not eaten or rested since our return, and I'm beginning to feel the exhaustion."

"Of course, my prince." Toani laid a loving hand on his shoulder. "You get some food and some fresh air. I will make arrangements for the princesses to be brought back to the palace to be reunited with their families. After your wedding and coronation ceremonies are complete tomorrow, we will send the armies to Miquitz." Then he lowered his voice so that only Ahkin could hear. "Say your goodbyes to her now. I'll even send her to your rooms if you wish. But we both know the only way to move forward. Give yourself a moment to grieve and then shoulder the responsibility as your father would."

Ahkin nodded, not trusting himself to speak. Before he decided anything, he had to speak to Mayana.

———

The stone across their prison had been rolled away. But instead of the princesses being dragged to a sacrificial altar, they were escorted back into the palace itself. Yemania gave Mayana a bewildered look of concern before the guard shoved her down a hall toward the residential guest rooms. Mayana, however, was led up the stairs toward the emperor's personal residences. She now stood outside the beaded curtain, hovering on the verge of indecision. Was Ahkin really on the other side, or was this some kind of trap? Should she make a run for it?

The low rumble of Ahkin's voice sounded from within, and Mayana's heart lightened. He was inside. He could finally explain everything, *everything* that had happened since he retook his throne. She threw the curtain aside and rushed in. She barely glimpsed the expansive room, walls decorated with images of the gods, bed mat overflowing with the most luxurious-looking furs she'd ever seen, before Ahkin swept her into his arms.

He held her so tightly it was as if he wanted to take her soul into his own. He tipped her head back and found her lips, devouring them like a starving man set before a feast. She devoured him back, his response burning away every doubt and fear she'd let creep into her heart since their separation. Tears streamed down her cheeks, lacing their kiss with the taste of salt. She wanted to relax into him, to know to the depths of her being that everything was finally going to be okay. But the memory of her father's disgusted face and the throbbing of her bruised cheek hovered over her. *No one cares what you think. You are fighting a war that cannot be won.* Like a vulture circling a dying fawn, her thoughts continued their descent. Toani setting her up to fail with the dog sacrifice just as Ahkin wanted to announce their engagement. *I cannot allow such a demon to lead this empire by your side.* The lord of Millacatl insulting her in front of his entire city-state. *You cannot honestly think the council, let alone the empire, would support your marriage to the disgraced daughter of Atl? What kind of empress would she be?*

She broke their kiss, pulling back suddenly and gasping for air. Ahkin, however, leaned back in and rested his forehead against hers. She tried with every last shred of hope still in her heart to fight back against the darkness clouding her mind. She needed to understand, to hear from him that all her worries were unfounded . . .

They cascaded out of her mouth. "What happened? We were

arrested and told the selection ritual was taking place again, that you were going to marry Teniza, then you attacked Ehecatl—"

Ahkin wrapped his arms around her again. "I know. I know. I'm so sorry. None of this was supposed to happen."

Mayana slipped her arms around his waist and turned her cheek to rest against the warmth of his chest. His heartbeat thudded beneath her ear. "What happened?" she asked again, shuddering as she drew in a calming breath.

Ahkin sighed, his exhaustion making his body slump into hers. "I tried to stand up to the council, to tell them everything that happened to us in Xibalba. What the Mother goddess told us about the rituals."

Mayana stiffened. Obviously that conversation had not gone well. "What did they do?"

Ahkin laughed and hugged her tighter. "Toani had Ochix imprisoned, and then he declared me insane in front of all my advisors. I was imprisoned in my rooms. For my 'own protection,' of course."

Mayana gasped. "I'm surprised, but at the same time, I know I shouldn't be."

"Toani then ordered you all arrested in order to continue with the selection ritual and the war with Ehecatl."

"How did you get out of your rooms?"

Ahkin looked toward the doorway to make sure no one was listening. Then he dropped his voice to a whisper in her ear. "Toani told me the truth about everything. My ancestor created the rituals to ensure his power and keep the city-states united beneath him. Their purpose is to hold everyone hostage to fear. You were right all along: the original codices were altered and added to by the priesthood. All on my ancestor's orders. My blood isn't even needed to raise the sun."

Mayana's eyes went wide. "But I've seen you control it."

"I can control it, yes, but the sun would rise regardless. Just as I imagine our cities would not be flooded if your family stopped their quarterly sacrifices."

Rage burned hot within her belly as she remembered the endless fights with her family about her refusal to sacrifice her own blood. The lectures she'd endured from her father about her selfishness risking the lives of the entire empire. After all, it wasn't *her* selfishness; it was the selfishness of Ahkin's ancestor and the priesthood. They'd taken what was supposed to be a beautiful relationship with the gods and turned it into a system that manipulated people through their greatest fears.

"Toani does believe he is protecting us in his own way. He thinks the world ended because of our fighting among ourselves and forcing the gods to take sides. So I made Toani think I understood, or at least that I was willing to work with him. I've been secretly trying to maneuver my own agenda since. He's been watching me like a hawk, though, so I'm not sure he trusts me entirely."

Mayana scrunched her nose. "So you went along with what he wanted? Marched to Ehecatl to force them to submit?"

"No, no, no!" Ahkin said. "I went along, yes, but I sent Ochix to Omitl to rescue Metzi and try to get some of his own people to turn against Tzom while I handled Ehecatl. It was always my intention to negotiate peace, to meet Ochix at the base of the mountains with a united army ready to fight against either his father or the star demons. Or both, I guess. Then the storm prince was captured, and I—"

"Patlani was captured? Is he okay?" Mayana squeaked.

"He's . . . fine." Ahkin looked at her with his eyebrows pulled together. "I helped him escape to earn goodwill with his father. It's the whole reason they agreed to come here and negotiate. I . . . just didn't realize you cared so much."

"I don't," Mayana said quickly. She dropped her gaze to her feet, her stomach burning with shame. She had no real feelings for Patlani, but she was lying to herself if she said she wasn't curious. "He helped us escape and was kind to us. That's all."

"How did you end up back in Tollan, then? Teniza said you were all captured."

Mayana flinched at the memory. "We jumped into the sea to escape and washed up on a beach where my father was camped."

Ahkin closed his eyes, as if her words caused him pain. "So you were captured by your father and his men."

Mayana's answer came out barely louder than a whisper. "Yes." Her eyes began to burn. "I failed."

"You haven't failed." Ahkin's hand came up to rest against her cheek. "I'm the one who has failed you."

Mayana pressed his hand harder with her own. "No, you haven't. You stopped the war. You got Ehecatl to agree to peace negotiations. You're going to march a united army to stop the world from ending."

Ahkin dropped his chin. Now he was the one who refused to meet her gaze. "They haven't agreed to peace just yet."

"I'm sure they will. You are willing to give them the religious freedom they want, aren't you?"

Ahkin began to worry his lower lip between his teeth. "It's not their religious freedom I'm going to refuse."

Mayana tilted her head, not understanding. "What else do they want?"

Ahkin's gaze captured hers. "Something I don't think I'm willing to give up."

"And that would be—?" His sudden nervousness seeped into her like something contagious.

Ahkin took a step back. He rubbed his hand nervously along the back of his neck. "They agreed to peace under the condition that we end the selection ritual and—" He cut himself off, turning away from her.

She was going to kill him if he made her wait in suspense a moment longer. "Ahkin, tell me, or I swear to the gods I'm going to drown you with my necklace."

He whirled back around, his hands clenched into fists at his side. "They demanded I secure the alliance with a marriage. *Your* marriage. To the storm prince."

CHAPTER

41

Mayana blinked at him. Then blinked again. She was furious. Ahkin just knew it. So enraged that she couldn't even find the words to scold him as he deserved. Ahkin waited, watching every micromovement of her face for some indication of what her response would be.

Her lips pursed. He could almost see the thoughts swirling around in her head, but he couldn't tell what they meant. Finally, he couldn't handle her silence a moment longer.

"I won't do it. I don't care what it costs us. I can't lose you." He knew as he said the words that they were true. He couldn't lose her. Perhaps that made *him* selfish. He had everything he needed right at the tips of his fingers, waiting for him just to grab and take hold. Peace with Ehecatl. The selection ritual is called off. A way to unify his army and save his empire from destruction.

But at the cost of losing her to Patlani? To watch as she married someone else . . . No. He couldn't even stomach the idea.

"They are willing to cancel the selection ritual?" she asked carefully.

"Yes, the council has agreed. The ritual would be canceled so that Yemania can marry Ochix and secure our alliance with Omitl, and then you'd supposedly marry Patlani to secure Ehecatl."

"Toani agreed to cancel it?" Her tone sounded low, hollow, as if there were no life inside her. "None of the other princesses would die?"

"I don't think he wanted to, but the temptation of securing Ehecatl *and* Omitl as part of the empire was too much for even him to let pass. And yes, the other princesses would be spared."

"Hmmm." Mayana kicked at the ground, shuffling her sandaled foot against the stone.

"But it doesn't matter," Ahkin assured her. "We can find another way to save them. And the empire."

"What other way, Ahkin?" She lifted her shimmering eyes to his. "What other way is there?"

Ahkin's breath rushed out of his lungs. "I—I don't know yet. But I will think of a way. I just need time."

"There is no time," Mayana said. The dead hollowness to her voice was beginning to make his palms sweat again. Defeat was already hanging heavy on her slumped shoulders. "The eclipse starts in two days. Everyone is here. And there is a perfect solution to everything staring us in the face."

"Everything except allowing us to be together!"

Mayana turned away from him, pacing toward the open window that looked out over all of Tollan. Though it was evening and the stars winked against the endless expanse of darkness above them, the city itself was still bathed in light, the many torches reflecting off the golden surfaces below. Ahkin carefully moved to stand beside her.

"You can't honestly be thinking of saying yes," he said.

Mayana shrugged a shoulder. "Why not?"

He grabbed her shoulder and forced her to face him. "Because I love you! You love me! We are each other's dualities! We are destined to rule the empire together, side by side!"

Mayana gave a laugh as empty as her tone. "Ahkin, your council, the entire empire, would never let that happen."

"It's not up to them. It's up to me!"

"Is it, though? Is it really up to you? It doesn't seem to me like it is. Ahkin, I'm *tired*. I'm sick of fighting to change something that refuses to change." She turned back to the window. Then, she crossed her arms over her chest as though her heart ached. "We are fighting a war that cannot be won."

He couldn't believe what he was hearing. Mayana had always been a fighter, someone who refused to submit her will to the wishes of others. Yet here she was, saying she didn't want to fight anymore. "Because we haven't been able to fight together! Fight with me! Change it with me! We can burn the whole thing down together." He reached out a hand to her in invitation.

But she refused to take it.

Ahkin dropped his shaking hand back to his side. "You can't mean this. The Mayana I know would never give in like this."

"But maybe it's not giving in. Maybe it's just choosing another path that makes more sense. I've been to Ehecatl. I saw what they were like. Ahkin, I've never in my life been somewhere I felt so accepted. They appreciated me. They saw me for who I am and didn't shame me for it."

"Patlani did, you mean." Ahkin's voice was tight.

"So what if he did? Ahkin, I may not love him, but who knows! I could someday. I could be happy there. Away from Toani, away from Tollan, away from all of this!"

"Away from me!" Ahkin shouted. He didn't know when his temper had snapped. "You aren't just giving up on the system. You are giving up on *me*."

Mayana drew in a shuddering breath. "Maybe I am."

She could have stolen his dagger and shoved it through his chest and done less damage. The pressure he felt crushed the very air from his lungs. He could fight for her, defy the council, the empire, the gods themselves, but if she wasn't willing to fight by his side . . . then he couldn't force her. He couldn't make her fight a battle she didn't want to fight. He wasn't sure there could ever be a pain strong enough to drop him to his knees, but this nearly did. He nearly begged her not to do what she was doing.

"Th-this—" Ahkin cleared his throat, fighting back whatever emotion was clawing up from his chest. "This is really what you want?"

Mayana rubbed her hands up and down her arms for a moment, staring out across the shining golden city of Tollan. "Yes. I think it is."

Ahkin sniffed and used every ounce of strength he had left to choke back the feeling rising in his throat. "Fine," he said coolly. "Fine.

I will notify the council of our decision. Tomorrow morning at sunrise, I will marry Teniza. And then you can go to Ehecatl and marry the storm prince."

"Fine," she said.

The pain of looking at her, the memories that flooded through his head of their tender moments together, the triumph of surviving literal hells together, was too much to bear. He turned away and headed for the door.

And then he left her there—staring out the window and holding a piece of his heart he knew he'd never get back.

———

Yemania searched every guest room she could find, but Mayana was nowhere. She patted her hands nervously against her thighs. Think. Think. *Think.* Where could she be?

The idea burst through her thoughts like a sunbeam through a cloud bank. Of course! Where had Mayana always gone when she was upset? The pleasure pools in the gardens.

Yemania lifted the hem of her dress, a clean one in her native red that had been waiting for her in her rooms, and sprinted through the labyrinthine halls. Her dress hadn't been the only thing waiting for her either. The bag containing the jade bones of Quetzalcoatl had been sitting upon her bed mat. She didn't know how they'd gotten there, but the black-and-white owl feather she'd found resting beside it told her *who* had brought them. She could almost hear the Mother's voice whisper on the wind, scolding her to *stop losing these.* Although she'd been relieved to see them, her first reaction had been panic. Where was Mayana? Why were the bones given to her and not the daughter of water?

Yemania's intuition flickered with unease. Something was not right.

She flinched at the first group of Eagle warriors she saw pass by, but they did not try to stop her or chase her down. Something had recently shifted in the world around them, and Yemania needed to find her friend. And there was still a much more pressing issue. She now had the bones bouncing along against her hip, but they only had two days to resurrect Quetzalcoatl. If they didn't leave soon, they would never make it before the eclipse. At least they were much closer now than they had been in Ehecatl.

She skidded to a stop at the entrance to the pleasure gardens. The land behind the palace sloped in gentle terraces to the edge of the plateau itself. Paths of multicolored painted stones wound their way through the fruit orchards, and jungle blooms released their tantalizing scent into the night air. The sound of bubbling streams and gentle waterfalls mingled with the chattering of night animals hiding in the foliage. Clouds obscured the nearly full moon, adding an extra layer of darkness to the heavy, humid night.

Yemania searched along the paths, checking each of the pleasure pools for signs of the daughter of water. Even the steam bath at the garden's center was empty. Finally, tucked along the edge on an out-cropping of rock, she found her.

Mayana was curled in on herself, hugging her knees so tightly against her chest it was as if she was afraid she'd fall to pieces if she let go.

Yemania delicately sat down and wrapped an arm around her friend's shoulders. "What's going on? Are you okay?"

Mayana did not answer. She only shook her head.

"Where did they take you? They took me back to a guest room. None of this makes sense. Why would they capture us, throw us into the holding cell, and then change their minds and treat us like royal guests again?"

Mayana turned her head so that her cheek rested on the top of her knees. "Because the selection ritual is over. They aren't going to sacrifice us anymore."

Yemania gasped and pressed a hand against her heart. "That's good news, isn't it? Why do you still look so crushed?"

"Because in order to secure peace with Ehecatl they made an agreement. An agreement that ends the ritual for now . . . among other things."

Yemania chewed the inside of her cheek. "What other things?"

"I should have known," Mayana said suddenly. "I should have

known from the start that there was no way Ahkin and I could ever be together. The council was never going to allow it. So he will marry Teniza come sunrise, and I am now promised to Patlani of Ehecatl."

"No, that's not right. Ahkin loves you!" Yemania cried.

"It doesn't matter who he loves, Yemania! You all keep saying that like I don't know. I *know* he loves me. But in the end, it doesn't mean anything. He has to do what's best for the empire. And that includes sending me away."

Yemania frowned. She remembered Ahkin's anxious pacing on the riverbed while they waited for Ochix and Mayana to return from the Miquitz palace. She couldn't imagine Ahkin ever choosing to let Mayana go. "Is he sending you away, or are you sending yourself away?"

"Is there a difference?"

"Yes! Of course there's a difference! Mayana, he's not the one choosing someone else. You are! Do you want to go to Ehecatl?"

"I could be happy there. Truly be myself for once. I wouldn't have to fight to change a world that refuses to change."

Yemania rose to her feet. "So you're giving up?"

Mayana shrugged. And Yemania's heart cracked in half as she realized that hopelessness had finally claimed her friend completely.

"And what about the bones? You are just going to give up on them too?" Yemania lifted the bag at her side for emphasis. "What about our mission from the Mother? We still need to resurrect Quetzalcoatl!"

Mayana's voice cracked as she threw a hand toward the distant horizon. "Then you go. You are the healer. Your blood is needed, not mine. You and Itza take them. I'll stay here to do my part. I will marry Patlani to keep Ehecatl in their alliance. That is the role I am meant to play."

"No," Yemania said, her voice going cold. "That is the role you are *choosing* to play. And if you refuse to do what is needed, then I will have to do it for you. Is that what you want?"

Mayana just curled back into a ball and did not answer. Although, Yemania realized with aching clarity, Mayana's silence was her answer.

Ochix had been traveling for days with the dullest companions he could have ever imagined. First, having to travel all the way to the mountains, then to sneak a group of Chicome warriors into his father's city, all without any real interaction beyond grunted orders and responses from his fellows . . . he was about to start throwing berries at someone's head again.

Not that he expected the Jaguar warriors to be particularly entertaining, but it would have been nice to be treated with some modicum of respect. Especially on an assignment he was supposed to be *leading*. Instead, Ochix continually felt like an unwanted tagalong, a fly buzzing around the ears of the Chicome that they kept trying to swat away.

At the edge of the city, they'd found an abandoned stone structure, its woven roof on the verge of collapse. "I need you to wait here and stay hidden," he told them. "I am going to sneak into the temple and see if I can find out where Metzi is being kept. Once I get a better idea of what we're facing, I'll come back here, and we can figure out a plan."

His pronouncement was rewarded with a series of noncommittal grunts.

"Lovely talking with you all, as usual." Ochix rolled his eyes and slipped back outside.

After weeks of living in enemy territory, he was finally able to take a breath here in his home. He knew his city better than anyone, from the steep mountainside terraces to its curving stone streets squeezed between buildings and its endless alleyways of steps. Omitl was wedged between rising mountain peaks on all sides, perched upon its own hilltop like a fat bird perched upon a branch. Above the city itself loomed his father's palace and temple, the tiered stone pyramid framed with the waterfall backdrop that cascaded behind it. Ochix prayed that their escape this time would not involve another plunge. He'd really seen enough of that waterfall to last him a lifetime.

He kept a steady supply of blood collecting in the palm of his hand and possessed the soul of anyone who came too close. Ahkin's gift of invisibility would have been a handy tool to sneak into the palace, but his own gifting was useful enough.

He forced the guards at one of the side entrances to turn their backs as he walked inside. He was tempted to make one guard he never cared for pick his nose, but then decided against it, figuring that would fit under the "abuse of power" category. He had a purpose here, and that was not it.

It felt strange walking into the palace he'd known his whole life, not as the emperor he always thought he would be, but as a fugitive.

As a traitor.

The word tasted bitter on his tongue. Was he a traitor? Ahkin had promised his priest that Omitl would submit to the Chicome, but then he promised Ochix he would expect no such thing. It was supposedly a ruse, an excuse to release Ochix and march their armies to the base of the mountains. Ochix trusted Ahkin to keep his word, but not the men *around* Ahkin. Had he made a deal that would lose Miquitz their independence like Ehecatl?

Well, at least their independence wouldn't matter if everyone fell to the jaws of ravenous star demons, so there was always that.

He made his way deep beneath the palace and into the halls of the holding chambers. The lack of guards was not encouraging, but he knew he had to check anyway. He popped his head into each of the cells, but no sun princesses were lounging upon the rank stone floors.

His hand raked through his long hair in frustration. Where were they keeping her? This was the only place they kept prisoners . . . unless . . .

Unless she *wasn't* a prisoner.

As he made his way up the steps to the residential palace halls, the risk of seeing his father rose with each floor. He finally rounded another corner and saw a pair of guards positioned outside one of the guest rooms. That had to be it. He reached out with his divine senses, feeling for the life force of the guards beside the door. Once he sensed their spirits, he tightened his fist and grabbed hold. He could see their eyes misting over even from this distance.

Walk, he told them. *You're hungry and have just realized you'd like to get something to eat.*

The guards obeyed without hesitation, turning on their heels and marching out of sight. Ochix looked around to make sure there was no one else before he sprinted the length of the hall. He slipped inside, his bone-handled knife ready in his hand.

Metzi was there—the most pampered-looking prisoner he'd ever seen. She lay stretched across a bed mat overflowing with feather-filled pillows, dropping berries one by one into her open mouth. Her room was comfortably furnished, and the open window exposed a beautiful view of the moonlit valley just beyond the veil of the waterfall.

"Well, don't you look comfortable?" Ochix said, crossing his arms across his chest.

Metzi scrambled to her feet, sending the bowl of berries rolling across the floor. "Ochix? What the hells are you doing here?"

"Um, saving you?"

Metzi frowned. "Saving me? From what?"

Ochix let his gaze wander around the room. "I'm starting to ask myself that question. Why aren't you in one of the holding cells?"

Metzi trilled a laugh. "Because I am a guest here, prince of death. I think the better question is, why are *you* here? Last I heard, Ahkin adopted you as his little pet and had you eating out of the hand of the Chicome now."

"It's a generous hand, I will admit. Certainly more so than the hand that stabbed me in the stomach. Speaking of which, have you had the lovely pleasure of meeting my father?"

Metzi leaned around him to see where her guards had gone. Her eyes narrowed when they were nowhere to be found. "I did have the pleasure of meeting him, yes. We are in agreement about our next steps moving forward."

Ochix shook his head, trying to dispel the confusion buzzing through his thoughts. "You are in agreement about you dying to unleash the Obsidian Butterfly and her star demons? Can't say I ever saw you as the suicidal type."

Metzi scoffed and placed her hands on her elegantly curved hips. "Ahkin's blood will summon them, not mine. The Obsidian Butterfly has a plan, and I—"

"Ahkin is on the other side of the empire trying to end the war that you started with Ehecatl." Ochix flung a hand toward the window.

"*I* did not start the war with Ehecatl! My father tried to sell me to keep them appeased. Ahkin refused to bend on the deal, even after our father died. I told them I wouldn't do it. The war is *their* fault, not mine."

He didn't have time to argue with her. Ochix gritted his teeth and reached for her arm. "We can play the blame game on the road, but we need to get you out of here before your blood paints my father's altar."

Metzi yanked her arm back. "I'm not going with you. I am staying here."

"Why?" Ochix threw his hands into the air. "You can't honestly trust my father? The man is insane, Princess. Has he shown you all the creepy little drawings he does on the walls of his rooms? Or have you watched him stab a servant just for bothering him during his manic little study sessions?" He pointed to the scar across his abdomen. "Or seen him stab his own son for daring to question him?"

"It doesn't matter," Metzi said, smoothing out her dress. "He's not part of my plan anyway. When I am empress of the Miquitz, he will be disposed of."

Ochix let out a disbelieving laugh. "Is that what *she* promised you? That you would become empress of the Miquitz Empire?"

Metzi tilted her chin into the air. "She promised me more power than I could ever imagine. The power to crush my enemies and finally take what I deserve."

Ochix laughed again. "They are going to *kill* you! Do you understand that? He's making you comfortable and letting you think—"

Metzi took out her knife and pointed it at Ochix's chest. "I am not going anywhere with you, death prince. I am demanding the respect I should have had from the beginning. They didn't value me, so now they will fear me."

"I'm not trying to keep you away from power, Metzi. I'm trying to keep you and a lot of other people away from death." He tried to grab her arm again. She slashed down with her knife and drew a shallow cut across his chest.

Ochix hissed, his hand flying to cover the wound. "Gods, Metzi! Are you going to make me possess you and force you out? Because I will. I'm not going to let you die no matter how determined you seem to be to make that happen!"

"Go ahead! Take away my will! Take it away like everyone else has!" she screamed at him. Anguish and rage hovered around her like an aura. He hesitated. He didn't want to take her will away from her, but she was being an utter fool. She refused to see the danger that she—all of them, really—were in because of the Obsidian Butterfly. He didn't want to, but he knew it was essential for the greater good.

His blood was already exposed, both on his hand and in the fresh cut on his chest. "I'm sorry," he said. And he truly meant it. The last thing he wanted was to take her will away from her. He reached out a hand, stretching out with his divine senses until they brushed up against the glow that was her life force. Gritting his teeth, he closed his fist as he tried to clamp down upon it, to force his will over hers. Her eyes began to cloud with mist, but then she screamed again. She grabbed at her head, her own teeth gritted in concentration. Her dark eyes cleared, and the grip he had on her life force recoiled as if he'd been burned.

Ochix gasped, stumbling backward. She glared at him, her chest heaving, a triumphant smile growing on her lips. "Go ahead, death prince, bend me to your will. What are you waiting for?"

Ochix felt his eyes go wide with wonder. What the hells? He'd never met a will like hers. Ever. The strength, the power it possessed. There was no bending it. There was no forcing her to follow him. "I . . . I can't. Your will is too strong."

Her face broke into a grin that raised the hairs on the back of Ochix's neck. "Then I will repeat myself one more time. I am not going with you, prince of death. I am staying here."

There was shouting coming from the floor above them, the sound of thundering feet. Someone must have heard her scream and summoned more guards. He had to get out of here before he was captured. Now. He ran to the door, but turned back for one last warning.

"I won't leave without you, Metzi," he told her. "I will be back."

Yemania was furious. She knew Mayana was stronger than she was acting. She was tempted to grab Mayana by the shoulders and shake her until she realized the truth.

But there wasn't any more time. The Mother had left the bag of bones on *her* bed for a reason. *You have an important role to play*, the Mother goddess had told her beneath the temple, and Yemania knew from the top of her head to the tips of her toes that this was her responsibility now. This was the role she was meant to play.

She always thought she had to step aside and let Mayana be the hero, let Mayana be the one to save the empire. But the challenge was being placed before her, and if Mayana would not or could not rise to meet it, then she would have to. Her heart ached for Ochix and the dangerous mission he was on, wishing he could stand beside her as she made this choice. But he was doing what needed to be done, and she would do the same.

She marched into the guest room where Itza was staying and was unsurprised to find her on her knees in prayer. "Are you ready to put those prayers to the test?"

Itza rose slowly to her feet, turning to Yemania with a grin pulling at the corner of her lips. "Just asking for a quick blessing before we depart."

"Excellent. When do we leave?" Yoli's voice said from the doorway behind them. "I saw you come in here and thought I'd follow. You looked pretty determined about something."

Yemania beamed. "Then let's go. Together. They aren't guarding us like they were, but I still doubt they will let us just walk out of the city."

"If they try to stop you, then they will answer to me." Zorrah's voice came from the hallway behind Yoli.

"Oh, I invited her too. I hope that's okay." Yoli jerked a thumb toward Zorrah with a teasing smile.

Tears of joy burned behind Yemania's eyes. "I don't think we could do this without you both."

"Where's Mayana?" Zorrah asked, her catlike eyes darting around the room as though expecting Mayana to announce herself too.

Yemania swallowed hard. "She has to stay and . . . help negotiate peace with Ahkin." She wouldn't give up hope on her friend just yet. Mayana still had time to change her mind. "She asked me to take the bones instead. They are preparing to march the armies to the base of the Miquitz Mountains."

Zorrah narrowed her eyes slightly, but she nodded in understanding. "Then we leave now. The Caves of Creation are not as far from Tollan as they were from Ehecatl."

Yoli looked out the window to where the night sky obscured the appearance of the moon. "This is going to be cutting it close. We might not make it in time before the eclipse begins."

Zorrah straightened her jaguar cloak across her shoulders. "I will get us there in time. Or I will die trying."

———

"Oh, Ahkin, your mother would be so proud," Atanzah said, looking at his reflection in the polished obsidian mirror. She beamed with the pride of a mother as she adjusted the crown of yellow and white feathers upon his head.

Ahkin touched the golden carved chestpiece hanging across his shoulders. It was still heavy, so heavy he wanted to rip it off and toss it away. But he supposed, like everything else that felt like it was suffocating him, he had to bear the burden as best he could.

"I never thought this day would come." Atanzah wiped a tear from the corner of her eye. But then she twittered, "Literally. First, I thought you died, and then when you came back, I thought Teniza's demands would never let us get here." She drew in a calming breath. "But here we are. Where you were always destined to be."

Ahkin's gaze dropped to the golden straps of his sandals. "Thank you, Atanzah. Even if my mother cannot be here, I'm glad that you are."

"Oh, my dear boy." She patted his cheek lovingly. "You look as handsome as your father did on his wedding day."

Ahkin clenched his jaw and did not speak.

The sky outside the window was still as dark as charred wood. He tried not to think about where Mayana was or what she was thinking right now. Would she come to his wedding ceremony? Or would she avoid it altogether? It didn't matter. She'd be attending her own in Ehecatl soon enough.

The servants were already in a frenzy, preparing for the morning feast that would take place after the ceremony. The scent of roasting meat with peppers hung as heavy as the anticipation in the air. Prince Ahkin had finally chosen a wife. The entire empire wanted to celebrate.

Toani had been busy in the royal zoo and aviary, selecting animals for the ceremony that would replace the coronation sacrifice of the other princesses. He was making his concession to ensure peace and unity within the empire.

Now it was Ahkin's turn.

He swept through the halls of the palace, a flowing cloak of white and gold billowing out behind him as he walked. His ankles danced with the sound of tiny golden bells. As he passed, every servant and noble alike bowed in respect as if he were the sun god himself. He certainly felt as separated from the people around him as a deity was from humans—not because he was any better than them, but because they couldn't possibly understand the burden he carried. The sacrifice he was making for them.

Atanzah brushed a swift kiss across his cheek. "I am going to get Teniza. I'll see you at the top of the temple."

Ahkin nodded and made his way toward the golden steps of the Temple of the Sun. The tiered pyramid loomed above the city of Tollan like a mountain, dwarfing even the royal palace that sat in its shadow. The lords of the other city-states paused in their own ascents to the top as Ahkin passed, just as his ancestor intended. The submission of the other cities. The blood of Huitzilopochtli, ruling over all.

A group of red-cloaked Tlana priests were waiting beside the ever-burning brazier, various beasts ranging from monkeys to small jungle cats to birds gripped in their hands. Toani was already standing behind the golden altar where Ahkin performed his daily ritual to raise the sun. The pillars surrounding them had been encircled with vines and blooming jungle blossoms, a fitting tribute to the joining of the city of suns and city of plants. It really was beautiful. Ahkin wondered how it would feel to actually be excited for his wedding, to feel joy at the prospect instead of guilt and grief. He knew Teniza was heartbroken, also having to sacrifice her heart and the man she loved to make this commitment. The marriage altar would be painted with both of their tears.

Perhaps it wouldn't be as much of a sacrifice as it seemed to be. Teniza wasn't as spoiled and stuck up as he'd always imagined. In fact, he'd been surprised at the generosity and cleverness he'd seen beneath her polished exterior. Perhaps like Mayana and Patlani, they could learn to love each other someday.

The lords of the various city-states crested the steps next, followed by other nobles and judges from across the empire. Then, some members of the royal families—sons and daughters of Atl, Papatlaca, Millacatl, Pahtia, and Ocelotl. Finally, the lord of Ehecatl joined them with his son, Patlani. He expected the Storm Lord and his son to seem triumphant, perhaps even flaunting their victory, but they both appeared calm, collected, even reserved. Ahkin nodded his head in greeting to the storm prince, with a silent plea: *Love her as I couldn't.* Patlani returned the gesture, nodding his head with a fist pressed against his heart as if to say, *I will, I promise.*

"Are you ready, Ahkin?" Toani lightly touched his elbow to guide him toward the altar. "We will begin with the marriage itself, and once you are bonded before the gods, we will offer the sacrifice and crown you emperor, officially. It will culminate in you performing the daily ritual at sunrise to display your power and signal the dawn of your reign together."

Ahkin swallowed the lump rising in his throat.

"You are doing the right thing, Ahkin," Toani went on in a low voice. "I know it was hard to say your goodbyes, but the gods will reward you for your dedication. Women are not worthy of our hearts anyway. They do nothing but squander them and play with them like the cats they are."

Ahkin's eyebrows pulled together as he watched the priest adjust his many jeweled necklaces. To speak of women in such a way, with such bitterness, Ahkin couldn't help but wonder . . . who had broken this man's heart?

"Ah, here comes the daughter of Millacatl now. Let's begin, shall we?"

Ahkin straightened his spine. "Yes, let's begin."

CHAPTER

44

Mayana watched the pinkish light grow more pronounced from behind the distant mountain range. The marriage ceremony would be beginning soon, if it hadn't already. Tendrils of doubt began to sneak into her mind like caterpillars eating their way through a leaf. Had she made the right decision? She guessed it didn't matter now. It was too late. And what would changing her mind accomplish? The empire would never let them be together.

After Yemania left the garden, Mayana had slipped down to the edge of one of the small pleasure pools. She took off her sandals and dangled her feet into the water, watching as the tiny silver fish nibbled at her toes.

"You're not jumping in? I thought you loved the water," came a voice she was beginning to know all too well.

Mayana looked up to see the wizened form of the goddess Ometeotl taking off her own sandals. The old woman teetered dangerously as she maneuvered herself down beside Mayana. She dipped her wrinkled toes into the pool. The silver fish immediately left Mayana's feet and flocked to Ometeotl's.

"Well, they know who made them, what can I say?" She grinned at Mayana with crooked teeth.

Mayana drew her feet out of the water and hugged her knees against her chest. "Why are you here?" She didn't want to sound disrespectful, but she was tired—so tired. She felt like the pool in Ehecatl, drained when her father attacked the city with drought. Or better yet, like one of those fish that had been left on the bottom, gasping for air.

"The better question, daughter of water, is why are *you* here?" The goddess lifted her foot and dropped it back into the water with a small splash.

"Don't worry, Yemania is taking the bones to the caves."

"I know she is, but that's not what I'm talking about."

Mayana hugged her knees tighter but didn't answer.

"I mean," the Mother goddess continued, "why aren't you stopping the wedding?"

Mayana gave a hollow laugh. "Why stop the inevitable? You may have made us dualities, but you told me yourself, that it isn't destiny. We still have to choose to be together."

"And yet you aren't choosing him."

"No, I'm not."

"Why?"

Mayana groaned in frustration. "What do you mean, why? Can't you see everything going on from that heavenly realm of yours? You know exactly why."

"*I* know why, but do *you*?"

Mayana rose to her feet and dusted her hands off on her skirt. "Leave me alone." She turned and stomped back toward the palace. If the Mother goddess wouldn't leave, then she would. She was so sick of everyone telling her what to do. Who to be. Who to love. This was her choice, and she didn't want to have to explain it to anyone else. A monkey screeched somewhere nearby and Mayana felt tempted to mimic it.

With a flash of light, the Mother goddess appeared in front of her, blocking her way down the paved garden path she'd chosen. "I asked, do you know why you aren't choosing him, child? The real reason?"

"Because I'm sick of fighting! I'm sick of fighting a war that cannot be won!"

The Mother goddess shook her head. "Those are your father's words, not yours."

"My words don't matter. My thoughts don't matter. I can't choose Ahkin, no matter how much I want to!"

Ometeotl lifted a finger. "That is where you are wrong, my dear. You can choose whatever you wish. There will be consequences for whatever you decide, but don't let fear choose for you."

Mayana turned and headed down another path. A flock of birds condensed like a storm cloud to block the way forward. Mayana gritted her teeth and chose another one.

This time, a growth of branches rose from the surrounding bushes. They began to weave themselves together, forming a gate that blocked the path ahead.

"Stop it! Let me go!" Mayana cried. She was so tired of everything, of everyone. Instead of turning around, she ripped at the branches with her bare hands. The thorns cut into the flesh of her palms, but Mayana did not stop. She channeled every ounce of frustration—every memory of someone else tearing her down, every feeling of anger she'd ever felt at her helplessness—into her hands. When she was nearly through, her fingers already covered in blood, she summoned water from the amulet of Atlacoya. She condensed the stream of water that rose from the skull's mouth and blasted the remaining branches aside, as powerful as a river cutting through a mountain. Pride pounded inside her chest alongside her frantically beating heart. The path ahead was finally clear, and she turned around to gauge the Mother's reaction, to declare victory over her attempt to block her.

But the Mother goddess was already gone.

Mayana fell to her knees, staring at the open path ahead, tears streaming down her cheeks.

A warm breeze gently played with her hair. "There's the fighter I know," Ometeotl's voice whispered.

And Mayana rose back to her feet.

———

The Eagle warriors stood silently at the city gates. Though the princesses were no longer prisoners, Yemania highly doubted they would be allowed to just walk out and into the jungles below, especially at night. The Chicome had strict rules about curfew, and there was no chaos of a star demon attack this time to distract them.

Zorrah slowly withdrew her knife.

Yemania yelped and put her hand on Zorrah's wrist. "I don't think fighting our way out is the answer."

Zorrah sighed in frustration. "Sometimes, daughter of healing, fighting is the only way."

"Let me try something first." Yemania threw her head back and tried to hold herself with a confidence she did not feel.

She strode toward the gates, acting as if she was just heading out for an evening walk.

The nearest guard eyed her with suspicion. "Excuse me," he said, stepping in front of her. "Where are you going?"

Yemania's heart leapt into her throat. "Um, I am a healer of Tollan, and I am just going to gather some—"

The guard was already shaking his head. "I'm sorry, princess. You are not permitted to leave the city, especially at night."

Her pulse began to flutter like the wings of the moths darting around the flaming torches. "I'm afraid it's a bit of an emergency."

The guard on the other side of the engraved golden pillars carved with hieroglyphics came to stand beside his fellow.

"You heard him. Scurry back up to the palace like a good little mouse."

The back of Yemania's neck burned, and she opened her mouth to protest, but before she got the chance, the guard crumbled to the earth before her.

Yemania's mouth fell open as she beheld Zorrah standing behind him, her dagger raised from where she'd struck the guard on the head with the handle.

"Too much talking. This is faster."

The second guard roared and lowered his spear toward the princess of beasts. Zorrah smiled and raised a bloody hand. The guard paused, tilting his head in confusion. Then a troop of lithe-bodied black monkeys erupted from the darkness beyond the gate and engulfed him. They became a mass of writhing fur and teeth. Several set to ripping the spear out of his hands and snapping it to pieces. The others dragged the guard off his feet, their feral shrieks mingling with his as they pulled him back into the darkness.

Yoli stared after him, her eyes wide. "Well, that was utterly terrifying."

Zorrah waved a dismissive hand. "He'll be fine. They'll just keep him distracted for a bit."

Yoli shook her head slightly. "Uh, sure."

"There are more coming," Itza hissed, lifting the skirt of her purple dress and sprinting down the path toward the bottom of the plateau.

Yemania gasped as several more guards appeared in the distance, clearly responding to the shrieking of the monkeys and their fellow Eagle warrior. "Run!"

All four of them broke into a sprint, the dark night making it nearly impossible to tell the borderline between the rocky dirt path and the edge, which tumbled down the cliffs to the jungle floor below. Itza slipped on a loose rock, taking a hard tumble. Yemania wrenched her to her feet to keep them running. Shouts echoed behind them as the shadowed forms of the guards followed, their feet slipping and sliding down the steep path. Yemania couldn't tell how many there were, but they were faster and stronger, and soon they were closing in.

"We aren't going to make it to the bottom before they reach us," Yemania cried.

Yoli stopped so suddenly that Yemania almost ran into her. "Unless they *can't* reach us," she said, turning slowly to face them. She lifted her hands into the air, blood already dripping from one of her palms. Flames erupted across the path in front of them, blocking their pursuers from coming any closer.

"That should slow them down," Yoli said, the corner of her mouth turned up.

"Sometimes you have to fight," Zorrah repeated. She lifted an eyebrow at Yemania.

"All right, fine. Yes. Sometimes you have to fight," Yemania sputtered. At least now they didn't have to worry about Eagle warriors hunting them down. Their greatest obstacle now was time.

The moment they reached the bottom of the plateau, Zorrah dug her hands into the earth and brought the soil to her nose.

"This way," she said, pointing toward the southeast before striding purposefully into the trees.

45

Ahkin took a breath to calm himself. Teniza looked like an empress as she followed the torchlit procession of priests guiding her to the ceremony. She wore a flowing cape of gold over her green dress, its train trailing behind her and dotted with live blossoms. The headpiece of gold and white feathers she wore matched Ahkin's own. Her face and arms had been painted with tiny shimmering crystals so that she sparkled like an orchid covered in morning dew. She held her head high as Atanzah and the procession of priests led her toward the golden altar. Though to the rest she appeared regal, Ahkin did not miss the sheen coating her eyes. He took her hand and squeezed it reassuringly. She squeezed back, but a single tear traced down her cheek before she swiped it away. They lowered themselves to their knees upon the wedding mat.

The smell of the incense rising from the bowls around them teased Ahkin's nose as Toani spoke about the significance of the marriage alliance. Drums and flutes added to his melodic chanting. Then, the priest called forth four of the elder priests to speak blessings over them, calling upon each of the four cardinal directions. When they were finished, Toani signaled for Teniza's father to step forward.

"Do we have the gift for the bride's family?" Toani asked.

"Right here," Atanzah said in a sing-song voice. She snapped her fingers at the two servants standing beside her holding baskets. She lifted the lid for all to see the golden contents of the baskets glitter in the torchlight.

Toani clapped his hands together. "Excellent. Lord Millacatl, please accept your gift from the groom and his family."

Lord Millacatl nodded. "We accept with gratitude for the emperor's generosity."

"And your gift for the emperor?"

Two more servants came forward with baskets of cacao beans and maize.

"I accept Millacatl's gift," Ahkin said.

Toani nodded approvingly. "As Ahkin's mother is no longer with us, I will ask the matchmaker to perform the next steps of the ritual."

Atanzah giggled with excitement and came forward. She grasped the corner of Teniza's skirt and the corner of Ahkin's cloak and tied them together into a knot. Ahkin felt a knot forming in his throat as he watched her. Teniza's shoulders shook with silent sobs. Then Atanzah took the bowl of foaming pulque from the altar and lifted it toward Ahkin's mouth. Once he took the drink, Teniza would take it as well, and the wedding portion of the ritual would be complete. They would next move on to the coronation ceremony before being sent to a bedchamber to consummate the marriage officially. Usually a feast of several days would follow, but Ahkin insisted the armies leave immediately after to ensure enough time to reach the base of the mountains. They could celebrate after the war with the Miquitz . . . if they were all still alive to do so.

Ahkin pursed his lips, everything inside wanting to refuse the drink, to reject this final step of the wedding. The bowl moved closer toward his lips. Teniza closed her eyes, accepting the finality of their fate with a shuddering breath.

The music of the drums and flutes suddenly ceased. Atanzah froze and lowered the bowl back to the altar, a look of confusion crumpling the round features of her face.

A wave of whispering washed across the gathered guests. Ahkin spun around, his eyes searching for what his heart dared hope to be true. Beside him, Teniza gasped in relief.

Mayana was there, standing at the top of the temple steps, panting as though she'd just run the entire way up. She clutched at a stitch in her side, but then straightened. Standing tall and proud and entirely alone before every noble and leader in the empire, she ignored every set of staring eyes except for his. Her hands clenched into fists at her side as she threw her chin into the air. A warm wind swept up the side of the temple, whipping at her hair.

"I want to fight," was all she said.

And it was enough.

Ahkin leapt to his feet. His cloak fell from his shoulders, crumpling to the ground as he closed the distance between them in a few strides. He cupped her face in his hands, savoring the blazing fire he saw reignited in her eyes.

"Then let's fight together," he whispered before crushing his mouth to hers.

And the world around them erupted into chaos.

———

What a waste of time. Ochix was furious that Metzi refused to leave. But as he ran past his father's room, he couldn't help but wonder if there was a way to make this trip to the palace a little more worthwhile. A strange feeling in his gut told him that he needed to go inside. Perhaps he could find and steal some of his father's notes? Could there be some secret hidden in his papers about how to defeat the Obsidian Butterfly?

He reached out to feel for the presence of any life forces within his father's rooms, but they were empty. His father was likely checking on Metzi or murdering a servant somewhere, so he tentatively stepped inside. He didn't know what he was looking for—perhaps he could steal his father's star stone? But no, he knew his father carried it with him at all times like a pet cat, stroking it and talking to it as though it could understand him.

Again, how the rest of the empire didn't see his father as unhinged was baffling.

The tables were cluttered with odd contraptions his father had built, drawings upon drawings of that same disturbing image of a skull with eyes like stars, his collection of random trophies of his conquests. A glint of torchlight caught upon a golden sun engraved upon a wooden shield, and a warm breeze caressed his cheek.

He recognized that shield. He'd seen Ahkin emerge from the underworld with it across his arm. A shield that could supposedly summon the light of the sun itself.

Well, if he couldn't get Ahkin's sister to come with him, at least he could get Ahkin's shield. It wasn't quite the same, but if the star demons needed the instability of night for an eclipse to descend to the earth, wouldn't it make sense that light could be used to fight against them? He grabbed the shield and slipped out before his father could come back.

———

"What do you mean, she doesn't want to come?" the Jaguar warrior repeated as though Ochix had not just explained it to him.

Ochix took a breath through gritted teeth. "She refused to come with me and insists on staying here."

The warrior looked around at his fellows. "So, what are we supposed to do now?"

"I don't know," Ochix admitted. "I can go around and try to convince some of the warriors to defect with me, explain to them my father's crazy plan, but the problem is, everyone else thinks my father is a god. But I'm going to try. In the meantime, pray Metzi realizes she's being an idiot."

"So your trip to the palace accomplished nothing?"

"Well, I wouldn't say *nothing*." Ochix tossed the shield to the ground, where the golden sun stared up at them. "If it's as useful as I think it might be, I imagine Ahkin wants that back."

Yemania and the princesses did not stop. The going was slow, especially in the dark of night as the land began to slant upward, rock formations jutting out of the ground like gods of rock reaching hands up through the earth. The cave was supposedly located at the southernmost tip of the Miquitz mountain range. It was not a far journey from Tollan, but she was already so exhausted after their trek to retrieve Itza and their march back to Tollan as captives. Every muscle in her legs burned. Her side ached, and her back and neck were drenched with sweat, but she kept her feet moving. One step after another after another.

Zorrah kept her typical grueling pace, forgetting that the others were not as trained as she was. Finally, they stopped beside a stream for everyone to catch their breath. Yemania fell to her knees and brought the cool water to her lips.

"You think Ahkin is marrying Teniza right now?" Yoli asked, glancing up at the star-flecked sky. The depth of the night's darkness was beginning to soften. Dawn would be soon approaching, and with it, the conclusion of the wedding ceremony.

"I hope not," Yemania said.

"I don't know. I think Mayana made the right choice," Itza said, stripping off her sandals and rubbing at her feet. "She will feel much better in Ehecatl."

Yoli frowned. "Yeah, she seemed to like it there. Though, to be honest, I was surprised you still performed so many different rituals. Like the priestesses blessing the food."

Itza sighed and leaned back on her arms. "Rituals themselves are not bad. They can be a way to connect with our history, with the gods, and others around us. Like prayer, they can take us out of ourselves and into something bigger. There is comfort and familiarity in rituals."

"But then why does your family fight against them so much?" Yoli asked.

Itza smiled and closed her eyes. "We don't fight against rituals. We fight against the tyranny of Tollan. Of them using fear to force their version of certain rituals upon us so that they can maintain their power and control. We perform our rituals out of worship, not blind obedience."

"Huh." Yoli plopped down beside Yemania on the stream bank.

"I'm just glad they canceled the selection ritual," Zorrah grumbled, scrubbing at her face in the water.

"Didn't fancy marrying the prince?" Yoli wiggled her eyebrows. "Got someone back home like Teniza and Itza?"

"Why do I have to fancy marrying anyone?" Zorrah splashed more water over her arms. "I'm not interested in that sort of thing at all."

"Well, I think the Jaguar warriors are lucky to have you," Yemania said, mimicking Zorrah and cooling off her skin in the stream. "And so are we."

Zorrah gave her a tight smile. "You are all much different than I expected. Not as weak and pathetic as I thought."

Yoli threw back her head and laughed. "Aw, that's the nicest thing you've ever said, Zorrah."

Zorrah hissed at her, but Yemania noticed that she was smiling as she sloshed her way back onto the sandy shore. Much had changed between all of them over the last few days, and the thought warmed Yemania's heart.

Zorrah shook her head out like a soaked dog, ponytail whipping her in the face. "All right, enough talking. Let's move."

"How much farther is it?" Yemania asked after several more minutes of hiking. She kept thinking about what Lord Ehecatl had said . . . about Itza and Yemania sacrificing their blood to resurrect Quetzal-coatl. She desperately hoped that their "sacrifice" didn't mean *all* of their blood. Surely the Mother wouldn't ask that of her . . . would she?

Zorrah slashed aside a palm branch hanging in her face. "We should be getting close," but then she stopped and held up a hand for the others to stop.

"What is—?" Yemania started to ask before Zorrah hissed at her to be quiet.

Yemania strained her ears. There was no sound, not even the chirp of an insect. "I don't hear anyth—"

Zorrah threw a hand over her mouth. "Exactly," she whispered. "The jungle is too still. Something is not right."

Bumps rose along Yemania's arms. She had heard too many legends and tales of demons that waited in the jungles during the instability of night. Minions of the lords of Xibalba sent to wreak havoc upon the world above. Creatures escaped from other layers of creation . . . lone demons escaped from the stars.

The silence was deafening as they huddled together, watching the space between the trees for any sign of movement. Then, Yemania heard it—the snapping of a branch, a rustle of dried leaves, and finally the rattle of a skirt lined with tiny shells.

Yemania's skin suddenly felt as if it were too tight. Her stomach clenched.

"You will not reach the caves, little princesses," came a voice. It was cold, inhuman, and yet distinctly female.

Yemania fought back a whimper behind Zorrah's hand still closed around her mouth. The animal princess lifted her blade higher, head turning frantically to locate the source of the voice.

"Give me the bones, and I might let you live," the voice purred. "Do not, and I will pry them from your lifeless fingers."

Then, from behind the trees stepped a creature that Yemania had only seen in nightmares. Skeletal thin, frighteningly tall, and with limbs far too long to be human, the demon towered over them. Her bare skin was covered with a chestpiece of feathers, while her skirt rattled with tiny seashells clacking against one another. The pale skin stretched tight over its ribcage heaved with excitement, while its bony face leered at them from beneath a feathered headpiece.

A tzitzimitl. A star demon, like the one that had killed her brother. Her heart frantically beat against her ribcage as if it wondered why they were not already running. She hugged the bag of bones tighter against her chest.

The star demon beckoned with a blood-stained finger that elongated into a claw. "Give me the bones," it rasped.

Zorrah positioned herself in front of Yemania and nodded at Yoli. A wicked grin split across Yoli's face before the space between them and the demon erupted into flame.

"Run!" Zorrah screamed, wrenching Yemania to her feet.

They sprinted into the darkness, a darkness that was beginning to lighten with hints of the impending dawn. The frustrated shriek of the demon faded behind them. Yemania was not as fast as the others, but she pushed her body harder than it had ever been pushed before. Branches whipped across her feet, and she tried not to stumble on the uneven ground. Her breath came in gasps as what little energy she had left began to fade. Then, something yanked her back, as if her bag had caught on something. Yemania turned to dislodge it, but she came face to skeletal face with the star demon. Its claws pierced the canvas of the bag, ripping it away from her. Yemania screamed and kicked the demon in the face, but not before the claws of its other hand sank into the flesh of her calf. Pain seared its way up her leg as if it were on fire.

"Give me them to me!" it hissed. "Or I will suck every drop of blood from within your body!"

Something collided with the demon, throwing it away from Yemania. Its claws ripped out of her leg, taking chunks of her flesh with it. Yemania screeched in pain. Then Itza was there, helping her onto her feet. Yemania looked back to see Zorrah wrestling with the demon, her knife connecting with wherever it found the demon's flesh. But the demon seemed unfazed by the obsidian blade. It did not have blood to spill. Then, it grabbed Zorrah by the hair and threw her against a tree. She gasped in pain and crumpled.

Yemania tried to hobble along, Itza supporting her over her shoulders. A blast of wind forced the creature back, but it scrambled forward on its hands and knees like a deadly crab. Yemania screamed again before an explosion of fire engulfed it. Yoli appeared at Yemania's other side, adding her strength to pull Yemania forward. The blood from her wounded leg coated the jungle floor behind them.

The demon rose to its feet, covered in flame. It began to walk forward, its body glowing like a true star, burning claws outstretched. "You will not succeed in bringing him back. The Obsidian Butterfly will conquer this land and devour all, just as I will devour you."

The roar of a jaguar echoed around them, and a spotted beast hurtled out of the trees. It tackled the demon just as Zorrah limped up beside them. "Keep going!" she ordered. A deep wound along her hairline dripped blood down the length of her face.

With a yowl, the jaguar's body went limp, and the demon stepped over its body. Nothing seemed to be able to stop it. Yemania wanted to curl into a ball and cry, to give up and stop fighting, but she knew she couldn't. As much as she wanted to, she had to keep fighting. The sweaty and determined faces of the girls helping her forward gave her the strength she needed to push herself harder.

Even if it weren't enough, they would not fail for lack of trying.

"What is the meaning of this?" thundered the lord of Millacatl. He stepped forward and ripped Mayana and Ahkin apart. "You are marrying *my* daughter. It's already done."

Ahkin's temper flared. He opened his mouth to let the lord of Millacatl know exactly what the *meaning of this* was, but Teniza beat him to it.

"No, it's not," she cried from beside the altar. She ripped the white and golden cloak from around her shoulders and threw it to the pavement. "We didn't finish the ceremony, and we aren't going to. I'm not marrying him. I never wanted to marry him."

Atanzah gasped and fanned herself with a chubby hand.

The other lords and nobles turned to each other, and their mutterings grew into yells, each blaming the other for something that had nothing to do with them. Toani lifted his arms and tried to quell the chaos, his eyes darting about in panic, but everyone ignored him.

And Toani did not like to be ignored.

"STOP!" the priest roared. "Ahkin, get back up here and finish the ceremony or else!"

But Ahkin had had enough. This had gone on far too long. Perhaps his ancestors would curse him forever for what he was about to do, but it was time the empire knew the truth. Toani's attempts to hide everything for the sake of unity were an obvious failure. He had only to look around at the lord of Millacatl screaming at the lord of Atl, the lord of Papatlaca lifting his fist at the lord of Pahtia, the lord of Ehecatl staring at them all as if they'd gone insane. Fear was not enough to keep the empire unified, and it was time to burn the lie to ashes once and for all.

Ahkin squeezed Mayana's hand and led her toward the altar.

"Ahkin, leave this viper in the pit she crawled out from," Toani hissed, stepping back. "You need to finish the ceremony and raise the sun. *Now*."

"No," Ahkin said. If he truly wanted to lead, he needed to do what he thought was best. He'd listened to Toani's advice for long enough.

"It is time the empire knew the truth," Ahkin yelled, drowning out the voices all around him. Dozens of curious faces turned toward him, the anger and fear and frustration as heavy on the air as the smell of the incense.

"Ahkin, what are you doing?" Toani whispered harshly, reaching for Ahkin's arm.

Mayana slapped his hand away. "You've done enough. How about you hold your tongue for once and let your emperor speak for himself?"

The priest blanched, but his shock at Mayana's audacity momentarily stunned him into silence.

Ahkin grinned and continued. "The city of Tollan has ruled the Chicome Empire for generations, ensuring the obedience of the other city-states and uniting us in our desire to avoid the disasters of the past."

The lords and nobles continued to listen, though many of the eyes fixed upon Ahkin were narrowed and suspicious.

"But we have not learned from the past. Instead, we have taken it upon ourselves to be our own salvation, forsaking the true will of the gods for our own ambitions. The rituals that we perform to supposedly save our world are not necessary—in fact, they were created by Tollan to manipulate you all by fear. If I am to lead this great empire, I will not have it be because you are afraid. I will have you follow me because you trust my leadership, and because I am worthy of following."

He watched the distant horizon grow ever brighter, the sun

supposedly waiting for his blood to call it into day. But he knew the empire needed to witness for themselves the truth of what he spoke.

Toani screeched from somewhere beside him. *"Ahkin, the sun! You need to raise it now!"*

Ahkin lifted the ceremonial knife, the same knife he'd used almost every day since his father died, except when Metzi had performed the ceremony herself. The same ceremony a member of his bloodline had performed since the beginning of the age of the Seventh Sun. Toani groaned with impatience, while the crowd below seemed to hold their breath.

Mayana met his gaze and nodded. "Burn it down," she whispered.

And Ahkin threw the knife to the ground, shattering the obsidian blade into a thousand tiny shards of darkness.

Toani screamed as if he were being burned.

The entire top of the temple, all of Tollan and the empire itself, blazed in the golden light of the sun.

And Ahkin had not raised it.

Silence followed as every face beheld the Seventh Sun, alive, without the need for Ahkin's blood. Then, like a wind gathering before a storm, a muttering began to build, and the suspicious gazes turned toward Toani.

———

The demon closed in, reaching for Yemania's wounded ankle.

At that moment, a burst of brilliant morning sunlight illuminated the jungle around them. The tzitzimitl froze, tips of its clawed fingers raking the sole of Yemania's blood-soaked sandal. The sunshine shot through gaps in the leaves above like beams of hope escaping from the heavens. Wherever they met the star demon's skin, smoke began to rise. The demon writhed in agony, shrieking as it tried to scramble back into the shadows. But it could not escape the light of the Seventh Sun.

The creature burned to death before their eyes, leaving behind nothing but the foul stench of charred flesh and a glittering, pockmarked gray stone the size of a fist. Yemania had seen one like it only once before, in Metzi's chambers.

A fallen star stone.

Yoli and Itza collapsed to the ground, gasping for breath and dragging Yemania down with them. Yemania retched as her stomach tried to upend itself. The wound in her leg throbbed with fresh, stabbing pains. But when she looked at Zorrah, who wobbled before she fell to her knees, all worries about herself faded to the background of her mind. The wound on Zorrah's head was severe, and if she did not tend to it immediately, Zorrah might not ever reach the caves.

Yemania dragged herself forward and laid a hand on Zorrah's forehead, willing the power of her already exposed blood to heal the damage she sensed. The wound closed, and with it Zorrah's eyes as she relaxed. Her breathing eased as her pain began to fade.

"Thank you," she whispered, then sat up and fingered the freshly healed skin. Her gaze dropped to Yemania's mangled leg. "What do we do about you?"

Yemania grit her teeth and looked down, and what she saw threatened to make her retch again. The flesh was torn to bits around three deep puncture wounds. The blood coating both her skin and the dirt beneath her explained why she was beginning to feel so dizzy. And of course, she was unable to heal herself.

"Um," she said, her voice trembling. "I need some cloths. In my bag. And the jar of—" She hissed as she moved her leg, "—maguey leaves. I need to put the sap on the wounds before we wrap them. To keep out infection."

Yoli was already digging through the bag, pushing aside the jade bones to find the few supplies Yemania had packed in a rush before they left Tollan.

Itza, however, was rising to her feet, her eyes focused on something ahead.

"I think . . . I think we found it," she said softly, pointing with a shaking hand.

Through the underbrush, they could just make out the steep side of a hill rising up from the jungle floor. A curving hole resembling the shape of a woman's body scarred its side like a gash. Vines dangled down across the entrance—the entrance to a cave. From its mouth gushed crystal-clear waters into a pool the color of the bluest sky.

The bones in Yemania's bag seemed to grow heavier, as if they knew they had made it to their final destination.

They had finally reached the Caves of Creation.

48

"Priest, you knew that Ahkin's blood was not needed to raise the sun?" The lord of Atl's deep voice was simmering with fury. "Is what he says true?"

Toani confirmed everyone's suspicions when his eyes turned crazed. He sputtered incoherently, searching for words he could not find. The lord of Atl shook his head in disappointment. But then, Toani dug into the folds of his robe and withdrew a bone-tipped knife. "You heathen!" he screamed suddenly and ran at Mayana. "You've ruined *everything*!"

Ahkin's heart froze as he turned, ready to jump between Mayana and the priest's knife, but before he got the chance, the priest's body jerked. Blood spurted from between his lips, and a blade protruded from his chest. The priest's body slumped slowly to the floor, the jade hilt of a dagger in his back. Oztoc, the lord of Atl, stood above Toani's twitching body, his hands shaking. "Don't you dare hurt my daughter," he said.

The head priest answered with a gurgling sound and then went still.

Mayana's father looked up at her, tears shining upon his cheeks. He opened his hands, exposing his palms to her. "I'm sorry, Mayana. I'm sorry I ever doubted you."

Mayana made a choked sound somewhere in her throat before throwing her arms around her father's neck. The lord of Atl's eyes went wide with surprise, his hands hovering above her back as if unsure how to proceed. But then, he lowered his arms and wrapped them around her, embracing her tighter and tighter. Mayana's brothers ran forward, each embracing their sister in turn, muttering apologies for their own behavior.

"What do we do now?" the lord of Atl asked, coming to stand beside Ahkin. The other lords and nobles still gaped at the risen sun, some shaking their heads in disbelief, others turning to Ahkin as if waiting for answers on how to proceed. Ahkin remembered how it had felt on that beach on Xibalba when the Mother goddess had told him the truth about everything: as though the ground he was standing on had crumbled to dust beneath his feet. He hadn't known what was real and what was not, or how to even tell the difference between the two anymore. Then, he remembered Mayana taking his hand, a source of solid strength amid his inner turmoil.

Ahkin cleared his throat to address everyone. "I know the fear and confusion that everyone is feeling right now. I was there too, when I first learned the truth from the Mother goddess herself. That is a tale you deserve to be told. But I'm afraid we will have to discuss what this means at a later time. Right now, I must inform you of a greater danger we all face. Tzom of Miquitz kidnapped Metzi and seeks to use her blood to unleash the Tzitzimime upon us all during tomorrow's eclipse. I sent Ochix and a group of warriors to try and save her in time, but even if they succeed, I know we will unleash the fury of the Miquitz as they pursue her. I do not know if we will be facing demons or man, but I will march out with whoever is willing to follow me. But I cannot fight alone."

Ahkin's gaze immediately shifted to the lord of Ehecatl, who stood beside his son in pensive rigidity. Ahkin had just broken *another* engagement to Patlani by declaring his love for Mayana. He knew he likely lost Ehecatl's alliance for good with such a decision, but the consequences would be what they were.

But it was not Lord Ehecatl who first unleashed his rage upon Ahkin.

"I will not stand silently as Tollan insults us!" The lord of Millacatl towered over Ahkin, his face as red as cinnabar. "You manipulated me with false promises of a wedding, just as your sister did to Ehecatl. I hope you are happy with your decision, prince of light, because you have destroyed an empire that has stood for generations. My armies and I are leaving."

He whirled, his green cloak smacking Ahkin in the chest. Ahkin's stomach soured, bile rising into his throat. Did the man not understand what was at stake? Millacatl was the closest city to the mountains. They were the most at risk of them all.

"Your city will be the first to fall," Ahkin cried after him. "Do not let your pride and stubbornness cost you the lives of your people!"

"I will worry about my own people, Ahkin. You are no emperor of ours." And he disappeared, descending over the edge of the temple's stairs. Several of the lesser lords followed after him.

Ahkin turned to those remaining. "Will you please fight with me?"

"My prince, I know you are convinced of this threat of star demons, but Ocelotl has seen no evidence of such. We can defend ourselves if any threat does present itself." The lord of Ocelotl rubbed at his golden eyes. "But in the meantime, we will retreat to our city and discuss the best way to move forward." And he followed the lord of Millacatl down the temple steps.

Ahkin's chest felt as though it were collapsing in on itself. Ocelotl's soldiers were their greatest warriors, the naguals able to command beasts in battle. Was the empire truly going to fall to pieces in his hands like sand?

"Lord Pahtia," Ahkin began. He lifted a hand in invitation toward the lord of healing.

But Yemania's father did not even answer. He turned his nose into the air and left with a swish of his red cloak.

Ahkin dropped his head, fighting the doubt and hopelessness nipping at his heels. A strong hand settled on his shoulder.

"Atl will fight beside you," Mayana's father said.

"As will Papatlaca," rumbled the Fire Lord.

"Thank you," Ahkin said. "I will be honored to fight with both of you."

All eyes turned to the lord of Ehecatl, who had remained silently observant. He exchanged a glance with his son and then slowly came to stand before Ahkin.

Ahkin sucked in a breath. "Lord Ehecatl, I will understand if you wish to leave with the other lords that have abandoned us at our time of greatest need. Please know that I never intended to insult you, but I cannot let Patlani marry Mayana. I am not willing to use the woman I love to barter for peace. I hope that you can find it in your heart to forgive me."

The lord of Ehecatl pursed his lips and then nodded slowly. "I told you on the battlefield that I needed to see that you were different from your father. Your father was willing to trade away his daughter—to use her, as you said yourself, to barter for peace. The proposal I made before the council was a test, young prince. To see if a son could learn from the mistakes of his father." Then a smile broke out across the older man's face. "A test that I am happy to see you have passed. You are not your father, Ahkin. And for that reason, Ehecatl will stand beside you and fight against whatever threats loom on the horizon."

Mayana gasped, a hand flying to cover her mouth as she turned to Ahkin with tears of joy. "Thank you, Lord Ehecatl. Your loyalty means more than you know. It would have been an honor to join your family."

"Not that my son was not taken with you, my dear." The lord of Ehecatl bowed before her. "But Ehecatl will be honored to serve the emperor with you at his side as our empress."

The opening to the cave was narrower than Yemania expected, though she knew appearances could be deceiving. A large, clear pool covered its entrance, which meant the only way to enter would be to swim. Zorrah's nervous pacing confirmed Yemania's suspicions.

"I never thought I'd say this, but I really wish Mayana was here." Zorrah sniffed.

"We can help you. Itza can swim just as well as she can," Yemania reassured her. She turned to Itza for confirmation, but the wind princess was too focused on the sky to pay attention to anything else. The ghostly image of the moon was already high in the morning sky, inching its way toward the Seventh Sun like a wolf stalking its prey. It would only be one more day until it would be in position to obscure the sun entirely.

Yemania cleared her throat. "Right, Itza?"

"Oh, yes. I can help." She brought her attention back to earth. "Though I am more worried about you."

Yemania grimaced at her leg. The maguey sap had stung like the hells when she spread it across the wounds, and although they'd tied strips of cloth around them, blood still oozed through the wrappings.

"Maybe the cool water will help with the throbbing," Yemania said.

Yoli, however, was eyeing the smooth, thick trunk of a tree. "Do you know what kind of wood that is?" she asked.

The other girls exchanged glances and shrugged.

"In Papatlaca," she continued, stepping forward and running a hand along the tree's bark, "we make the weapons for the empire. Many of the weapons we make are not for the royal families, and we use different kinds of woods for the handles. My father invented a knife that could float if dropped in the water. He used balsa wood because it is so light . . ."

Yemania could see where she was going. "Is that balsa wood?"

"I think so." Yoli stepped back and eyed one of the thicker branches. "Stay back. I want to try something." She unleashed a jet of flames from her hands, severing the branch from the main tree. It fell to the earth with a resounding crash that sent nearby birds screeching for the skies. It was not large, only about as long as Itza and thick enough that Yemania could wrap her arms around it. Yoli strode forward and began snapping off the excess foliage, burning away thicker branches that proved more challenging to remove.

Finally, a relatively smooth chunk of wood remained.

"What are we supposed to do with that?" Zorrah narrowed her eyes at the branch as if she didn't trust it.

"Well, I don't think we have time to make a boat, and I highly doubt one would fit in there anyway, but you can at least hold onto this while we swim in."

"I think that's brilliant," Yemania said, watching as Yoli dragged the branch to the pool's edge. With an almighty heave, she shoved it into the water. Yemania held her breath, but the branch bobbed back to the surface, its weight buoyed by the water.

Zorrah sighed and removed her jaguar cloak. She folded it delicately and laid it in the shade of a nearby tree. With the heartbroken look of a mother leaving behind a child, she turned her back on it and waded into the stream. "All right, let's get this over with."

Itza helped Yemania hobble into the pool. The coolness of the water did ease the swelling, but the slickness of the rocks beneath her feet nearly sent her face-first into the branch. She wrapped her arms around it instead, using it to catch her fall. "Gods, it's so slippery."

"The algae covering the rocks cannot grow without light, so it won't be as slippery inside," Itza assured her. Yemania hoped she was right. With the motion of heaving a boat off from a dock, the girls eased the branch forward, Itza swimming ahead and guiding them toward the cave opening. Yoli swam at the rear, a protective hand at Yemania's back. The water was a beautiful shade of blue, so clear Yemania could see all the way to the sloping bottom of the pool. The bodies of tiny silver fish darted around them, nibbling at their exposed skin. Zorrah's nails dug into the wood, and the muscles of her neck were rigidly tight.

"We are fine, Zorrah. You're not going to drown," Yemania said, her heart aching at the sheer panic gripping the princess of beasts.

Zorrah gripped the branch tighter as they passed beneath the cave's overhang. "It's not just that. In Ocelotl, we are taught . . . to stay out of caves. They are incredibly dangerous."

Yemania swallowed hard as the shadows of the cave enveloped them. "I know," she said, her stomach tightening with the reality of what they were doing. "I've always been taught the same thing."

The pool itself did not reach very far into the cave. Soon the sloping bottom rose to meet them, and they stumbled onto a narrow beach of pebbles. The air inside the cave was much cooler than the air outside and smelled of wet rock. Yemania's good foot scrambled for a foothold against the tiny shifting rocks, wincing as they slipped between her foot and sandal. Yoli steadied her against an outcropped boulder, and Yemania sighed with relief.

Itza walked ahead, but the darkness obscured their way forward.

"Where do we go now?" Yoli asked.

Itza pointed into the inky blackness. "I think it would be that way. Caves are carved by water, so if we follow the water, it should lead us to the deepest part. We just don't have a torch or—" but then she turned back to Yoli with an eyebrow arched.

Yoli nodded, not even needing encouragement before her arms ignited. "Who needs a torch when you have a child of Papatlaca?"

"We don't have enough," Mayana said, watching the dust kicked into the air by the armies packing up their camps at the base of the plateau.

"It will have to be enough," Ahkin said. His grip tightened on the handle of his macana sword. "If we are only facing the Miquitz, we will stand a fighting chance, but if the Tzitzimime come down the mountain slopes with them . . ."

He didn't need to finish. Mayana swallowed hard. Perhaps it didn't matter that Ahkin chose her to become empress over the shattered remains of the Chicome Empire. She wouldn't get the chance if they did not survive tomorrow.

"I'm going with you," she said, keeping her eyes on the horizon. "You will need every soul you can find to fight, and my power will be useful on the battlefield."

Ahkin loosed a sigh. "I had a feeling you'd say that."

"If we are going to die anyway, Ahkin, then I'm going to die fighting by your side, not waiting and wondering if you're going to come home."

Ahkin's face lit up as though he had a sudden idea. "What about the bones? The Mother said we needed to resurrect them. Where are they now?"

"Yemania and the others left with them last night. They will be lucky to make it to the caves in time, so we'll probably have to hold off death and star demons alike until they can succeed."

Ahkin closed his eyes and pinched the bridge of his nose. "You think Yemania can do it?"

"I know she can." And Mayana truly believed it.

What armies remained at Tollan began to pack—not to return home, but to prepare for battle against Miquitz. Mayana would have been nervous enough with all of the armies of the Chicome united against the star demons. She'd seen what a single demon did to the guards in the temple. But to have only half of the empire behind them . . . Mayana just prayed Yemania was successful.

Shame burned inside her stomach at the memory of sending Yemania off without her. She should have been on the trek with them, but she couldn't change that now.

Teniza had left with her father, but not before embracing Mayana and giving her a cryptic encouragement. "I will do what I can," she'd said with a squeeze of her hands.

And at least Mayana had her family. Never in her life had she felt closer to her father and brothers as they prepared their city's armies to leave. Her brothers teased her and laughed with her as they had when they were children, and her father kept smiling at her with something that resembled pride. It was more than she could have ever hoped for. Certainly more than she'd experienced from him before. Atl was one of the larger city-states, contributing about three thousand warriors. Combined with Papatlaca's two thousand, Ehecatl's three thousand, and Tollan's own Jaguar and Eagle warriors, they had nearly as many as had marched to Ehecatl. Combined with the godly abilities of fire, water, wind, and light, it had to be enough.

Just as the Seventh Sun tipped over its peak into afternoon, the remaining armies of the fractured Chicome Empire began their march to the mountains.

CHAPTER

50

Yemania had never been fond of tight spaces, but as she wedged her way through the narrow passages of the cave, it took every ounce of her strength not to descend into full-blown panic. Wading chest-deep in water, she turned her body sideways, squeezing between the layers of rock wall on either side. Without the light emanating from Yoli's elevated hands, they would have been making this journey in total and complete darkness.

Her breath came in short gasps, but she tried to focus on the physical sensations around her instead. The extraordinary smoothness of the water against her flushed skin, the shuffling gravel beneath her sandals, even the beauty of the swirling mineral grains on the rock wall. Anything to take her mind off how utterly trapped and helpless she felt.

"Watch out for—" Yoli started to say.

Zorrah yelped in pain and then growled, "The boulder sticking out there? Yes, thank you. My shin managed to find it just fine."

Itza continued to lead them through the twisting maze of boulders, climbing up out of the water only to slide back down once another obstacle had been cleared.

"Gods, Itza, you're lucky you're so small," Zorrah complained, turning her head to avoid cracking it on a low-hanging rock.

"The ground drops off again here," Itza called back from the front. "Hold on to the wall to get across if you can."

"Fantastic," Zorrah said.

The cavern finally opened up into a room the size of a banquet hall. Towering rock formations lined the room like pillars, glittering with tiny crystals embedded on their surface. The pale gray body of a long-legged spider scurried across one of the walls.

The room was dimly lit by a single beam of light escaping through the ceiling far above their heads. Forgotten shattered bowls and pottery lined one of the walls, offerings to the gods from generations far older than their own. Though, Yemania noticed, some of the bowls were newer, and she remembered Itza saying her family made a yearly pilgrimage to the caves. Ahead, the dark mouths of several different passageways gaped open, waiting to swallow them whole.

Itza bent down and fingered the broken edges of one of the newer pots. "This is the farthest I've ever been inside." Her gaze lingered on one of the pitch-dark passageways. The air within it seemed to hang heavier than the air in the cavern, as if it held a thousand secrets. Yemania swore she heard faint whispers of voices coming from within, making the hairs on the back of her neck stand on end.

"Why?" she whispered.

Itza rose to her feet and brushed her hands off on the soaked skirt of her dress. "I don't know. When we came to make our yearly offering, we were forbidden from going any farther."

"Well, that's comforting," Yoli said.

"How do we know that's the right passage?" Yemania asked, rubbing her hands along her arms to smooth down the nervous bumps.

Itza did not answer. Instead, she lowered herself onto the floor and folded her body into a praying position. The others looked around at each other, unsure what to do other than just wait. After several minutes of tense silence, Itza finally stood back up.

"May I see the bones?" she asked.

Yemania blinked, but held the bag out to her.

Itza closed her eyes and hovered her hands over the glittering jade bones, mumbling prayer after prayer under her breath. Finally, her eyes snapped back open.

"My blood is calling me this way." She nodded, Yemania noted with a twinge of dread, toward the opening that seemed to whisper with unseen voices.

"Well, you heard her." The flames along Yoli's arms glowed a little brighter, and she marched inside. Yemania and the others followed.

The passageway was much bigger than the one they'd followed from the entrance, the water trickling along like a stream beneath their feet. They walked for nearly thirty minutes until the passage suddenly ended.

Yemania studied the rock around them. Though the wall in front of them rose straight to the ceiling, the wall of the cave to their right sloped upward in layered terraces, their edges smoothed and bulbous as sap running down the side of a tree.

"Flowstone," Yoli said, running her hand along the nearest terrace ledge, which reached out just over their heads. "The water came from up there somewhere; that's what makes the minerals calcify on the rocks. The cave continues up that way."

Yemania lifted her chin. "Up there? You mean we have to climb?"

Yoli was already wedging her sandal into a crevice and hauling herself up.

Yemania took a deep breath and mimicked her. The scratchy surface of jagged rock beneath the flowstone bit into the flesh of her palms. She tried to put weight on her injured leg and gasped as pain shot up her whole body. Her foot slipped. Yemania screamed as she fell backward.

A sudden burst of wind embraced her like a pillow, forcing her back to her original position. She clambered for a hold, her pulse thrashing inside her ears.

"How about I help you up?" Itza asked with an arched brow.

"Yes, please," Yemania whimpered.

With Itza's added support, Yemania made it over the lip of the first terrace. They continued to climb, leaving the flowing water below and entering the dryer realms where water had initially carved the older parts of the cave. The smell of dirt and dust replaced the smell of wet rock. Yemania hauled herself up the last ledge and felt her eyes go wide.

Yoli was already there, lifting her flaming hand higher to illuminate a massive cavern. The ceiling hung low, bulbous and curved as though a giant of some kind were sitting on the land above. The distant walls illuminated by Yoli's flames were narrow and spiked as though covered in thorns of flowstone, but it was the floor that had Yemania's brows pulling together in confusion. Small ridges twisted and meandered like snakes across the surface. The hollows between them looked like they should contain water, but they were empty, filled with nothing but compacted dust. Compacted dust and—upon Yemania's closer inspection—fragments of human bones. The unmistakable jointed bone of a finger rested partially covered in the nearest hollow, and in another, the rounded shape of a skull, a large crack in its cranium.

"Uh, keep your feet on the ridges?" Yoli suggested, kneeling to get a closer look at the exposed finger bone.

"How do you think they got here?" Yemania whispered, eyeing the ground with increasing mistrust.

"I wonder if the bones of sacrifices from the altar washed down here and just settled in the cracks between the ridges," Yoli said. "Can you see the curves of the stone? The swollen shape of some of the bones? That indicates the presence of water over long periods of time. This must be the right way."

"How do you know so much about rocks?" Zorrah asked. "I just see rocks."

Yoli rose back to her feet, the corner of her mouth tugging upward. "We study rocks in Papatlaca. The mountain of fire provides more than just fire glass. Our people have studied the earth for generations, using what it gifts us for tools and weapons alike. Some rocks come from cooled magma." She lifted her obsidian blade as if in demonstration. "Other rocks come from water or from pressure deep within the earth."

"Hmmm," Zorrah said. "Are the ridges sturdy, at least?"

Yoli tapped one with her sandaled foot. "I think so. Just don't step into the hollows, or you might get a finger bone through your foot."

"How lovely," Yemania grumbled, teetering up onto the nearest ledge.

———

Ochix tried to approach several different groups of warriors he'd trained with to beg them to see reason and help him stop what his father was planning. But so far, all he'd managed to do was piss a lot of people off.

For the third time that day—the last before the eclipse began tomorrow—he was forced to possess the warriors long enough to let him escape before they stabbed him. His people were being just as stubborn as his father, convinced their moment of victory over the Chicome had finally come.

It didn't help that his reputation as Ahkin's "pet" seemed to have spread farther than just his father's palace.

"This isn't working. Perhaps we should just bust into the ceremony and grab Metzi before they can kill her?" Ochix half-heartedly suggested, squatting down before the small fire the Jaguar warriors had built in their little hideout.

One of the warriors gave him a flat look.

"Fine, I won't lead you all to your deaths on a suicide mission. But we can't just leave without her. The ceremony starts tomorrow, and if they spill her blood, we are going to have a lot more to worry about than my father's soldiers."

"I never worry about death demons," one of the Jaguar warriors grunted.

"Fine, yes, you are strong and brave and do not fear us, I get it." Ochix waved a dismissive hand. "But that's not my point."

"Why can't we try and fight our way in to save her? It would be an honorable death if we failed."

Ochix clenched his jaw. "Because I'd rather succeed than die an honorable death, to be quite frank."

"Then think of a better plan, death prince. If you cannot, then we will fight with or without you, and let the gods decide if we succeed or not."

Ochix rubbed his face in frustration. "No pressure," he mumbled. He slapped his thighs and rose to his feet. "I do have one idea, but I don't think you're going to like it."

Yemania fought to keep her balance along the winding ridges that lined the cavern floor. The maguey sap she'd slathered across the wounds in her leg had mostly washed off in the water. The burning and throbbing she felt beneath her bandages was worrisome, but there was nothing she could do about that now.

Yoli led them across the rising slope of the cavern floor until they came to an archway spiked with frozen drips of flowstone. Another pile of boulders waited for them, along with an ancient-looking wooden ladder leading up into the darkness.

"The water flowed from somewhere up there." Yoli eyed the ladder with mistrust. "You think this thing can hold our weight? It looks as old as the First Sun." She reached out a hand to give it a little shake. The ladder creaked in response and rained down flecks of decayed wood.

Itza lifted her hand and her small knife. "I've got you if it breaks."

"All right then." Yoli shrugged and settled her foot on the first rung.

Yemania held her breath as Yoli climbed. The ladder groaned but held her weight, and finally, Yoli disappeared over the lip of the rock ledge above. The flickering light of her arms faded with her.

"Gods . . ." she whispered. "You all have to see this."

"Working on it," Zorrah grumbled and followed Yoli up the ladder next.

Yemania tested her weight on her leg, hissing in pain.

"I've got you," Itza reminded her. "If you fall, I can catch you." She summoned a little wind and gently nudged Yemania toward the ladder as if to prove her point.

Yemania swallowed and placed her hands on the splintered wooden beams. Tiny bits of rotted wood pricked beneath her palms. She tried to keep as much weight on her good leg as possible, relying on her arms to make up the difference. Muscles burned as she hauled herself up one step at a time. Zorrah's hands found her shoulders and helped heave her over the last step. Yemania flopped nearly on top of her, but Zorrah steadied her and helped her stand. Itza appeared last, and her eyes went wide with wonder.

The chamber they'd emerged in was smaller than the cavern below, only about the size of Yemania's bedroom back in Tollan. Here the walls were smooth, solid, and reflective, as though a thin layer of volcanic glass had been laid across every surface. At the end of the room was a raised stone platform like an altar. Its edges were plain and perfectly polished, catching the flickering light of Yoli's flames. She could see deep brown stains through the dust around its base.

But it was not just the room itself that was different. The whispers Yemania had heard before grew louder, as if unseen spirits could not contain their excitement. Were they observing from another layer of creation, separated by the thinnest of curtains? Did they know whose bones resided in Yemania's bag? What they planned to do?

Itza's eyes shone with tears. "Is that where . . . ?" She removed her sandals and stepped forward as if in a trance. Her hand ran delicately across the surface of the altar. "This is where he saved us. All of us," she whispered.

The Caves of Creation were sometimes called the womb of the mother earth, and Yemania could see why. There was a subtle power that seemed to hover in the air like a presence, waiting for a conduit source to channel itself into, a vessel in which to pour its life-giving properties. This was where Quetzalcoatl had brought the bones he'd stolen from Xibalba after humanity was destroyed. He used his own blood to resurrect them, then sacrificed himself to birth the Seventh Sun. This was where the seventh age had begun.

Where they hoped to stop an eighth age from needing to begin.

Yemania glanced around at the other princesses. Each had played such an essential role in getting them here. Mayana rescued the bones from the underworld in the first place. Zorrah had led them here and protected them from demons, determined to prevent this very moment from happening. Yoli had lit the way through the darkness of the caves, guiding them through the winding tunnels with her knowledge of the earth.

Now it was Itza's turn. And Yemania's. Itza's blood, the blood of Quetzalcoatl, would resurrect him, and Yemania's healing blood would heal his divine body.

Hopefully.

"What do you know about the actual process?" Yemania asked, moving to stand beside Itza at the altar.

"The codex sheets in Ehecatl only recount how Quetzalcoatl resurrected us. He did not need to spill all of his blood to do so, but he was also a god, so I am not entirely sure how it compares. I think we should start by mimicking what he did and hope it is enough."

Zorrah and Yoli came closer to watch, but kept a respectable distance to allow Yemania and Itza to work. Yemania opened the bag and one by one removed the jade bones of Quetzalcoatl. They were slightly larger than the bones of a human, and there were nowhere near as many. Hopefully it didn't matter that they didn't seem to have his complete skeleton, just important bones like landmarks to map out his body. A skull, two arm bones, two femurs, several ribs and smaller appendages, a section of spine. Yemania had studied the human body under her aunt Temoa, so she knew exactly where to place each one—as long as the bones of gods resembled the bones of humans. Itza chanted over the bones with mumbled prayers. With each clatter against the surface of the altar, the faint whispers grew more frenzied, their excitement building. That had to be a good sign.

"What next?" Yemania asked.

Itza closed her eyes. Her fingers tapped her ear, her tongue, her palm. "The legends say he pierced certain parts of his body and sprin-kled the bones with his blood, so I think we should imitate those wounds and try the same thing?"

Yemania lifted her shoulders. Itza and her family knew more about their ancestor than she did. "It's worth trying."

Itza lifted the tip of her blade to the lobe of her ear, the tip of her tongue, and finally reopened the wound already across her palm. With her thumb, she gathered blood from each location, smearing it on the side of the jade skull, on its chin, on one of the bones of the hand. Yemania mimicked her, inflicting the same wounds on herself and placing drops of her own blood in the exact locations.

And nothing happened.

Yemania's pulse began to pound inside her ears. "It's not working!" She tried to keep the desperation from seeping into her tone, but her voice cracked anyway.

A crease formed between Itza's eyebrows.

Behind them, Yoli shuffled her feet against the dust. "Perhaps more blood is needed?" she suggested.

Itza squeezed out more blood from her ear, her tongue, and her palm. The red beads of crimson swelled before her thumb harvested them and applied them to the jade surface of the bones. Yemania did the same, adding more of her blood on top of Itza's. Yemania gritted her teeth and called deep into her spirit, willing the healing power of her ancestor to pull from the power housed in the room and funnel it into the bones laid across the altar.

Still nothing happened.

Her heart began to beat even harder, throwing itself against her breastbone as though it wanted to escape. "What else does the legend say? We have to be missing something."

Itza's chest rose and fell with short, panicked breaths. She scrunched her forehead and smacked her head with her hand. It left a bloody im-print from her palm above her eye. "Maybe it isn't the blood that's the problem. Maybe it's the bones themselves. In the original legend, I think he grinds the bones of humanity on a metate grinding stone and places them in . . ." She screamed suddenly, making them all jump. She dove for the floor beside the altar and emerged with a dust-coated jade bowl in her hands. "He placed the ground bones in a bowl. A jade bowl!" Her eyes went wide as if she only just realized what she was holding. She dropped the large bowl onto the altar as if it had burned her. The clatter echoed all around. "Oh my gods, I think that's the actual bowl he used to resurrect our ancestors." Tears of awe tracked their way down her cheeks.

Yoli poked the bowl with a finger. "You'd think it would be bigger."

Itza shooed her back with flapping hands. "This is a holy *relic*!" she shrieked. "Don't poke it!"

Yoli shrugged. "You dropped it."

Itza shushed her and began looking around for something else. "Where is the grinding stone? Help me find it."

They searched all around the base of the altar, and sure enough, they found a flat round stone on the other side. A smaller grinding stone sat within its gently curved sides.

"Will it be strong enough to grind jade?" Yoli leaned down to inspect it. "It's made of a material I don't recognize."

Itza nodded sagely. "The metate from the legend belonged to the goddess Cihuaoatl. She lent it to Quetzalcoatl to save humanity. I don't think it is from the earth, or even this level of creation."

Yoli rubbed her hands together. "Excellent! Who wants to use the goddess's grinding stone first?"

But Yemania placed a hand on Yoli's wrist. "Are you sure this is what we are supposed to do? Once you grind the bones, there will be no getting them back."

Itza worried her lower lip between her teeth. "I think this is what we are supposed to do. The bowl and the metate are both still here. That has to be a sign from the Mother, right?"

Something felt unsettled in Yemania's gut, but then again, Itza did know more about the legends than she did. "All right. Let's get started then."

They each took turns, rotating, working the grinding stone until their arms ached and sweat dripped from the ends of their noses.

"I bet . . . a goddess . . . could do this . . . faster," Yoli panted on her second rotation.

Yemania massaged the aching muscles in her wrists. "We are making progress. I think Cihuaoatl's metate is making this easier than a normal one would."

"You call . . . this easy?" Yoli slid the stone back and forth across the glittering jade powder.

It took them several hours, but finally, the bones of Quetzalcoatl had been completely ground down. Itza swept the powder into the jade bowl and placed it back upon the altar.

"Now, let's try this again," she said, reopening the wounds on her ear, tongue, and palm. This time, when each drop of blood made contact, it hissed and smoked. Itza cried out with relief. "I think it's working."

Yemania copied her, dropping her own healing blood into the jade bowl, watching the puffs of smoke rise into the air and filling the room with the herbal scent of incense. The smoke rising from the top of the bowl grew thicker, filling the room entirely until Yemania stumbled back and covered her nose with her arm. She coughed the burning herbal smell out of her lungs.

Then, from within the bowl, a figure began to rise. He rose from the ashes, head first, then torso and legs, human in shape, but with skin scaled and green like a serpent's. His face was not human, but some cross between reptile and bird with a broad snout, flaming nostrils, and knife-sharp teeth. He wore an elegant collection of feathers atop his head and across his chest that reminded Yemania of rainbow-colored macaws.

Quetzalcoatl. The great Feathered Serpent.

Itza threw herself onto the floor before him, prostrated in an act of worship and submission. Yemania couldn't force her body to move.

"G-g-great Feathered Serpent," Yemania tentatively addressed the god. "We have resurrected you to defeat the Obsidian Butterfly and her star demons."

She didn't know what she was expecting, but certainly not what happened next.

Quetzalcoatl fixed her with his yellow eyes oddly tinged with sadness. "I am sorry, daughter of healing. It is not my purpose to defeat her." With a swish of his rainbow-colored cloak, his body transformed into that of an actual serpent, elongating and sprouting wings that matched his feathered adornments.

Then, with a roar that shook the walls of the caves, he rose into the air. A great rush of wind swept over them, so intense that Yemania braced herself against the floor to keep from being pushed back down the ledge into the cavern below. Then, as quickly as it began, it stopped. The smell of incense and smoke began to fade. Yemania sat up, her ears pounding with her pulse, and looked around.

Quetzalcoatl was gone.

"W-w-where did he go?" Yemania asked, unsure if everything she'd just seen was real or a hallucination brought on by the smoke.

"I . . . don't know." Itza rose onto her knees.

Yoli snorted. "Gods, what did he mean that it isn't his purpose? Isn't he supposed to help us defeat the Obsidian Butterfly?"

"Did we do something wrong?" Yemania's lip quivered despite her attempts to stop it. They had succeeded in resurrecting Quetzalcoatl, but had it accomplished anything at all? Had he just abandoned them to their fate?

"Did Ometeotl say she wanted to save *us* or humanity in general?" Zorrah said slowly, exposing her pointed teeth. "What if the Mother's plan is to have him resurrect humanity after we are already gone?"

A tense silence grew between them. Yemania's stomach tightened into a knot. *These bones are our last hope to save humanity*, the Mother had said.

Humanity. Not the Chicome.

Morning dawned for the second day without the use of Ahkin's blood, and he prayed it would not be the last. He had hoped they would intercept Ochix and Metzi somewhere on their march toward the base of the mountains, but so far, the prince of death was conspicuous only in his absence. They'd bypassed Millacatl entirely, trying not to reopen the wounds of the city-state's disloyalty. Finally, they reached the expansive field where Ahkin had battled against Miquitz forces a lifetime ago. He tried not to think about the blood of his people that already fertilized this flat stretch of earth. It would be the perfect position to defend against anything descending from the mountains. They did not need to seize the higher ground, merely defend against it.

He ordered his leaders to begin stationing their warriors at the agreed-upon locations, maximizing use of the space they'd have to fight with their limited numbers. Ehecatl's and Atl's forces took the front, while Papatlaca's forces and some of their more creative weapons waited at the back.

"He might still be coming," Mayana said, coming to stand beside Ahkin and gazing toward the trees edging the base of the mountains at the other end of the field. Between them, low grasses waved in a gentle wind. The humid heat of the day was beginning to intensify, along with the buzzing of the cicadas. He knew she was hoping that their friend would appear and prove them wrong. But he still hadn't, which to Ahkin meant one of two things—Ochix was still trying to save Metzi before the eclipse began, or he had been captured. Either way, they had to be ready.

Ahkin tracked the moon's proximity to the sun, barely visible in the light of day but inching ever closer. By his calculations, the eclipse would begin around midday, just as the sun reached its highest peak. Ochix only had a few hours left, and if he failed, at least they still had Yemania resurrecting the bones.

———

"What do we do now?" Yemania squinted up at the bright sun shining overhead. Cicadas buzzed in the gathering heat of the jungles outside the cave. Their journey back out had gone much faster than their journey in. Had it really been only a few hours since they'd entered the cave? Now they rested along the stream that poured out from the cave's mouth, not sure where to go next. Part of her still hoped that Quetzalcoatl would appear and prove their suspicions wrong.

But he didn't.

Yemania's bag was much lighter, but the burden on her heart had never felt so heavy. How foolish they had been to think the Mother intended to save them before the world ended. Now that the reality washed over her, she was angry she had not seen it before. When had the Mother ever stepped in and prevented an apocalypse before? Every legend from their past told the same story. The gods destroyed them. Then the gods saved them again.

"Do you think when our bones are resurrected, we will remember this age? Or will our souls remain in Xibalba while a new generation starts over?" Yemania tried to sound conversational, but she couldn't hide the flat hopelessness from seeping into her tone. What would the legends of the eighth people say about them? Their end would be written in history as the apocalypse of darkness. The Seventh Sun, devoured by the stars.

Zorrah crushed a clump of leaves in her hand. "I'm not giving up that easily," she growled suddenly, jumping back to her feet. "Who says we can't defeat them? I mean, Ochix might still save Metzi and prevent them from even descending in the first place."

"Perhaps," Yemania said half-heartedly. She picked up a stone and tossed it into the stream. It broke through the surface with a soft *plunk*.

"We should join Ahkin and the others and fight. If we are going to die, then I want to die fighting."

"Sounds good to me," Yoli said, playing with the flames on her fingertips again.

"What do you think, Itza? Do you want to go back and fight with us?"

Itza sat in reverent silence, her arms wrapped tightly around her knees. She hadn't said a word since Quetzalcoatl abandoned them inside the cave.

"It's not your fault your ancestor is a jerk," Yoli said, slapping her on the shoulder.

Itza wiggled out from Yoli's hand. "This is not how his return was prophesied. I just don't understand." Her head snapped up. "Do you think he's already gone to the front lines? Maybe he is already there, preparing to fight with Tollan and the others?"

"Either way, that's where I'm going," Zorrah said. "The armies are probably gathering at Millacatl. It's the closest city to the mountains. If he's there, then I'll fight beside him. If he's not, then I'll still fight anyway."

Yemania groaned. Even though she had applied fresh maguey sap and rewrapped her leg, it would not be an easy trek. And Yemania was so exhausted already, physically and emotionally. They'd already walked countless miles, traveled across the empire and back again, and had nothing to show for it.

Worst of all, she had no idea how to tell Mayana and Ahkin that the plan to resurrect Quetzalcoatl wouldn't save them. Ochix was now their final hope.

———

"Absolutely not," the Jaguar warrior grunted, and threw the black cloak into the dirt at his feet.

Ochix pressed his fingertips into his temples to ease the ache that was beginning to form. "I'm not asking you to join the damn Miquitz Empire. You just need to look like one of us to get close enough. You *all* do." He glared at the grimacing faces of the other warriors, most of whom handled the Miquitz warrior costumes Ochix had stolen like venomous snakes prepared to bite.

"I earned my jaguar pelt, and I will proudly wear it into battle." The warrior closest to him sniffed and turned his nose into the air.

Ochix gathered the black cloak off the floor and threw it back in his face. "Then wear it over your bloody jaguar pelt. I don't care. If you all condemn the Seventh Sun to die because you won't change your clothes, I swear to the gods . . ." He blew out a heavy breath and stomped to the doorway of the stone cabin. If his own people didn't kill these stubborn sun worshippers who always thought their way was best, then he was going to do it himself.

They continued to mumble amongst themselves, holding up the cloaks by the tips of their fingers and shaking their heads.

Somewhere in the distance, the sound of a shell horn called out through the capital city—the signal for the people to join Tzom in the amphitheater for the ceremony to sacrifice Metzi. Ochix nearly choked on his tongue. He leaned his head out of the doorway and checked the position of the moon. It was nearly time.

"Nine hells, put them on and let's go! If I have to possess you to do it, I will. The ritual ceremony is about to begin."

"You will not take my will away from me, death prince," the warrior said with narrowed eyes. "Fine, we will wear the cloaks of our enemies, but we will not enjoy it."

Ochix grabbed the ends of his hair and pulled just to keep himself from screaming. This was too much, too much responsibility that Ahkin left upon his shoulders. Ochix jammed the prince's sun shield onto his arm. "Ahkin, you *owe* me for this," he said to the shield as if it could answer. The golden sun glinted up at him. "Stubborn sun worshippers," he mumbled, and followed the newly disguised Jaguar warriors out into the gathering crowds.

Ochix's stomach soured as he watched the celebrations of his own people, men laughing and jeering, women throwing flowers and dancing with their young children, all at the prospect of the destruction of an entire empire. Ochix didn't care that the Chicome were supposedly their enemies. Just as Yemania had not cared he was an enemy when she found him washed up on that riverbank. He thought of the women and children he'd seen strolling the streets of Millacatl, the first city that would fall in the destructive path of the Obsidian Butterfly. They did not deserve such a fate.

No one did.

He led the Jaguar warriors toward the amphitheater, but they continued to glare at everyone that passed as if they were star demons themselves. "Try not to look as if you hate everyone, please? They are supposed to be your people," he begged them.

The plastered attempts at grins they gave him were not reassuring.

We are all going to die, Ochix thought savagely. There was no way they would pass as Miquitz warriors. He had to find another way. And quickly.

"New plan. I will hide you just outside the amphitheater while I go in and try to get her. Watch from there, and once you see me come out with Metzi, come help us fight our way out of the city. Got it?"

"You do not trust us to go into the amphitheater with you?" one of them asked.

Ochix crossed his arms across his chest. "Nope. Not really, no."

The warrior withdrew a blade and waved it threateningly in front of Ochix's nose. "Hurry, little death prince, or we will do this our way."

Ochix sighed and adjusted his black cloak. "Just . . . don't do anything stupid." He sprinted back out into the masses of people flooding the amphitheater entrances. He would need to maneuver as close to her as possible, which would, unfortunately, require being close to his father as well. Then, he would just throw Metzi over his shoulder and run if he had to.

The seats were already beginning to fill. In the center of the amphi-theater, a black altar stood upon a raised stone dais. Metzi and his father were still nowhere to be seen, but he knew they would be here soon. He was reminded strongly of the last time he'd been here, frantically trying to find a way to save Yemania from the sacrifice to his ancestor. A lone guard wandered past, heading in the direction of the altar, and Ochix had another idea. It had worked before when he needed to get close to Yemania; perhaps it could work again to get him close to Metzi.

He pricked his finger and grabbed hold of the guard's life force. *Give me your spear*, he ordered. The misty-eyed guard handed it over without a moment's hesitation. Another shell horn sounded. Cheers rose from the stands. His father and Metzi appeared in one of the entrances and made their way toward the altar. His father was dressed in his finest black robes, his chest bare and painted to match the skull-like pattern on his face. His headdress fanned out behind him, the glossy black tou-can feathers shining in the sun. Metzi was dressed equally as regal, this time in a sleeveless gown of dyed black cotton that plunged down her front all the way to the jade beaded belt she wore around her waist. Upon her head sat a crown of golden-yellow feathers. A thick stripe of black had been painted across her eyes to match the paint on her lips.

How could Metzi look so calm? His father did not have Ahkin. She had to have some idea of what was about to happen, of whose blood was about to flow across the altar.

Ochix ducked his head and joined the group of soldiers stationed along the side of the raised stone dais. It would be just close enough for him to leap up and grab her. A shoulder pressed into his, then another on the other side. Ochix jostled against them, trying to keep his range of movement free.

His father lifted his hands to signal for silence. "All hail the great Obsidian Butterfly! Because of her generosity, our time of living in the shadows has finally come to an end. We will finally conquer the sun wor-shippers once and for all. We will show them the might of the Miquitz, and they will pay for their oppression with the blood of their own people."

The crowd's cheers rose in response, and Ochix swallowed back his disgust. Did they even really understand what they were cheering for?

"But before we begin," his father continued, "we have an honored guest among us who I think would enjoy a front-row seat to the festivities."

Then his father turned his face right toward Ochix and smiled. Metzi met his eye with a knowing smirk.

Ochix's stomach dropped. His father knew he was here. But before he could react, hands closed around his arms, and a blow to his knees knocked him to the ground.

Yemania had thought she'd never make it to Millacatl. They'd hiked through the jungles almost without rest, grabbing only two hours of sleep before continuing the rest of the night. Just as the Seventh Sun appeared, the city's gates appeared in the distance in the last dawn before the eclipse later that day. Yemania leaned heavily against Yoli and cried in relief.

"Where are the rest of the armies?" Zorrah's catlike eyes scanned the rolling fields surrounding the stone city, but the only camps they could see were at the base of the city walls. The warriors wore cloaks of green, but no other color or ranking was present.

Yemania felt as if she'd swallowed a stone. Why were Millacatl's armies here but none of the others?

They hobbled their tired, aching bodies past the camping army and toward the main gates, looking and undeniably smelling as if they'd been traveling for days. They asked to speak with emperor Ahkin, and the guards at the entrance led them immediately to the palace. Ahkin and the other lords were likely busy formulating their strategies and preparing for the battle against either the Miquitz or the Tzitzimime. Yemania wanted to assail the guards with questions, but she chewed the inside of her cheek to keep them to herself. She could ask Ahkin when they saw him. Perhaps Mayana and Patlani were even here somewhere.

They were led into a comfortable guest room filled with bowls of fruit and luxurious pillows. Yemania immediately collapsed upon them, barely listening to the guard, who said he would fetch the lord of Millacatl to speak with them as soon as he was able. The healer of Millacatl, one of her uncles stationed at the city, came and tended to her leg.

Yemania sighed with relief as the skin mended itself under her uncle's ministrations. He too remained quiet, and Yemania didn't have a close enough relationship with him to feel comfortable asking where the rest of the armies were.

After he left, Zorrah jumped to her feet and started pacing. "Something isn't right," she said, absently clicking her nails together as she paced.

"What do you mean?" Yemania asked.

Zorrah whirled around to face her. "Don't you think it's strange that none of the other armies are here? Why did the guards say they would get the lord of Millacatl when we asked to speak to Ahkin?"

A throat cleared, and Yemania turned to see Teniza standing in the doorway. "Because he isn't here," she said.

Teniza held her chin proudly in the air, but the puffed skin and redness of her eyes confirmed Yemania's unease. Something was not right.

"Congratulations," Yoli said, inclining her head at the princess of plants.

Teniza's eyebrows pulled together. "Congratulations?"

"On your wedding?" Yoli looked at Teniza, mimicking her look of confusion.

Teniza's eyes went wide with understanding. "Oh! You haven't heard? No wonder you all expected Ahkin to be here."

Zorrah crossed her arms over her chest. "What happened? Where are the armies?" Her tone was sharp, militaristic.

Teniza looked taken aback. Her hand fluttered to her chest. "We didn't get married. Mayana stopped the wedding, and Ahkin refused to raise the sun. He exposed the priest's lies about the rituals and essentially destroyed the empire."

Yemania's mouth fell open. "What do you mean, destroyed the empire?"

"Pahtia, Millacatl, and Ocelotl left Tollan without any intention of following Ahkin. But from what I can gather, he's taken the armies of Tollan, Atl, Papatlaca, and Ehecatl to the base of the mountains."

Zorrah picked up one of the fruit bowls and threw it across the room. The wall splattered with grapes and bits of mango. "And why aren't your people out there fighting with them? The eclipse will begin any minute. If the demons descend, they are going to devour *all* of us, not just Tollan!"

Teniza's eyes shone with defiant tears. "I've been trying to convince my father of that very fact, and he won't listen. I've been holding on to the hope that you all managed to resurrect the bones of Quetzalcoatl."

Zorrah hissed and kicked at the already discarded fruit bowl. "Well, we did, and he isn't going to help us. He left. Disappeared. Apparently the Mother intends is to have him resurrect humanity *after* the Seventh Sun is already destroyed."

Teniza shook her head. "No, no, that can't be right."

Zorrah spread her arms wide. "Do you see him anywhere? He's gone. We are on our own. We need to get your men out to the battle-field to support the others, or we are all going to die."

"I've been trying! He won't listen to me!" Teniza stomped her foot in frustration. "My father doesn't believe there's a real threat. He thinks Ahkin is crazy and that the eclipse will just pass."

Zorrah prowled to the window and glared out at where the moon's faded face inched ever closer to the sun. "Then he's going to have to learn the hard way. I just pray it isn't too late when he realizes Ahkin was right."

———

"Welcome home, my son." Tzom motioned for the guards to bring him onto the stage. One of them ripped the sun shield from Ochix's arm and threw it lazily behind the dais. It skidded to a stop in the dirt, sending a small cloud of dust into the air.

Ochix arched and struggled against his captors, but he was not strong enough to fight so many. They pushed him to his knees before his father. The death priest yanked Ochix's hair back to force his face up.

"You did not think I'd let you get away with that little trick of yours again, did you? Metzi told me of your little visit, and my generals relayed your failed attempts to recruit warriors to your cause. I figured I would see you here eventually."

Ochix gritted his teeth. His scalp screamed in response to his father's hands. "Does Metzi know you plan to sacrifice her? Or have you lied to her about that as well?"

Tzom laughed. "Is that what you think? That we could not get Ahkin's blood and so we would spill all of Metzi's instead?"

Metzi trilled a laugh. "They do not know the power and cleverness of our goddess," she said. "But they soon will."

Ochix stared at her in disbelief. This could not be happening. He could not fail Ahkin—or Yemania and the others. He could not let the entire Chicome Empire fall beneath the claws and teeth of the Tzitzimime. Nor did he want to become their first victim. Ochix roared and arched again, but a ball of cloth was shoved into his mouth, and more hands joined to hold him still.

A shadow began to fall across the amphitheater, across the world itself. The light around them changed, day turning not quite into night, but something halfway between the two. The sky's blue deepened, while a haze of yellow hung to the horizon. Stars blinked awake, their attention fixed upon the earth below. The temperature dropped, and bumps rose across Ochix's skin. He lifted his eyes and watched in horror as the black disc of the moon, forever jealous of its glorious brother, finally began its revenge. The eclipse had begun at last.

"It is time," Tzom said, offering a jet-black blade to Metzi. He placed his beloved star stone on the altar . . . and then stepped back. Ochix's pulse pounded inside his ears, almost blocking out any other sound.

Metzi nodded and then moved to stand at the altar by herself. With the obsidian blade, she sliced deep into both of her palms. Blood welled, bright and sensuous. Then, she placed each of her palms on the surface of the fallen star, coating the pockmarked silver stone in red.

She took it in her hands and lifted it toward the heavens, throwing her head back in reckless abandon. She began to chant, a mysterious phrase in an otherworldly language that Ochix did not recognize. Slowly at first, but then with increasing intensity. Her voice grew louder with each repetition of the chant, and the heavy silence hovering over the theater soon filled with the sound of her voice.

The stone began to glow as though the star itself were being reborn. Her chanting ceased, and Metzi did not scream—did not even flinch—as the blinding white light began to consume her, inching down her arms until it covered her body completely. Ochix wanted to turn his eyes away, the light almost too intense to bear.

From her back, the shape of wings began to sprout like seedlings from the earth. But they were not feathered wings like a bird's. They were two pairs of wings covered in shimmering, iridescent scales of red and black and yellow. They pulled her off her feet and into the air as the star stone dropped back onto the altar with a metallic thud. Metzi's hands and feet elongated into claws with nails as sharp as flints. The glowing light around her began to fade, or at least condense, until only her eyes remained as bright as stars.

The crowd's cheers rose to an earsplitting crescendo. Ochix's pulse thrashed inside his veins, and a cold sweat broke out across his skin. It was still Metzi . . . but not, somehow. They had summoned the goddess to them, and Metzi had become her vessel, hosting the divine form of the Obsidian Butterfly from within. She lifted a clawed hand to the sky just as the eclipse reached its apex, the sun nothing more than flaming edges around the moon, and clenched her bloodied fist. The flaming white edges turned deep cinnabar, tinting what little light remained over the earth with shades of red.

Ochix waited for the moon to continue its journey, to release the sun from its prison, but it did not. The Butterfly had frozen the sun in place, using—Ochix realized with a start—the blood of the sun god still coursing through Metzi's veins. She had not taken just Metzi's body. She had combined Metzi's power with her own.

The crowd gasped, though in awe or horror Ochix could not tell.

His father began to laugh, a high cruel laugh that betrayed the mania lurking within. He threw his arms wide in victory, tears streaming down his cheeks.

"My goddess!" he cried. "You have joined us at last! Unleash your wrath upon the Chicome, the descendants of those who imprisoned you! Feast upon their blood! Destroy our enemies!"

Metzi—or the Butterfly? Ochix had no idea what to call her—turned her star-bright eyes to Tzom. She bared pointed teeth. "You do not command me," she purred, her voice deep and cold. She reached down and grabbed Tzom by the throat, lifting him off the ground. His sandaled feet dangled pathetically.

"You—you—promised—" he gasped. His hands floundered across hers, but her grip remained tight.

"I promise many things, priest of death. Humans with ambitions of power and revenge are always easy to manipulate. But I am not a tool for you to use for your own purposes. *Your* purpose is to feed my Tzitzimime, and nothing more."

She squeezed her fist and crushed his neck as if it were made of straw. The crack echoed through the pregnant silence of the amphitheater. Then, she threw him aside, his usefulness to her complete. Ochix watched in horror as his father's lifeless body flew across the stage, eyes popping, skin purpled. Ochix's face burned, and the muscles in his neck went rigid as rage washed over him. Rage at the Obsidian Butterfly, yes, but also at his father for being foolish enough to trust her.

The Butterfly rolled her shoulders as if adjusting to her new body, and then lifted her arms toward the glittering stars watching from the inky blueness of the sky. "Awake, my children. The sun is now the one imprisoned, and you are finally *free*!"

The stars began to move, growing in size and streaking toward the earth like comets. All around the amphitheater, the fallen stars crashed, sending clouds of dust and smoke rising into the sky. And when the debris cleared, each impact revealed a tall, thin skeletal body of a star demon. A dozen, then two dozen, until an army of Tzitzimime filled the empty space between the crowd and the dais.

The guards holding Ochix dropped him and scrambled away, their instincts correctly telling them to run. Ochix's back hit the stage, knocking the wind from his lungs. He gasped for breath, clutching at his painfully tight chest. His frantic gaze focused on the Butterfly. For a wild moment, he wondered if he could try and possess her. But if he hadn't been able to master Metzi's will, her will combined with that of a bloodthirsty goddess would be impossible. Expectant tension hovered in the air like the inevitable moments before a snake struck, making his heart race.

Screams rose from the crowd as the mass of people writhed like a turbulent sea, rushing for the exits.

The Butterfly's mouth split into a wicked grin. "Let the feast begin."

———

Mayana's stomach clenched as tight as stone as the moon began to move across the sun. She stood on the edge of the field, Ahkin by her side. The general chatter and preparations of the army ceased, a great wind of silence sweeping across the battlefield as every face turned skyward. The light around them began to fade, the moon stealing both the sun's light and heat from the world.

She reached out and squeezed Ahkin's hand. This was it.

Her throat tightened as the moon continued its slow progression . . . until the eclipse was total and complete, a thin band of light around an empty hole of darkness. Stars grew bright in the deep navy of the sky, hints of yellow light teasing the horizon.

She swallowed hard, waiting. *Keep going.* She begged the rebellious moon. *Keep moving.*

But instead of continuing its journey, the moon remained in the same position, obscuring their source of life from the sky. The ring around the eclipse grew suddenly red, casting a bloody shadow across the land.

A cry of fear broke out among the warriors. Panic now replaced the silence as it swept across their forces. The sounds of preparations returned and intensified.

Mayana turned toward Ahkin, tears pooling in the corners of her eyes. "He didn't save her in time."

She didn't have words to describe the rush of emotions rearing up inside her. She nearly gasped under the pressure she felt building in her chest. Ahkin laid a hand upon her cheek, reaching for her as if she were the only source of strength he had left. She lifted her hand to cover his. Whatever was coming, they would face it together.

Their love had survived so much: the selection ritual, Xibalba, the foolish council, their own doubt and insecurities.

Could their love survive the end of the world too?

CHAPTER

54

It had to be a nightmare. It was the only explanation Yemania had for what she was seeing. It had to be a figment of her imagination, her mind dredging up her greatest childhood fears. The moon had devoured the sun, covering its glowing face in darkness, but then it did not spit the sun back up. The eclipse was frozen in place. The princesses all gathered at the window beside Zorrah, gasping as the edges of the sun's remaining light turned red. The hungry stars awakened in the sky. Then, the stars began to fall, plummeting toward the earth like thousands of tiny comets. A meteor shower of demons raining down upon the Miquitz Mountains.

Zorrah turned and looked at Teniza's tear-stained face. "Do you think your father will believe us now?"

The star demons screeched with glee and charged, a pack of starving wolves unleashed. Ochix rolled, his body slamming into the ground behind the dais. He lifted his head, gasping for breath from the impact. Ahkin's shield rested inches from his face. He reached out and slid his hand beneath the hide strap just as the Butterfly materialized above him.

"As for you, prince of death, your blood will be the first to pass my lips." She lashed out with her clawed hands, but he lifted the shield between them. Her claws collided with the golden image of the sun, sizzling and smoking where her skin made contact. She screamed and withdrew her hand, cradling it to her chest, the skin charred and blackened. Ochix stared down at the golden sun, wondering how in the hells he'd done that, if he had been the one to do that at all. But he wasn't going to let her moment of distraction go to waste. He rolled again, back onto his feet, and sprinted for the exit.

"I will find you, prince of death!" she screamed after him, her flint-tipped wings beating against the air. "Just as I will find Ahkin!"

Ochix barreled out of the amphitheater, but what he found outside its stone walls feasted upon his heart just as the Obsidian Butterfly had planned to. The star demons had chased the people, *his* people, into the city itself. Chaos reigned. Bodies of young and old alike littered the streets, chests ripped open, bodies pale and drained of lifeblood, the sounds of screams and demon screeches filled his ears, while the salty scent of fresh blood hung heavy.

Ochix didn't know which way to turn. His breathing grew shallow, panic overwhelming his senses. His father was dead. He was technically the emperor of the Miquitz now. Except that very soon, there might no longer *be* a Miquitz. How was he supposed to protect his people against an enemy such as this?

At the end of a long alleyway, a star demon turned and noticed him, straightening to its full, terrifying height. Ochix swore and ducked into the closest doorway, only to find a family huddled together in terror beside their extinguished fire. The father held his wife and two older children close. The mother's hands covered the children's mouths to keep them quiet. Tear trails glistened on their cheeks. Ochix shuffled them all to their feet.

"Run," he commanded them. "Run down the mountain and get out of the city. Take as many as you can."

"Into the valley?" The father seemed even more terrified at the thought. "But the Chicome—"

"The Chicome will protect you."

"But they—"

The demon screeched from the alleyway outside, making the man and his family flinch.

"There is no us or them right now!" Ochix hissed at him. "The only enemy that matters is death, and the only way to fight it is together."

The man nodded his head in understanding. Then, he reached into his cloak and withdrew a simple obsidian knife. "I only have one weapon, but I know it will be more effective in your hand than mine, my prince."

"Technically you can call me your emperor now." Ochix tried to laugh, but the sound came out hollow. He shoved them toward the back of the house. "Climb out a window if you can. Stay off the main alleys. I'll distract it as long as I can."

A skeletal torso atop spindly legs and a shell-lined skirt obscured the doorway. The demon bent at the waist and wedged itself inside. Ochix backed away with quick, jerky steps, trying to focus over the thrashing pulse inside his ears. His fingers holding the knife trembled, but the thought of helping the family escape kept him from bolting from the room.

"Ah, death prince," the demon rasped from its fleshless face. "I imagine your blood will taste *divine*."

Then Ochix did either the stupidest or the bravest thing he could think of—he charged directly at it.

Ochix collided with the demon, his knife finding the space between its ribs. But the demon snaked its long fingers around his throat and tossed him like a child bored with a doll. He slammed into the wall. His head swam with the force of the impact.

The demon wheezed a laugh. "We are not hurt by blades or fire, arrows or spears, death prince. I have no human soul for you to possess. There is nothing you can do to stop us." It bent low, its skeletal face grinning—well, could a skeletal face grin more than it already was? Ochix wasn't really sure, but either way, it looked pleased to have him cornered.

Ochix dropped his gaze to the golden sun on Ahkin's shield. An idea leapt into his head. "Nothing except this," he said. He thrust the face of the shield against the face of the tzitzimitl. Just as he anticipated, smoke rose from where the gold met its pale white flesh. The demon roared in agony, slashing at the shield with its hands, only to have them sizzle and burn where they touched the golden sun. It screeched again, then stumbled back as its hands and arms began to crumble into dust.

Ochix jumped to his feet, head spinning, and kicked it in the chest. The demon crashed into the extinguished fire pit. He threw his weight behind the shield and brought it down upon the creature's chest, trying not to vomit as the smell of burning demon flesh stuffed itself up his nose. He gagged, pressing down with every ounce of strength he had until the body disintegrated into dust beneath him.

Ochix clambered unsteadily back to his feet, chest heaving with both exhaustion and exhilaration. A cold lump of metallic stone sat where its body had been—a fallen star stone for a fallen star demon. The bloody things could be killed after all. Not by blades of bone or obsidian, but with *gold*? Holy gift from the gods or excrement of the sun, it didn't matter where it came from. All that mattered was that if his theory was correct, it could potentially be used to fight back.

He suddenly understood why Tollan might have built their whole damn city out of the stuff.

"Prince of death," came a voice.

Several figures clad in black cloaks appeared in the empty doorway. The Jaguar warriors he'd left hidden outside the amphitheater. "You didn't save her," one of them said flatly.

Ochix shook his head to try and stop the spinning. "Obviously. But I need to get back down the mountain to Ahkin."

One by one by they shed the black cloaks, exposing their proud jaguar pelts beneath. "We will get you back to the emperor. Or die trying."

He eyed the golden adornments some of them carried upon their weapons. "Excellent. And on our way, I have a little theory I'd like to try out on some of the star demons."

———

The tension that hovered over the Chicome forces was palpable, especially in light of what was likely making its way down the mountain toward them.

"Prepare yourselves." Ahkin lifted his macana sword. "We fight for the empire!"

A cacophony ran down the front line of warriors as they yelled in agreement and beat their weapons against their wooden shields. Ahkin's chest swelled with pride. He would proudly die fighting alongside them.

"Remember," Mayana mumbled, giving him a tense smile. "Just because the sun doesn't need you, doesn't mean I don't. Please don't be stupid."

Ahkin arched a brow at her. "Same goes to you, daughter of water."

She thrust out a hip and summoned water from her skull pendant. It wove around her chest and down her arm like a tame silver snake. She condensed it into a sphere, where it hovered at the tips of her fingers. "Together?"

"Together," Ahkin agreed.

A scream echoed across the length of the field. A human scream. The foliage that lined the sloping foothill across from them began to thrash, as though great beasts moved beneath. Ahkin's throat bobbed. Because great beasts *did* move beneath the leaves.

The trees closest to them shifted. Ahkin's muscles tensed, waiting for the first of the demons to appear. But what spilled out from the trees at first was not Tzitzimime. They were citizens of Miquitz. Faces painted with panic, parents running with children, wives running with husbands. They stumbled onto the open field, straight toward their lifelong enemies.

"They're Miquitz refugees." Mayana leaned forward, and Ahkin knew from her tone that she was fighting the urge to run out and protect them herself. What horrors had they just escaped in the mountains?

The first of those horrors appeared out of the trees behind them. Its skull-like mouth opened as it unleashed a roar. Then it sprinted for the nearest victim, its prey finally out in the open. A young woman fell beneath its claws in a flash of crimson.

Mayana turned her tear-filled eyes to Ahkin's. The order came to his lips before she even said a word. "Protect the Miquitz! Bring them behind our lines!"

The shell horn to begin the battle rang out, and the warriors charged across the field. Their feet beat against the earth like thunder before a coming storm. The first citizens they encountered crouched low, hands over their heads as if expecting the Chicome to attack *them*. Ahkin's heart nearly cracked in half. Did they really think so poorly of the Chicome? That they would attack innocent families fleeing from demons?

"Get behind us!" Ahkin doubted they could hear him from across the field, but he yelled anyway. "We will protect you!"

His warriors continued to usher as many of the refugees to safety as they could, but the first star demon had closed in. More demonic screeches echoed down the slope of the mountain. The hairs on the back of Ahkin's neck stood on end. Soon there would be even more.

A group of Jaguar warriors intercepted the tzitzimitl, which had been ripping at its victim. With a sweep of its long arm, the demon knocked half of them clear off their feet. The remaining warriors charged, stabbing and hacking. But one by one they fell beneath its pointed claws. The obsidian blades did nothing to the demon's bloodless body. It lifted one of the fallen soldiers and drank the blood flowing from a wound in his neck. Its eyes glowed a menacing red.

The warriors around it began to stumble back, their fear getting the better of them. Two more demons stumbled out of the trees, adding their roars to that of the first. Ahkin didn't even need to give the command; the men he'd sent out began to retreat.

The three demons started to give chase, greedy claws swiping after the men and remaining refugees fleeing like scared rabbits. But then, the demon on the right screeched and writhed as though in pain. Smoke rose from its towering form as though it had suddenly caught fire. Then, its body crumbled to ash, just as a figure sprinted over its smoking remains. It was Ochix. A group of about six or seven Jaguar warriors followed after him, golden jewelry and adornments flashing in their grasps. The two other demons turned their attention toward the disturbance; their hungry eyes now focused on the death prince. Ochix was yelling something as he ran, but it was impossible to hear him over the chaos and screams.

Ahkin ripped a bow out of the hands of the closest warrior. He nocked a flint-tipped arrow and let it fly, striking one of the demons right in its glowing eye socket. The demon stumbled back from the impact, then ripped the arrow out of its eye as if it had been nothing more than an irksome fly.

If Ahkin didn't do something immediately, his friend would never make it across the battlefield.

55

Mayana nearly cried with relief when Ochix appeared, but her relief evaporated as she watched him and the Jaguar warriors with him sprint for their lives. The two remaining demons were closing, their long legs outpacing the much shorter ones of their human targets. Ochix was shaking his head as he ran, pointing and gesturing to the shield around his arm, still screaming words that were impossible to make out. But Mayana recognized the golden sun etched onto the shield's surface. Ahkin's shield. The shield of his ancestor, Huitzilopochtli. The shield that could call forth the light and heat of the sun itself with the power housed in Ahkin's blood.

"Ahkin!" Mayana yelled, realizing suddenly what Ochix was trying to say. "Light the shield!"

"What?" He was already nocking another arrow.

"Forget the arrows and light the damn shield! He has Huitzilopochtli's shield!"

Ahkin's eyes went wide with understanding. He removed the arrow from the bow and raked its tip across his palm. He threw his palm toward Ochix, gritting his teeth in concentration.

The golden sun began to glow until it unleashed a beam of light so powerful it nearly blinded them. Ochix smiled triumphantly and turned it around to face the demons chasing him. The beam of light focused on the nearest one. Where it illuminated, the demon's flesh began to char. The demon shrieked and clawed at its body, its fellow slowing down and taking a defensive stance as it realized the threat. Ochix threw the shield over his back and kept running, the light protecting him like the quills of a radiant porcupine. The last demon crouched low, as though waiting for an order from an unknown source. Instead of continuing its pursuit, the demon then slunk back into the darkness of the distant trees. Mayana knew better than to take it as a victory. The demon was likely waiting for reinforcements to arrive, the other demons still feasting upon the city of Omitl.

Ochix ran right for Ahkin, who finally dimmed the blinding light emanating from the shield. The death prince collapsed at Ahkin's feet, removing the shield and rolling onto his back. He lifted the shield with both of his hands like an offering. "Here," he wheezed. His chest rose and fell with heavy breaths as he gasped for air. "I think this is yours."

Ahkin took the shield into his hands as gingerly as a newborn baby. "Where did you find it?"

"My father had it in his rooms from when they captured you." He coughed and took a few more deep breaths. "I'm sure as hells glad I found it. The demons are hurt by gold. It's the only reason we made it out."

Mayana's heart jumped into her throat. "The demons are hurt by gold?"

"Excrement of the sun, good for something other than just looking pretty." Ochix waved a weak hand toward the golden sun.

Ahkin shook his head, amused. "It's not—never mind. How do you know they are hurt by it?"

"Because, you shove it in their faces and their faces burn. Quite effectively, too."

One of the Jaguar warriors that had gone with Ahkin nodded in agreement, lifting the golden bracelet he clutched like a weapon in his hand. "It's true, my lord. The gold seems to affect them far more than obsidian."

"Gold!" Ahkin called down the lines of warriors suddenly. "We need gold!"

But Mayana knew they needed time more than anything. Ahkin

ripped the golden chest piece he wore off his chest and handed it to the lord of Papatlaca. "We need to get as much gold as we can on our weapons. Whatever jewelry, whatever adornments anyone has, melt them down and coat the weapons. Have every soldier dip their sword or arrows."

"Not many men bring gold to a battlefield," the lord of Papatlaca mumbled. But he took the golden chestpiece just the same. "But I'll find everything I can."

Mayana slithered her bracelets off her arms and shoved them into his hands. Some men did indeed possess small golden trinkets, bracelets or necklaces, adornments for their shields or helmets. Someone even ripped out an inlaid golden tooth. Ahkin's general, Yaotl, collected every scrap from the Eagle and Jaguar warriors, including those who had arrived with Ochix.

The lord of fire dropped the gold pieces into a stone smelting bowl and unleashed flames from his bloodied fingertips. Heat rushed out in a wave, hitting Mayana in the face. She shielded her face and stepped back while his flames melted the gold into molten sunlight.

Ahkin and the generals shuffled the men into lines, rushing them through to dip the edges of their weapons. It wouldn't be enough for all of them, but the more weaponry touched with gold, the better.

Another screech of a star demon cut through the air, slicing through each and every one of Mayana's nerves. The trees across the field began to thrash again. The demon's reinforcements had finished their meals in the mountains and were making their way down to quench their thirst in the valley.

"They're coming!" Mayana cried.

A line of skull-like faces materialized through the trees, their numbers multiplying as more and more demons made their way down the slope. Mayana fought back against the terror slowly freezing her insides. The few refugees who had made it out of Omitl had taken cover with the Chicome, but would they be safe even here? How were they supposed to protect those fleeing from another empire when they couldn't even protect their own?

"Shields up!" Ahkin yelled.

The men did as they were commanded, lifting their wooden shields with shaking arms and bobbing throats. It took great courage to follow orders in the face of fear.

The lord of Ehecatl and his son Patlani stepped out, standing in front of the line of shields with no protection whatsoever. They threw their arms out wide, unleashing hurricane-force winds that raced across the field. The demons flew back, many of them knocked clear off their clawed feet. Again they surged forward, only to be met with a solid dome of air that would not let them through.

Blood dripped in earnest as the Storm Lord and Patlani continued to expend enormous amounts of energy to hold the wall of wind in place. Their blood would eventually stop—or their lives would.

Mayana's heart raced. "They can't hold them for long. Do you think the gold will be enough to stop them?"

"We can't stop them, Mayana." Ahkin dropped his chin.

Her shoulders slumped. She hadn't expected him to be so blunt.

"My goal is to slow them down," he continued. "We have to give Yemania and the others enough time to resurrect the bones."

Mayana choked back a sob, guilt pooling in the pit of her stomach. They should have made it to the caves by now. But what if they hadn't? What if something had gone wrong? If she'd just gone with them . . .

"They will succeed," Ahkin said.

"How do you know?"

"Because if I don't believe they will, then I won't have the strength to keep fighting. And we have to keep fighting."

On the field, the Storm's Lord's arms began to shake. Slowly at first, but then they trembled as if he were battling chills. Ahkin used the rest of the time Ehecatl had bought them to set men digging trenches and filling them with thick tree sap. The lord of Papatlaca walked between the freshly expelled earth, igniting the sap until small rivers of fire flowed across the field. Smoke rose like an early-morning fog. They had all the warriors they could gather, weapons coated with every ounce of gold they could find, traps of smoke and fire set in the terrain between them. But still Mayana worried.

Would it be enough to slow the Tzitzimime?

Hundreds of demons now lined the barrier the Storm Lord and his son were creating. Some cast themselves upon it, only to be thrown immediately back. Each impact followed by a shriek raked along her nerves. She shivered and rubbed at her arms. She, along with every warrior the Chicome had, waited anxiously for the moment the Storm Lord's strength would fail.

Finally, with a cry of defeat, the Storm Lord collapsed in exhaustion. Perhaps the smoke became too much for him to take, or he'd finally lost too much blood to remain conscious. Patlani held on longer than his father, feet braced against the earth, sweat pouring down the length of his back. Then, even the storm prince collapsed to his knees. The dome of air collapsed with him. The air rushed off the field, blowing Mayana's hair back from her face. A group of warriors rushed out to drag their tired bodies back behind the front line.

The demons began their charge across the field. The Chicome forces held their collective breath, sending a prayer to the heavens that the fire would stop their advancement. At the first line of fire, the demons slowed, but did not stop. They carefully walked through the flames, which ignited the feathers atop their heads and hanging from their chests. Now they resembled demons of fire escaped from one of the hells.

Mayana's palms were so slick with sweat she wiped them on her skirt. She tightened her grip on the handle of her knife, its steadiness giving her the strength she would need. Beside her, Ahkin adjusted the grip on his macana sword. The sharp edges of the obsidian shards wedged into the polished wood reflected the flickering flames on the field.

Ahkin threw out another encouragement, trying to rally the remaining forces. "Fight to protect your families. If we fail, there will be nothing standing between your children and the wrath of the stars!"

His words seemed to stir the hearts of most. Heads and shields lifted a little higher; stances braced a little firmer. Mayana realized that it was hard to find the will to fight unless you knew what you were fighting for. When you were fighting to protect the ones you loved, the ones who gave meaning and purpose to this life, you realized why you were living at all. Death did not seem as terrifying as the thought of losing loved ones, of having to go on without them. She looked over at her father, standing beside the other men clothed in blue, and held his gaze. He gave her a small smile, and a warmth spread to the tips of her toes. A wound between them had finally begun to heal. Next, she looked at her brothers, twins Achto and Aquin standing beside Chimalli. Chimalli also caught her eye and nodded. Unsaid declarations of love, promises to protect each other, passed silently between them. She would fight for her family, just as she would fight for her younger brothers Tenoch and Mati, both waiting back in Atl. For Ahkin. For Yemania. For Zorrah, Yoli, and Itza. The friends and family who gave her a reason not to run.

Suddenly, as she watched death march toward her with each flaming step, she wasn't afraid.

Ahkin gave the signal. With the call of a shell horn and the answering cry of the warriors, the first line of the Chicome forces charged. He led alongside Yaotl and Ochix at the front, melding into the group of warriors, their cries rising together as one. What fear he felt dissipated as the adrenaline took its place. He was not alone. He was one tile in a much larger mosaic.

With a burst of light from his shield, Akin scorched one demon after another until nothing but lumps of rock remained. But where one demon fell, a dozen more rushed in to take its place. They were a living, breathing wall of flames and claws. He had to remember to ration not only his strength but also his blood. He lashed out, catching one demon in the back with his macana sword, the gold lacing its edge digging into its pale flesh. The weapons coated in gold did at least seem to be having an effect. All around him, demons screeched and roared, clutching at blackened wounds that smoked. Their tactics of attack became more careful, more calculated.

Mayana had moved to fight alongside her family, uniting their powers of water with terrifying effectiveness. The lord of Atl bent down to the earth. With a single touch of his hand, streams of groundwater burst forth like geysers across the field. Mayana and her brothers were there, manipulating the water into battering rams that knocked the demons off their feet, even encasing them in glittering crystal sphere prisons. He watched in awe as Mayana mimicked her father and bent to the ground. She closed her eyes and ran a bloodied hand along the dirt, summoning water to turn the soil beneath a group of demons into mud. The demons sank up to their bony knees before she pulled the moisture back out. They were instantly trapped within the hardened earth. Warriors of Atl made quick work of the trapped demons, shearing into them with their gold-tipped weapons like farmers harvesting wheat.

Ochix, on the other hand, whirled like a dancer, his gold-tipped spear plunging and striking with the effectiveness of a rattlesnake. Ahkin secretly thanked the gods they had never met on the battlefield.

Fallen star stones began to litter the ground, but still, they did not outnumber the bodies of the warriors that joined them. Ahkin watched in horror as a star demon's claws ripped through two men's stomachs at once, pinning them together and then flinging their bodies away with a single lashing strike.

Ahkin bent what little light around him remained, hiding himself from view. He ran at the closest star demon, his sword and shield raised. With a spindly arm, it swiped at him as though it could see exactly where he was.

He narrowly missed getting hit, but the sudden change in momentum threw him off balance. Before he could recover, it lashed out again with whiplike speed, knocking his shield off of his arm. Ahkin flew back, landing hard on his spine. He gasped for breath. The tzitzimitl appeared above him. It could most definitely see him. A searing pain shot across his shoulder as one of the demon's claws pierced through it. He pulled at the claw, trying to free himself, but the creature pressed down even harder. Blood dripped from the sharpened teeth in its skull-like face, matching the color of its eyes. It cocked its head. "I wonder how much power the blood of Huitzilopochtli will give me."

A geyser of water erupted from the ground and blasted the demon away from him. Ahkin yelled as its claw ripped itself out of his shoulder as quickly as it had gone in. Darkness clouded the edge of his vision.

Warm blood soaked his arm and chest. He looked up, expecting to see Mayana standing above him.

But it was the lord of Atl.

———

Mayana kept her distance from the demons themselves, not trusting her skills with an actual weapon. Though she had faced her share of horrors in Xibalba, she'd never been on a real battlefield before. That was something she'd have to remedy if they survived this. Perhaps Zorrah could give her lessons. But her water itself was a powerful weapon. Mayana mimicked her father and brothers, studying how they used their divine gift to help them fight. A surge of pride rushed through her, filling her lungs to their fullest with a deep breath of satisfaction as she watched them.

Achto and Aquin took turns using their gift to force a demon toward the other's waiting macana sword. Chimalli fought beside her father, manipulating every burst of water the lord of Atl brought forth from the earth. Their city-state's warriors were a blur of blue and gold as they moved across the field.

Her head grew heavier as more blood flowed from her veins. A warning sounded within, cautioning her to pace her strength. One of the demons set her in its sights. She summoned water from the amulet of Atlacoya and engulfed it, lifting the sphere of water into the air before slamming it back down. The demon was expelled flat upon the earth with an almighty splash. Ochix appeared from nowhere, his gold-tipped spear already impaling it in the back.

"Nice work, daughter of water," he said, panting with exhaustion.

A scream suddenly rose above the chaos, a scream Mayana knew to the depths of her bones. Ochix's head whipped around. Recognition sparked in his eyes too.

Ahkin.

A demon had him pinned, his shield lying useless, yards away. Mayana's stomach clenched painfully. He was so far. She and Ochix would never reach him in time, but they sprinted toward him anyway.

A geyser of water knocked the demon free, and her father was there. He reached down to lift Ahkin into his muscled arms. But before he could, another demon appeared. Time seemed to slow. Mayana was running as if through water, unable to force her limbs to move any faster. It grabbed her father by the shoulder, wrenching him around. Her father's eyes went wide as the demon lifted its claw like an arrow about to release from a bow. Mayana screamed. Her father lifted his hands, but he was not fast enough. The demon's hand plunged clean through his chest. Blood bubbled up through his lips. Life slowly drained from his eyes until nothing remained. Mayana didn't remember falling to her knees, but she was suddenly there. Smoke from the fires burned at her eyes and nose, but every thought was wiped clean from her mind, every sound faded to a dull buzzing.

The demon retracted its claws. Her father's lifeless body swayed and then crumpled, landing on top of Ahkin. The prince of light yelled and tried to wriggle out from beneath it. The demon turned its face to him, hunching over like a stalking cat. But then Chimalli was there, a scream of rage erupting from his core as he unleashed his fury upon the demons around them. A wall of water rose between Ahkin and the demons. They lunged forward, clawing at the rushing water that kept pushing them back.

Someone dragged Mayana back to her feet, was yelling something in her ear, but she saw nothing beyond her father's slack face, the empty stare of his eyes that—even in death—seemed to fix upon her. Chimalli wrenched Ahkin up and struggled to carry him away from the battle. Something blurred in front of her vision. Ochix's face came slowly into focus. He was yelling, but she could not hear him. She pulled her gaze away from him and found the rest of the world crumbling to pieces along with her. Many of the men had collapsed to their knees, and some bent forward cradling their heads in their hands. Others retreated toward the trees entirely. Fear and hopelessness were sinking their claws into her people as effectively as the demons themselves.

They were retreating.

They were losing.

Ochix's voice finally cut through the buzzing in her ears. "Mayana, we need to get off the field!"

Ochix's words echoed as if from a great distance, but she let him drag her back toward the line of trees. She had hands, had feet and arms and limbs, but they felt suddenly detached from her body as if she was nothing but a heart. A bleeding, breaking, helpless heart. The second wave of warriors rushed past them, ready to take over for their battered brothers.

But how long until their line crumbled too? How long until the demons cleared the field and began their sweep across the empire? The truth fell heavy upon her shoulders. They could not defeat the Tzitzimime. They were only humans. Humans fighting against gods.

Ochix half carried her to where Chimalli had Ahkin propped up against a tree. Bloodied bodies and screams assailed her from all sides—warriors nursing wounds and helping fallen brothers find temporary respite in the jungle's shade. It was far worse than Mayana ever imagined war could be. She struggled to pull in breaths, terror and hopelessness closing around her throat like suffocating fingers.

Her brother pressed a hand against the wound in Ahkin's shoulder, trying to staunch the bleeding. Mayana gasped as her mind flashed back to Xibalba. Ahkin's stomach bleeding out into the ocean of the dead. The snake fang sinking into his shoulder just before he lost consciousness—the boulder crushing his hand as she frantically tried to free him.

She had lost her father. She would not lose Ahkin too. Her fumbling fingers ripped the fabric of her skirt. She crawled toward him, shoving a bunch of the fabric against his bloodied skin. Her hands shook, so Chimalli helped her tie it in place. Then, her brother pulled her into his arms.

The grief, the terror that had been thrashing inside her chest, finally broke free. She embraced Chimalli back, choking on sobs that wracked her body like spasms.

"It's okay," he whispered, rubbing her back assuringly. "It's okay."

But it was *not* okay. Their father was gone. The armies they'd gathered were not enough. Her brother's arms were warm and solid, and they held her together as she let herself cry, unable to hold back the tears any longer.

"I should have helped him," Chimalli said at last, his voice thick with emotion. "Can you forgive me for not saving him?"

Mayana pulled back. "Chimalli, there is nothing you could have done. I don't need to forgive you, because there is nothing to forgive. Besides," she said, blinking back the tears clinging to her lashes. "You're the lord of Atl now."

Her brother stiffened. "You're . . . you're right. I—" His worried gaze scanned the injured men around them. But then his eyes returned to Mayana, worry and concern just as apparent.

"Go," Mayana told him. "I'll be fine. Take care of your men. Ochix and I can handle Ahkin."

Chimalli embraced her one last time. When he rose to return to his men, he did so with his back a little straighter, his head held a little higher.

Ahkin shifted against the trunk of the tree, hissing in pain at the movement. "I'm so sorry, Mayana. Your father saved my life. Without him, I would already be with Metzi in the underworld."

Mayana nodded, not trusting her voice. Her face throbbed with emotion, and she didn't want to lose the fragile control she'd just mustered. As it was, she carried her strength like a glass vase that might slip from her fingers at any moment and shatter.

Ochix dropped to the ground beside Ahkin, his hands gripping his hair.

Mayana's heart lurched. "This isn't your fault either, Ochix. I know you did the best you could to save Metzi in time. And without you, we never would have known about the gold."

Ochix leaned back against the tree. "I didn't save her. But my father didn't kill her either."

Mayana's hands covered her mouth. "She's still alive? Where is she? Why is the sun still frozen behind the eclipse?"

Ahkin leaned toward his friend, waiting for an answer.

The sound of the screaming around them intensified. A warrior raced past them. Then another. The second line of warriors was rushing back to the trees; horror painted across their faces. But Ochix's breathing seemed to stop as he focused on something over Mayana's shoulder. Something on the field. Mayana leapt to her feet. A cold feeling trickled down the back of her neck as she scanned for what caused the sudden shift upon the battlefield.

Through the smoke, a figure appeared. Feminine in shape, but with hands and feet tapering into knife-sharp points. Two enormous sets of wings sprouted from her back, elevating her above the chaos of the demons writhing for her to unleash them below. A sleeveless black dress plunged down her front to a beaded belt around her waist. The skirts of it flew out around her in the buffeting wind of her wings. Blank paint covered her eyes and lips, but her eyes themselves burned as bright as the stars in the heavens.

"Um," Ochix said, his throat bobbing. "She's right there."

CHAPTER

57

The creature that had just materialized on the battlefield was his sister . . . but also wasn't. Ahkin scanned her terrifying form: the wings protruding from her back, the pointed tips of her clawed hands and feet, the glowing stars in her eyes. It was Metzi, but it was also the Obsidian Butterfly.

"What happened?" Ahkin demanded. His shoulder gave a painful throb, and he winced.

Ochix had now joined Mayana, watching Metzi's slow progression across the field, her demons flocking around her like drone bees protecting their queen. She took down warriors—*her own people*—with vicious glee. She was taking her revenge against the empire that had crushed her dreams.

"She performed some kind of ritual using her blood and the star stone," Ochix said. "The Butterfly took over her body, like her spirit was being possessed. Then the Butterfly used her power combined with Metzi's to hold the eclipse in place."

"So she was forced?" Mayana asked. She could not keep her eyes away from the hideous female figure.

"No, I think it's what she wanted. I tried to possess her myself when she refused to come with me, but I couldn't override her will. It was too strong. If she's letting the Butterfly possess her, it's because she wants her to."

Ahkin's heart fluttered with fear as he watched his sister crush the skull of an Eagle warrior between her clawed hands. How had Metzi gotten here? To this place of such rage and revenge? Where her desire for power had consumed her to the point that nothing else remained?

He glanced over at Mayana, at the beautiful, strong, stubborn soul he loved. He'd watched her battle against a system that nearly crushed the life from within her. He'd seen it, that hollow hopelessness that had shadowed her eyes when she told him she didn't want to fight anymore. It had terrified him, almost separated them forever. Had Metzi also reached such a place? Had her powerlessness and hopelessness sunk deep enough to corrupt a soul that had once been so joyful and full of life? Ahkin's heart ached for her. How could he have let this happen?

And now his men were suffering. The entire empire was suffering from the mistakes of *his* family. Mistakes that traced back to the beginning of the age of the Seventh Sun. He would not let those same mistakes bring about its end as well.

"We need to retreat to the trees," Ahkin ground out through clenched teeth. The wound on his shoulder demanded his attention with each painful throb. He fixed his eyes upon Ochix. "Find Yaotl. Tell him to call all the men back. We can't face them on the open field like this."

"You think the trees will really be any better?" Ochix asked.

"What other choice do we have? They are slaughtering us in the open."

He could tell Ochix disagreed, but he left to find the general anyway. Not long after, the sound of the shell horn ordering retreat sounded three short blasts.

His gaze met Mayana's. "I'm sorry," he said, his throat thick with emotion. "For your father, for even bringing you here. For everything."

Mayana bent down and helped him to his feet. "I wouldn't be here if I didn't want to be. It was my choice, to fight for my people. It was my father's choice as well."

Ahkin leaned heavily against her. Ochix reappeared and took Ahkin's other side. Together, they retreated alongside the last remaining warriors.

———

Mayana wondered if they were just prolonging the inevitable. Were they retreating into the jungle just for the demons to hunt them down again? Her answer was the victorious screeching of the demons at her back, the cries of the warriors falling beneath their onslaught.

Mayana and Ochix dragged Ahkin through the underbrush, their pace as fast as they could manage. But the sound of the screeching was getting closer.

They had nowhere to run. No one left to help them.

A demon crashed through the trees, roaring with glee at the sight of them. Ochix dropped Ahkin's weight entirely on Mayana as he turned to face it, catching it in the stomach with his gold-tipped spear. Ahkin summoned light from his shield. The demon crumbled to ash and stone, just as two more appeared where the first had fallen.

Ochix engaged the closest, but the second slipped around him and headed right for Ahkin and Mayana.

Mayana screamed, trying with all her strength to pull Ahkin away while his attention and shield were focused on assisting Ochix. The demon reached for his leg, its pointed teeth and chin already dripping with the blood of its other victims. Ahkin turned his attention back just a moment too late as its claws sliced into the flesh of his foot. His scream of pain lanced through Mayana's chest.

Vines suddenly erupted from the surrounding foliage. They wrapped around the demon's arms, pinning them to its sides. More vines wrapped around its legs, dragging it to the jungle floor with a crash. Mayana choked out a sob of relief as Teniza appeared above them, her bloodied hand outstretched, her face contorted in concentration.

But Teniza was not alone.

Someone reached down to pull her and Ahkin away.

"We need to get you out of here," a hurried whisper said in her ear. But Mayana recognized that voice.

"*Yemania?*"

Yemania was already moving her hands across Ahkin's foot, his mangled shoulder. Ahkin gasped in relief as his wounds healed beneath her divinely gifted hands.

Zorrah appeared next, her face wild, her eyes untamed and focused on her prey. She launched herself at the demon, digging her obsidian spear into its back. The demon screeched, but her attack did nothing but anger it further. The demon lashed against Teniza's vines, nearly ripping itself free.

"Gold!" Ochix yelled, tossing his spear to Zorrah. "They are injured by gold!"

The animal princess caught the spear and, in one fluid motion, drove the golden tip where her first had been. The demon arched its back, claws gouging deep into the earth as smoke rose from its burning flesh. Zorrah stabbed again, and again, until it was nothing but a star stone sitting amongst the leaves.

Panting, Zorrah eyed the spear with appreciation. "Gold, huh? Where can I get one of these?"

Ochix delicately plucked it out of her hands, as if worried she would break it. "Well, this one is mine. We'll find you your own."

Zorrah bared her teeth. Mayana laughed a little hysterically. Yemania threw herself into Ochix's arms next, holding onto him as if he were a kite tether in a gale-force wind. The passion of their reunion reignited a flame of hope inside Mayana's heart. Maybe they would survive this after all.

Another volley of yells rose from the trees behind them, as thousands of soldiers dressed in green charged toward the front line. The appearance of reinforcements stirred the courage of those remaining. Word of gold weapons spread quickly as the new arrivals bent to retrieve the spears and shields of their fallen comrades.

Teniza motioned for Mayana and the others to follow her. The jungle was much darker than it normally was during the day, but the red-tinged light that filtered down through the trees still made it possible to see. Mayana didn't know where Teniza was leading them, but it was away from the main battle.

"What made Millacatl decide to fight?" Ahkin called after her as they sprinted away from the main action and deeper into the jungle itself.

"Well . . ." Teniza lifted the skirt of her dress, somehow still elegant as she ran from the starving demons of death. "My father finally believed you once the eclipse stalled. It took us a little while to get moving, but better late than never, I suppose."

She led them to a small protected copse of trees. The screams of men and demons were still close enough to raise the hairs on Mayana's arms. The lord of Ehecatl had recovered his strength and stood beside Patlani and Itza. This time, they protected the small wooded grove with bursts of wind that kept anyone from approaching without their permission. He eased his shield of air to let them pass. Inside the copse, they found the lord of Millacatl pacing impatiently as though waiting for something. The lord of Papatlaca was melting more gold beside a line of Millacatl's warriors, helping them prepare their weapons. The absence of her father sent a pang through Mayana's heart.

The lord of Millacatl snapped his head up the moment he saw Ahkin. He wrung his hands like a naughty child caught in an act of disobedience. The sight of such a proud, large man cowering made Mayana's stomach lurch. All the money and power in the world could not stand up against an apocalypse.

"Emperor Ahkin, I am sorry for not believing you. You have been out here protecting my city while I have done nothing but question your judgment and legitimacy to rule."

Ahkin took a step back, his jaw going slack. "I—um—this isn't the time to—"

The lord of Millacatl grabbed his hand and knelt before him. "If I face Xibalba today, I will not die without offering my apologies."

"Or die without trying to earn himself more favor with the gods," Yoli's dry tone said at Mayana's shoulder.

Mayana turned and threw her arms around Yoli's neck. "You're safe! You're all safe!" She pulled Yemania into an embrace next. All of the princesses had returned, which meant only one thing. Hope unfurled like a blossom inside her. "You did it! You resurrected the bones and came back to us!" She looked around, expecting to see Quetzalcoatl preparing for battle. But no gods were standing amongst the leaders of the empire . . . only mortals.

Yemania dropped her gaze to her feet. She rubbed a hand nervously up her arm. "We *did* resurrect the bones, but . . ." Her voice faded to a whisper too soft to hear.

The hope Mayana felt shriveled before it got the chance to fully bloom. "Then . . . where is he?"

A single tear trailed down Yemania's cheek. "He's gone."

"Gone? How can he be gone?"

Yemania lifted her face and met Mayana's eyes. "He told us that stopping the Obsidian Butterfly was not his purpose, and then he disappeared. I think—do you remember what the Mother told us in the holding chamber beneath the temple?"

Mayana didn't understand. "That the bones were the last chance to save humanity, right? We are fighting for our survival right now! This is the moment to save humanity!"

Yemania drew a shuddering breath and closed her eyes, as if she couldn't bear to look at her again. "Mayana, how has the Mother always saved humanity in the past? Does she ever stop the end from coming? Or does she provide a way for humanity to be reborn after they've already been destroyed?"

Every breath of air rushed from Mayana's lungs. Yemania's words struck her like a blow to the gut. Not because of their absurdity, but because of their brutal, undeniable truth. Yemania spoke them as if it had been the answer all along, a solution so obvious now that shame burned inside Mayana's stomach for even daring to believe something different.

Quetzalcoatl was not going to save them.

The Mother was not going to save them. She was going to let them be destroyed.

The burning in her gut flared even hotter, rage singeing away the shame. If the people of the seventh age were going to go down, they would go down with a fight. They would take as many star demons down with them as they could.

A lifetime ago, her father had scolded her. *"You, born into a time of privilege, do not know the pain of drought or famine. You have not watched your family swept away by waves of fire or water. You have not seen whole cities succumb to sickness or fall to the jaws of ravenous beasts. Thank the gods I have not, but I can imagine . . ."*

Now she did not have to imagine. Her father's warnings had always felt as distant as birds soaring high above their heads, too far away to be of any consequence to them here on earth. But now her father's words circled like descending vultures. The end he'd always feared had finally come upon them. It had cost him his very life.

Was this how the people of the other ages had felt? When they watched their world being destroyed around them? Had they given into hopelessness, overwhelmed by the weight of their world ending? Or had they raged? Had they fought back against their ends, no matter how dire the circumstances became?

She knew what it felt like to want to give up, to feel so tired of fighting that it just seemed easier to lie down and let the world step over you. But she knew now she could never do that. No matter the odds, no matter the cost, she would fight. Perhaps it was a war they could not win, but she would rather die standing, staring the end in the face with her chin held high, than ever lie down on the ground again.

CHAPTER

58

"So you stopped their wedding? That's a story I want to hear." Yemania arched an eyebrow. The sounds of battle continued outside the clearing, but Mayana was glad to think of something else for a moment.

The back of her neck grew warm. "You were right. I should have kept fighting for what I wanted," she admitted. "I just needed a little help to remember that."

"I knew you'd figure it out eventually. I want to hear all the details someday. You know, if we survive this."

"If we survive this . . ." Mayana repeated, picking at her thumbnail.

"I always wanted us to die together, remember?" Yemania gave a half-hearted smile. "Maybe that wish will come true after all."

Mayana reached out and squeezed her hand. She was so glad to have met her dear friend. "If we do, I promise it will be together."

"We all will," Zorrah said from Yemania's other side. A bee buzzed around her head, and Zorrah knocked it away with a furious swat of her hand. She then glared at the bee's fallen form as if it had done her a great personal harm. Zorrah rarely allowed herself moments of connection like this, so perhaps she wanted to punish the bee for daring to interrupt her. The memory of Zorrah taking control of the entire swarm of bees back in Ehecatl popped suddenly into Mayana's head, the image of her directing them as if she were their queen . . .

"Ahkin!" Mayana screamed suddenly, rushing to where Ahkin was still awkwardly trying to fend off the continued apologies of the lord of Millacatl so that he could strategize their next move with Ochix. The sounds of the battle were raging ever closer, and just as before, the Storm Lord, Izta, and Patlani were beginning to lose strength. Men were again beginning to retreat around them, though where there was to run to, Mayana didn't know.

Ahkin looked up at her, his head cocking to the side.

Mayana skidded to stop, struggling to find her breath. "Bees!" she gasped.

Ahkin stared at her as if she'd gone insane. "Bees?" he repeated flatly.

"No, not—never mind," Mayana waved an impatient hand. "The demons flocked around Metzi like drone bees around a queen, remember?"

Ahkin's brows knit themselves together. "I do . . ."

"We are focusing on killing and holding back the drones when we need to be putting our energy into killing *the queen*. She is the one who brought them here. If we can kill her, the eclipse will end, and the sunlight will destroy the rest of them."

Ahkin blinked, then yanked Mayana toward him for a swift kiss. "I think you're right." He looked at Ochix.

The death prince nodded. "I think she's right too. We need to hit the enemy right in the heart."

"Then we need to find her." Ahkin stretched out his newly healed shoulder and tightened the strap on his sun shield.

———

Ahkin knew he might not survive the encounter, but if he were going to leave this world, he'd do so the same way he'd come into it. He would take his twin with him.

Just as his plan solidified in his mind, Itza, Patlani, and their father all slumped against one another. The dome of wind protecting their copse of trees collapsed in a rush. Dozens of demons that had been waiting just outside the barrier rushed in. Their skeletal smiles stretched wide in triumph. Zorrah and Yoli rushed to Itza's side, defending the royal family of Ehecatl with their abilities while Yemania tried to tend to their wounds. A demon slipped past Zorrah's whirling spear, headed straight for Yemania's back as she bent over the lord of storms. But then Ochix was there. His own spear thrust up through the tzitzimitl's jaw.

"Go! Find the Butterfly!" Ochix yelled. He jerked the spear out of the star demon's skull and rammed it into the chest of another.

Ahkin bolted for the trees. He intended to go alone, but Mayana followed, her face set in such a way that he knew it would be pointless to argue. Warriors continued to run past them, heading away from the battlefield. He felt like a fish swimming upstream against the current of their retreat.

All around him bodies littered the jungle floor like husks of fallen fruit, some still freshly bleeding, others drained of blood entirely. The Tzitzimime gained more strength with each drop of blood they consumed. The longer the battle raged, the smaller their chance of victory became. The reinforcements from Millacatl had helped, but ultimately the tide was shifting again in favor of the stars.

One terrified young Eagle warrior lay before them, a wound in his thigh leaking his life's essence onto the jungle floor. Ahkin knelt beside him, clasping his hand. "You fought bravely, my brother. I know you will find your place in paradise. Do you know where the Obsidian Butterfly is?"

The man nodded, gasping for breath, his lips paled with pain. "I think she's that way. I heard the—" he swallowed hard "—the screams."

Ahkin squeezed the young man's hand with a pang of regret, and followed the direction he pointed. He felt as though they'd stepped into a nightmare, or fallen back into the realms of Xibalba. Bushes thrashed where demons stalked them through the semidarkness, the blood of his people running thick across the leaves. Movement and sound assailed him from all sides. It was utter chaos. If he had any hope of finding her, let alone defeating her, he needed to draw her out of the shadows. He needed a clear path to see what was coming. They finally stumbled into a small clearing of grass. It was not ideal, the ground sloping sharply beneath their feet, but it would at least afford the visibility they'd need. Mayana caught his eye and nodded as if she already knew what he planned to do. Her confidence gave him the strength for what he did next.

"Metzi!" he yelled, his voice echoing through the trees. "I know you're here!"

A hissing sound swept through the clearing, a wind of whispered laughs from the thrashing greenery surrounding them. Then, the thud of beating wings. A high, cold laugh as dark as spaces between the stars. Mayana cried a warning. He turned his shield just in time to block a blow intended for his spine. The impact knocked him off his feet. Breath rushed from his lungs.

The Obsidian Butterfly lowered herself to the ground before him, her bare, clawed feet settling upon the grass. Blood coursed down her arms and coated her chest.

An unknown emotion tightened his throat as he studied her familiar, yet drastically altered features. The face that had once laughed with such mischievous joy. Feet that had dragged him onto the dance floor at feasts. His voice cracked as he stumbled back to his feet. "Metzi, what happened to you?"

Her star-bright eyes flared red, and she bared her pointed teeth. "I am not Metzi. I am Itzpapalotl, the great Obsidian Butterfly, mother of the darkness and stars!" She paced toward him with slow, deliberate steps—a jungle cat in the moments before it pounced. "I will devour you just as I have devoured every soul that has stood in my way. You humans are nothing but playthings of my mother's favorite children. And now, I want to play with you myself."

Ahkin charged, swinging his macana sword in an arc over his head. With a rush of wings, she returned to the sky, laughing as she rose out of reach. She lifted a hand like a signal, and more demons slinked out into the clearing. He and Mayana were entirely surrounded.

"Where are your allies, Ahkin?" Her laugh was malicious. "Where are those who swore to fight beside you? Have they seen the truth of how weak and foolish you truly are?"

Ahkin's macana sword found the chest of a nearby demon, but not before its claw found his first. Sharp, searing pain. Warmth flowed down across his stomach. He pressed a hand against the wound to staunch the flow. Mayana cried out beside him, grasping at blood streaming from her shoulder. She collapsed to her knees. Ahkin screamed and unleashed a desperate blaze of light from his shield that cut across the field.

The Butterfly appeared before him, sending the demons into retreat with a wave of her hand. They prowled the edges of the clearing like scavengers waiting to clean up whatever their mistress left behind. This was undeniably the Butterfly's plan, to end him herself.

She lashed out with whiplike speed. Ahkin braced himself for the blow, but her aim was careful, calculated. Her claws avoided the gold altogether and connected with the wood around the edge. The shield fractured into pieces, the golden sun shattering like glass. He flew back and landed hard on his back. His macana sword flew out of his grasp.

Mayana tried to summon water from her necklace. But the Butterfly struck her across the head. Mayana's head whipped to the side. Her body crumpled to the ground. Blood poured from a cut above her eye.

"M-mayana!" Ahkin cried. He struggled to pull breaths into his lungs.

The Butterfly stalked toward him. "So much concern for the daughter of water. Where was that concern for your sister? Your own flesh and blood!"

Ahkin looked around, desperate for any help he could find. His macana sword had landed several feet away. He lunged for it. But the Butterfly's clawed foot came down on his wrist, smashing the bones with a sickening crack. Ahkin screamed as pain burned its way up his arm like flames.

"Who has the power now, Ahkin?" She ground her foot down harder.

He screamed again.

Mayana's ears were ringing. The edges of her vision blurred, and her head swam. She touched a stabbing pain above her eyebrow—her fingers came back coated in sticky blood.

But Ahkin's scream dragged everything back into sharp focus. It was a knife cutting through the fog obscuring her thoughts. Mayana tried to sit up, but everything around her tilted dangerously to the side.

The Butterfly stood over Ahkin, her foot crushing his wrist. Ahkin writhed in pain beneath her. Blood coated his chest from a nasty-looking gash. Occasional bursts of light shot helplessly into the sky from where the pieces of his ruined shield lay too far outside his reach. The beams of light glinted on the golden edge of her knife lying beside her. The one she'd dropped when the Butterfly had struck her. Mayana reached for it and gripped it tightly in her hand.

"You brought this on yourself, Ahkin. The favored sibling, everything handed to you on a golden platter. You had the chance to change things, to undo everything your father did to Metzi, and you didn't." She grabbed Ahkin by the throat, her divine strength lifting him as easily off the floor as if he were a stalk of wheat. "You aren't any different. You were ready to sell me to Ehecatl just as easily as he was!"

Mayana's ears perked up. Sell *me*, the Butterfly had said. Not sell *Metzi*.

Metzi was still in there, somehow. She was raging, angry at Ahkin and everyone else who had tried to control her and force her into a system where she didn't feel she had a voice. But she was wrong. He was willing to stand up, to burn down the system that had done this to *all* of them. Hadn't he already done that? Ahkin had stood up and said no. He had refused to raise the sun, and as a result, he'd brought every lie his ancestor had carefully crafted crashing down. He had chosen to give up that power, not sacrifice those around him to keep it.

The Butterfly lifted a clawed hand over Ahkin's rapidly rising and falling chest.

"Stop! You're wrong, Metzi!" Mayana yelled.

The Butterfly's hand hesitated. "I'm not Metzi! Metzi belongs to *me* now!"

Mayana stumbled to her feet, a hand pressed against her swimming head, the other gripping her knife's handle for stability. "No, Metzi, I know you're still there. And you're wrong. Ahkin isn't like your father. He did change things."

The Butterfly hissed and turned her star-bright eyes to Mayana. "You are a fool, daughter of Atlacoya. I've seen you in Metzi's memories, and I have watched you from the stars. You hate the empire and all it stands for. You, too, have suffered under the burden of its lies and oppression. Ahkin was ready to sell you to Ehecatl just as he was willing to sell his sister."

"Is that what she's told you, Metzi? That Ahkin tried to sell me to barter for peace too? Because that isn't what happened. The Butterfly is hiding the truth from you. She's using you. She doesn't have your best interests at heart."

The goddess's eyes flickered for just a moment, as if a hint of Metzi's brown eyes lurked beneath. Something about those final words had struck a chord inside her, as though she'd heard those words somewhere before but hadn't quite believed them yet.

"*Lies!*" the goddess hissed through Metzi's lips.

But Mayana sensed the weak spot and pressed it even harder. "You think you have true freedom and power? Do you really feel free right now, Metzi? With the Butterfly controlling you like this? With her lying to manipulate you, feeding upon your anger and pain? This isn't what freedom looks like."

The Butterfly dropped Ahkin and stalked toward Mayana instead. Ahkin fell to the ground, clutching at his assaulted throat.

Mayana refused to back down. She wouldn't cower in the face of lies, of those desperate to keep their power. She'd done enough of that to last her a lifetime. "He had the chance to sell me to Ehecatl, and he *refused*. I was the one who wanted to go. I was the one willing to give up under the pressure of the empire's traditions, until I decided I wanted to be with him no matter what. Instead of rejecting me, he refused to raise the sun. He showed everyone the truth, and it cost him everything. He made a *different* choice than your father."

"NO!" The Butterfly struck Mayana across the face again. Lights blinked behind her eyes as the ringing in her ears returned. Claw-tipped fingers closed around her throat now, forcing her chin up. Mayana dropped her knife. Her hands flailed uselessly against the Butterfly's grasp.

"If he loves you so much, then the best punishment I can give him is to make him watch as I drink every last drop of blood from your body."

"He loves you too, Metzi," Mayana choked out. "He always has."

The brown in her eyes returned for the briefest of moments. Her fingers loosened their grip, dropping Mayana to the ground. But then the stars returned, and Metzi gripped her own hair in her clawed hands.

"*She lies! He never loved you!*" The goddess's voice poured out from Metzi's mouth.

Metzi screamed, an agonized scream of soul-deep suffering. The color in her eyes shifted back and forth from blinding bright to simple brown.

Ahkin tried to crawl closer. "I do love you, Metzi," he said, reaching a hand toward her. "You are my sister. I was wrong to treat you as I did. Please forgive me. I knew you didn't want to go to Ehecatl. I knew your heart belonged to someone else, and I was going to force you to go anyway. Forgive me for being a fool and not allowing you the freedom you deserved."

Metzi's brown eyes filled with tears, and she gasped, clutching at her heart. But the goddess's star eyes returned just as quickly. "She will do as I command! Metzi is *mine!*" The Butterfly bent down and retrieved Mayana's fallen knife. She turned and stood over Mayana, lifting the knife into the air. Her bloodred lips split into a triumphant smile and her wings fluttered with anticipation.

"NO!" Ahkin screamed.

Mayana covered her head and tried to roll away, bracing for the bite of the obsidian blade into her flesh.

Another scream, but this time it was cold, inhuman. A scream of rage, of terror, of defeat. Mayana glanced up through her arms.

The knife blade had penetrated Metzi's chest. Her eyes were again brown and focused, even as blood bubbled from between her lips.

"I'm sorry . . ." Metzi whispered. Her hand fell away from the hilt. And then she collapsed.

"Metzi!" Mayana cried. She crawled toward the princess of light, the ground beneath her turning a deep crimson. Smoke rose from around the hilt of the dagger that protruded from the Butterfly's ribs, the gold along the blade having found its way into her heart. Her beautifully intricate wings lay crumpled and broken against the grass, like a real butterfly someone had crushed beneath their foot. The demons encircling the clearing shrieked with rage. Mayana expected them to charge, to seek revenge for their fallen goddess, but they remained where they were, hovering as if waiting for another order.

Mayana knelt beside her, lifting Metzi's shoulders into her lap. She was heavy, like a bag of grain. Her head lolled against Mayana's chest. Mayana searched for any flicker of light remaining in her eyes, but didn't see any. She pressed her fingertips into Metzi's neck, already slick with the princess's blood—but found no sign of her beating heart.

Tears burned their way down Mayana's face. She guessed she shouldn't have been surprised. Metzi's will had been too lofty to bring back to earth, too solid in its strength to bend. But she'd fought back against the Butterfly in the end, using what control she had left to set herself free once and for all.

Mayana prayed Metzi would find peace and forgiveness in paradise.

CHAPTER

59

Metzi was dead. Ahkin's bruised throat felt tight, the pressure on his chest suffocating. She had taken the final strike against the Butterfly. In the end, she'd tried to make up for her mistakes. But the truth settled heavily in his stomach. His sister, his twin, was gone.

He rose to his feet. The pain in his crushed wrist shot through his arm and nearly made him black out. He held it to his chest, watching as Mayana cradled Metzi's head in her lap. She didn't even notice that Metzi's blood was covering her hands and legs. She just whispered a prayer of passing over his sister's body, then gently reached up and closed the lids of her open, glassy eyes. The demons surrounding them clawed at the earth, still holding their position where the Butterfly had commanded them, but impatient somehow. What could they be waiting for?

A cold wind swept across the clearing. The short stalks of grass bent and rippled out from where Mayana held Metzi's body in her arms. The waiting demons growled like a pack of ravenous wolves. Ahkin's stomach tightened with unease. They needed to get out of here before the demons broke through whatever bonds held them back. Mayana's spine, which was still facing him, went suddenly rigid.

"Mayana?"

She did not respond. The demons began to chatter excitedly.

"Mayana, please, we need to—" He reached out for her shoulder.

Her skin felt cold beneath his hand. He turned Mayana around to face him, but then scrambled back as if she'd burned him.

Her eyes shone as bright as newly awakened stars. From her shoulders, the shape of glorious butterfly wings began to unfurl.

———

A rush of power unlike anything Mayana had ever experienced flooded through her. Every ounce of fear, every shred of doubt, disappeared in the white-hot sensation that burned across the surface of her skin. She could do anything, defeat anyone. All of her dreams could finally be hers. She just had to reach out and take them.

This is power, daughter of water, the voice of Itzpapalotl purred in her ear. *You have only caught glimpses of what it means to be a goddess. Let me show you what it really means.*

A goddess. Not a shadow of the divine, not a part-blooded descendant, but a true, fully realized goddess. All her life her power had been limited—limited to the godly blood in her veins, limited by her human frailty and how much blood she could afford to spill. She had watched as the royal family of Ehecatl fought to keep those barricades of wind in place, only lasting as long as their bodies would allow.

With my power, I can enhance your abilities as I did Metzi's. My power does not end. It does not tire or grow weary. The eclipse can hold because my power combined with hers will not fade. Not even Ahkin is strong enough to move what Metzi and I created together.

What would that look like? Mayana tried to picture it, to imagine unlimited use of her ancestor's power.

Why imagine? the goddess said. *Try it for yourself. Surely you can feel the water all around us. Call it to you, Mayana. Make it obey . . .*

The goddess was right. From the moisture condensing in the clouds, to the rivers and streams weaving through the forest like arteries. Mayana could sense it all. Water was all around her, waiting for her to call upon it.

And she did.

Mayana lifted her hands into the air, and from all around, water flowed through the trees and descended from the sky. Rivers and streams became airborne, heeding her call. She pulled it all together, a crystalline mass that stretched the length of the sky as far as she could see, holding it just above the jungle canopy, an almighty wave about to break. She didn't need to prick her thumb or slice into her palm. The power was no longer just her ancestor's that Mayana called upon in times of need. This power was entirely *hers*. She could release it if she wanted. Let it fall and drown every soul in these jungles with the flick of her finger. Screams rose from all around them at the sight of the wave, but Mayana barely heard them; she was lost . . . marveling at the possibilities.

So many possibilities. No one could ever force you to choose between your heart and their expectations ever again. You would get to decide.

It was as if she held a delicate baby bird in her hands, its very life depending on her whim. She could close her fist and crush it, or let it go free. But for the first time in her life, there was no one forcing her to choose. It was a decision she could make entirely for herself. Her fate was completely in her own hands, not Ometeotl's.

The Mother had abandoned her, left her to die along with the rest of the Chicome Empire. She never had any intention of saving them from the start . . .

Yes, the voice said, *the Mother does not care for you. She never has. You were a tool for her to use and discard. She cares only for her favorite children, nothing more. But you can take your revenge against Ometeotl. Help me destroy the ones she loves, just as she has done nothing to protect the ones you love.*

Images flashed before Mayana's eyes. Her mother's broken body lying at the foot of those stairs. Her dog Ona crumbling to ashes in the sacrificial fire. Her father's body bleeding upon the battlefield.

Where is her divine love now, daughter of water? Where is her concern for her creations? More images: the broken, bleeding warrior who had told them where to find the Butterfly, Ochix sprinting across the battlefield with demons hot on his heels, Itza collapsing in exhaustion while Zorrah and Yoli fought to protect her, tears running down

Yemania's cheeks as she worked to heal Itza's wounds. The Mother had abandoned them all, tricked them into a false sense of security with the bones of Quetzalcoatl when she never intended him to save them. Had she just used the princesses to get her favorite son back? Were their human lives a price she had been willing to pay for her own selfish goals?

She made you give up the bones of your mother to save her son, didn't she? She asked you to pay a price she wasn't willing to pay herself . . .

Her gaze fell on Ahkin. He stared at her as if he did not recognize her. His mouth was moving—shouting something, his eyes darting from the mass of water hanging over them to Mayana's face and back again. But she could not hear him above the goddess's whispers in her ear.

You could do it, you know. Destroy the empire that refused to allow you to be together. Even now, where are Pahtia and Ocelotl? The lord of Millacatl is only here to save his reputation, to earn himself favor in the underworld should he perish.

It was true. The other cities had left. Millacatl had arrived at the last possible moment. She had watched their lord grovel at Ahkin's feet in a show of false humility.

They have called you selfish. But they are the selfish ones. They have allowed this empire to build itself upon lies. Burn away the rotted flesh this empire has become and start anew. They are too corrupt to continue the way they have. You have the power now, Mayana. Your power combined with my own. My demons are at your disposal, you need only lift your hand, and they shall do whatever you command.

Whatever I command?

Whatever you command. Take your revenge, daughter of water. You were never enough for the Chicome. They rejected you over and over. They demanded your very life. Now demand theirs. You and Ahkin can create a new world together once this one has been cleansed. This empire is a plague. Burn it to the ground.

"Burn it to the ground," Mayana whispered. The goddess was using the very words Mayana had spoken to Ahkin on top of the temple. And as horrible as it was to admit . . . the goddess's logic seemed sound. Ahkin had showed the empire the truth, and yet, the city-states could not agree. Still their empire was in ruins. Each lord had his own agenda, his own selfish desires. Could she and Ahkin really save a world already so broken to begin with? Wouldn't it be easier to just start anew?

A flash of light cut through the clearing. Mayana's attention snapped back to Ahkin. He stood before her, holding a fractured piece of the once-golden sun from his shield. He did not direct the beam of light at her, but up at the mass of water above their heads. Where the light met the water, it split, breaking into tiny beams of every color. A feeble, flickering rainbow that reflected briefly across the sky.

His voice drowned out the Butterfly's whispers for just a moment. The searing light at the edges of her vision cleared.

"Water and light, Mayana," he yelled. Tears glistened upon his cheeks.

"Together they can create something beautiful," she whispered back.

His strength suddenly gave out, and Ahkin dropped to his knees. The broken shield shard fell to the earth with a thud. The faint rainbow disappeared, but Mayana could still see it, as if the colors had burned into the back of her eyes.

Ahkin had been just like the lords . . . broken, lost in his ignorance and blind acceptance of what he thought was true. But he'd learned. He'd seen the truth and become one of her greatest allies in fighting for it. Could the rest of the empire learn as he did? It would be difficult. It would be the fight of her life.

She looked down at her hands, the hands that had ripped away the bushes the Mother had placed in her path when she'd tried to escape her in the garden before Ahkin's wedding. *There's my fighter.* Yes, the empire was broken. Yes, her people had done horrible things. But they were still her people. And hadn't she already made up her mind to fight for them? To never give up again? She could have walked away that night too—chosen Patlani and Ehecatl and given up on ever saving the Chicome Empire. They hadn't wanted her to be their empress, and she had known it.

But a true empress fought for her people, not just for herself. Even broken, even confused, her people were still hers. A true empress would be willing to make the hard choices it took to do the right thing, no matter the cost. An empress would not burn her world to the ground, but fight to build it into something worth fighting for.

Together she and Ahkin could bring color back to the Chicome's stark black-and-white world. They *could* create something new. Something beautiful. And they didn't have to destroy the world to do that.

Mayana lowered her fisted hands. As she did, she dispersed the mass of water stretching the length of the sky into a thin mist. Then she opened her palms, releasing the mist to fall across the entire jungle as a gentle rain. The distant rushing sound of the water against leaves felt as comforting as home.

Stop! What are you doing? the voice in her ear hissed.

"You said I had the power to make them do whatever I want," Mayana said, a smile tugging at her lips.

The power coursing through her veins throbbed. Her skin burned. But Mayana thrust her hand upward toward the sky.

Toward the stars.

The Obsidian Butterfly screeched inside her head, but Metzi was not the only one with a will too strong to bend. The demons began to shine, their pale skin radiating a light so bright they illuminated the trees around them. The first one shot into the air like a comet in reverse, this time rising instead of falling. Then another. And another. One by one, the star demons returned to the skies, twinkling back in their heavenly prisons.

No! the goddess screamed inside her head.

Mayana then summoned water from the amulet of Atlacoya, encasing herself in a glittering cocoon of glass. The water coursed over her skin. Its cool caress pulled away every trace of Metzi's blood and relieved the burn of the Butterfly's power. As the blood and dirt and grime washed away, Mayana felt the Butterfly's dark presence wash away as well. The power slowly faded from her veins, until it was gone entirely. The Butterfly's cruel laughter disappeared with a final warning in her ear. *You haven't saved anyone, daughter of water . . .*

The water finally crashed down around her feet. She gasped for breath, drawing deep gulps of air into her lungs.

A final flash of light raced across the sky until it found its place next to the eclipsed sun. Without a host to feed upon, the Butterfly had returned to the stars.

Ahkin's body crashed painfully into hers, wrapping her in an embrace. His warmth seeped into her cold, wet skin. His arms held her steady as she shivered.

"Thank you for reminding me," she whispered, and pressed a kiss to his lips.

She expected him to look relieved, to kiss her back in celebration, but his narrowed eyes remained skyward.

"She's gone," Mayana assured him, even though the Butterfly's final warning still rang in her ears. "I forced her out, and she didn't have another host to take."

Ahkin's gaze finally lowered to hers, concern creasing his mouth into a thin line. "She's gone, but then why isn't the eclipse?"

Mayana's stomach clenched in panic. He was right. The world around them was still cast in the ominous reddish shadow.

Like the Obsidian Butterfly, the sun remained trapped in its celestial prison.

The chill that already clung to the air seemed to sink deep into Ahkin's bones. The shadow of the eclipse, of everything the Butterfly had just put them through, still hung heavy upon the empire. But if Metzi was gone, and the Butterfly was gone, perhaps the power in his blood would now be enough to move it.

He was already covered in blood from the wound on his chest. Ahkin lifted his unbroken hand and concentrated. He willed the moon to surrender, begged the sun to come back to them.

But it did not move.

Ahkin screamed, trying to force it, but the moon was as stubborn as a boulder. His strength was not enough. He reached for his knife—perhaps he just needed more blood, more power from the sun god—

Mayana's hand came down gently on his wrist and lowered the knife. "Ahkin, it's not enough."

"It has to be enough," he argued. "My blood has to be enough. If it's not, then . . ." He couldn't even finish his thoughts. They'd defeated the Obsidian Butterfly, banished her and her demons back to the stars, but the Chicome Empire would die anyway. Without the life-giving power of the sun, every plant, every creature, would eventually succumb to darkness. Water would not evaporate into the clouds. The temperature would eventually drop to levels unable to sustain life. It wouldn't be a quick death at the claws of demons, but a slow, excruciating death of starvation, freezing, and drought. They thought they'd saved their world . . . but had they damned it instead?

"It won't be enough," Mayana repeated. The exhaustion that tainted her tone pulled at his own strength, reminding him how incredibly exhausted he was too.

"But Metzi is the one who did this, which means maybe I can—"

"The Butterfly combined her power with Metzi's." Mayana pressed her fists into her eyes and slowly lowered herself to the ground. He could see her waging a war against the hopelessness threatening to overwhelm her. Ahkin knew exactly how that felt. He wanted to rage, to fight, but how could you fight when there was no longer an enemy you could defeat? He lowered himself down beside her, wrapping an arm around her shivering shoulders.

"You're right," said a deep voice Ahkin did not recognize. "You would need the power of a god."

Ahkin and Mayana both looked up. Standing above them, scaled green hands outstretched, stood a godly figure he'd only ever seen in codex drawings. The dragon-like face, the elaborate headpiece of rainbow feathers that cascaded down his back. The conch shell amulet sitting above his breastplate. The scales of his skin, shimmeringly iridescent despite the lack of sunlight to illuminate them. Ahkin recognized him immediately. Quetzalcoatl. The Feathered Serpent. The god of wind and air himself.

Ahkin and Mayana tentatively took his offered hands, and the god lifted them back to their feet. He smiled—or, at least Ahkin *assumed* it was a smile on his serpentine face.

Ahkin bowed low, wincing at the pain that flared across his chest. Mayana mimicked him, her eyes wide with wonder.

"Ahkin, before you try and needlessly sacrifice yourself *again*," the god's yellow eyes sparkled with humor, "I want to assure you that I am here to help you in your task, as was my purpose in the Mother's plan from the beginning."

"Thank you," Ahkin said, feeling breathless.

Quetzalcoatl dropped his gaze to the shattered shield of Huitzilopochtli. "I can't say my brother would be too happy with what you did to his shield, but I can at least take care of that for you before I leave." With a wave of his scaled hand, the shattered fragments of the shield, including its golden face, came back together as if it had never been broken. He handed the shield to Ahkin then slapped his hands together. "Thank the Mother we do not need to create a new sun altogether; I would not be thrilled to have to sacrifice myself again. This time, I will use my power to blow the moon forward on its path, and when I do, use your blood to set the sun back into motion."

"I—I will, my lord Quetzalcoatl."

"And please, tell my descendants that I am proud of them for standing firm in their faith, but I am also proud they have decided to remain part of their divine family. It is truly where they belong. Atlacoya and Huitzilopochtli would also be proud of both of you."

Quetzalcoatl transformed into a great serpent with a blink of an eye, wings of rainbow feathers sprouting from his back. A great wind rushed over them as he took flight into the sky. Ahkin's heart filled with hope as the serpent disappeared from view. Several heartbeats later, the sky began to lighten as the dark disc of the moon began to move, rays of the sun's light escaping from behind it. Finally, the moon cleared the sun entirely, bathing the valley in its warmth. Ahkin savored the feeling across his skin as he lifted his hand into the sky. With the moon out of the way, he felt the sun's easy compliance with his will. He nudged it with his power until—like the moon—it was set back on its original path.

Mayana slid her arm around his waist and squeezed. He draped his arm across her shoulders.

"We did it," she said. "We saved the Seventh Sun."

"We did." He pressed a swift kiss to the wet hair on top her head. He could stand here in the freshly reborn light of the sun with her forever.

Mayana suddenly snorted. "Ometeotl knew all along that we needed Quetzalcoatl to end the eclipse. She could have at least *told* us that from the beginning."

"Do you think you'd still have made the choices you did if you had known?"

Mayana smacked him gently in the stomach. "Yes," she said defiantly. But then she smiled at herself, as if she knew the honest answer to that question.

Ahkin laughed. "Stubborn till the end."

Mayana arched an eyebrow at him. "Who says this is the end?"

———

Yemania always imagined what a royal wedding would be like to attend, but she'd never imagined it would be her *own*. After Ahkin and Mayana's wedding and coronation the week before, she didn't think anything in the world would ever be so beautiful . . . until she saw Ochix waiting for her at the top of Miquitz's temple. He stood silhouetted against the waterfall, a billowing cloak of black accented with tiny crystals like stars. His crown of toucan feathers was enormous, and she secretly thanked the gods that the crown waiting for her on the altar was much smaller in size. Still elegant, but much more to her liking in its simplicity. Mayana and Ahkin stood at Ochix's side with the other princesses, all of whom had traveled from their city-states to witness her become empress of the Miquitz.

She still squealed internally at the title. *Empress.*

A million years ago, when she'd walked through the gates of Tollan for the selection ritual, she'd given up any dream of holding such a title. It would be hard work, cleaning up and healing the devastation the Miquitz Empire had endured from the Tzitzimime's attack. Many buildings had been destroyed. Many lives had been lost. The wound to the heart and soul of the empire had been unfathomable.

But if anyone knew anything about healing, it was Yemania.

The ceremony itself was short and quick, an exchange of gifts and vows before their closest friends, Ochix placing the crown upon her head, a kiss that curled her toes. But the celebration—oh, the celebration—lasted well into the night. After many drinks, and dances with every distinguished guest from both empires, Ochix finally led her away from the chaos of the feasting guests to a dark, secluded room.

"Close your eyes," Ochix said, taking her by the hand and leading her inside.

"Why? I already know what I signed up for when I agreed—"

"Just do it," Ochix teased.

She breathed in the heady scent of dried spices and herbs. He stepped away, and she listened to the crackling sound of igniting torches. The light of the flames danced against her eyelids. Anticipation fluttered in her stomach.

"Okay," he said after several agonizing minutes of waiting. "Open them."

Yemania did. And then she gasped, her eyes immediately filling with joyous tears.

Ochix spread his arms wide, proudly displaying his handiwork. "What do you think?"

Every wall of the expansive room was covered with bowls of different herbs and plants. Mixing pestles and empty jars sat waiting upon the worktables. Stone shelves boasted an endless supply of codex sheets and documents for her notes and remedy instructions. "You . . . you made me a healer's workshop."

"Of course! You always told me you wanted to bring your healing to the people, not just the royal families. Now you can."

Yemania threw her arms around Ochix's neck. "What could I ever do to thank you for how good you are to me?"

Ochix wiggled his eyebrows. "Well, I'm sure I can think of something." And lowered his lips to hers.

———

"So did you ever think you'd be attending a Miquitz royal wedding and coronation?" Mayana asked Ahkin. She swirled her bowl of pulque and tilted her head at him.

Ahkin was dressed in his finest gold chest piece and armlets for the occasion. The sight of him looking at her the way he did still left Mayana marveling that this wasn't all a dream. That she wouldn't wake up back in her room in Atl. But no, she was here, celebrating Yemania and Ochix as Ahkin's wife. As the empress of the Chicome Empire.

"No, I can't say I did. But the Miquitz and the Chicome will certainly have a better relationship now than they ever had in the past. I'm looking forward to our alliance."

"Mostly because you know Ochix will pester the hells out of you if you don't stay friends." Mayana smirked and took a sip of her drink. The burning liquid warmed her tongue and throat.

Over Ahkin's shoulder, Mayana noticed a familiar figure standing on the expansive balcony overlooking the waterfall—the same waterfall she and Ochix had plummeted from weeks ago.

The drums and flutes had taken up a frenzied new song. "Care to dance?" Ahkin set down his drink and lifted a hand in invitation.

Mayana smiled at him. "I'll join you in a minute. There's something I need to do first."

Ahkin left to join the other dancers, where Itza twirled with Nitia and her brother. Teniza laughed with her new husband, the handsome young guard she'd married against her father's wishes, as she fed grapes into his mouth. Yoli strolled past, hands clasped with a ferocious-looking Miquitz woman who looked as if she could crush a man's skull between her thighs. Zorrah prowled proudly around the perimeter like a lone jungle cat, nodding a greeting when she met Mayana's eyes.

But Mayana left them all behind and went out onto the balcony, the cool mist of the waterfall coating her exposed arms. An old woman stood gazing into the cascading wall of water. Her hair swirled with white and gray. She leaned heavily upon a walking stick.

"Hello, daughter of water," Ometeotl croaked, not taking her eyes off the falls. "I knew you would join me eventually."

"How long have you been out here?" Mayana asked, crossing her arms across her chest.

Ometeotl grinned at her with crooked teeth. "Not long."

They were silent for several moments, the sound of rushing water filling the peaceful silence between them.

"You were right," Mayana said finally, rubbing her arms. "About everything."

"I usually am, but about what in particular this time?"

The corner of Mayana's mouth twitched. "I had a lot to learn before I was ready to become empress."

"You were always destined for great things, Mayana. I knew from the moment you were born. But greatness often comes at a price, as does everything in the universe. There must always be balance. Duality. You have suffered greatly, wrestled with incredible hardship. But hardship is what prepares you for greatness. Rainbows usually shine the brightest after the darkest storms."

Mayana nodded. "I'm sorry I questioned you so much. Questioned your love for me and your creation."

Ometeotl shrugged. "Love is not always easy. It does not always feel good or look pretty. Sometimes it is messy and painful. But it is always worth it in the end. Wouldn't you agree?"

Mayana turned around to where Ahkin stood waiting for her in the doorway. He gave a low bow to the Mother in greeting.

"I do," Mayana said, her heart filling to such capacity she feared it might burst.

Mayana then threw her arms around the Mother goddess and hugged her. "Thank you," she whispered in the old woman's ear. "Thank you for never giving up on me, even when I wanted to give up on myself."

The Mother patted her gently on the back. "Of course, my dear. Now, go have some fun. Goodness knows you both deserve it before the real work begins. You have a world to rebuild together, after all." The goddess winked and shooed her back toward the party.

Mayana walked back to Ahkin and took his hand. His eyes danced with hope and love and promises as he brought her hand to his lips and kissed it.

They did have a world to rebuild together, but this time, they would make it better than the one before.

EPILOGUE

Mayana knew the end was near. But if it was to be her final end, she could think of no better way than to be surrounded by her family and descendants.

Ahkin had already passed on several years before, and her place beside him in their burial temple was already prepared and waiting. There would be a grand funeral, a celebration as the city-states mourned their empress together as one. The Chicome Empire had thrived for generations, growing and changing under Ahkin and Mayana's rule. It would be a legacy etched into her people's history. An empire remembered not for blind obedience and power, but for its love and dedication to each other and the gods they served.

But their greatest legacy surrounded her now. Their children, grandchildren, even great-grandchildren. She knew the work she and Ahkin had done would continue long after she left this earth. Her family's smiling faces were the last image she saw when she closed her eyes for one last time and took her final breath.

When she opened them again, her body was no longer stiff, no longer in pain. It was younger, stronger, more energetic than it had been in years. A body that was as familiar as it was foreign. But the black sand beach she now stood upon was also familiar, though it had been decades since she'd last stood upon this shore.

She looked down at her hands, silvery and transparent as a spirit.

"I've been waiting for you."

His voice was so dear, so familiar. Mayana's heart ached to hear it again after so many years. How she'd missed him.

Ahkin stood before her, dressed in a simple white wrap and head-piece, his spectral form as young as it had been in the days when they'd saved the Seventh Sun.

"Actually, we both have," he said.

Beside him sat a smooth, nearly hairless dog, tongue lolling as Ahkin scratched the top of his head. Ona barked, and his tail thrashed against the black sand.

Mayana cried out with joy.

Ahkin reached out a hand toward her, just as he had all those years ago when he'd asked her for their first dance during the selection ritual. "Are you ready to do this again?"

Mayana wove her fingers through his and rubbed the smooth top of Ona's head. The dog leaned into her touch.

"Together," she said.

And once again they began their trek through Xibalba, this time anxious for the peace and paradise that awaited them at its end.

There are so many people to thank for the fact that this book (and the whole series!) exists. First, I want to thank my personal higher power, God, for not fitting into any of the boxes we as humans try to force Him into. Thank you for teaching me that loving you and loving others is what matters above all else. My faith is such a huge part of who I am, so naturally that is going to come through in my writing. So much of this series wrestles with spiritual questions and I love that because spirituality is rarely cut-and-dry. Like with Mayana, I love seeing others be able to search and come to conclusions on their own without having those conclusions forced on them by others. Especially as a teen, I was always asking questions and exploring my spirituality. Faith is such a unique personal journey, and I hope these books have helped you on whatever journey you find yourself on.

I also want to thank my amazing agent, Samantha Wekstein, for walking alongside me every step of this publishing journey. I am so grateful that you believed in me and believed in this story! You are always there for me to cheer me on and answer my random questions with professionalism and compassion. To my editors, Betsy Mitchell and Courtney Vatis, I can't tell you how much your enthusiasm for this series meant to me. You both helped me make all three books the strongest they could be. Mandy Earles and Samantha Benson, my rock-star marketing team, you have both been so fun to work with! To Rick Bleiweiss, Josie Woodbridge, Jeffrey Yamaguchi, Megan Wahrenbrock, and everyone else on the Blackstone team, you are the absolute best! Blackstone Publishing has been like a family to me, supporting my writing dream and caring about me as an individual as well as an author. I feel so blessed to call Blackstone my publishing home.

This book would not exist without the support of the writing community and the author friends that came alongside me while I was writing it. Devri Walls, if you had not gotten on Zoom with me for weeks at a time during the pandemic to hold me accountable, I might still be trying to finish my first draft. I cannot thank you enough for brainstorming with me and forcing me to sit down at my computer at a time when the whole world was falling apart. I am convinced every writer needs a friend like you and I cannot put into words how grateful I am that as two introverts, we both took that chance to room together at a writing conference when we didn't know each other yet! To my writing group, Rachel, Tanager, Angela, MaryAnn, and Margo, you all inspire me so much. I love our conversations and the way we build each other up while challenging each other to be the best writers we can be. To Nikki, Meg, and Elizabeth, for always being willing to meet me at a coffee shop to write together. To all the authors I've met through Kid Lit Net, Realm Makers, Romance Writers of America's Coeur du Bois chapter, LTUE, and SCBWI Southern Idaho/Utah, I love all of you and cherish your feedback and support. To all my beta readers and friends who read early versions and gave me feedback, thank you, thank you, thank you!

My incredible husband has supported me every step of my publishing journey and has always believed in me, even when I didn't believe in myself. My mother always taught me that the man is supposed to be the setting that allowed the diamond to shine, and you have absolutely held me up so that I could sparkle to the best of my ability. To Raelyn, Zachary, and Wyatt, you all inspire me and give me so much strength. Thank you for calling me mommy and sharing me with my book children. I hope that you learn to always follow your dreams no matter the obstacles that stand in your way! To my mom, stepdad, sisters, and in-laws, thank you for supporting me in this dream as well! I know I couldn't have done this without each and every one of you!

And lastly, thank you, dear readers! I hope that Mayana and Ah-kin's journey has inspired you as much as it has inspired me. May you always have the courage to follow your heart!

Like The Seventh Sun and *The Jade Bones, The Obsidian Butterfly* draws inspiration from a variety of diverse ancient Mesoamerican influences for its setting and mythology. Though it is a fantasy world, and the kingdom and the rituals performed by the characters are fiction, many of the motivations behind those rituals are influenced by history. For example, the New Fire ceremony that is mentioned is a historically based ritual that was an important Mexican festival believed to have prevented the events that take place in the story, specifically the descent of the Tzitzimime star demons!

As always, it is my hope that this story inspires you to research and learn more about Mesoamerican history and culture! I highly recommend the book *Handbook to Life in the Aztec World* by Professor Manuel Aguilar-Moreno. Also, please check out the "extras" page on my website, www.LaniForbes.com!